PRAISE FOR *R...*

"Acclaimed author Kelly J. Ford spins a propulsive, sophisticated, and fearlessly queer tour de force in *Real Bad Things*. Ford's richly drawn characters and breathtaking storytelling create an inescapable undertow of menace that will not let go until the shocking final page. This is gothic suspense at its most haunting."

—P. J. Vernon, author of *Bath Haus*

"Ford's follow-up to her devastating debut novel, *Cottonmouths*, is a moving meditation on misplaced loyalties, love, and the legacy of violence and abuse, all wrapped in a mystery filled with guy-wire tension."

—John Vercher, author of *Three-Fifths*

"A powerful, grounded, and dark dose of rural noir, *Real Bad Things* is a tale of a homecoming gone wrong. Kelly J. Ford evokes the work of superstars like Gillian Flynn and Daniel Woodrell in this story of dark secrets coming back to roost and pulls it all through the prism of her own potent voice. This is a down and dirty crime novel that nods to the masters while keeping both feet firmly planted in the present. I loved it."

—Alex Segura, acclaimed author of *Secret Identity*,
Star Wars Poe Dameron: Free Fall, and *Blackout*

"*Real Bad Things* is a down and dirty, gravel-road-gritty story that pulls no punches while it blows kisses. Kelly J. Ford is the moonshine-soaked voice rural noir has been looking for. *Real Bad Things* is really damn good."

—S. A. Cosby, *New York Times* bestselling author of *Razorblade Tears*
and *Blacktop Wasteland*

PRAISE FOR *COTTONMOUTHS*

"Ford's novel features a lesbian protagonist, yet sexuality is only one facet of her strongly drawn character. Emily suffers from unrequited love, from betrayal, and from a longing for meaning and acceptance. Her struggles, as well as those of her family and community, are universal struggles set in a brutal reality where choices are scarce. Read this debut novel for its ability to go beneath the surface, striking impressive depths of character and setting."

—*Los Angeles Review*

"We talk about the need for diverse books in America; *Cottonmouths* shows us a version of our country seldom given its own narrative. Kelly J. Ford writes with honesty, subtlety, and grace."

—Patricia Park, award-winning author of *Re Jane*

"Gripping and atmospheric. A tense tale of the specific gravity of the places and the people we come from and can never fully leave behind."

—Kate Racculia, award-winning author of *Bellweather Rhapsody*

"Filled with foreboding and anguished desire, *Cottonmouths* is a perfectly paced drama of the perils of loyalty, love, and homecoming. A terrific novel by an exciting new queer voice."

—Christopher Castellani, author of *All This Talk of Love*

"A compelling story of unrequited love, identity, and the power of letting go."

—Heather Newton, author of *Under the Mercy Trees*

"A taut page-turner trembling with desire and regret, Kelly J. Ford's debut, *Cottonmouths*, strips away nostalgia for person and place when the return of one young woman reveals the rotting core of a small southern town, unraveling with the ferocity of addiction, and forces a painful lesson—she must learn to let go of her delusions in both love and friendship before it's too late."

—Michelle Hoover, author of *Bottomland*

"A fierce first novel—startling in its grip and authenticity. It's a novel about desire and desperation and the perilous danger of loving broken people in broken places."

—Travis Mulhauser, author of *Sweetgirl*

"Part noir, part southern gothic, *Cottonmouths* is far more than the sum of these parts, an original story that haunted me after I read it. Kelly J. Ford's unflinching prose plunges readers into the town of Drear's Bluff, where what's familiar isn't what's safe and where desire proves deadly."

—Stephanie Gayle, author of *Idyll Threats*

"An astonishingly assured debut from Kelly J. Ford, a writer who daringly plumbs the depths of both love and despair in a new and chilling South rendered with taut and pitch-perfect detail. Trust me, this is a book you will remember."

—Kimberly Elkins, author of *What Is Visible*

"*Cottonmouths* is a wonderfully harrowing debut full of shady characters and bad choices—two things that make every novel more satisfying . . . Kelly J. Ford delivers a sharp punch to the gut with this tightly spun modern noir tale. I can't wait to read more from this author."

—Tiffany Quay Tyson, author of *Three Rivers*

"With prose as lyrical and languid as a hot Arkansas summer, Kelly J. Ford explores the myopia of desire—and its tragic aftermath. I found myself torn between wanting to rip through these pages to find out what would happen and a need to slow down and savor Ford's sentences. A remarkable debut."

—Lisa Borders, author of *The Fifty-First State*

"Kelly J. Ford's *Cottonmouths* is a heartbreaking debut about the lies we tell ourselves to brave the past—and the truths we hide that hurt us most. An honest, unflinching portrait of yearning and loss."

—Andy Davidson, author of *In the Valley of the Sun*

"*Cottonmouths* is not a love story; it's a tale of resentment, venomous betrayal, and the wounds hidden beneath familiar surfaces. Through a kaleidoscope of characters, Ford's dark novel shows us the choices people make when the world denies them good options, and the consequences of complicity."

—*Lambda Literary*

"Kelly J. Ford's novel *Cottonmouths* captures life in backwoods America like a fish in a frying pan. Ford takes her young, raw, flailing characters and rakes them over the heat of a high-octane plot until their vulnerable insides sizzle on the page."

—*Shelf Awareness*

"This debut novel from Kelly J. Ford is sensitive yet brutal . . . A terrific new voice in the genre."

—*Shelf Discovery*

"*Cottonmouths* paints a disturbing picture of deep darkness lurking just below the surface of small-town America."

—*Mystery Scene*

REAL
BAD
THINGS

OTHER TITLES BY KELLY J. FORD

Cottonmouths

REAL BAD THINGS

KELLY J. FORD

THOMAS & MERCER

Text copyright © 2022 by Kelly J. Ford
All rights reserved.

Published by Thomas & Mercer, Seattle

www.apub.com

Amazon, the Amazon logo, and Thomas & Mercer are trademarks of Amazon.com, Inc., or its affiliates.

ISBN-13: 9781662500091
ISBN-10: 1662500092

Cover design by Rex Bonomelli

Printed in the United States of America

For Sarah, who would bury the bodies.
And for Jesse, who would not (but who did ruin his
favorite metal Hulk lunch box over the head of my
kindergarten bully).

Prologue

Away from the bridge, the river smells of the cottonwoods that grow along the banks. Cattails brush your calves and ankles. A lone whippoorwill calls out. The distant water sounds of white noise, a lullaby for sleep.

Closer to the dam, the song turns.

Closer. Tires thump when they hit different sections of the bridge. The water churns. Closer, closer. The concrete and steel structure sucks the water into its mouth, makes it scream.

Leaves the words, the world that came before, behind.

Oar plunges into the water. Your teeth chatter. Your arms ache. Wind hits the skin. The night warm, the water cold. You navigate the boat past the faded sign warning of danger. Cut across the half-sunken string of red buoys that span from one side of the river to the other like holiday lights.

The current tickles the bottom of the boat, eases it toward the locks. The boat lurches forward. The oar, gone. The roar, loud. Louder.

Jump.

Jump.

Leave the boat behind. Before it's too late. Before the turbulent water catches and curls its fingers into the boat, onto your limbs. Yanks you with him, sucks you to the bottom, under the dam gates. Legs and arms kick. Water wants inside your lungs. Terrorizes and tatters your light summer shirt.

Then.

Relief, at the top. Light lets you know it's there. Your fingers scrape the surface. Your heart fills with hope. Your lungs beg for air. But the light tells a lie. The water pulls you down. Covers your nose. Whispers to sleep as it drowns you with him in the deep, deep, deep.

One

JANE

It wasn't wise or polite to wish ill of once-loved ones, but there Jane Mooney sat, entertaining violent scenarios in her mind and thinking that oft-thought phrase: *I wish y'all were dead too.*

At first, the thought had horrified her. But thoughts weren't actions. They were only words. If he were dead, Jane wouldn't be on a plane. And she wouldn't be waiting for Jane in the Maud Regional Airport with words like *justice* and *I told you so* spitting out of her mouth like knives.

Those people probably wished Jane dead too.

The single runway lights flickered blue and white. In Boston, there were lights everywhere, except for the edge of land that broke into the ocean. Jane liked living on the edge of the continent. She liked knowing that at any moment she could hop a plane, head east over the Atlantic, and disappear. In Maud, there were scattered lights, like pebbles thrown onto a riverbank. The littlest plane, the littlest airport, the littlest she'd felt in her life, wrapped up in this one place.

When the pilot asked the flight attendants to prepare for landing, she squeezed her eyes and braced for impact. The calm of the night flight gone, along with the soothing baritone of Luke Bryan on the

Hot Country playlist she'd put on repeat because nothing really bad happened in a country song. Just tears and beers. Easy enough to switch the pronouns, and she did. *He* rhymed with *she*, and *them* worked just as well as *him*. Those songs also gave her an education on a standard-issue southern upbringing. Homemade rolls prepared with bacon grease, rope swings launching people into swimming holes, tailgate drinks and dalliances—little details she peppered into conversation with fellow southerners when she felt homesick for a life she'd been denied.

Bits of rain streaked the window. She wound her headphone wires and tucked them into their carrying case. She'd need to be fully present and on guard given who awaited her. As she neared the exit, heat crept inside and nipped at her bare ankles. One step back onto Arkansas soil and she'd be back in this life.

She descended the wobbly plane stairs onto the tarmac. Below the smell of stale airplane coffee and fuel and concrete: rain, grass, wildflowers, and freshness. Country living had its appeal if you could afford the land and no one minded that you were different. Almost instantly, the humidity stole her breath and energy. As soon as she left the tarmac, she peeled off her hoodie and shoved it into her backpack.

She'd seen bodegas bigger than the boarding area. Gate agents yawned. The gestures of talking heads from muted ceiling-mounted TVs screamed. A swarm of belt-buckled and decked-out-in-Razorback-red passengers waited for their long-delayed flight on the plane she'd departed. Panic bloomed in her bloodstream, as it had when she'd received those texts from Diane a few days prior, a hot blur of a barely remembered exchange. As always, her mind wandered back to the blood. The body. The headlines. The nickname.

Jane hoped it had been forgotten by now.

Guess who.

They found him.

I TOLD YOU THEY WOULD.

Time to come home.

Time to pay for what YOU DONE.

Let me know when you're here.

What's your flight number?

What time you getting in?

And then the last one: And don't think about running!

A normal person would get back on that plane. Disembark in Dallas or take off to a new destination. Maybe Idaho, Montana, somewhere desolate and boring. Change her hair. Change her name. Even if she had it in her to run away once more, the math would show it wasn't an option. The highest balance in her accounts belonged to credit cards, not savings or checking. Over the past month she'd lost her job and her girlfriend, which also meant she'd lost her home. Bad things came in threes. She hoped the lost home would count as the third strike in the equation and that her new home wouldn't be a cell in McPherson Unit. But then again, that was why she had returned to Arkansas.

In Boston, no one knew about Warren, about the gap in Jane's life, the hole she filled with lies. When the conversation shifted to family, she typically smiled, said they weren't close, downed most of her wine, and drowned any convulsive need to confess that she'd been small-town famous once on account of a crime.

They'd all sworn—Jane, Georgia Lee, Jason, Angie—to never tell another soul about that night. Then Jane had gone and broken that promise.

She clutched the handle of her suitcase to steady herself, gathered some air into her lungs, pulled the T-shirt away from her neck.

"You all right, honey?" A woman who looked older than her years due to cigarette lines around her lips offered a look of concern. "You look a little pale."

"I'm fine," Jane lied. "Thank you," she added with a smile when the woman was taken aback at Jane's clipped reply.

Past the security gate, women with large purses and men in bent-bill caps welcomed loved ones with bear hugs. Snatches of that comforting yet assaulting accent met her ears, like the letters shuffled across tongues only to fire out of the mouth once they hit the tip. No one greeted her. But she could swear they did a double take despite her changed appearance, even though nothing had shown up on the local news or social media channels yet. She'd checked.

Jane hadn't seen Diane in so long she wasn't sure she'd recognize her. Before the slew of texts a few days previous, they'd rarely communicated; they hadn't spoken on the phone in years. She wasn't sure she'd recognize Diane's voice if she heard it. Her body would know, though. A biological link to her mother, like some primal response to a predator.

She reached the restroom and braced herself. Women startled when she walked into restrooms, as if they'd never seen a woman with short hair and hips not built for birthing. Arkansas being a concealed carry state, she decided not to correct the person should the situation present itself. As soon as she walked into the restroom, the automatic air freshener clicked on and spritzed its floral scent, nearly scaring the shit out of her. But no one else occupied a stall. She considered that good fortune, a sign of things to come. She splashed her face, avoiding the mirror and any desire to compare and contrast the girl she'd been to the woman she'd become. No need. The limp hair and white skin that screamed malnutrition were things of the past. At least, she hoped so.

Her hands shook. She had to pull herself together.

Five minutes later, she'd traversed the length of the airport, from rental cars to baggage claim to ticket counters. No sign of Diane.

Outside the building, she texted: Where are you? She stared at her phone. A notificationless screen stared back. Not that she expected Diane to respond. She couldn't help but wonder if Diane had no intention of picking her up and had asked for Jane's flight information just to mess with her. There was a fucked-up comfort in that, in wishing for something from her mom and confirming that Diane didn't care. That felt like home.

She mapped out her destination. No buses that ran at reasonable times. No Uber or Lyft or cab that could or would arrive in less than an hour. A rental car, out of the question. Over an hour to walk. She'd walked farther, but not with a suitcase and a backpack. And not across the bridge, the one she'd had so much trouble crossing after her release that she'd left town to avoid navigating it altogether. After another glance at her phone, she hefted the backpack onto her shoulders, gripped the suitcase, and stepped off the sidewalk.

Empty fields surrounded the barren service road that wound its way to town. At the four-way stop, she paused. If she took a right, she'd eventually reach the hill towns of the Ozarks, where she was as likely to trip across an artist colony as a blown-out meth trailer. Ahead of her, in the distance, the lights of Maud Proper beckoned with promises of deep-fried savory and sweet delights, a small indie bookstore, brewpubs with live bands most nights. Probably shitty food, she reasoned, to soothe a sudden ache. Any other Thursday night, she'd occupy a bar seat at her favorite restaurant, inhale the warm-hug scent of a Parker House roll, let a fine rare sirloin melt on her tongue, a beefy red coat her throat. Luxuries for a life she hadn't thought possible when they arrested her at seventeen. She cursed herself for not indulging in one last meal before leaving Boston.

And to the left, down in the river valley, Maud Bottoms: ugly sibling to Maud Proper. Devoid of anything warm or fine. Prone to both varietals of flood—slow onset and flash—and to tornadoes that never touched the gilded houses up on this hill. The wrong side of the river, with its sad lack of trees or functioning streetlights. Its flat stretch of land and plethora of one-story metal buildings that housed dead or dying industries reminiscent of Rust Belt towns. Apartment complexes constructed like bunkers with their concrete walls and flat roofs and linoleum floors that lacked heat and walls that lacked color. Chain-link fences, broken windows. No fancy restaurants. No mini mansions or curb appeal. Always looking up at that other part of their city on a hill.

That's also where they kept the jail. Couldn't spoil Maud Proper with something as base as that.

After one last pull of Maud Proper air, she made the turn onto the one-lane highway toward home.

More than once, she tripped and nearly twisted her airplane-bloated ankles as she made her way steadily down the hill. Lush, manicured cemeteries for the old families gave way to lush woods with well-maintained trails, which then became scattershot forest before all vegetation over six inches ceased where the trees had been cut down.

Her suitcase kept rolling into her shoes, which made her arms hurt from bracing for impact. Her toenails banged against the hard toes of her Converse. A blister raged on her right heel, and her back cried out for rest.

While waiting to exit the plane, she'd texted Jason I'm baaaaaaack!, thinking maybe he'd offer a *haha* or even a grimace emoji in return. But she should have known better. He never answered the phone and barely texted. The silence remained an open wound. She'd been his first friend, the one who understood him better than anyone. She was maybe—probably—on her way to prison. The least he could do was say hello.

Back in elementary school, when the tornado sirens went off, they'd lie in the tub for hours, after the sirens had quieted down, long before Diane would come home from wherever the night had taken her. Jason drowsy beside Jane, his limbs crammed among the blankets she'd thrown in to soften the plastic surround shell. Jane's head near remnants of generic bar soap that masked the smells of other transient families who had used the shower they were sleeping in, had splattered cheap vegetable oil onto the wall behind the stove, had stained the floor inside the closets with the soles of their shoes, bringing the whole world into the apartment with them.

Jason, just a nugget then, cuddled against her and asked her to tell him stories about his father. Jane didn't even know her own, so she told him nice things she'd heard about fathers from books and TV—never the *Jerry Springer* reality, which was that his father could be any number of Asian men who had settled in or roamed through Maud in the nine months before he was born. Maybe he'd come through Fort Chaffee during the Indochinese resettlement program back in the '70s, or maybe he'd come from California or New York. Maybe he'd been born in Maud and still lived there. Maybe he was dead. There was no way to know. But they were blood, she'd always reminded him. She was his sister, and he was her brother. No matter what people said.

Thoughts of Jason nagged her, no matter where she walked or how far she'd moved from this town.

As she continued walking, she turned her thoughts to shows that dramatized small-town crimes on the "investigation" channel. All the best shows focused on the victims and their lives—before, after, or interrupted. She changed the channel when they focused on the criminals or court proceedings. Too close. As she walked, she was reminded of those old rumors. Back in the '80s and '90s, a bunch of men had gone missing and were never found. Jane had always assumed that they had wisely left town or had wandered drunk into the river and drowned. But even then, Maud loved the smell of a scandal. Some folks had stood outside the Safeway with clipboards and a public petition to get *Unsolved Mysteries* to investigate. Nothing had come of it. The men must have stopped going missing because when she confessed, the town was eager to focus on her.

Out of nowhere, a truck came up behind her. The driver inched past. Then he stopped in front of where she was walking. Her pulse ratcheted up. No emergency blinkers, just taillights and a stuttering motor. She veered into the safety of the weeds, thoughts of that fabled killer fresh in her mind.

Sometimes, as a kid, she had thought, *Think something, and it'll come true.* On those occasions when it did, the result felt magical. Like when she imagined really hard about TV dinners, the kind with the gooey fudge brownie that never quite cooked all the way, and then sometimes they'd be in the freezer. Diane would even offer a semismile at her and Jason's delight. Those moments made it hard to hate her all the way through.

Sometimes, she thought, *I wish you were dead.*

At the time, she had believed she'd manifested Warren's death. Except if that were true, Diane would have been dead a thousand times over. Now, she couldn't help but wonder if she'd nearly manifested her own. Maybe this guy thought she was a man? No women she could remember had ever gone missing. Only men. Maud was the one town where women were safer than men. She laughed at the absurdity.

She didn't want to become the latest tragedy dramatized for TV. Bad enough that everyone in Maud knew her name. But then again, she hadn't become a household name on account of her "crime," nor would she become a national tragedy if she were murdered on the side of the road. A queer, androgynous woman over forty? Being white, she had a leg up. Still, her untimely demise would only nab her a ten-minute segment on KMSM's five o'clock news. There was something romantic and tragic about dying at night by pickup truck in Arkansas. It'd make a great Lifetime movie.

She crossed to the other side of the road, away from the truck. *Don't let him see you panic,* she told herself. *No one fucks with you, Jane. No one.* The universe, however, seemed particularly up to fucking with her of late. Part of her wanted to ignore the murderer in the truck and keep going, but another part of her rallied. *Don't look away. Let him know that you know he's not going to slaughter you.* Not today. Perhaps tomorrow. After he'd tortured her for twenty-four hours. She curled back her instinct to run.

But he took off. Oblivious of her presence. Irritated by her own foolish fear, she stood in the middle of the road, in the drizzle, both hands up, giving him double birds, hoping he would see her in the rearview mirror.

God, she hated this fucking town.

Deep breaths. Georgia Lee's words came back to her. Jane had thought of her often over the years. Impossible not to. Their fates were tied thanks to one dumb night when they were teenagers.

Her legs ached, and the multiple bags of complimentary cookies and pretzels she'd consumed on the plane cemented in her gut. She pushed on. Gravel antagonized her feet through the thin soles of her shoes. She pushed on. Soon, the thrum of water through the dam intensified and joined the steady roll of her suitcase and the squeak of her wet sneakers. She pushed on against the darkness and the dread until she finally came to the long bend in the road and the riverfront park that demarcated Maud Proper and Maud Bottoms. Families used to gather there for picnics and reunions, probably still did despite the recent discovery.

Her breath labored at the sight of the bridge over the lock and dam, the expanse of it, the knowledge of what awaited her at the end. Even before everything that had happened, that bridge had signified reentry into a world she wanted to leave behind. Affirmations she'd normally mock ran through her head: *The only way to it is through it. One foot in front of the other.*

Head down, she charged forward, allowing happy memories to fill her mind—like field trips to the dam facility. The big engine room. Sunny afternoons in the grassy picnic areas and snacks at the bright red tables. Walks along the river's edge with Jason, who obsessed over finding driftwood and arrowheads and other items in the mud. Hours spent on a threadbare towel in a swimsuit, trying to get a tan so she could look more like Jason, but all she did was burn. Fishing with her best friend, Angie Pham, who'd slipped the worm on Jane's hook like a pro when the thought made Jane queasy.

Jane had come here with Georgia Lee too. They'd sat near the lock. Stars lit the sky, and the lights of the dam lit the bridge. They hadn't yet touched. Georgia Lee told her to close her eyes. *That's close to what the ocean sounds like,* she'd said. When Jane listened closely, it was almost like she'd managed to escape.

A breeze drifted by, and Jane could almost feel, see, smell the salty ocean water permeating the air. A wish for Boston or a dream of that long-ago day, she didn't know. But that wasn't salt water. The river smelled of what people couldn't see: things that were dumped, things that got caught in its currents, things that decayed.

They'd gone there often. They'd gone back that fateful night. All four of them. They hadn't known that would be the last night they'd spend there on the riverbank. But Jane had known that eventually the past would catch up to her. She had known that one day she'd have to return to Maud to face the consequences of her confession.

When she came to the end of the bridge, she paused and bent over to touch her toes to relieve her back, catch her breath, clear her mind of the memories that churned with the sound of the water rushing through the locks, the smell of the river, the darkness along the riverbank where she'd stood twenty-five years before and pushed a boat and a man to his end.

Two

Georgia Lee

Another dead night at the pharmacy. All the same songs filtered through the outdated music system, and it nearly drove Georgia Lee Lane mad. She had recommended an upgrade several times over the past several years. Had anyone listened to her, the store manager? No. They had not.

Billie leaned on the register and picked at her nails. Dr. Irwin had already pulled the shutter down and headed home for the day. Georgia Lee worked the floor in the event those nonexistent customers finally decided to show up. Nothing but a trickle since the superstore went in across the street after the Harper family sold their land. Gone were the horses and the haystacks, in were cars and congestion the one-lane highway could hardly handle, especially since they'd shut down low bridges due to the recent flood, the likes of which the town hadn't seen in decades. One more complaint Maud's citizens added to their ever-growing list of things to blame the city council for. Mostly her, the only member up for reelection that year. The only one they seemed to blame for anything. Even her three fellow council members—all from and representing Maud Proper, mind you—treated her like a leper, barely talked to her outside of meetings, as if they might catch the town's resentment too.

With the election only two months away, Georgia Lee had to make calls and distribute flyers. She had to find hands and shake them. None of which were things Bollinger—her boss, her nemesis, the pure bane of her existence—had to do. He had the means to run commercials on the local news and radio channels. He bought billboards on I-40 and every out-of-the-way dirt road within their district. He gave away lollipops. Sponsored ads in the high school yearbook. Bought every candy bar, candle, magazine subscription, and silly whatnot from every schoolkid he could find. All this, for the first time since never. All this, because someone had told him he ought to run for city council. Against her. For what reason, she couldn't fathom, other than he was a man of a certain age. Sports cars and busty new girlfriends weren't enough to boost a man's ego these days, she reckoned.

Let's Talk About Maud had stirred up the trouble. People should know better than to take the word of a Facebook group run by a couple of auto body guys. Christlyn and Susannah had repeatedly warned her not to read the comments, but she couldn't help herself. Fred "the Body" Baker wrote that the city councilors ought to be taken out behind the abandoned K-Parts factory and shot, execution-style.

Shot!

People liked his comment. Reacted with smiley-face emojis. K-Parts had promised them jobs. It had built the factory. And then it'd changed its mind after the building and land flooded, like everything else in Maud Bottoms. What was the city council supposed to do? They couldn't force businesses to stay or shareholders to pick Maud instead of Mexico (mind you, it was Dayton, but nobody in Maud was interested in the facts). As if they could control the weather.

She ran her hand along a shelf of condoms and knocked them all onto the floor.

"Everything okay?" Billie appeared at the corner of the aisle, her skin all young and supple. Georgia Lee could've ripped it right off her.

"Everything's fine."

Billie chewed her hair and gave Georgia Lee an odd look before wandering off.

She took her time returning the condoms to the shelf. If it were up to her, she'd march into Maud Senior High—and the junior high—and give them all away. Birth control too. If it was too late for birth control, she'd give them the address for a clinic down in Little Rock. Off the record, of course. On the record, she was a Southern Baptist woman, and that was that in the great state of Arkansas. She, too, knew better than to get pregnant so young, but back then she'd also believed romance meant marriage and babies equaled maturity.

Deep breaths. Things would work themselves out. They always did.

The election would be over soon. Still, she felt compelled to unleash a good old-fashioned cussing. But her momma had told her it was like having a dirty thing in your mouth, cussing. Like everyone could not just hear but also see your filth. Georgia Lee knew her mother meant it figuratively, but she couldn't help but think about a few of the dirty things she'd had in her mouth. She pressed the thought down into the deepest corner of her mind. That was then; she liked to stay in the now. Focused on the future. Being and doing different.

She straightened the hair dye and other health and beauty aids. Then she wandered down aisle eight. After a quick glance toward the endcaps, assuring herself of Billie's presence at the register, she snatched the newest Jasmine Guillory, which she'd been reading during those times when she couldn't focus on productive work, and headed toward the office. Reese's Book Club had yet to steer her wrong!

Not five minutes into the climax came Bollinger—hollering hellos to Billie and Cassidy and Georgia Lee—like he had a sixth sense for when her attention drifted from store duties. Wouldn't surprise her if he'd installed hidden cameras to go along with the ones he'd trained on the pharmacy counter after they'd been robbed of all their pseudo-ephedrine back in 2003.

She set her book aside and wandered out of the back office. Bollinger peeked his head around an endcap, then ducked back into an aisle.

"Good evening, Mr. Bollinger." He insisted on being addressed formally even though they were the same age. He looked ten years older, though. Too much time in the sun without protection. Her smooth white skin looked better than that of her forty-something peers. Everyone said so.

He bared the bleached, straight teeth he'd gotten at a discount from a dentist friend and hesitated at her appearance. She wore the white smock required of all employees. He responded to such vocational costumes from a deep pubescent desire. Nurses, maids, the waitresses at Sizzler with their ill-fitting brown slacks and white button-downs. All were subject to the salacious mind of a man who didn't know better than to superglue his thumb instead of using a Band-Aid.

He pushed the skin shut, then squeezed the clear liquid and let it dry for a few seconds. "Did you know they invented superglue during World War II to seal injuries?" Dubious. She would confirm on Wikipedia later. "Better than Band-Aids. I kept losing them in tight, dark places."

Vile man. Georgia Lee scanned the shelf and handed him a box. "They make liquid bandages, which I imagine are far less irritating to the skin." He claimed to be a pharmacist. A lie. She'd looked it up. But he owned the pharmacy. His daddy got it from his daddy. And his daddy's daddy before him probably got the land for free from the government after they stole it from the Osage.

He leaned against the shelf, leg kicked back like the Marlboro Man. She couldn't fathom how anyone saw Bollinger as anything but a two-bit businessman. He strutted into the spotlight without a lick of general know-how while she had to prove herself worthy of the council position she'd held for fifteen years. But Georgia Lee had paid attention in history class and Bible study. She knew better than to think folks couldn't be swayed by someone's charming stupidity.

Some days, she had a mind to drop out of the race. Let Bollinger try public service on for size and see how he'd do. But that wasn't her way. She never quit. Not even in the worst of circumstances. She'd been through the worst already and come through.

A shock of memory disarmed her. Beer and onion breath. Spit on her neck. Blood on her tennis shoes. The images dislodged and scattered her thoughts. She recalled a dream from the previous night about being in a fight. The feeling of anger and fear, a tight ball in her stomach all day.

Rusty had suggested she might be overextended. Working too hard. Imagining people were out to get her. But this was simply the situation during election season. She had promised him she'd talk to Dr. Irwin about her insomnia, but she hadn't. Deep sleep only led to harrowing dreams about fighting and not being able to breathe, and she didn't like that. She preferred the little catnaps that refreshed her. Sleep apnea. That was probably the problem. She'd read the risk of developing it increased with age in women.

Bollinger stared at her long enough that she worried she'd had a stroke and wasn't yet aware of it. She pushed the images and the previous night's dream aside, put them in the box in her mind where she placed anything unpleasant that threatened to disrupt her focus.

"You owe the store three dollars for that superglue," she said after taking a moment to remember what they were talking about.

Bollinger laughed. "I own this store."

"I own inventory," she said, annoyed at the interruption of the book she wanted to return to. "And you should set a better example. You don't want the kids up front thinking it's okay to steal, do you?" Billie and Cassidy, a couple of rich white teenagers, had gotten their jobs because their daddies golfed with Bollinger. Irritations lined every minute of her day. "I'll cover the superglue so it doesn't screw up the count. You can drop off what you owe anytime."

He'd never pay. He treated the pharmacy like his own personal stock. Not bothering to mention to her the things he took, messing up the inventory and people's lives. She'd accidentally fired a girl for stealing only to discover Bollinger was to blame. Georgia Lee still felt just awful about it.

But she wasn't about to let him think that she didn't keep a running tally of his infractions. She set her sights on the back office, where she'd wanted to read until closing.

She sensed him behind her, greasing his gears with bad news or an inappropriate comment.

"Wild story from the lock and dam, ain't it?"

Her heart raced in response to those words. There was no way to avoid the bridge if she required a touch of civilization up in Maud Proper. But every time she drove across the lock and dam—even now, thinking of that drive—her body temperature plunged, and she struggled to breathe, coughed on her own saliva, told herself to ignore the fear. *Go. Go. Go.*

Georgia Lee clutched a shelf. "What?"

"Did you hear the news?" He stared at her. "Did you hear about—"

"I heard you the first time," she said and focused on straightening the crossword puzzle magazines to steady her nerves. "I haven't had time to catch up on the news. I have a job. Two, to be precise." Ever since he had announced his election bid, she'd tried in vain to scare him with reminders that a council position required actual work, what with meetings and email newsletters and documentation review.

"Hoo boy, have I got some dirt for you then." Before she could interrupt him, he said, "They found a body at the dam when they were doing cleanup."

"A body?"

"Well, bones, more like it. You remember that guy that went missing?"

"Which one?" There had been several over the years. Capsized and carried away with a current. Theirs was no lazy river, no floating or swimming river. The Arkansas River could kill you. But Maud's citizens didn't like facts, they liked fun. So they blamed any and all accidents on a bogeyman instead.

"The famous one. You know, back in high school. What was his name? Anyway," he continued when she didn't answer, "somehow old what's-his-name ended up in the lock chamber. Finally found him after the waters receded."

Her face heated as the words finally plugged in to her memory and booted up a name: Warren Ingram.

Jane confessed to his murder. The words popped into her head unbidden. *Jane. Jane Mooney confessed to Warren Ingram's murder.* Jane's face fuzzed in Georgia Lee's recollection, despite them having once been so close. The whole of their acquaintance a dream, a figment of her too-vivid imagination.

A hit of dizziness forced her to grip the shelf again. She stood still, blinked several times. Composed herself. Almost smiled, but thought better of it.

That was all wrong. Surprise. A hand to the chest.

Better.

"My goodness," she said. *My fault.* The images returned. *My blood.* She cleared her throat. Regrouped. "Yes, I remember. They suspected he drowned like the others. Makes sense someone would turn up. We haven't seen a flood like that in years, what with the water running high and fast—"

"Mmm. Climate change." He'd denied its existence six months prior. "I guess they talked to the wife and confirmed it."

The wife. Diane Ingram. Jane's mother.

Names and associations flung around her mind. She closed her eyes and swallowed. *Swallow it down. Whatever this is.*

Breathe.

"I haven't heard a word about this on the news," she said. "Where'd you get this information?" Someone was sharing confidential things with Bollinger, things they used to share with her.

"Guess it pays to play golf with the chief of police." If they were in a movie, he would've twirled his mustache and a star would have twinkled off his fake incisor.

She wouldn't know. John hadn't invited her to golf. She could swing just as well as Bollinger. Better. Hit him right in the head.

Her mind tunneled to the past with remembrances of a stormy sky, a headache that portended rain, the rush of the river. Warren on the ground, splayed like one of those chalk outlines, only without the chalk and before they took away the body. Blood on his head. A rock in her hand.

And one question on her mind: What did the others remember about that night?

Three

Jane

Nothing grand had occasioned the name change from Maud Bottoms Trailer Park to Maud Bottoms Estates. The laundromat still sat at the entrance to the neighborhood with the same cracked window that had been repaired with masking tape year after year. The management office door still held a laminated sign warning folks not to drop by but to CALL FIRST!, followed by a reminder about the consequences of not paying rent on time: ONE STRIKE YOU'RE OUT! Maud Bottom Feeders—the moniker citizens in this part of Maud clung to happily—still pulled the curtains wide and without discretion to investigate strangers like Jane walking along the road. They still sat on porches and spit to the side when she rolled by with her luggage.

They'd recall her name soon enough.

With each clack of her suitcase wheels on the pavement, panic shot through her. Beat at her temples. Told her to run. She should've taken the flight to Dallas. She should've run when she could.

Run. That's all she had to do. But then what? Coming home had always been the prediction, if not the plan. Her head didn't even know how to change course. Her return—and Warren's—felt fated.

Once she reached Diane's trailer, she paused. Jane had lived here for almost two years. The longest of any place up to that point. The trailer still sat in darkness against the neighboring trailers. The grass was still overgrown and patchy. No trees or flower beds or wind chimes like some of the others. Of all the places for Diane to call her forever home after a life spent hauling them here and there and everywhere, an inexplicably itinerant existence within the confines of Maud, skimming the bottom. They'd inhabited apartments, houses, trailers. More than one night, when they'd been between places and Diane had been between jobs, they'd slept in the car.

It's an adventure, Jane recalled Diane saying when she was near to crying, Jason already going at full throttle. And then: *You'll never remember this night.*

She did remember. At least Diane had sheltered Jane and Jason a bit, offered something to keep their fears at bay. It had been an adventure. Potted meat cracked right from the can. Saltines and orange soda. Diane even let them eat some of her bridge mix while Jane read old issues of *People* magazine to Jason in the back seat with a flashlight before they both dozed off.

In Boston, people used to ask Jane if she was an army brat. No, she would say, we just moved a lot. She'd never even thought to question why they moved so much until people cocked their heads in confusion. She'd always assumed people just moved every year. She and Jason had drifted in and out of the three elementary school options Maud Bottoms offered. There was only one high school in the Bottoms, until its roof got ripped away by a tornado. But here Diane stayed. Probably because the trailer was paid in full and she only had to scrounge up rent for the lot.

On the porch, she ran her hands along the top of the door and along windowsills, under chipped ceramic flowerpots with dead plants, and in between cracked lawn chairs, looking for a spare key but finding none. She should've known to head to Cloverleaf Liquors to find Diane.

She sat down at the railing like she and Angie had done most days and nights, bored and hoping for something exciting to happen—until it did. She picked through a package of nuts she'd swiped from the airplane snack cart that morning. Mindless eating. She wasn't even hungry. Her stomach cramped, but it gave her something to focus on other than her current situation. She shoved the empty package in the pocket of her jeans. Exhausted but wide awake, she waited.

If she'd watched her mouth, as Diane had always warned her to, Jane wouldn't have had to leave Boston on a flight that morning. She might not have left Maud in the first place.

Low thoughts and hovering anxiety swarmed. On one otherwise ordinary Sunday, Jane and Angie had sat here on this same porch in their usual spots, legs dangling off the side and chins lodged on the rails. Their feet swung high above the overgrown grass below them. Jason sat next to Jane, singing softly to himself as he stripped the bark off a stick. His hands always had to be moving, doing. Tapping or clenching. He was sweet and sensitive, unlike other fourteen-year-old boys she'd known, all ratcheted up tight from hormones, itching to fight or fuck or both.

Light from the TV flickered through the white lace living room curtains behind them. The windows of the neighboring mobile home were covered with faded pages ripped from the *Maud Register*. Angie claimed a hoarder lived there, but Jane couldn't confirm. The central AC unit underneath the kitchen window a ways down clicked on and off periodically, disguising the sounds of summer bugs and yonder dogs tied up in yards and Diane yelling at "all them ignorant folks" on *America's Funniest Home Videos*, which she was blasting in the living room.

Angie swung her legs and chewed her gum. With her bored frown, bright-pink skirt, black leggings, off-the-shoulder black shirt, and bangle bracelets, she would have fit perfectly in a John Hughes movie. Angie, so different from other girls Jane had known. She was kind and generous and smelled good. Things Jane had never been accused of. Once they moved to a new place, Jane couldn't help but cling to the first person who said something nice to her. That person usually turned out to be the weird kid in school, weirder than Jane, the New Kid. Angie wasn't considered weird. She was considered something else entirely. Outsider. Other things.

Jane wormed a hand into Angie's pocket and extricated a piece of Juicy Fruit, only to be punched in the arm and scolded to ask next time. Jane laughed and popped half the piece into her mouth. She gave the other half to Jason before resting her chin back on the rail. He ran his fingers over the smooth surface of the now naked tree branch he'd stripped, as if whittling with his fingertips. She ran her hand along his hair as she'd done when he was little, his head all warm and slightly damp. He swatted her away. She grabbed his hand in midair.

"What's the magic word?" she asked, holding on. He tried to wriggle his way out but couldn't. "Say it."

"Fopp u copp kopp yopp o u." Oppish. The secret language they used around Warren.

She squeezed his hand harder until he laughed and surrendered. "Okay, okay," he said. "You are the smartest and strongest person I know."

"You bet your ass I am."

"Even though that's more than one word." He braced himself for the smack he clearly expected in return for his insolence.

"Sopp hopp u topp u popp."

Jason laughed and returned his attention to the stick. He focused on sharpening it into a spear by scraping it back and forth on the porch.

Angie shook her head at them. She didn't engage in their games. "Have you heard from Tiffany?"

Jason groaned in response.

Since Angie had started mooning over Colin, a skateboarding punk with long blond bangs in their art class, they talked extensively of the assorted emotions their crushes induced. Jane didn't mind. No one else asked about her crushes. No one else knew. Well, Jason knew. But they didn't talk about it.

Jane shook her head. It was nothing, she'd told Angie. But the mention of Tiffany's name still intoxicated her and made her flush at the remembrance of hands besides her own within the confines of elastic and fabric that cloaked her body. How easy it'd been. How thick and heady. How she wanted more of it.

But Tiffany was long gone. Back to Hot Springs after spending the summer in Maud with her grandparents. There wouldn't be any late-night calls or letters. Jane knew the drill. If there was one thing she excelled at, it was how to pack up her heart and move along.

"You know that girl Georgia Lee?" Jane chewed without lifting her head off the railing, causing her jaw to pop. A chipped piece of paint poked her chin, and she rubbed the spot. All Jane knew of Georgia Lee was she was cute if you could endure the ever-present pastel and smile she wore—like nothing bad had ever touched her family tree—the overbearing desire to win school elections and have her photo featured more than anyone else under the "Most" designations in the yearbook, and the strange way she had of talking, like she'd stepped out of *Steel Magnolias*. Every time Jane saw her, she wanted to yell *Shelby!* She also looked at Jane and Angie all the time, like they were some kind of science experiment. It was weird, and attractive.

Angie took the gum wrapper out of her pocket and stuck her chewed gum inside. She folded it into a tight, neat package and slipped it back into her pocket. "She's not a nice person."

Before Jane had a chance to interrogate Angie about her comment, Warren's car rumbled into the drive.

Beside her, Jason muttered, "Fopp u copp kopp."

Jane's pulse always quickened at the thought of what Warren might say or do in Angie's presence.

"Jason and I should go in and do some homework," she said, checking to see how close Warren was to stepping out of the car. "We both have big tests tomorrow."

"You don't have to lie." Angie looked toward Warren's car and then back at Jane. "We live in Maud. I'm not stupid."

Jane reached over to grab Angie's hand, but Angie slipped out of her grip.

"I know you're not stupid," Jane said. "I don't want him to . . ." Speak. Look at Angie. Hurt her the way he hurt Jason with his crude remarks, even though Jason swore he didn't care. "I'm sorry."

Warren watched them from behind the wheel. He wore sunglasses, but Jane could tell from the set of his jaw and the way his mouth turned down that something had already set him off and it'd be best to steer clear.

Angie slipped through the porch rails. "I'll see you at seven?"

She asked every night during the school week, even though she walked with them to the bus stop every morning. Maybe Angie knew more than she let on. Like if Jane and Jason didn't show up, she might call the cops. Like that would do any good.

"See you at seven," Jane said.

Jason waved goodbye.

Angie paused and then rounded the hoarder's trailer, back to where she lived on the other side of the trailer park, the sunny side. It wasn't but a minute's walk, maybe a little more, but it felt like a hundred miles some days.

"Just stay quiet," Jane told Jason. He continued to sharpen his stick.

The car door shut, and Jane returned her attention to the empty window across from her. She wondered if the woman inside was dead or alive. If she heard things. If she was the one who sometimes called the police.

The wooden boards creaked under Warren's weight, even though he wasn't a big man. Tall, but not big. Stringy looking. Mean. He banged a pack of cigarettes on his palm.

"What are y'all doing out here?" On his bad days, he'd add, *Y'all stupid or something?*

If they sat outside, it was wrong. If he found them inside, it was worse. They were too loud. Or too quiet. Too visible. Or too absent. There was never a right place or way for them to be.

"You hear me? You deaf or something? What are you doing?"

Jane sat still. Jason's sharpening slowed. "Nothing."

The light hit the window just right, bright enough that Jane could watch Warren light his cigarette and blow smoke into the air. "All you kids do is nothing. Must be good at it."

Smoking kills, and I hope you die. Jane said nothing. Nothing was the best move.

Warren walked behind Jane and poked Jason with the toe of his boot. She could feel Jason stiffen beside her. Fight or flight, she'd learned in biology. *Run, Jane. Run.* But she'd never run without Jason. And he never seemed ready for that. His patience surpassed hers.

Jane risked a glance at Warren. The end of his cigarette glowed orange when he inhaled. Ashes flickered down to lightly singe her skin. She scratched at the spot.

"Did you want something?" Jane tried to tamp down the tremble in her voice. She felt incapable of anything but the smallest of breaths. If she didn't take a big gulp of air soon, she worried she might pass out.

"You better watch yourself, girl," Warren said.

"Yes, sir," she said, and hated herself for it. Hated that he could waltz into their lives and control them all, and Diane let him. But Jane wouldn't let him think he'd scared her, that he had some sort of control over her. Not even if it meant getting a kick to the face. Maybe she'd let him. Maybe he'd go to jail. Maybe that wasn't a bad plan.

Warren smiled and blew a smoke ring. "Get inside the house. Help your mom."

With what? Picking out a skintight top for another late night at Crawdaddies, her favorite bar? She watched Warren's reflection in the hoarder lady's window. Him standing right behind her. Over her. Threatening.

"We'll go inside when we're ready."

Before Jane could react, Warren lunged toward her. She yelped and scrambled back toward the screen door, banging the metal at the bottom. Warren's hand landed on her jaw, his grip one second shy of tight. Heat emanated from his body like a just-stoked fire. *Go on. Bring up a bruise.*

"You little cunt," he whispered.

Over Warren's shoulder, she saw Jason in the corner of the porch, the sharpened stick held tight, his fist shaking.

The porch light flicked on. Warren released his grip and straightened. The door hit Jane in the back, releasing another metallic smack into the air.

"What are y'all doing out here?" Diane's voice rang with suspicion and dread.

Jane watched Warren; he watched her. The sweat on her skin chilled with the shifting wind. An owl hooted in the distance and seemed to quiet the other creatures, including the incessantly barking dogs. Everything seemed to pause for her response.

"Nothing," Jane said, eyes locked on Warren's. For years, Jane had been able to slip by and out of sight of people who could harm her, whether her mom's boyfriends or kids at school. But something in that moment unleashed her mouth. A feeling rushed through her. She wanted to hurt Warren, to put him on the opposite side of all the pain he and other men tried to inflict on girls like her and Angie, boys like Jason.

"Warren's in one of his moods," Jane said. *Must be on the rag.* She kept Warren's shitty words out of her mouth.

Warren yanked the screen door open, and the handle flew out of Diane's grip. He shoved past her and disappeared into the house.

Diane grabbed at the shoulder he'd knocked on his way in and gaped at Jane. "What the hell's going on?" *What'd you do?* her expression asked.

When Jane refused to answer, Diane eyed Jason. "He hurt you?" Meanwhile, Jane's back was on fire, and she rubbed it, but Diane didn't seem to notice. If she did, she definitely did not care.

"No," Jason muttered.

"You got to learn to stick up for yourself. Ain't always gonna be someone around to protect you. You gotta learn to hit back." Diane had never offered that advice to Jane. It was always *Keep your mouth shut and stay out of the way.*

"I know how to hit." Anger crept into Jason's voice.

Diane smacked a mosquito on her arm and then scratched at the skin. "Y'all stay out here awhile. Don't come in till I tell you to." She grumbled and shut the door, complaints trailing behind her about the AC, the cost of electricity, unnamed but knowable trouble Diane would endure because Jane had the audacity to open her mouth.

Jane arched her back to release the tension and ache from where the door had clocked her spine and Warren had gripped her. Jason sat rigid in the corner of the porch, the stick still clutched in his fist, but the shaking subsided. His eyes wide, jaw set tight. The look he always got after her fights with Warren. Wanting and always unable to do more.

"It's nothing," she said. "Don't let him get to you." She smiled away the tears brought on by adrenaline and the fear that this time, somehow, she'd gone too far.

"I'm not the one he got." Jason broke his stick in half, threw it to the ground, and left her on the porch alone.

Four

Georgia Lee

Rusty stretched his limbs along the length of the recliner, sleepy eyed from one of his extended underemployment naps. He checked his watch and then frowned when he noticed what Georgia Lee was cradling in the crook of her arm.

"Again?"

Georgia Lee dropped the bucket of fried chicken on the too-expensive dining room table. Golden crumbs scattered across its espresso sheen. Jesus on his iron crucifix accused her from across the room. Groceries were the last thing on her mind. She tossed her purse onto the long buffet that completed the dining room set and grabbed a bottle of wine from the liquor cabinet. Tim and Tate, the twins, lumbered down the stairs and nearly knocked her down, as if she were a player from an opposing team. They raced toward the table like a couple of heathens who hadn't been raised right. Didn't even say hello or *What's for supper?*

Not for the first time, she fantasized about what it would be like to come home to an empty, quiet house. Forever.

Amid the disarray of the living room and noise of the boys, she paused. Her heart raced. The blood. She kept thinking about that night, that spot of blood on her shoes.

Rusty hoisted himself out of the recliner. "Guess I'm on supper duty again."

"Guess you are," Georgia Lee said, not meaning to sound as harsh as she did. She let the spring door to the deck slam and shut her family behind her.

She slumped into an Adirondack chair, one hand holding the wineglass, the other the bottle. Both shook like she was craving a fix. She set them down and placed her head between her knees.

Deep breaths.

Some days it felt like trouble hung around her like a coat she couldn't cast off, weighing her down, no matter how good or kind or helpful she tried to be. It made her sweat. Restricted every forward motion so much that past deeds and present resentments swelled inside her.

Jane Mooney. She'd not thought of her in years. Now, the name afflicted her every twenty minutes like contractions.

Fuck. She mouthed that forbidden word, holding on to the belief her still developing preteen mind had produced that that was better than making the sounds, even though God knew her mind, her soul.

Fuck fuck fuck fuck fuck.

When she lifted her head, stars spotted her vision. The moon was almost full, bright enough for some clear thinking, but all she could think was: What if I'd left school just five minutes later that one day? Her whole life would be different. She wouldn't be sitting here worried about what her mind showed her on replay. Snatches of memory that didn't amount to anything but trouble.

But she'd gone through the school doors at that specific time on that day, bent on enjoying her last year of high school. Those hot days before fall, she often ruminated on what might come next. Homecoming, prom, graduation, summer, yes. But after that, she wasn't sure. Even with college on the list of Things to Do, the months ahead presented a blur of uncertainty. As she walked along the concrete sidewalk toward the parking lot, worry crackled through her veins. She should've known. She should've seen Jane Mooney and walked in the opposite direction.

Jane sat in the passenger seat of Angie's car with the door open, a Dr Pepper bottle dangling from her hand. She looked up but didn't move as Georgia Lee neared her own car and the narrow space that separated it from the one Jane sat in alone. Jane's stare—no, assessment—made Georgia Lee nervous, especially when coupled with her silence. She dropped the car keys on the ground in her efforts to finesse the key into the lock. Finally, she asked Jane if she could move.

Jane swung her arm out Vanna White–style with a smile and nudged her legs to the side.

Despite the afternoon heat, the sensation of Jane's closeness chilled her skin. Georgia Lee thanked her and opened her door after retrieving her keys from the ground.

Jane asked for her name and then propped her arm on the open window frame and slowly repeated it with a level of fascination that made Georgia Lee's insides tingle. She wasn't sure what to say. Georgia Lee had long known Jane's best friend, Angie. When Angie was in first grade, her family had moved out of Fort Chaffee and up to Maud Proper after being sponsored by a local Christian missionary family, and later moved to Maud Bottoms. One day, Susannah's boyfriend had called Angie an ugly word during lunch. The rest of their friends had laughed, but Georgia Lee had to force a lump of mashed potatoes down her throat. She hadn't known food that mushy could go down that hard, leaving a raw trail in her throat.

Once Jane came along with all the other kids from Maud Bottoms, dropped into the middle of the school year after a tornado tore up their high school, Georgia Lee began to watch Angie and Jane so much she worried others might notice as well and call her a different kind of bad name. When she stared, her brain crowded with the words *Stop looking stop looking stop looking*, but she couldn't look away from their ease with one another, how they laughed like they didn't care what anyone else thought. Georgia Lee couldn't remember ever feeling that way herself.

Jane had left Georgia Lee feeling sore all up in her body that day—sore from wanting something she shouldn't want; sore from knowing it was wrong.

She rubbed her eyes and breathed in through her nose, out through her mouth. Three seconds in, six seconds out.

The last time Georgia Lee had seen Jane was on the five o'clock news, after she'd confessed to Warren's murder. Twenty-five years ago now.

When reporters crowded around Jane after she exited the police car, her wrists in handcuffs, she had looked straight at the camera and said, "I killed Warren Ingram. Alone."

Confusion. That's what Georgia Lee remembered. The only thing she could really remember. It'd been so long ago. But wait: That was why her parents had locked her in her room. She remembered now, startled that she'd somehow forgotten.

Her parents had already expressed their "concern" with the friendship before Jane confessed to killing Warren. They certainly weren't going to allow it after. But she didn't expect they'd go that far.

Her body shook at the memory. Her father's drill squealed into the wood of her doorframe four times. The freshly installed padlock knocked against the door when her mom unlocked it to bring her lunch or the homework that Christlyn or Susannah dropped off every Monday afternoon. Georgia Lee pressed against the door like some doomed fairy-tale princess, locked away to protect her from her own impulses. Fingernails scraping the wood till they were jagged, skin cracked. Not daring to complain lest her captors find some other creative torture to inflict on her. Christlyn's and Susannah's voices drifting upstairs, wishes for a quick recovery. Reminders from Georgia Lee's mom that she could be out of school awhile. Words of thanks for their concern and help. Promises to tell Georgia Lee that they'd stopped by.

The illness? Mono. The kissing disease. Georgia Lee hadn't thought her mom could come up with something so clever. That her dad's "concern" could manifest in something so cruel.

One month without contact from Jane. One month with only her bedroom walls and en suite bathroom. One month without news, friends, phone calls, TV, radio, anything. One month with Jane's face and words on repeat in her mind.

By the time Georgia Lee's parents let her out of her room, Jane had left town and Georgia Lee had lost ten pounds and any chance of a scholarship, academic or otherwise. At church, she smiled weakly when the preacher thanked the Lord for her recovery. She got saved. Rebaptized. And buried thoughts of Jane and all they'd done, including that night. The Maud police had even moved on. Corpus delicti—no body, no evidence, no crime.

But now?

"Baby?" Rusty said behind her.

Georgia Lee planted a smile on her face, tried to mentally wash her thoughts in case they revealed themselves, and turned toward him.

He squatted behind her chair and wrapped his arms around her. Good and strong. A good man. She gripped his arm.

"I'm sorry," he said. "I know things are hard right now with the election."

"No, I'm sorry," she told him, and she was. About her behavior. About her recent and more frequent fantasies of living alone. About how this troublesome news could affect him and the boys. About how that one night when she was seventeen could ruin all their lives. "I'm sorry about supper. I'll come home early tomorrow. I can cook up that—"

"Hush." He kissed her on the head. "I don't care about supper. I want you to be all right."

"I am all right." She disliked insinuations to the contrary, even when they were correct. "I just had an annoying day at work. Can't nobody—"

"Keep Georgia Lee down," he finished for her. He laughed in that easy way that cracked her armor. He was her best friend. "Why don't you come inside?" he asked. "I'll turn off the TV. We'll sit and talk, and if the boys start acting up, I'll beat their asses for you."

She squeezed his arm. "You'd do that for me?"

"Hell, I'll beat their butts and lock 'em out of the house for the night."

"True love." She swiped at her eyes. The tears were real. She hoped he could see. She hoped he knew she was still in there. That good girl. The one he'd married, so far from who she'd been with Jane.

He gave her one last kiss on the head. "Let's get a move on, Miss *Lane*." Though his tone was kind, the words cut. She wouldn't change her last name when they married, and it still bothered him. But she couldn't. Though she was barely aware of it at the time, she knew she needed to keep something of her own before being swallowed by the future and all its unknowns.

Disquiet yawned and stretched within her like long-dormant fault lines, cutting through his kindness. She released her grip and patted his arm. "I'll be there in a sec."

He made a move toward her bottle of wine. She clutched it.

"I'll be there in a sec," she repeated, trying to keep her tone friendly. He didn't like it when she sounded angry, even though he could sound angry. He didn't like her drinking, even though he drank. Didn't like her close-to-but-not-quite cussing, even though he cussed. There were rules for women, and there were rules for men.

He held his hands up in surrender, offered a warm smile she couldn't bring herself to return. Instead, she turned her focus to some random point ahead of her.

After he closed the door, she took three deep, cleansing breaths. She would do what she always did. She would remain calm. She would manage the situation. Like old times. Like always.

She unscrewed the lid on her wine. Drinking was her reward for positive thinking. But then she paused.

She set the bottle of wine on the deck floor and steepled her hands for prayer. The wine could wait until she entered the house, closed the door, and drew down the blinds on the pressures of a public life and the frustrations of the private one.

Dear Lord . . .

Thinking better of it, she slipped out of the deck chair and onto her knees, facing the yard, the moon. This latest news from the lock? Nothing but a hurdle. Every winner had those.

They could see things, and they could tell their stories, but they would never know what was in her heart. They would never hear the words she whispered.

Dear Lord, please forgive us for what we did to that man.

Five

JANE

Jane woke with a start. Dreams and memories clung like a film across her mind. Every bone in her body complained from sitting, then walking, then sitting some more. She shielded her eyes from the headlights in the drive.

Diane eased out of the car, purse clenched tight. She peered into the shadows where Jane sat. "Who's there?"

"Jane." Then, after a pause: "Your daughter."

Just speaking the words made Jane shake all over. The last time they'd seen each other had been the day of the confession.

Fry her ass.

She could still hear Diane screaming those words as the officers walked Jane out of the trailer in handcuffs after Jane confessed to Warren's murder. When they eventually let her go for lack of evidence, Jane had broken into the trailer while Diane was at work and Jason at school. She'd grabbed whatever she could fit into a bag and hauled ass out of town.

Diane approached Jane slowly, like she might be a stranger hoping to fool her and carry out some violent action. Jane got this reaction all the time walking in the city. When other women realized she wasn't a man, they slowed their steps, their bodies releasing the tension. They slipped the keys out from between their fingers, fists no longer ready to fight.

Diane walked up the steps and took in Jane's appearance when the porch's motion light flickered on. Her body relaxed. "Well, if it isn't the infamous Lezzie Borden herself."

The cases weren't even similar. But Jane felt a kinship with her nick-namesake's desire to deliver forty whacks to her mother. Diane looked like hell, like she hadn't eaten or drunk anything but pork rinds and pickle juice for years. Underneath, there was still that rugged beauty. Her voice still plucked at Jane, making her crave the tender moments Diane rarely gifted her.

"I thought you were going to pick me up. I sent you the flight number, the arrival time."

Diane yanked the screen door open and fiddled with the front door lock. "You didn't say specifically you needed a ride. And you didn't say you was planning on staying here."

"You asked me to come."

Diane gripped the handle and shouldered the door until it swung open. She snorted. "Not 'cause I missed you."

Jane flinched but let the comment go and followed Diane inside. The country-craptastic fabric on the couch and the chairs near the windows had faded from the sun. The chandelier Diane had inherited from her grandmother and insisted Warren install still hung above the kitchen table, collecting dust on each prism. The wood paneling and wall-to-wall carpet caved Jane in and compacted her back into a teen-ager. She'd sat right there under the chandelier at the kitchen table with Jason and made him do his homework before bed. She'd read books with Georgia Lee on those backbreaking couch cushions when Diane and Warren were gone—Stephen King for Jane, Danielle Steel for Georgia Lee. She'd opened a can of pork and beans in that kitchen. Cut chunks of hot dogs with a dull knife from that silverware drawer.

Thrown them into a burnt-bottom pan she bet she'd still find in that cupboard. Called it supper and served it to Jason like it was something special.

Diane plunked her purse onto the scratched kitchen table. They both stood there and looked at each other, waiting for the other one to go first, like a game of chicken. Jane chewed on her bottom lip, trying to think of what next. What now. She wanted to sink into sleep, real sleep, deep sleep. The kind of sleep she couldn't remember ever being graced with.

"I'm gonna head to bed," Jane said and made her way toward the hallway.

"I got rid of your bed. Wasn't no sense in keeping it." Diane flicked a cigarette out of its pack. She kept her eyes on the flame of her lighter and the tip of the cigarette, not once looking up at Jane. "Jason doesn't come around, so what's the point?" The absence of Jane's name stung, even though she understood why. Why would Diane want the person who confessed to killing her husband to visit?

"I wouldn't expect you to keep it."

"Well, I couldn't. I don't have enough room to be storing all the crap you left and mine too." Diane exhaled, adding another layer of precancer to her lungs and stench to the room.

Jane adjusted her backpack and grabbed the handle of her luggage. "You got any clean sheets? A blanket?"

Diane glared at her.

Jane tossed her backpack onto the couch and released a long sigh. She'd slept on worse.

◆ ◆ ◆

Sunlight streamed onto Jane's face. She yanked out the rolled-up sweatshirt she'd used as a pillow and pulled it onto her head. She always had a hard time waking up because she always had a hard time falling asleep. The slightest noises elevated her heart rate. Terror spiked when she imagined someone sneaking around outside, peeping in the windows with ill will, even though Diane had always told her, *People don't break in to steal from people who don't have nothing.* Then again, she didn't have a window in the Sebastian County Juvenile Detention Center, and she had learned how much worse it could feel without windows and with thirty other criminally minded girls surrounding you.

During the night, she had dreamed of Georgia Lee. But they weren't dreams. They were replays of their time together. The edges of one moment gathered in her mind and then came into focus.

The air had been ripe for a thunderstorm. A breeze blew in through the living room window to cool their skin. Georgia Lee nudged Jane awake after she'd fallen asleep reading. She'd been making sounds, tossing. Georgia Lee asked what was wrong. Jane told her it was nothing. Just a dream. Georgia Lee propped her head on her hand and asked about the dream. Her golden hair drifted across her face.

Jane tucked it behind Georgia Lee's ear and stretched.

"Hard to wake up." Her head felt groggy, her body like cement.

Georgia Lee nudged her with her toe. "Is it a secret?"

"What?" Jane rubbed her eyes.

"The dream." Georgia Lee leaned in. She smelled like green apples. A smile, a spark in her eyes. "Was it about me?"

Jane laughed. Things were so much easier with Georgia Lee, like the light came on in a room. Joy in human form. Like nothing could ever be bad and whatever problem came her way could be fixed with the right attitude. "No."

But it was. Jane couldn't remember the contents, but she could recall the feeling. Lying there with Georgia Lee on the couch, the rain tapping at the window and some far-off wind chime relaying a song, Jane let herself believe all the hurts and the harm were in the past and all that lay ahead for her were easeful days full up with Georgia Lee.

Georgia Lee sucked on a Jolly Rancher and then grabbed Jane's left hand. She took the last little bit of candy out of her mouth and stuck it on Jane's ring finger. An almost emerald, sticky mess.

"Gross," Jane said and laughed, examining the candy-cum-gemstone's placement on the fourth finger of her left hand. She wished she could afford a class ring. She wished Georgia Lee could wear it on her left hand. She wouldn't need to wrap it in embroidery thread and nail polish to make it fit. "How many girls have you proposed to like this?"

Georgia Lee punched her. "None! I'm barely seventeen."

Jane held out her hand and let the overhead light sparkle in its limited capacity against the green candy on her finger. They could never marry. Not in their lifetimes. They'd have to be like those sad women in the movies and books Jane sometimes consumed. Doomed to fight. Doomed to tragedy. Doomed to sorrow.

Those were adult worries. First, Jane had to survive trigonometry. Georgia Lee, her swim meets.

Georgia Lee nuzzled close. "Do you like it?"

Jane held out her finger. "I'd prefer something a little more tasteful."

"It is!" Georgia Lee wrestled for the "emerald," but Jane popped it into her mouth before she could grab it.

"You're right. It's pretty good."

Georgia Lee rested beside Jane again and clasped her hand. "You'll be mine, though? No matter what?"

Underneath that green apple goodness lingered the sense that nothing would ever come easily to Jane, not without reaping some other sorrow. Not without payment in kind. Joy required a price.

Jane let the last bit of candy melt on her tongue. She swallowed it down and kissed Georgia Lee on the head.

"I will," she said, mimicking words she'd only ever heard on TV. "Till death do us part."

Agitated by the recollection and the state of her back, Jane shoved the sweatshirt aside and rubbed the sleep out of her eyes. She twisted her hips to crack her back, rolled over, and wrangled the previous day's bra on under her shirt. She didn't miss much about youth except a body that could handle some extra weight and a walk in nonsensible shoes longer than a mile without feeling like she needed a crank and grease to set it right. Her most recent ex had tried to get her into yoga, but it had only made her more tense. All that breathing. That quiet time. The clock ticking in Jane's head and filling the emptiness with anxieties. Her ex was probably at yoga right now. Taking deep, cleansing breaths. Inhaling a new life, exhaling Jane.

Pills would help.

She wandered into the bathroom. Diane had always preferred booze to numb her feelings, but that'd been years ago. Maybe the alcohol no longer worked for her. She opened the cabinet. Made a wish for Xanax, Prozac, Valium, Ativan, Adderall. Something. Anything. She'd once stolen all the Klonopin prescribed for an ex's dog when the night terrors of the time she'd spent in juvie had hit.

The dog was fine. He got a refill.

She rifled through an assortment of cold sore remedies, dried-up nail polish, disposable flossers, and mostly empty jars of what looked like face cream with worn-off labels. No pills. Of course not. Pills would require a prescription and a prescription would require a doctor and a doctor would require insurance, which Diane never had, which meant Jane and Jason had never had it either.

She shut the cabinet door, and the whole shelf came down with it.

"God. Dammit." She breathed in once, twice, three times to calm the rising irritation.

When she opened the cabinet, all the contents tumbled out into the sink, including the broken shelf. At least it wasn't glass.

Diane slept soundly through it all. At times, it was hard to know if Diane was blackout drunk or just slept like a baby, unbothered by the world.

Cleanup complete, she sat on the toilet and lost track of time wading through old news articles about Warren's disappearance on her phone and debating whether the local police would immediately arrest her or let her sit around for a while. She certainly didn't want to show up and offer herself as she'd done before. So stupid.

No word online about the discovery of Warren's body. Yet. As soon as it hit, she had to be prepared. For what, she wasn't quite sure. But one thing felt certain: a second arrest.

After her first arrest, no one had visited her. Not Jason, not Angie, not Georgia Lee. Would they now that they were adults? Now that they were clearheaded, mature, and fully aware that Jane could be sent to prison, for real this time?

She googled Angie. She tried Facebook first, searching the listings for Arkansas. Too many girls had been named Angie the same year. Too many results to sort through, even when looking for a Vietnamese woman named Angie. She'd probably gotten married and taken her husband's last name. Probably moved out of Arkansas.

Maybe she was dead. That would certainly be helpful. One less accomplice to keep quiet.

She had to stop wishing other people dead. It wasn't good for the spirit.

She set up RSS feeds and Google notifications to alert her to news that mentioned *Angie Pham* along with the one she'd already set up for *Jason Mooney*. Then she added one for *Warren Ingram*. She tossed her phone onto the bath mat and waited for her bowels to relax after a night of poor dietary choices.

No need to check on Georgia Lee. For years, Jane had kept tabs on her under the guise of mildly stalking old high school friends. Everyone did that; therefore, she reasoned, no one could peg her as suspicious should anyone care to dig around in her browser history. She knew all about Georgia Lee's job at the pharmacy, her city council position, her marital and parental status. No way she'd admit to being linked to a murder. And Jane didn't want to open any doors where Georgia Lee was concerned. Best to keep some things in the past.

After thinking more on it, she stretched to reach her phone from where she'd tossed it onto the mat, removed the Google Alerts, and deleted her phone's browser history even though nothing ever truly disappeared online. The thing she really wanted to search—*Is a confession and a body enough to convict a person of murder, or no?*—would probably reveal she was fine.

Goddammit, she thought. She really should have changed her name. Gone into hiding when she had the chance. But Jason. Always Jason. Jane never should've left him alone with Georgia Lee that night. She tapped out a text, asking him to call her. As always, the screen stayed blank.

Everything will be fine. If she repeated it enough, maybe it'd come true.

After her shower, she threw on some jeans and a vintage *The Lost Boys* T-shirt she'd swiped from a one-night stand years ago, slicked her hands with gel, and proceeded to fix her hair even though she had nowhere to go. The routine soothed her and made her feel less unemployed and look less indigent. In the kitchen, she made herself a cup of store-brand coffee she found in the cabinets and waited for Diane to wake. She took one sip and dumped it in the sink.

Bored, she wandered into the bedroom she and Jason had shared. Diane hadn't lied. Wasn't but a foot of space clear on the floor. The room smelled of mildew.

When she turned to exit, she busted her pinkie toe against the leg of an old chair. Diane kept so much unnecessary shit. Tin cookie cans full of thread and needles and denim patches Diane had never used despite the frequent holes in the knees of Jane's and Jason's jeans. Fringed purses and frayed tops. A set of faded purple dumbbells from Diane's brief Jane Fonda workout phase before she'd said to hell with it and switched to SlimFast for breakfast and lunch followed by dinner at her favorite bar, whose phone number Jane could still recite. She bet someone would answer. Bars tended to stay open in towns where everything else died.

She knew better than to expect anything of hers in the bedroom, locked in time and place as it had been in her memory. Still, she looked. The only photos she found were in a shoebox that held assorted memorabilia of random men Diane had dated before Warren. Twenty-three in all. None around longer than three months, by her recollection. Some she'd seen occasionally in nearby towns or at gas stations. Others seemed to have fallen off the face of the planet—no doubt in hiding from Diane. Of the boyfriends in the box that Jane remembered, she and Jason had only liked one. He taught them penny poker and chased them around the house, them screaming in terrified delight. Diane was nice when he was around. Somehow, Jane couldn't recall his name, only that she liked him and he had a missing ring finger. The photo she found of him and Diane had been taken one blistering hot day, out near the river on the Maud Proper side. Jason skimmed rocks across the water, Diane nearby saying something to upset his aim. Jane sat with the guy on a beach towel. She asked him what had happened to his finger. He laughed, leaned in conspiratorially, and whispered, "Your mom." Before she had a chance to ask what she considered to be an important follow-up question—a knife, a hammer, a car door, her teeth?—Diane appeared out of nowhere, took his hand, and teasingly led him toward the murky water. He never came around again.

She flipped through the odd collection and set aside pictures of Asian men who might be Jason's dad, a smaller pile than the one she sorted of white men for herself. That pile held several options, such as the bare-chested, long-haired guy in the red bandana, which she found at the bottom of the box. Or the snap-shirt cowboy, whom she suspected once owned the turquoise-and-silver ring that dwarfed her thumb. Or the smiling blond in a red shirt and jeans and a giant gold belt buckle in the shape of Arizona, whose smooth surface she ran her fingertips across. Briefly, she mused about that missing ring finger and whether she'd find it at the bottom of the box too.

All she knew of her father was that Diane had gotten knocked up at sixteen by a guy nicknamed Tough, who was out there somewhere without any idea he had a daughter named Jane.

Diane's parents didn't disown her after she got pregnant with Jane, but apparently they were heavy handed with the shame and the *I told you so*'s because they were Christians, the kind who actually went to church and didn't believe in abortion, not even in secret to save face. Jane suspected Diane had only kept Jane to spite her parents. Like most men, Tough loved Diane and then left her. Tough hadn't lasted, but the parental estrangement had.

Maybe Tough was dead too.

One of her exes had gotten her a DNA test, back when no one worried about cops arresting their relations for heinous crimes they'd committed when they were young and stupid. Jane had declined the gift but hadn't explained why she didn't want her DNA anywhere someone could find it.

At the bottom of the box was one last photo. In it, Diane wore a yellow tube top and skinny white shorts. Warren stood behind her with his left forearm providing additional support for her breasts. Both smiling. No other photo had ever captured Diane that happy.

She returned all the photos to the box, shut the lid, and shoved it back where she had found it. Nothing of Jane remained in the house. None of Jane's drawings from childhood. No photos she could find. On the way out of the room, she slammed the door closed.

◆　◆　◆

By the time the sun hit its midday peak, Diane wandered out of her room, hair askew and day-old foundation collected in the lines of her face. The thin T-shirt she wore clung to her bony frame. Daylight was a harsh judge, but Jane didn't draw any joy from that. Many of those lines were Jane's doing.

Diane poured herself the remainder of the coffee Jane had made and abandoned. The chair she plopped in creaked, though she wasn't but a hundred pounds, if that. Her thinness had been a gift as a young woman. Now she lacked the fat that gave other women a healthy glow and plump cheeks. Before taking a sip of coffee, she looked at Jane, as if to question what poison she'd put in her cup. They sat in silence for a while, not even looking at each other.

"Did you sleep well?" Jane finally asked.

Diane looked at her like she had five heads. Silence was more comfortable than even the lowest form of conversation.

"Have you talked to Jason?" she asked after Diane didn't respond to small talk.

"Course not. He used to come around, but . . ." A thought seemed to darken Diane's mood and then cleared. She fluttered her hand in the air and let the gesture fill in the rest, then sipped her coffee and grimaced. "The only way anybody'd know I had kids is because of the stretch marks." Diane released a phlegmy cough. "Why you asking?"

Because she worried about what Jason might tell the cops if they came knocking. "Because I haven't talked to him since you texted me about Warren," she said. "That's what families do. Talk."

Diane crushed an empty pack of cigarettes she'd retrieved from the purse hanging on the back of her chair and sent it skittering across the table like a tumbleweed. She glared at the empty pack before redirecting that glare onto Jane. "Forgive me if I'm not itching for a conversation with you."

"Then why'd you ask me to come and stay with you? Why'd you forgive me?"

"You think I forgive you?" Diane laughed and held Jane's stare, challenging her. "I don't forgive you. You should never have been allowed to leave. I want to make sure you don't skip out on serving your time now that they've found Warren's body. You're the idiot who agreed to come back."

Meanness. That's what Jane remembered, stitched onto every wound that didn't work its way out of her skin and all the ones that did. Even before Warren. For years—her whole life—Jane had wondered what defect she possessed that made Diane hate her so much. Was it that she had ruined Diane's life at sixteen by being born? Was it because she was queer? Was it that Jane didn't follow the Game of Life, with all the right pegs and all the right spaces, cutting Diane off from an easy and early retirement filled with grandchildren and someone to wipe her ass and feed her Ensure when she got older? But that wasn't something she could ask, not even in the heat of the moment. Maybe because the answer would be too painful to hear.

"I won't skip town," Jane said. "I confessed, remember?"

Diane smirked. Jane paused to consider what she would say next. "Did the police say anything about what happens next? Now that they found him?"

"You tell me."

"I haven't talked to them."

"Then you best get on it. You need the number?"

Jane tried to shake off her hurt, sound normal. "No." The news about the discovery still hadn't gone live. She couldn't say why she hadn't called the police or gone straight there from the plane. Maybe a part of her hoped that she'd still get away with it. The explanation, an accident, after all these years.

The phone rang and made her jump. She hadn't heard a house phone in ages. Diane let it ring a few times.

"You gonna get that?" Jane asked.

"Probably just a bill collector. Let it ring." Diane paused until the rings subsided. "How much you reckon a funeral is gonna cost?"

Jane had never buried anyone. At least not in the traditional sense. "Two thousand, five thousand? I don't know. I'll have to look it up."

"I hope you didn't spend all your money on some last hurrah." She examined Jane's clothing and clearly reconsidered that accusation by the way she smirked.

So that's why she called.

"So do you?" Diane asked.

"Have the money? Yeah. I have money." To pay for her abusive stepfather's funeral? Sure. Why not? She closed her eyes and choked back emotions she'd prefer to suppress.

"Well, good. It's the least you can do after what you already done. That'd take me weeks, maybe months, before I could haul up that kind of cash. Even if it were my responsibility. Lord knows I can't afford a service right now with everything going on around here—"

"What's going on around here?"

"Everything. Nothing good." She flung her hands into the air, as if the house swarmed with obligation. "The car's been giving out on me. And then the AC. The fridge is on the fritz. I can't even get the goddamn toaster to act right. You name it, it broke down."

"That's some bad luck."

"It is bad luck. I've had nothing but bad luck. My whole life." Diane's voice trailed off as she likely remembered every bad thing that had ever happened to her since Jane, the first bad thing.

The phone rang again. Again, Diane ignored it.

"Don't you have someone to help you out? A boyfriend?" There was always a boyfriend. Never in the history of Jane's life had there been an absence of men in Diane's.

"My God. You think I could date after all that? The shit you put me through?" Diane's eyes glistened, and Jane softened, even if a small part of her questioned the sincerity of those tears, if not the words. How quickly and easily tears came when something Diane wanted or lacked was on the line, with family and friends and boyfriends. With Warren. With Jane.

Jane waited for the tears to end. When the phone rang for the third time, she got up to answer it, but Diane swatted at her. "Leave it be. They'll stop after a while."

"It could be an emergency."

Diane delivered a withering stare. "Like learning my husband's been beaten to death by my daughter?"

The morning after, Diane had made a racket in the kitchen, cursing Warren's absence. She called everyone, it seemed. The bar. His workplace. His shitty friends. Her shitty friends. Made a big show of how he'd decided not to come home after a big fight they'd had at the bar. Even changed the lock on the front door the next day to "teach him a lesson about leaving" even though it was his trailer.

The ring agitated. "I didn't mean for any of this to happen." Much as Jane tried to muster emotion to match the statement, she couldn't. Not after Warren's shouting at her and Jason for talking while he watched TV, accusations that they'd broken his beloved Johnny Reb commemorative football mug, curses that they dared to even exist at all. Not to mention Freddie and Charlie, their parakeets. The only pets Diane had ever allowed. Pretty, chirpy birds they'd been given by a departing neighbor who had to move to a new place. Jane and Jason had sworn to take care of them and to love them. They had. And then one morning both birds were gone. No warning. No reason. Just gone.

Jane fought a strong and sudden urge to lash out. She wasn't sorry Warren was dead.

Diane's tears welled again.

Jane checked her watch. A habit. A distraction from Diane's emotions. Of course she was mad at Jane. What mother wouldn't be?

She mentally calculated the cost of a coffin, a funeral director, and whatever else people had to pay for and the rapidly diminishing amount in her savings account. The unemployment checks would still come for at least a month, but she wanted to hold on to every penny in the unlikely event she got lucky and could leave Maud unshackled. Or in case she could somehow draw on that money in prison for commissary snacks. Or tampons.

Diane wiped her nose on her sleeve and sniffled. "We best call the funeral home today and get things moving along."

The phone rang. Jane closed her eyes and swallowed down her pride. "Okay."

Diane's face brightened, but then she paused. "You promise you'll take care of the funeral? The costs?"

Always a catch, a confirmation. "I'll call in a bit and see when they might be able to release the remains."

Diane near sucked the air out of the room with her gasp. "My God, Jane. The remains?"

"Sorry. I just . . ." *That's the proper terminology,* she muttered under her breath.

"To you, maybe, but I loved him. He's a person."

Was. Resentment rose like bile.

A click interrupted them, followed by the robotic female voice of Diane's antiquated answering machine telling the caller that the person they wished to reach was not at home.

"Jesus. They could've left a message five tries ago," Jane said.

"Ahh . . . ," said the deep-voiced man on the line. "Sorry to bother you at home, Mrs. Ingram. This is Detective Hampton with the Maud Police Department." Jane froze. She didn't hear what else he had to say over the sound of her ears ringing and her head pounding at the realization that the inevitable had finally come to pass.

Six

GEORGIA LEE

Diane had been manning the register at Cloverleaf Liquors since Georgia Lee could remember. She didn't know how she could stand it. Probably 'cause she got a discount. Georgia Lee hated coming in this warehouse full of booze. Handwritten, misspelled signs indicating markdowns. She preferred one of those cute little shops like they had up in Maud Proper, with mood lighting and free Friday night samples. All her anxiety gave way to annoyance. What was the point of being friends with the chief of police if not to get the most up-to-date dirt on one's friends and neighbors?

Diane pushed aside a case of wine she'd been attacking with a box cutter, tucked an errant swath of bleached hair behind an ear, and rang up some boozy seltzer and Flamin' Hot Cheetos for a customer. She thanked the man and flashed one of those quick retail-worker smiles, exhausted and bracing.

Georgia Lee had once credited Diane as some kind of something. Trashy but seductive, braless in her tight tank tops and short shorts. All flash and glitter, good perfume and good hair. But that was a false memory. Diane was always nothing. Waiting for and wanting a man to throw her over his shoulder and take care of everything. Even if it meant beating the crap out of each other—as long as he kept her rich in booze, Marlboros, and bridge mix. No wonder Jane and Jason had always looked so ill. Nothing to eat but what they could scrounge. They'd reminded Georgia Lee of those *Flowers in the Attic* kids, all pale and poisoned, looking five years younger than they oughta. Minus the incest, of course.

She released a long breath full of spite and made her way to the counter, but a guy clutching a pack of Milwaukee's Best against his uniform made it there first. He looked familiar. Gerry What's-His-Name. That was it. Rusty had sold him a house early on in his career. Something small. Nothing fancy. Nice fellow. Took care of his momma. Worked at the lock and dam. Probably found the body. Wouldn't be the first. It'd been a while since the last one. Early spring, an older man out fishing. She was surprised they'd not found more bodies after that flood.

Georgia Lee refocused on the two of them. She wondered if Diane knew that he'd likely found the body. She'd add it to her bulleted list of items to ask John about later if he felt up to talking instead of continuing with his annoying tight-lipped stance on an "active" case.

If she wasn't mistaken, Gerry was sweet on Diane. His eyes stayed focused on her face instead of traveling down her body. Fine time to woo a woman. Diane didn't seem to mind. In fact, she bared her teeth and smiled, something Diane rarely did. She could use some of that teeth-whitening stuff.

Diane said something and Gerry laughed, shifting his stance in the process and bumping into Georgia Lee. She had a mind to educate him about standing too close and invading her personal space.

"Oh goodness. Pardon me," he said in the sweetest, thickest accent before casting his eyes to Diane. He looked uncertain as to whether he should leave or not.

"Good to see you again," Diane said to him, all formal-like, as if they hadn't been flirting two seconds prior. Then Diane gave Gerry a closed-mouth smile and a little wrinkle of the nose, like she'd tasted something off in the casserole at a dinner party and didn't have the heart to tell the host. Though Georgia Lee doubted Diane had ever been invited to one of those.

"Oh, I think I forgot something," Gerry said, doing a poor job of faking surprise in the service of spending more time with Diane. "I'll just take another spin around the store." Diane practically vibrated with irritation, though Georgia Lee wasn't sure if it was because of Gerry or her.

"Diane Ingram, is that you?" Georgia Lee looked over her *Breakfast at Tiffany's*–style sunglasses—used for slipping in and out of liquor stores without her constituents noticing.

Diane swiveled Georgia Lee's way and did a double take.

"It's Georgia Lee. You remember me?" She took off her sunglasses. Less suspicious that way. Kindly. Thoughtful. "I'm on the city council. Perhaps you've seen my posters. There's an election coming up—"

"I'm voting for Andy Bollinger."

"Oh," Georgia Lee said. She could walk away, wait and see if an image of Jane being escorted to jail crossed her TV once more. But sitting by wasn't Georgia Lee's style. "I was friends with Jane. Your daughter." Maybe Jane didn't remember her. Maybe Diane wouldn't either. The last thing she needed was to be associated with Maud's confessed killer.

"I know who you are." Diane gave Georgia Lee the once-over. "I ain't stupid."

Georgia Lee bit down on a retort. "I was passing by on my way home from a council meeting and thought I'd stop by to pay my respects. I heard the news. What a shock that Warren has been found after all these years." She paused, swallowed, smiled. "Did they say what happened? I remember it being such a mystery, especially after the confession." She couldn't bear to say Jane's name. "Was it true? Did she kill him?"

Cold rushed through her. She clasped her arms against her chest and rubbed at the goose bumps that had risen. *Stay focused,* she told herself.

Diane began to speak but hesitated, and her bottom lip got all quivery like she might cry. Well, she wasn't the only one. Georgia Lee would prefer to read about the details of Warren's demise and Jane's fate in the news instead of hunting them down in the bad part of town, but they still hadn't released the information to the public. Granted, it was her town. But that was why she'd initially become a city councilor. To beautify! Make Maud Bottoms as good as or better than Maud Proper!

Stay calm, she reminded herself. She needed Diane.

Diane searched the store for a customer to help, but she was trapped behind the register. She looked at Georgia Lee, and Georgia Lee looked right back. Diane scratched at her head, and that made Georgia Lee want to scratch her own head. She wondered what kind of shampoo and conditioner Diane bought. That cheap stuff, probably. Might as well use bar soap.

"You trying to make me feel some kind of way?" Diane had always seemed uneasy around her. Like Georgia Lee might tell on her or something. Call the cops on her for being a bad mother.

"Of course not." Georgia Lee smiled harder, clenched her jaw. "I wanted to see how you're doing."

"How the hell do you think I'm doing?"

"Look, Diane . . ." Georgia Lee clenched her fists and smiled. "I know we weren't always on the best of terms, but I truly am sorry for your loss. That can't be easy, having this come up again after all these years."

"Well, it's not easy," Diane said. "That's a fact."

"I'm sure you're relieved. As are the cops. Have they mentioned any next steps?" Georgia Lee couldn't help but get to the point. Questions swirled. Were they planning on issuing a warrant for Jane's arrest? Did they already conduct an autopsy? Did they know how Warren truly died? She straightened her posture, tried to keep her body from shaking.

"I know why you're here."

Flashes of memory shot through Georgia Lee, the fog of what she'd remembered at the pharmacy clearing in her mind: Warren's breath, his mouth, his fingers.

Diane's voice startled her. "What?" Georgia Lee asked.

"I said," Diane strung out the words, "your parents paid a pretty price to keep your name out of the press. Apples don't fall far from the tree. Ain't that what people say?"

Georgia Lee saw herself standing there, stunned and blinking, as if she were having an out-of-body experience. "What are you talking about?"

"They didn't tell you? I guess they wouldn't. Probably wanted to protect you." By the crooked smile Diane gave, Georgia Lee knew she'd opened a door she should've left closed. "But protection comes at a price."

"What did they do?" Georgia Lee asked.

"Well, I don't want to go talking out of turn. If you want answers, you ought to talk to them."

Confusion mixed with anger. "They're dead."

Diane frowned. "That's too bad. Or maybe it's good. They were so desperate to keep their good name out of the papers, especially when it came to Lezzie Borden. They'd be right disappointed about now."

Georgia Lee had only learned of Jane's nickname and the town's frenzy to learn the identity of her mysterious "gal pal" after Jane was released and left town, after Georgia Lee's parents had removed the padlock on her bedroom door and released her.

The nickname jarred Georgia Lee's senses and told her everything she needed to know about what was to come as soon as the news got out. "Sad that even now you'd stoop so low. Especially when it comes to your daughter."

Diane dipped her head so that her eyes looked sinister under the veil of her eyebrows. "The only ones who stooped were your parents."

"Lies."

"You want evidence? I got it."

"I don't believe you."

"I don't give a shit if you do." Diane challenged her, a smile on her face that Georgia Lee wanted to rip off.

"What exactly did they do, then?" Georgia Lee asked again.

The cigarette lines around Diane's mouth crinkled as she considered an answer. "They paid me to keep quiet about you and Jane." She raised her chin in defiance. "But that offer's expired. And if you want the same courtesy, it's gonna cost you."

Before Georgia Lee knew what she was even doing, she grabbed Diane's hand where she'd rested it on the counter. Diane startled and tried to remove herself from Georgia Lee's grip, but Georgia Lee held on to her dry, rough hand and squeezed so hard her wedding ring cut into her own skin. Diane needed Gold Bond. She needed to make this easy, give up the information Georgia Lee wanted in a normal, conversational manner without making her beg for it, keep her secrets without forcing her to pay for it. Georgia Lee would admit she wasn't great at not being defensive. She made a mental note to work on it and released her grip.

"I best be going." Georgia Lee checked her watch and slipped on her glasses. "You're in my prayers."

Diane rubbed her hand in dramatic fashion. "I don't need your prayers."

"Well, that's not how it works, honey. I'm praying anyway."

Diane snickered. "You come all this way. Ain't you gonna ask about Jane?"

Georgia Lee glanced at Gerry, who'd wandered up behind her. She wished he would go find some other register. There were three additional lanes open, but he had to hang around here, listening in on private conversations. She gave him another glance, but his focus was on the assortment of cigarette lighters and candy that lined the checkout lane.

"Jane?" Georgia Lee asked, not willing to commit to any other word in regard to that subject.

"Figured you'd want to see her before she goes to prison for real this time. Who knows what other information might come out now that she's had some time to think on it."

Georgia Lee looked directly at Gerry without saying a word. He hugged his beer closer to his chest and slunk off toward a moonshine display.

"Seems your memory isn't quite what it used to be," Georgia Lee said. "Jane and I were just friends."

Diane's gaze drifted to the box cutter beside her hand and then back to Georgia Lee.

"My memory's just fine," Diane said. "It don't take a genius to know you two used to be—" she searched for the word—"close."

Georgia Lee's whole body warmed.

Diane smiled and tilted her head. "Here's something else I remember: Jane was a good girl before you came along. Used to mind me. I'd tell you to stay away from her, but I guess y'all can get up to whatever the hell you want to now for whatever time you have left. Just don't do it on my couch this time." Before Georgia Lee could find the words to respond, Diane continued, "The funeral service would be a fine time to drop off what it'll take to bury him, if you catch my drift. Otherwise, I'm gonna have to ask you to leave." She clicked a nail against a laminated sign. "No loitering, ma'am."

Diane motioned for Gerry to step up to the register.

Lightheadedness swept through Georgia Lee. She straightened her sunglasses, smiled, and speed walked out of the store and to her car. She fumbled with the keys, unlocked it, threw herself into the seat, slammed the door, and gripped the wheel.

Fuck.

Seven

JANE

Adult contemporary pop played low on the radio. As soon as Jane turned the dial to a country station, Diane told her, "Turn that shit off." Jane conceded rather than fight.

The songs weren't that bad. Seemed there was a station like that in every region of the country, no matter how small, usually with *Magic* in the name. Fitting, as the tunes lulled Jane into almost forgetting about the phone call from the detective, her impending imprisonment, and the fact that the car she drove had belonged to Warren, another thing Diane kept around because it required no payment other than regular servicing when it broke down. Or maybe she had an emotional attachment to it. Jane got that. She still had a friendship bracelet Angie had made her.

The AC didn't work, so she let the hot highway wind envelop her. Diane responded by throwing a hand to her freshly shellacked hair. She had asked Jane to drive on account of a headache. Jane wondered if she'd already started drinking. Not that driving would stop that.

The wind also helped to air out the lingering smell of Diane's cigarettes and White Shoulders perfume, a smell Jane would forever associate with desperation and hunger and another breakup. Diane back on the hunt, back at Crawdaddies. She could almost hear the click of Diane's cheap black heels down the hallway. See her open the fridge to pull out a beer from among the empty shelves and condiment containers. She could see herself there on the floor. Pen marks on the tips of her fingers. Strands of hair stuck in the dried sauce of her SpaghettiOs. And Jason there, too, beside her, his little digits clutching the crayon in his fist, not looking up from the storm of dark colors he'd circled over and over on the page. Little bits of paper torn off from the violent swirls. Humming the whole time.

And there in the kitchen, Diane downing the beer and dropping it into a paper bag under the sink, where it clocked the bottle she'd drunk after she got home from work. Diane facing the empty cabinets, hands on hips, looking for a quick bite to eat that wasn't there because she'd neglected to go to the store. Diane pausing, noticing the quiet, the fact that she wasn't the only one in the room. Looking over her shoulder, seeing Jane there, and pausing to take in this girl, her girl. A pen in each hand, head up, mouth drawn tight. Thinking about doing harm. Plunging those pens into Diane's throat. A thought so bright and clear, like it was the right and true thing to do.

"Sonofabitch," Diane muttered.

Jane glanced at her in the passenger seat. Diane sighed loudly, typed out a message on her cracked phone with its fake crystal case, and then sighed some more.

"Everything okay?"

Diane nodded and then stared out the car window, not saying anything more.

"Maybe we could head over to Jason's after. See if he's up for lunch or something." Still no word from him after multiple calls and texts, which worried Jane. It was one thing to ignore her when she lived hundreds of miles away, another when she was in Maud because their dead stepfather's body had been found. If she knew Jason—and she did, in that deep, familial way that didn't dissipate no matter the minutes or miles that separated them—he was avoiding her for one particular reason. "You got his address?"

"Not since he moved." Diane looked up, pointed at the road, and then returned to her phone. "You missed the exit."

◆　◆　◆

Diane insisted on a casket instead of the much cheaper option, cremation.

She also insisted Warren be treated like a real person with a family, not some homeless guy. Jane would've been happy to toss the remains in with the other unaccounted-fors in the city plot.

Chuck didn't meet Jane's expectations of a funeral home guy. He was too young, too tanning bed tan, too talkative. He wore a short-sleeve polo shirt tucked into heavily pressed khakis. She wanted the guy she always saw on TV, the one with a welcoming smile and kind eyes. A Wilford Brimley type who not only listened patiently but also offered mourners condolences and hard candies from a glass granny bowl. Not a former high school football star who pity smiled at Diane too much and was super interested in "the case" and having a true crime celebrity as a client—even if he didn't quite understand how she and Diane could be in the same room together. But according to the Yelp reviews, the price was as right as they could get in Maud Bottoms.

As for the case, it was all over town now. Jane had pored over the news items all morning, addicted to other people's opinions on whether or not she deserved to die. Most seemed to think she did. A local Facebook group called Let's Talk About Maud provided the most comments and votes for her demise after a "little bird" who claimed to be close to the family "revealed" that Jane had been planning to kill Warren for weeks as evidenced in "as-yet-unreleased journal entries!"

One. Jane didn't fucking journal. Two. They weren't a family. There was no such thing as getting or being close when it came to them.

As if reading Jane's thoughts, Diane positioned herself across the room from Jane in a stiff wooden chair, glared, and let Jane do all the talking. Jane examined a laminated copy—for the tears, Chuck explained—of package deals.

"What kind of options do we have for . . ." Jane paused, not wanting to make the same mistake again of mentioning the remains, even though that's what they were. "A simple burial."

"Simple?" Diane shook her head. "I don't think so."

Jane's blood pressure spiked. But Chuck took the opening and proceeded to outline the mechanics, construction, and stylistic features of various caskets. Poor Chuck. She suspected he never got out and talked to normal people anymore. Unfortunately, he didn't sell plain pine boxes. Not that Jane could get away with that.

"That's super interesting, Chuck. But listen. We need the cheapest thing you got."

"He deserves more than a cheap box." The words shot out Diane's mouth like gunfire.

Jane turned to her. "I'm happy to pay. But I'm not made of money." Chuck typed away without taking his eyes off them. Probably transcribing every word they said, thinking he had some inside scoop for KMSM or the *Maud Register* or that Facebook group. Jane held up the laminated sheet. "The cheapest thing he has is still *quite* nice and *quite* expensive." She cut her eyes at him.

He didn't miss the opportunity for an upsell. "There's a wonderful option from a company right here in Arkansas." He shuffled through a drawer and pulled out a brochure. "Their caskets are made to look like fishing boats." He turned to Diane while Jane looked on, stunned. "Was your husband an outdoorsman?"

"This one will do fine." Jane pointed at the cheap option while Diane sank in her chair.

"Wonderful." His tight shoulders belied his polite tone at Jane's rebuttals. "And the body, would you like a closed casket?" Now that they'd agreed on an option, he didn't look up from his calculator.

Diane clutched her purse and stared at Jane for an uncomfortable amount of time. Soon she started blinking back tears and turned her attention to Chuck, who clicked away. "An open casket's not an option, thanks to my daughter." She pushed herself out of the chair with one arm, leaving the chair to hobble awkwardly to one side and her to nearly trip in her rush to remove herself from the room. She would've done a fine job as an extra in Hollywood.

As soon as the door clicked shut, Jane eyed Chuck. "I don't think anyone's gonna want to see a skeleton, Chuck."

He looked up, realized his mistake, and clutched at his polo. "I'm sorry. I—"

"It's fine. You've got a script." His face went ashen, and she regretted her words. Dark humor had always been her coping mechanism. "Sorry. It's an honest mistake," she said, returning her attention to the coffin catalog. "Really. Don't worry about it." Surely there were discounts available to people who needed to bury bones, not bodies. There'd be no need for blood drainage or formaldehyde. No organs to deal with.

Chuck looked to the door, as if questioning whether or not he should follow Diane and try to comfort her.

"She's fine," Jane reassured him. "She just needs some time alone." She wasn't about to let him get Diane alone and swindle her into some custom Razorback-embellished monstrosity with a lifetime guarantee. And she wasn't about to turn over her last dime for a man who didn't deserve more than a shallow grave.

"Golly." She sniffled and wiped her dry eyes. She'd learned from the best. Might as well not let her skill set go to waste. "I didn't realize how awful that sounds when you say it out loud, to think about him as nothing but bones." But she'd thought about it. Many times over the years. And not without some sorrow. But not for him.

Attentive once again, Chuck pushed a box of tissues across the desk. She took one and blew her nose, even though she didn't need to.

"Sorry. It's hard. Accepting her forgiveness, though I've done her so wrong. But to have to handle the burial of the man who brought me so much pain? You don't even know. No one knows." Except Jason. She dabbed the tissue at nothing, head still lowered. "It's a lot."

Chuck kept repeating, "I know, I know." She kept expecting him to call her honey. "I just can't imagine what you're going through. You know, despite what you might be hearing or reading, a lot of us are on your side and think he deserved it. I'm a God-fearing man, but I tell you what, I would have done the same."

"You would have?" she asked. She hated how she craved that validation. That he'd deserved it because he was a bad man.

"Sounds like an open-and-shut case of self-defense, if you ask me." He smiled but then added, "Course it didn't help that you told everyone at the time you didn't regret it and wished you'd done it sooner."

"Thank you. I appreciate your support." She'd been so stupid. A dumb teenager. Angry and scared. She crumpled her dry tissue in her lap. "Back to the coffin. It's just a lot of money. I lost my job, of course. And my mom can't afford it, and we don't have any savings. And with my legal fees, I . . ." She waited for him to offer a discount, but he didn't bite. "I think I should probably check out a few other places, Chuck. Just to be sure."

Ten minutes later, she'd secured 15 percent off his services and a layaway plan for a pecan-colored coffin with brass flair. She could've done without the flair, but it wasn't optional.

"The last piece of business is to settle on a date." He tapped away at his computer, minus the cheer he'd exhibited ten minutes prior. "That all depends on when they release the body. Have the police indicated when that might be?"

Jane looked up from her phone, where she'd been working on her own set of calculations. "No. How long does it usually take?"

Chuck considered. "Rather quickly in most cases. In your case, it might take a while." The words Jane wanted to say weren't formulating in her mind in a way that felt innocent. Luckily, Chuck stepped in for her. "Because of the nature of his death."

"Right," she said and smiled weakly. "They need to confirm the manner of death."

Chuck slowly blinked his eyes to affirm her statement.

"About that discount. I appreciate it. I do. But I'm wondering if maybe there's any way you can speed things along?" The longer that body stayed unburied, the more likely they'd find something that created suspicion as to how Warren had died.

He tilted his head and blew air out his mouth slow and steady.

"What if I pay you extra? Like a rush fee?" she asked.

All smiles now. "How much we talking?"

"That all depends on how quickly you can make this happen." She stood. "But I'll make sure it's worth your while."

He shot out of his chair and followed her to the door. "What if they arrest you before I can get to it?"

She turned and shrugged. "Guess that means you better hurry."

"If I could just get that deposit—"

"Call me when you've got good news for me," she said and shut the door behind her before he could follow her.

The scent of orchids overwhelmed her nose. A florist had made a delivery and left it on a table near the entrance. In a room down the subtly lit hall, little sobs escaped to provide a mournful soundtrack. She walked toward the exit, bracing for the heat behind the glass doors and the burden of wondering *Now what?*

What were the cops looking for? Wasn't her confession enough?

Outside, it felt like she'd stepped into a sauna, but without the soothing lights or lavender aromatherapy. The grass had been burned of color and drooped against patches of dirt. Across the road, an old white woman sat on the porch of her shotgun house and fanned herself with a Frisbee. A couple of Asian women sat on a bus stop bench, their necks craned toward a bend in the road. A trio of Black and Latino boys walked along the side of the road in single file to avoid cars. Despite their presence, Jane had not experienced that much quiet in a long time. Every creature seemed to doze, including grasshoppers, birds, and Diane. She reclined in her seat, an arm flung across her eyes to block the sun.

Jane propped herself against the building for some thinking. A fly buzzed about her head, drawn by her sweat, she supposed. Though no one had ever sung "What Are Little Girls Made Of?" to her. She swatted at it and googled how long it usually took to get a body from the coroner. The results were useless, even after she added *because of murder* to her search string. Could be days, could be weeks. The need to take action overcame her, and the next thing she googled was the phone number she'd been avoiding.

As her thumb hovered over the green call button, she felt that same edge to her nerves that she'd felt calling Georgia Lee's house for the first time. Worried she'd pick up, worried she wouldn't. Worried about everything. Coming up with worst-case scenarios and preparing herself for rejection. What she wouldn't give for those worries now.

While Jane pondered whether she should call the detective back and if calling would mean she would sleep on a cot in a cell that night rather than a couch, someone in a Ram truck pulled into the parking lot. A handsome Black man in slim-fit jeans and a black polo shirt stepped out and greeted her.

"Jane Mooney?" He smiled and showed his badge. "Detective Hampton." The same guy who had called and left a message.

A badge, not handcuffs. Still, her stomach dropped. More evidence that she could manifest thoughts into being.

After she got her shit together, Jane glanced around her. "Could we go somewhere?" She motioned toward the car, where Diane dozed. The last thing she needed was for Diane to wake up or Chuck to walk outside and to have to start batting away their phones documenting her imminent arrest.

Detective Hampton nodded and nudged his head to the side. They walked behind the building to a spot in the shade.

"I meant to call you back, but I . . ." She scrambled for an excuse the same way she had after any number of one-night stands she'd run into at the few lesbian bars Boston had to offer back in the day.

"Please," he said, that gleaming smile aimed at disarming her. "Call me Benjamin." Like they were friends and she'd forget all about the purpose of his stalking her and catching her unawares. From his message, she had pictured him as a white former military man with a flattop chasing after the bad guy. Overworked. Oversmoked. Overdrank. Always complaining about how he got no respect. Definitely didn't work out like this guy. Didn't smile pleasantly.

"I'm sure I don't need to tell you I'm here about your father, Warren Ingram."

"Stepfather." Jane and Jason hadn't gone to the wedding. Didn't even know where they held it. Maybe at the courthouse, more likely a bar. Diane and Warren had pulled up to their apartment building in Warren's car after a weekend away. Diane had told Jane and Jason to pack their bags. They were moving. Again.

"Stepfather. Forgive me." He placed a hand on his chest, as if swearing to an honest mistake. "I'm new in town."

"Oh, it's fine." She threw on her best southern accent, though it'd been a while. When in Rome, especially when you're likely to be arrested any minute on a murder charge. After she'd disembarked in Massachusetts courtesy of a string of relationships that steadily moved her from the center of the country to the coast, she'd taken great pains to scrub the diphthongs and intonations. Those notes of her youth rolled back onto her tongue with an ease that surprised her.

"I'm surprised to find you here with your momma," he said.

Everyone assumed all mothers were mommas. That they loved and hugged and fed you. That they came home at reasonable hours and tucked you in. Diane was no one's momma. Jane was usually quick to correct anyone who suggested differently. This time, she made an exception. Before answering, she glanced at each corner of the building in the event Chuck or Diane decided to make an appearance.

"Momma . . ." She hated the sound of it. "She asked me to help with the funeral."

He smiled but didn't offer an opinion.

"Are you here to arrest me?"

Another smile—no teeth, all business. "No. Not yet."

She waited for him to explain. He didn't. "Why? I confessed."

"Why did you?"

"Confess?" she asked, confused. When he nodded, she continued, "'Cause I did it."

He narrowed his eyes. "See, here's the thing. I don't think you did."

She choked on her spit, and he whacked her good on the back.

"Jesus," she said and jerked away from him.

"Sorry. Instinct. You okay?"

"Yeah," she choked out. "Just got an itch." She coughed herself into something more akin to normal. "I did it. So if you're going to arrest me, get on with it."

"I would love to. But like I said, I'm not sure that's the case."

"Is this about my alleged girlfriend? That's a lie. She doesn't exist. That's just gossip. People letting their imaginations go wild." Then she realized what was different about him. He wasn't like other folks in Maud. He was like her. "You know how people are."

This time, his smile came tighter and quicker. Bingo. A Black police officer? A Black *gay* police officer? Oh, Maud would have a fit if they found out. She imagined they had not.

"It's not about that," he said. "It's about the fact they found no body, no evidence of a crime. Not one shred. And they looked. Allegedly."

He smirked. "Do you know of anyone else who might've had an issue with Warren?"

"I don't understand." Could they really be so dumb? But then, this was Maud. Most of their crimes were petty. Maud's only other reported murder case involved two guys back in the late '70s. The perpetrator had admitted he'd killed a guy who'd thrown a drink on him and then told him to "eat shit and die." The jury decided that wasn't so bad. Maybe they'd extend that courtesy to her. Maybe she wouldn't even go to trial if this Benjamin character got his way. She supposed it helped to have "family" on the inside. Maybe he'd go easy on her. *Sure,* she thought. *I'll play along.*

"There was this coworker. Warren and him had some trouble. You heard about him?" This had not been the plan. But why not use Warren's friends and all that macho male posturing in her favor?

"Yep, they looked into him way back when."

Was that good or bad? "I believe Warren was arrested for assault on that guy. What was his name?"

"Paul—"

"That's right." Details she'd forgotten rolled out of her brain and onto her tongue. They'd been at a company picnic. Everyone had been enjoying their free hot dogs and soda until Paul joked that Warren seemed to be awfully interested in the new press feeder, a young man named Thomas. The guy lied to his kids when they saw him after Warren got done with him, told them he'd visited the face-painting booth. That didn't stop them crying.

She couldn't stop herself, like her brain had decided to shit stories out her mouth now that he'd given her an opening. She blamed the heat, that oppressive Arkansas humidity. It made people stupid. "He always had trouble with folks. He'd invite them over to the house. They'd get to drinking and carrying on and then get into fights. Bad ones too. I hated my brother had to hear all that. All I ever wanted to do was run away. Even tried more than once but didn't stay gone long."

He leaned against the building, studying her.

Why wait for questions? Why not blurt out any old detail? "I think him and Paul became friends again, even after that." Paul was hardly a good guy. Maybe he could take the fall for what had happened. He'd probably done something to warrant getting locked away. She'd google him first to be sure. She wasn't a total asshole. "My grandpa was like that. He hit on his army buddy's girlfriend, and the guy shot him. Went to the hospital and everything. Even went back to the bar after they stitched him up." She'd stolen the story from an ex who liked to tell it to friends.

Benjamin chuckled. "What happened to the other guy?"

"Oh, nothing. They both agreed they'd had too much to drink and apologized. The girlfriend left. But they're still friends." She hoped he wouldn't ask for good old Grandpa's name or number or address. She didn't know but one of those off the top of her head. Hell, she wasn't even sure if he was still alive.

He laughed. "That sounds like something I'd hear in my family."

"We all got 'em." Each passing minute, her nerves regrew their endings from the frazzled tethers they'd been when he'd shown her his badge. Maybe Maud's finest would continue to do a poor job. Maybe they'd say to hell with it when they continued to not find any evidence—and how could they? Warren had been gone for what amounted to forever. What could they possibly scrape off a bunch of old bones? Though that didn't explain why they hadn't found evidence back then. Lord knows they left enough of it behind.

A fly buzzed near her ear. She probably looked deranged trying to get rid of it. "Are you really not going to arrest me?" She had only ever dreamed of her inevitable arrest, never that she could both confront what had happened and come out on the other side free.

"I thought about it. But then I found an eyewitness report buried in the files about a fight between your momma and Warren at a bar that same night. Did she say anything? Did Warren? Did you see anything on either one of them? Bruises? Blood?"

The only blood she'd seen was there when she arrived. Jason and Georgia Lee staring dumbstruck at where Warren's body sprawled on the ground. There had been a head injury. But she hadn't known how bad things were. Bad enough to put that body in a boat and say *sayonara*. Jane tried to remember anything odd about Diane but couldn't. Diane's entire existence was odd and unpredictable. "Not that I remember. But that whole night is a blur."

"Because you weren't there?" Silence. "Where was your brother that night?"

All those hopeful maybes began to swim with her dread. Every girlfriend she'd ever had had told her she didn't know how to stop when she was ahead. "In the house," she said and tried to keep the shake in her voice from escaping. She decided to keep her mouth shut for a change and wait for the questions.

"And he didn't hear a thing?"

"I don't know." *Ask him,* she thought. She had switched from chewing on a nail to chewing on the cuticle, which now ripped and bled. "Sounds weird, but when you're in that kind of situation, it almost becomes normal. I guess we got used to living in . . ." She didn't want to use the word, to be associated with it. "Violence. Hard to distinguish one fight from the next. They all run together." She had to get the conversation away from Jason. "Diane—" *Mom. Fuck.* She checked the building corners and lowered her voice. "My mom and I got into a lot of fights over Warren. She said I didn't want her to be happy and that I made him lash out."

"Did you?"

She paused at his meaning. "Maybe. I guess. I wanted her to stand up to him." Like that time Jane had called Warren an asshole. She'd said it under her breath, walking away, back to the bedroom. Then, darkness. The pain wouldn't come until after she woke up, Diane hovering over her, threatening Jane not to tell anyone what had happened or she'd regret it. Diane had told Jane, *You shouldn't have interfered in our affairs.* Those were the words she'd used. "She wouldn't. So I did." As she said the words, she knew they were wrong. Classic victim blaming. So many times, Diane could've chosen the nice guy. But she'd always chosen the guy who would give them a hard time. She was always loaning some guy money, and they drank and smoked whatever she earned while Jane and Jason went to school in last year's too-small clothes. Hard to have empathy for that.

"Did he hit her?"

Maybe it'd be better to leave out the truth, which is that they had beaten each other. "Sometimes."

"Did she go to the police?"

Jane wanted to laugh. Things back then had been no different than they were now. "No. She thought he'd change."

"They always do." Much as she resented Diane, she still wanted to put her fist through his face. "Did he ever hurt you again?"

What if he did? Would that make what happened okay? One time is fine, two is too much? He'd also constantly complained about how she ate too much—even though there wasn't much to eat—and took up too much space on the couch. How her hair clogged up the shower drain and polluted the bathroom sink. Told her she'd never survive on the streets because she was too ugly to sell herself.

That cursed fly sat on her arm, waiting. She smacked it and watched it fall to the ground. "He liked to ensure we never felt safe and that Diane never took her attention away from him."

"And your brother? Did Warren hit him?"

"I'm not sure."

Jason hadn't taken kindly to Jane trying to lift his shirt to confirm her suspicions. There were times when Jane had thought Warren had hurt him because of how withdrawn he'd become. Episodes, Diane had called them. They'd gotten worse over the years. When he was little,

Jason had been funny, outgoing. There were still moments—with her and Angie and Georgia Lee, with the handful of nerd friends he had at school but never brought home.

Something had happened to Jason late in elementary school. Something he never shared with her. That's when it all changed. Her thoughts raced. Where had they been living? Who were their teachers? Who had Diane been dating at the time? That last question made her especially nervous about what might have happened to Jason.

"Mostly, Warren liked to tease Jason about how he looked different, walked funny, smelled funny. Acted like a sissy," she added, gauging his response to confirm her suspicion. He was all professional, though. "I never saw bruises, but that doesn't mean anything." Why did the cops always have to wait until the worst happened? Why did they wait for bruises when they were all right there under the surface of the skin, the beatings occurring in any manner of ways, sometimes without a fist? She waited for more questions while he absorbed what she had said. Probably already had a bulleted list in his head. Reasons why she was no longer the suspect and someone else was. How selfish to believe her freedom meant freedom for her brother as well. That's what she got for being confident, telling stories. She'd probably manifest her brother's arrest.

"I think that'll be all for now, Miss Mooney."

She wanted to say more, do more, but she worried it would only lead him to Jason. She couldn't ask if they'd talked to him because maybe that would trigger some police hunch about her wanting to run over and get their stories straight, which was exactly what she would do if she had his address. And she couldn't ask how long this investigation of his would last, because she didn't want to sound too eager. If the investigation ended, that would mean one of two outcomes: jail or freedom. For now, she'd have to sit in the horrible in-between.

"How long do you expect until we can bury him?" She braced for his answer, hoping he'd say soon. Soon meant that maybe they would bury the investigation too.

"I know you all would like some closure. But it's still an active investigation."

No more *momma*. No timelines or reassurances. Only requests for patience and callbacks if they had questions. All that magic and optimism from earlier evaporated.

She uttered fake assurances of her cooperation and her story being true and overdone thank-yous with a smiling voice instead of a dying-on-the-inside one. He shook her hand, all business, and then made his way back toward his truck before pausing to face her. He didn't say anything, just stood there interrogating her with his eyes.

"What?" she asked out of nervousness.

"I'm having a hard time figuring out why you'd confess to a murder during a routine questioning at your home when the cops didn't even have a case. It's almost like you were making sure someone else didn't say it first."

She tried to find an ounce of hope inside her, something to hold on to. A cough from swallowing all wrong earlier tried to work its way out of her mouth, but she held it off.

"Well, you're wrong," she said.

He tilted his head. A smile danced across his lips before he turned to depart.

As soon as he disappeared around the corner, she yanked her phone out of her pocket. She needed Jason to call her. Text her. What was supposed to have been an easy confession and an easy burial had just become a lot more complicated.

Eight

GEORGIA LEE

Georgia Lee could barely breathe, and here Christlyn and Susannah sat, not only breathing but sucking down margaritas like it was half-off happy hour.

"First the gym and then a postworkout drink? What's gotten into you?" Christlyn laughed and looked to Susannah. "What's it been since you last came out with us? A year?"

"Ten?" Susannah joined in the laughter. "We can't vote in your district, sugar. No need to kill yourself on our behalf." She tapped her glass to Georgia Lee's and cackled. Georgia Lee nearly dumped her drink on her.

Earlier, Georgia Lee had laughed along with them while they pumped their arms, first on the ellipticals and then on the weight machines. She'd hated the whole experience. She'd not had a proper workout bra, one that didn't squeeze her insides out one end or the other, so she'd had to go to the store to find one. There was display after display of cute tops that would hide some of the curves she'd accumulated over the years. Then she saw a sign about something called compression tights, which promised to suck in her thighs like spandex, rendering all those unfortunate spots on her thighs and butt nearly invisible.

She couldn't say no to that. Especially in light of her conversation with Diane.

How dare she try to blackmail Georgia Lee! If her parents weren't already dead, she might murder them for falling for Diane's tricks the first time. They had negotiated with a terrorist. And now Georgia Lee had to pay the price, all because they couldn't bear the thought of anyone knowing their daughter associated with Jane.

Or maybe they had somehow learned the truth on their own? But how? Jane? Had she mentioned Georgia Lee when she was arrested and someone at the station told Diane, who then told Georgia Lee's parents? If only she could ask them.

Georgia Lee had searched her name in conjunction with Jane's on the internet and found nothing. Jane might as well not even exist. She'd given up after an hour. It did no good to imagine Jane's life now. Despite everything, she probably had a good life—an amazing life, to spite everyone. A great job, a good-looking wife, well-behaved children and pets, well-traveled friends she hadn't known since birth and who didn't make fun of her breath control and zip code. They'd only been together a few months before that business with Warren ruined everything. Maybe, even after all they'd been through, Jane would hear Georgia Lee's voice and struggle to put a face to a name. Maybe Jane had not only left physically but emotionally as well. Mentally, like one of those people who was so traumatized they forgot everything, including Georgia Lee. Or maybe she'd gone to therapy. Maybe she'd just moved on. And here Georgia Lee sat, fixated. Like a schoolgirl. Despite her best effort, her brain kept circling back to what Jane looked like now. Terrible, she hoped. She might learn soon enough. In the meantime, a workout couldn't hurt.

She gulped her margarita till the last drop hit her tongue and signaled the server for another. She'd likely regret it later, but she couldn't let Christlyn and Susannah think she'd lost her edge.

All she'd wanted was a break from the anger and confusion from her encounter with Diane and worries about the election and anxiety about whatever was going on with Warren's case—if there was one. She'd gathered no more information when she stopped by the station for another desperate attempt at a status update.

As for Diane, Georgia Lee would never give in. Never. Not one cent would leave her bank account and be placed into Diane's hands. Georgia Lee had to put it out of mind. She'd not give it any more attention. What Diane suggested was illegal. It had to be.

Her phone buzzed. She groaned at the text.

"Everything okay?" Susannah asked, margarita held in midair, as if disaster were about to strike and she needed to know whether she should down her drink or take her time.

"Everything's fine," Georgia Lee said. "Tim sent the latest draft of his college essay for my review. It's quite good." It was an embarrassment.

Christlyn checked her invisible watch. "Cutting it a bit close, isn't he?" Her kids had gotten into the U of A via early admission.

Georgia Lee flashed a smile. "He's a perfectionist."

"Sounds like someone we know." Susannah elbowed Christlyn and laughed. Georgia Lee laughed as well to be a good sport.

They all knew the boys would skate by as long as they showed up on time for their football games and didn't get caught doing drugs or committing larceny. Terrible as it sounded, she longed for them to be out of the house, a desire she wished she could express to her two best friends. But if they carried the same irritation and guilt about their own children, they didn't share it. Based on what they shared online, they were amazing mothers. Georgia Lee neglected to share anything, including photos, of her sons.

Christlyn and Susannah poked at their phones and gossiped about some new something or other, or someone. Georgia Lee nodded along like an active listener, but her mind kept wandering to the worst. What if Diane went through with it? What if Georgia Lee's name ended up side by side with Warren's? With Jane's?

No. She would not let Diane ruin her evening. She would put her anxiety aside. She would have some laughs. She would—or rather, she wanted to—order a giant plate of chimichangas, all smothered and delicious. But Christlyn and Susannah had both gone right to apps and drinks. They barely touched their loaded nachos while Georgia Lee practically drooled over tortilla chips like a cartoon wolf looking at prey. Why order food if you were only gonna eat a quarter of it and not even take home the leftovers? They'd been like this since they'd gotten boobs, like a switch had been turned on inside them. They'd both gone through bouts of bingeing and purging in junior high and high school. Georgia Lee would not judge. She had, too, after her parents had locked her away like some tragic character in a Victorian novel. It was a real sickness, worrying what other people thought about your appearance, one whose spell she'd not realized she'd fallen under until she and Jane started dating. Jane ate like a person who'd been lost in the woods for weeks. Georgia Lee joined her, not caring about calories at the Burger Depot. Or at the other assorted places she'd taken Jane in Maud Proper, like the Red Lobster or the Applebee's—all the good restaurants they'd not had, and still didn't, in Maud Bottoms. At first, Georgia Lee wondered if Jane only hung around her because Georgia Lee fed her and Jason. But Jane had loved Georgia Lee in the end. She had never doubted that.

She'd quietly place an order to go and pick it up after Christlyn and Susannah left. She deserved one good thing that day.

"Didn't you know her?" Susannah asked.

"Hmm?" Georgia Lee asked. She'd done such a good job of pretending to listen that she'd appeared fully engaged. "Who?"

"Jane Mooney. You know, Lezzie Borden? Have you been living under a rock, girl?" Susannah sipped her drink. "You need to get out more. Stop worrying about that darned election. Maud Bottoms ain't ever gonna change. I don't know why you try."

Before Georgia Lee could complain, Christlyn added, "You knew her. I'm certain of it."

Georgia Lee crinkled her brow in a show of deep thinking, all while trying to think of what to say and how to hide her shock at them not only paying attention to the news, but news that concerned her. Nothing came to mind. Nothing. Her mind blanked.

"No, I don't think so," she answered.

How could they possibly remember? Christlyn's and Susannah's capacities for recall had always been limited to fashion, pop songs, and boy crushes. Someone had to have fed them information. John? No. Too lazy to chase down a cold case. Diane? No. Not smart enough. The new hire, Benjamin? Perhaps he was investigating. Perhaps he'd asked Susannah and Christlyn to ask her about Jane. Georgia Lee leaned over to peek behind Susannah's hair, in search of one of those earpieces they used in TV shows when going undercover. But it was too dark to tell, even with the many string lights and red table candles everywhere. Also, they'd never be caught dead wearing sweatshirts in public, yet here they were.

"Is it hot?" She fanned her face. "Aren't you hot in those sweatshirts?"

Christlyn narrowed her eyes. "You started hanging out with her senior year." Emphasis on *hanging out*—or was that Georgia Lee's imagination? They hadn't answered her question.

"I can't remember every person I was nice to in high school. I was voted Most Popular." She pulled her shirt away from her skin and glanced at their bulky clothing again. "Aren't you hot? Just looking at you in those things makes me want to pass out."

Susannah looked at Georgia Lee quizzically. "I'm kinda chilly, actually."

Christlyn stared at the barely touched nachos in front of them, like her eyes were stuck to them, popped back into place, and landed on Georgia Lee. "You weren't voted Most Popular."

"Well, not in those exact words, but what do you think they meant by Best All Around? Everyone knew me. That's why they voted for me."

"They voted for you because you bribed them with candy," Christlyn said.

True. "The fact is, I knew a lot of people."

Christlyn scrunched her nose. "No, this was different. You actually talked to her." She paused and looked to Susannah for confirmation. "Like, a lot."

"Yes!" Susannah said, memory sparked. "You started hanging out with that new girl from Maud Bottoms. Back when they bussed them all up here after the tornado."

"We're talking about the same girl, Susannah," Christlyn said. "Keep up." Susannah's enthusiasm crumpled along with her posture. Her sweatshirt bunched around her waist.

Georgia Lee raced through the chips and salsa. Maybe she could crunch her way through whatever Benjamin might be able to hear in the wires they may or may not be wearing under their sweatshirts. Maybe he had Jane in a cell right now. Maybe Jane had told him everything about that night in exchange for a lighter sentence. And then what would Georgia Lee do? She could barely remember the details. But even knowing Jane was a mark on her character. The election ruined.

Christlyn tapped a long pink fingernail on the table. "You hung out with her while we were in that fight."

"Oh, right. I remember that," Susannah said.

As did Georgia Lee. She and Christlyn had argued about something stupid, an odd comment that sent both of them into extreme states of high school drama that morphed into an existential crisis. Eventually, Georgia Lee apologized to Christlyn, even though she couldn't remember the original offense. It had felt like the right thing to do to resolve things. But ever after, in the lunchroom or when they went out to the movies, she found her attention drifting.

She started to slip away from her old friends and their old routines. With Jane, she didn't worry about her clothing choices or whether her hair was too something or she had a foundation line she'd not noticed because she was in such a hurry to get dressed, eat breakfast, and get to school. She didn't wear makeup because they rarely went out in public, and her hair was pulled back in a simple ponytail. She felt pretty in a pure way she hadn't really felt before. Every other time she had tried to feel pretty, she'd felt miserable. She was never sure she wasn't trying too hard and being made fun of, even by her own friends, behind her back. With Jane, things had been easy. But hard in ways neither Christlyn nor Susannah would or could ever understand.

A hand landed on her forearm. Christlyn. "Did you stroke out?"

Georgia Lee shook her head. "I was trying to remember this girl you're talking about." No matter how much she wanted to ignore recollections of Jane, they came.

Christlyn tapped her fingernail against her teeth to think. Georgia Lee could practically see the germs run off her fingertips and into her mouth. A legion of illnesses danced in her mind. She pulled out her lavender-scented hand sanitizer and sprayed a good amount onto her hands.

"Oh, that smells like a dream." Susannah held out her hands. Georgia Lee offered it to Christlyn first, but she declined and tapped away at her teeth.

Georgia Lee spritzed Susannah's hands, tucked the sanitizer away, and checked the time on her phone. She hated to be the fuddy-duddy who left before everyone else, but she didn't want to endure their conversation any longer. Once Christlyn got something in her head, she'd bang away at it to prove she was right.

"I'm gonna head to the bathroom and then have the waiter ring up my portion of the bill."

Before she could stand, Christlyn spoke. "You got mono right after she was arrested." She grabbed a chip and bit the tip—just the tip—before slowly placing it on her plate. "And came back to school right after she left town."

Georgia Lee faltered. She inhaled and exhaled, slow and steady, to calm her body. "Well, maybe that's why I don't remember. I was very sick." She ensured the words were clear, loud enough for Benjamin to hear should he be listening.

"You should remember it soon," Christlyn said. "Rumor has it they're questioning anyone who knew her to see if—"

"They can find her accomplice!" Susannah said, earning her a smack on the arm from Christlyn.

"Don't interrupt me. You know how much I hate that."

"Sorry." Susannah pouted.

"What are you talking about?" Georgia Lee asked as they continued bickering. "Stop it."

Christlyn picked up her phone, clicked around, scrolled, and then slid it across the table to Georgia Lee, who groaned. Let's Talk About Maud. Nothing good could come of this.

LEZZIE BORDEN RETURNS!

The Good Lord has blessed us with some hot goss, y'all.
Maud's very own Murderess has returned to the scene
of her crime.
25 years after she hightailed it out of here after her
release,
she's back to pay her price. Ain't too bright if you ask
us. We'd of
run the minute them bones of Warren Ingram's were
found
floating around the Arkansas River. But there ain't no
accounting
for stupid. Some people just can't help themselves.

Real Bad Things

With a confession and a set of bones, will Jane Mooney
finally get her day in court?
Not so fast, folks! A little bird we like to call Lovelace
informed us
Maud's finest (BLUE LIVES MATTER! #BLM!) is talking to
a slew of women
who might have met that gal way back when, including
(wait for it, wait for it)
Holier Than Thou City Council Member Georgia Lee
LOSER.
Hoo wee! We bet she's wetting her britches about now.
Not only is she getting spanked by Bollinger in the
polls, she's
about to get spanked by the law. And, we gotta say,
WE LOVE TO SEE IT.
(Even though we don't believe it. Ain't a fun bone in
that woman's body.)

When we spoke at Bollinger yesterday and asked for
his comment,
he told us there wouldn't be none of this K-Parts BS on
his watch—
or murder!! MONEY QUOTE!!

Georgia Lee Loser could not be reached for comment.
Cause frankly we don't care enough to ask.
Hey! This is Facebook, it ain't the news!
(Real talk, tho: Based on what we heard,
Warren Ingram wasn't all that. But hey, a crime is a
crime,
no matter how much of a shithead a person is!
So stay tuned, Talkers!)

We may not know who helped Miz Borden with her
crime, but we DO KNOW
it's time we toss that CARPETBAGGER back to Maud
Proper.
Who better than a businessman to keep us Maud Bottom Feeders
out of bad business deals like the kind Georgia Lee got
us into—
and ensure Maud Bottoms don't become a den of
CRIME?

#LezzieBordenIsBackInTown #VoteAndy #GeorgiaLee-
LOSER #GiveHerTheBoot!

Little bird. Georgia Lee was right. Someone was talking.

And they had confirmed Jane was back in town. Jane had already confessed. Perhaps Jane's heart had turned to stone—and against Georgia Lee. Or could it be Angie or Jason, trying to keep the attention away from them? Or Diane, their so-called Lovelace? A warning shot if Georgia Lee didn't pay up?

Who else but these four would care, or want to see Georgia Lee take the fall?

She poked around Christlyn's phone in search of a browser to see if she could find a news posting about Warren or Jane or anything about her specifically. She gave up after scrolling through ten cluttered screens of app icons and reread the post before tossing the phone on the table.

"This is garbage. Do you really believe that I would have anything to do with a murder?"

"I mean . . ." Susannah paused and glanced at Christlyn. "No. Of course not. You only work. Who has time for murder with your schedule?" She laughed nervously.

"And you?" Georgia Lee asked Christlyn.

"I mean, they're kind of right." Christlyn chewed on her straw, that forever-bored teen look still present on her middle-age face. "You don't really like to have fun."

"I do too like to have fun. I went to the gym and I'm here, aren't I?"

"That's not fun. That's maintenance. Also, you're like, the straightest person ever. No one would believe you're the Bonnie to Lezzie Borden's Clyde," Christlyn said. "No offense."

What would she know of that? What would either of them know about anything?

Georgia Lee didn't know what made her angrier: the continued harassment of those Let's Talk About Maud knuckleheads, Diane's attempted blackmail, or the fact that Christlyn and Susannah didn't think her capable of being the person she actually was or doing things she'd actually done.

She stormed toward the bathroom but then returned to the table.

"You can't trust two auto body workers as a source for news! You need to be responsible citizens!" She smacked her hands together for emphasis. "You have to question the content!"

Susannah sank into the booth, wounded. Christlyn held her stare, almost like a challenge. As soon as she left, they'd laugh at her. For the first time in a long time, she decided she didn't care.

"Drinks and apps are on me." She didn't want to sit there and wait for the check in their presence.

She yanked her purse out of the booth and made her way to the server. She'd find this Lovelace. She'd ensure they learned exactly who they were dealing with. She wasn't some woman they could just roll over.

Nine

JANE

Though Jane had told Chuck they weren't interested in any of that religious mumbo jumbo, he stood next to the coffin for the graveside service sweating all over his Bible, talking about God and heaven and other things Warren hadn't given two shits about. This came after a lengthy recitation of lies courtesy of the chicken-scratch notes Diane had torn out of a spiral notebook that morning and handed to Chuck ten minutes before the service. He'd accepted it because grieving widow. But he'd been visibly flustered to have his well-thought-out and typed eulogy so unceremoniously hacked. He'd had no choice but to read off the paper, its little edges flapping in the wind, detailing how Warren was:

1. Loved
2. Not a dumbass who would fall into a river and drown (as originally reported when he first went missing)
3. Not a criminal

Even Jason couldn't suppress a laugh at that one.

He looked the same and different, like standing in front of a stranger she knew well. Gone were the tube socks with colorful stripes and hair in his face; instead he wore an ironed black button-down, mirrored sunglasses, and waxed black jeans. He looked like he could be an action star, or the handsome villain.

"Hey, kid," she'd said when he'd come walking up the cemetery path before the funeral. She motioned for him to join her under the shade of a tree while waiting to take a seat. She wasn't willing to sit in the front row and be stared at or stare at a casket any longer than necessary.

He didn't nod or wave back but course corrected in her direction, like a robot, which didn't match how he looked.

As he came closer, his lips lifted into a smile. She was reminded of watching movie stars walk the red carpet. That blink-and-you-miss-it hint of dread and annoyance, replaced with a warm smile as reporters and photographers approached.

She greeted him with a hug, which he accepted with a little pat on her back. His skin was cold from the air-conditioning in his car. He smelled expensive, like some of the guys she sometimes—used to—hung out with at Club Café in Boston.

She stuck her nostrils right on his neck and took a big whiff. He used to laugh when she did that.

"What are you doing?" he asked and pulled away from her, clearly not amused. First words she'd heard him say in years. His voice firm, mature, authoritative. His teeth so white.

"Lighten up," she joked. "It's just a funeral."

"What are you doing here?" His plaster smile returned, as if the world watched.

"Trust me. It's not by choice." Jane had offered to sit this one out, but Diane wouldn't hear of it. *You're gonna sit next to me and think about what you've done,* she'd said. Such a mom thing to say for a mother who couldn't be bothered half the time.

"There's always a choice," he said.

She didn't know what to say in return. She felt scolded, small. Now she was the weird, quiet sibling with all the outsize feelings.

She stuck her hands in her pockets and surveyed the crowd. A few reporters lurked along with their crew, but they didn't recognize Jane—at least not until Diane waved her and Jason over to take their seats. The plastic chairs squeaked as reporters and everyone else turned to stare.

"Ready?" she asked.

He stared at his phone, calculating responses in his head to whomever required his attention before committing them to ones and zeros. Finally, he looked up. "Let's get this over with."

Jane took a deep breath and stepped into the tent and onto the artificial turf, heading to the front row where Diane sat. Jason followed her. Whispers gathered as she passed. More than one phone camera clicked. The KMSM news crew hefted their cameras onto their shoulders. She could see the headlines. Hear the reporter's disbelief that Diane had the heart to forgive her, that Jane had the audacity to show her face at her victim's funeral, the question mark in the reporter's tone asking the audience if they could do the same. She considered giving them all a little pageant wave but decided against it at the last minute. This part would be over soon. No need to prolong it or give Diane or anyone else fodder for the next round of gossip.

Warren's family sat in the opposite row—cousins however many times removed, his parents being dead and sisters likely in jail for misdemeanor charges. Warren's relations stared at Diane and Jane and Jason. Mostly they stared at Jane in her black suit. She wondered if any of them had changed the channel beyond CBS or Fox or seen anything outside their opioid-and-Confederate-flag-filled bubble. Definitely had never read anything longer than a receipt. They all had that Ingram eyelid droop, making them look inbred, shit drunk, or both. They didn't come up to them before the service to hug Diane or give condolences. They wouldn't after. Warren might've been loud and violent, but his family was quiet in their hatefulness. They looked without turning away. Their looks told Jane exactly what they thought of her.

Jason greeted Diane like someone he was forced to work with on a group project. All forced smiles and then grimaces when they parted. Meanwhile, Diane clung to him like a parasite, hungry for attention or affection, which he didn't give. When he sat in a chair, Diane sat right next to him. But he pretended to have dropped something in the aisle, got up to feign a look, and managed to commandeer the seat next to Jane instead upon his return.

"Move down one," he told Jane.

She screwed up her lip.

"So it doesn't look weird," he said.

Jane had grumbled and reluctantly moved to the vacant seat next to Diane, leaving Jane stuck in the middle. She wondered what had happened between them.

Now, while Chuck droned on, she also fantasized about the inside of Jason's house and what it would feel like to cross the threshold of a world he'd built without her, to see if the walls were white and bare, the shades drawn down on the world, as they'd been in the roach-infested apartments they'd inhabited as kids, the oddly sweet scent of roach spray forever lodged in her nose. She wanted to believe Jason lived in one of the McMansions in Maud Proper, out near the golf course, where they'd gone trick or treating in the years when Diane remembered to take them. She wanted to believe he had hardwood floors instead of linoleum. Real art on the walls, not the shitty knockoffs you could buy at home stores. A dog with a human name—something like Bob or Harry—because Jason was too serious for cutesy names. A refrigerator stocked with steak and craft beer, not just condiments and stale white bread and Bud Light. A gym membership. A Netflix queue. A clean house, a backyard, neighbors who invited him over for barbecues, friends and colleagues who knew what made him laugh, what made him angry, what made him *him*.

For all she knew, he could have someone locked in his basement with a bucket and a bottle of lotion.

She noticed his foot tapping urgently out of the corner of her eye. The rest of his body, still. Maybe he had a prescription to help with his constant need to move. Or maybe he'd just been able to shake out most of the nerves that had plagued him in his youth. Most. Not all.

She shifted her attention away from him and returned to Chuck's eulogy, but that didn't last long. Her tolerance for religion and platitudes had always been low. That was one thing she was grateful for: an absence of religious family members to shame or scorn her. A feat for a queer girl in the Bible Belt.

Such an odd thing, burial. Preserving a body in a casket. And for what? The earthworms and microorganisms to applaud? Seemed like a waste of time and money. And the flowers. There weren't many, and they were from Sam's Club instead of one of the many florists they'd visited, but Diane had insisted on some even though Jane could picture Warren throwing them at the wall. Probably could resurrect an actual memory if she had the energy to go spelunking into personal trauma. Instead, she watched a couple of birds frolic in the trees. Or maybe they were fighting. Who even knew? Probably some bird scientist who'd been nurtured as a child and could spend their life on such questions instead of trying to shake off the indignities of a bullshit upbringing.

Diane kept looking behind her, a stare fixed on someone. And something else. Some look on her face. Jane twisted in her seat to see a handful of random men in the back row that Jane guessed had been Warren's friends. One guy looked familiar, but Jane couldn't place him. Maybe she'd gone to high school with him. Or he ran commercials on the local station for his car lot or something. When Jane focused on him, he looked away.

After the fourth time Diane glanced behind her to look at the men, Jane whispered, "Are you flirting at a funeral?"

"No." Diane ripped her focus away from them. But Jane thought she'd heard a crack in Diane's voice. She'd only ever let her guard down briefly before putting it back up the second someone might've discovered a way past her barrier.

"Then why—?"

"Pay attention."

"That's fucking rich," Jane muttered.

Jason sat quietly next to them, either oblivious to their movements or ignoring them. Probably the latter. She caught the last generic words out of Chuck's mouth as the coffin finally, blessedly entered its eternal resting state.

As soon as the last prayer ended, Diane rushed out of her hard chair and nearly knocked Jason out of his in the process of trying to get to him. He gathered his composure and waited for her to speak. Jane selfishly relished their discomfort around each other. Whenever Jane had ranted against Diane for something or other, Jason had countered she wasn't all bad. He said he remembered Good Mom, the one who came before Bad Mom. Good Mom took him for ice cream, tried to help him with homework, watched action movies with him on the couch. Jane had dug around in her mind but couldn't hook any of those descriptions to a memory. Maybe Jason's memory had finally hooked into reality.

"We should get something to eat," Diane said. "The three of us." Perhaps remembering some motherly instinct, Diane patted Jason's arm as if he was in need of consolation. Diane stole a look at Jane. "Might be the last time."

Jane's stomach plunged at the dissonance of her inclusion and then her exclusion. Her "last supper" on the outside could come at any time. Maybe Benjamin waited by the cemetery entrance.

As he'd done since he walked up to her, Jason avoided looking at Jane directly, his eyes cast downward or to the side. That cement smile returned, his hands revealing an imminent apology. "I'd love to, but I've got a lot of work to catch up on."

Diane grabbed Jason by the arm. He glanced at her hand. She let go.

Jane understood why he withdrew from Diane, but she couldn't help but wonder what she'd done to get her lumped in with Diane. Diane had smothered Jason with attention, like some heir to the throne. Always keeping an eye on him, always ensuring he was by her side. Stealing him sweets from the liquor store. Jason consuming them before Jane returned home from a friend's house or her shifts at Family Fun. The evidence all over their room. Sucker and candy bar wrappers. Jane had been so angry at the time. At Diane. At him.

Maybe Diane felt bad for whatever had happened to Jason as a kid that had made him sullen. Still, Jane would've saved a candy bar for him. She would've shared half. She would have sacrificed everything for him. She did sacrifice everything for him. She'd confessed to murder for him.

Was it guilt or indifference that kept him at arm's length? She hoped it was the former rather than the latter. She tried to imagine herself in his shoes. She wouldn't have an easy time with it either. She'd probably feel terrible. She'd probably avoid him, even though she didn't want that from him. Maybe he didn't want to associate with either of them anymore. They were both reminders of a life he had outgrown.

But she knew Jason. It'd be best to let him come around to her on his own. She would wait. At least she'd seen him today, the ice broken. And she'd been on her best behavior. She hadn't made any false moves. The day could end without incident, and then maybe Jason would feel it was okay to talk to her and she could get rid of her anxiety as well.

"Go. It's okay," she said, patting his arm in a warm manner and smiling and intonating like she meant the words. "I don't have much of an appetite, to be honest." She turned away from him lest her efforts failed to hide her disappointment.

Instead of walking down the aisle and toward the back of the cemetery, where a mob of mourners huddled inside and around the barrier of the tent, she made a beeline for the front, past Chuck's pedestal, where few people had wandered.

She escaped the tent's shade and felt the sun on her back, a welcome reprieve despite the continued heat wave. She'd almost made it to her previous hovering spot where she'd first greeted Jason when she felt a sharp push at her back.

Before she had time to turn and identify the culprit, her cheek stung like she'd been hit with a wooden paddle spiked with nails.

She swatted at the person but soon was on the ground. Feet surrounded her. Kicks, too quick, too many to avoid.

Her stomach flared with pain.

She rolled onto her back, kicking wildly and protecting her head, a tactic she'd learned in juvie when there was no point trying to fend off a horde of angry girls bent on her destruction for no reason other than she'd been in the wrong place at the wrong time.

Her ears fuzzed from adrenaline. Confusion. *What the fuck is happening?*

Feral grunts.

Nails in her scalp. Feet in her face. Pain and appendages everywhere. Until they weren't.

Air lashed her face. Cooled the sweat that had gathered. A firm hand gripped her under each arm and easily lifted her off the ground. She felt like a kid again, being lifted out of a playground melee by an adult, her feet barely touching the ground. Whisked away to safety, but not before she caught a glimpse of her attackers. The Ingrams. Faces red with rage, hair aswarm around their heads. Wow, had she been wrong about them.

Then she spotted Diane, standing in a large circle of onlookers, cameras flashing, boom mics hovering, people she hadn't noticed before holding on to the Ingram clan as they lashed out and tried to pull free. Diane, like in one of those reels where the world moves frantically around a stationary object, stared at Jane in silence, not moving, not emoting. Nothing.

"Go!" Jason yelled behind them. "Get them out of here."

◆ ◆ ◆

After stumbling through a gauntlet of headstones, they rested near a large weatherworn column someone had erected in centuries past, the family name barely legible. Jane spit blood near a tree that provided them with shade and wiped at her mouth.

"It's not that bad," Jason said, anticipating her reaction now that she had a moment to process what had just happened. "I don't think they got more than one or two hits. But if you need me to take you to a—"

"No. It's fine," she said, not wanting to appear any more weak or soft than she already felt. "I don't blame them."

"Why would you? Ingrams are gonna Ingram." He crossed his arms, face stern like a million school principals who wanted to know why she kept getting into fights. "What did you think would happen, showing up to his funeral?" When she didn't answer, he shook his head again and pulled a bleach-white handkerchief out of his pocket. "This is some redneck shit."

"Sopp o ropp ropp yop," she said.

Jason rolled his eyes at their childhood language but offered her a brief smile. "You're a mess." He proceeded to gently wipe at her face and smooth her hair. She doubted it would do any good, but the attention felt nice.

When he finished, he folded the handkerchief into a new square so that hardly any of her blood could be seen and then tucked it into his pocket. She chanced a look behind her, half expecting pitchforks and fists raised to chase the monster out of town. But the crowd had turned their attention to Diane, who reveled in the spotlight, placing a tissue to her eyes and nose, nodding along as reporters scribbled or thrust their mics toward her face.

"Sorry about dinner," he said. "I do have work. But this is just . . . a lot."

She nodded and smiled even though she hated being considered "a lot" along with Diane. "Shit, I wouldn't want to have dinner with us either. All she does is glare at me and remind me that I'm going to jail." She laughed. He didn't.

Jane had thought she'd known what to expect coming back to Maud. She'd been through all this before. But nothing could have prepared her for facing everything as an adult. Back then, all she'd focused on was survival. Just get through the day. Now, with time and maturity and true crime shows and books available to her twenty-four seven, she realized how much her teenage brain had protected her from the trauma and severity of the consequences of her confession.

They waited, awkwardly, as the crowd thinned. Unaccustomed to adult conversation with each other, they stayed silent. She hadn't eaten breakfast, unless the toothpaste she accidentally swallowed counted. Her stomach growled in complaint. He pulled a pack of what looked like candy out of his pocket and offered her some. She examined the package. Energy beans.

Jane took the offering. Tasted like jelly beans mixed with Sour Patch Kids. She nudged her head toward Diane. "You see her much?"

He chewed and paused before answering. "No. Not really." Maybe he'd finally realized that Good Mom had done the very least of a very low bar.

While they waited for people to leave, she tried to normalize and pretend that she hadn't just gotten the shit kicked out of her in front of everyone in a cemetery and that it'd be plastered on TVs and cell phones that night. She blotted her nose with her sleeve, and Jason shifted uncomfortably, gaze trained elsewhere. They briefly caught up as much as they knew how—the weather and basic, nonconfessional life updates. He had a job; she did not. He had a house; she did not. Neither of them was dating anyone. She avoided the word *girlfriend* in case he preferred men or no one at all.

He didn't ask any follow-up questions when she mentioned the loss of a job and a girlfriend and the discovery of Warren's body all in one month. There was no sarcastic exclamation of *That sucks!* Only a lifted eyebrow and a knowing nod. Taps on his phone screen to check the time—and presumably messages from other people besides her he chose to ignore. Jane's friends and exes had large families, siblings with whom they shared laughter and life details—or at least funny stories about how much they hated each other.

"What happened between you and Diane?" she asked, trying to be nonchalant so he wouldn't shut down. "Why'd you stop coming around?"

"Been busy." He focused on chewing but then added, "I left shortly after you."

"When?"

"After your release. Went to live with a friend in another town. His parents kept a camper trailer in the backyard. They let me stay there as long as I paid a little rent." He must've seen the question on her face. "I took on your shifts at Family Fun."

Jason had had this whole other life she didn't know about. He had never told her. She felt like she'd suddenly lost a limb, part of her literally missing.

"Why'd you leave home?"

"Well," he said, considering, "it wasn't exactly pleasant there. We killed the one she wanted to keep." The way he said the words—his use of *we*—chilled her.

Jason didn't offer any additional thoughts, leaving her to consider what life must've been like for him after she'd left. At least he'd had a friend and a place to stay. And a job. And Angie. Why hadn't Jane stayed? She could've gotten an apartment. Taken care of him. But she'd been too freaked out by it all, that nickname following her around, people staring at her, watching her every move.

Finally, she worked up the nerve to ask the question that nagged her. "Are you avoiding me? Because you think I might—"

"No," he laughed—nervously, it seemed. "No, of course not. I've been busy. There's this project at work." He checked his phone again. "You know how it is."

She did. But she also thought that he might extend a bit more courtesy toward her, understand the weight of what she faced on his behalf and put down his phone.

While waiting for his brush-off to stop stoking her anger, she noticed one of the cemetery workers who waited to put the casket in the ground kept shifting his position from behind a tree to get a better look at them. He walked toward them now, and her adrenaline hit overdrive, thinking the guy meant to start some shit.

"Excuse me," the guy said to Jason. Anxiety rushed through her. She hated conversation with strangers. Unplanned visitors. Random people who walked up out of nowhere in a cemetery. She liked to consume her drama from afar, or her couch. She guessed she couldn't expect any of that now. "Are you Jason Tran?"

Jason's face lit up in a way Jane hadn't seen, ever. He held out his hand and the guy broke into a giant smile. She only caught a few of the words they spoke: *match, Fayetteville, favorite, awesome*. When the guy left—after he'd taken a selfie with Jason, in a cemetery—the guy's words sunk in.

"Jason Tran?" she asked, confused. "Is that why I can't find you online?"

That charming smile dissolved, and he focused on his energy beans. "Why do you need to look me up online?" More nervous laughter followed. "You have my phone number."

Her nose started to bleed again, so she wiped it on her shirt. At least it was black. He dug around in his pocket and offered her his handkerchief. She declined.

"Which you barely answer." She slipped a hand in his pocket to steal his energy beans, sneaking his candy like when they were kids. But he blocked her hand with his arm.

"Ow."

"Sorry," he said, possibly remembering she'd just been pummeled.

"Dang," she laughed. "You never used to catch me."

"Yes, I did. You're thinking of Angie."

"No, that was you." He gave her a look. Had she mistaken them? "Anyway. What was that about? A match? What kind of match?"

"MMA." She must've made a face because he clarified. "Mixed martial arts."

That explained the block. No wonder he ate amped-up jelly beans. He'd be much better off in prison than her. "Hmm. Martial arts?"

"What?"

"Nothing." One of her exes had always joke complained about how white people assumed she knew kung fu. "Is that, like, your stage name?"

"No." He quickly poured the rest of the energy beans into his mouth. Hoarding them before she got a chance to steal more. There he was. Her little brother. Ensuring no one touched his food. Just like her. "It's my name."

"No, you're Jason Mooney."

"No," he said, a note of irritation layered onto the lilt in his voice. "That's your last name. Not mine."

"Why would you change your name?"

"To honor my father." He raised an eyebrow and gave her a look. "Don't roll your eyes."

"I didn't." She had. They were fatherless, the both of them. Together. "You don't even know him."

"And you don't know yours. Besides, you don't have to know your family to honor them. I took a DNA test—"

"You took a wha . . ." Her head and heart pounded. "Seriously?"

"It's no big deal," he said. "I wanted to know more about my ancestry and my father."

"The big deal is . . ." She looked around and whispered, "The big deal is your DNA could be matched to a crime is what."

Now he rolled his eyes. "I don't think that's going to be an issue."

"You don't know that." She didn't know either. But she assumed. An assumption that it could was safer than an assumption that it couldn't. She both hated and envied his blasé attitude. "Even if it's been too long, getting tested is risky. Your DNA could be stolen by corporations. Have you thought about that?"

He laughed at her. "Do you have a phone?"

"Duh. Of course I have a phone."

"Then DNA is the least of your worries. All your personal information is already stolen."

She muttered, arms across her chest. Some might call it pouting. She'd been accused of that often. Of all things, a DNA test. It was like he didn't even care. As if he went along in life without even thinking about what had happened. What she'd done to ensure no one else knew. She guessed she should be happy he didn't seem to carry a burden. That had been her goal. But it also irked her.

She raked the ground with the toe of her shoe and then stood next to him. Her body ached. A few hits? Felt like more. "Do you know anything else?"

"About what?"

"Your father."

He nodded as if he'd drifted off in a daydream during their conversation and suddenly remembered and could pick up the threads. "Not yet. I'm still trying to track down the details."

"You don't even know who he is?"

He exhaled way longer than necessary. "No, but—"

"Why Tran?"

"Why not? It's—"

"It's weird that you . . ." He crossed his arms again and tilted his head at her. Disappointed dad.

"Sorry," she said. "I interrupted you. I acknowledge that." She'd had to say that a lot in her life.

Jason swirled his tongue around his teeth, like he had to convince his mouth to keep whatever reply he wanted to say inside. She wished she had that ability. "I was going to say because that's the most common name among my DNA matches."

She nodded and futzed a hole in the ground with her shoe. "Vietnamese?"

He nodded.

What Angie had always insisted when they'd sat outside on the porch or walked to school together. He'd asked her once if she thought they could be related. Angie said she didn't know but called him little brother anyway. They'd always had a playful friendship. He'd laughed with Angie, smiled, teamed up against Jane just because he could. Asked her for help with things like homework. Throughout childhood, she'd always tried to shield him from feeling different. At school, at home.

She wanted to be happy for him. She should be happy for him.

She didn't know what else to say. She should probably say congratulations. But all she could do was wonder, selfishly, if he even felt bad about what awaited her.

"What if he's like Diane? You could go all this time thinking he's something special because he's your father, but he's really just a shithead like Diane and all you are is a biological outcome of the most basic human behavior."

He adjusted his perfectly cuffed sleeves. Was that silk? "And you wonder why I don't return your texts or calls."

She'd fucked it all up. She watched him walk to his car and told herself to respect his need for space from her. But then she ran after him, even though she knew people would be watching; they'd probably have their cameras at the ready. She hated to waste what time she had with Jason by fighting. "Wait."

When she caught up to him, he opened the car door and waited for her to speak. She wanted to say sorry, but he was just like her. It would only make him mad.

She paused to lean over and catch her breath. Jesus, the Ingrams had really knocked the shit out of her. "Have you talked to the police? Have they called you?"

Jason lodged his forearm on the top of his car, which by the looks of it cost more than anything she had ever owned. "Yes. They called the other day." His tone felt polite again. Like she was a difficult client who needed to be handled and he had just needed a break to blow off some steam before picking up their previous conversation.

"And? What happened?"

"They asked the same things as before: What do you remember about that night, did anyone help Jane, can you think of anyone else who might have had a bone to pick with him, anything else we should know, give us a call if you think of something, etc., etc."

"Did you get a weird vibe from them?"

He laughed, but she didn't find the question all that funny. "No. I think they're doing their due diligence. Checking every box."

He got in the car and pulled the door shut. Though he was older now and far more stable than she could ever hope for herself, she was reluctant to let him go, to let the outside world into their own, even if theirs wasn't great. Even if she wanted him to be brave and confess and tell everyone he had murdered Warren, not her. Save her this time.

She knocked on the passenger window, and he rolled it down. "Are you sure everything's okay? With us? I . . ." Words. Why were words so hard with him now? "I'm not gonna change my story, you know. I confessed. You don't have to worry about that, okay?"

He turned to her but still didn't really look her in the eye. More like a fleeting glance before shifting his gaze to the seat. Then he offered her his pinkie. "We're good, Jane."

She linked her pinkie with his and tried not to get all weird and emotional about it, but it was hard. "Good," she added and paused. "I love you."

He smiled, conciliatory. "I really do have to go." He held up his phone as if a client was on the line right then, waiting. "Tell Mom I had to take off, okay? I'll be in touch."

Before she could ask him to promise, the window hummed, and she yanked her arm out before it closed on her. His car disappeared down the road toward wherever it was he called home.

She'd made the decision to confess. To save him from having to pay for her decision to antagonize Warren in the first place. If she'd kept her mouth shut like Warren and Diane had told her, maybe Warren would be alive. But she hadn't. He hadn't asked her to confess. But she had.

The knock had come seven days after Warren disappeared.

For seven days, Jane had waited.

For seven days, she wondered what had happened and why Warren's body hadn't turned up. They had expected him to be found soon— maybe even the next day—the explanation a boating accident. Or that he had tumbled into the lock from the bridge after a bender. She fought the urge to walk along the riverbank to see if his body was tangled among the driftwood and mud. *Don't go to the river,* she told everyone. *And don't tell anyone what we've done.*

They all went to school like normal. Jane fixed Jason's cereal and supper. Gave him lunch money from what little she made at Family Fun. Angie didn't wait for Jane or Jason to walk to the school bus, though. She didn't save Jane a seat. She didn't nudge her or walk alongside her in the hallways when everyone started whispering once word got out. *Isn't that the girl whose dad is missing?*

Stepdad, she wanted to scream.

Georgia Lee tried to catch her attention before second period, but Jane rushed the opposite direction, as if everyone would know what they'd done if they saw them together. Georgia Lee resorted to calling the house repeatedly. But Jane didn't have anything to say, so she didn't pick up. Jane eventually pulled the cord out of the wall jack. She regretted that. She should've been more communicative, but she didn't know how. Everything in her froze with fear about getting caught.

For seven days, her heart hammered at every sudden movement or sound, every glance her way. She tiptoed around Jason, wondering what kind of permanent psychological damage he'd suffer from what he'd done. Guilt and terror. That's what she saw before he averted his eyes when she tried to talk to him.

Pretend nothing is wrong, she had whispered to him that terrible night and all the nights thereafter until she was gone. And hadn't he gone and done that very thing?

Life was great for Jason Mooney. Sorry, Jason *Tran*. He'd gone to college, learned how to program software, and become a professional fighter, recognized in cemeteries around Maud. Probably the state. No doubt under all the svelte black clothing there were rock-hard abs. Sweat and occasional blood, adoring fans.

He'd done exactly what she'd wanted. He had a life.

She tried to bat away her shame at being a shitty person and the disappointment of comparison. She'd always seen them as a pair. Two orphans against the world. Boxcar Children. Bitter and wondering what their lives might have been like had they been gifted a different mother in the great game of Life. There had been comfort in shared sadness.

She'd never felt so alone.

After a while spent staring at the sky, she wandered back toward Diane and the grave site, where a smattering of people still hung around smoking cigarettes and chatting. Probably related to the gravediggers. But the reporters and the Ingrams were gone.

Diane looked Jane up and down. There were smudges on Jane's pants. No telling what her face looked like. Finally, Diane ended her assessment and dug around in her purse for her keys while Jane shifted from one foot to the other.

"Should we head out?" Jane asked. The image of Diane standing there emotionless while Jane got kicked hovered in her mind. Diane would say she deserved it.

Diane scratched at the spot on her arm she'd been agitating all day. The skin responded in kind, angry and red. She settled her attention somewhere beyond Jane and got this look on her face Jane couldn't interpret. "What is it? That guy you kept looking at?"

"He keeps bugging me."

Jane didn't see him among the crowd milling about or the backs of people walking toward their cars. "Did something happen?"

"No." Diane glared at her. "And it's no business of yours if it had."

Jane launched her hands into the air. "Sorry. Okay." She dreaded the ride home. The night she'd have to spend there. Maybe she could borrow the car, head up the hill to the mall in Maud Proper. Binge on soft pretzels and soda from the mall food court. She wondered if the movie theater was still open. She could gorge on popcorn and nachos, way better than a night alone with Diane in her grief and anger. A terrible thing to admit, but there was no one to hear that confession.

Beside her, Diane sniffled. "I hate to cry."

Jane harbored so much hate in her heart for this woman who stood before her, for the times she'd left Jane and Jason to fend for themselves. And yet, a greater wash of responsibility told Jane, *You did this. Her pain is your fault. Jason might have killed him, but Warren's dead because of you.*

If only she'd stayed in the trailer with Jason and Georgia Lee instead of going for a walk with Angie. She could've calmed everyone down, even Warren. Or at the very least, taken the blows. She felt sure of it. She felt less sure of how anything would have changed with Diane if she had been able to avoid the events of that night.

"I'm sorry." No matter how many times Jane said the words, they'd never be enough. Maybe because deep down Diane knew it was a lie.

"You know when they're coming to pick you up?"

"No." It'd been five days since Chuck had called to say the coroner had released the remains. She expected Benjamin to show up any day now. "Would you like me to leave? I can head to the motel if you'd prefer."

"And miss them taking you away in handcuffs? Not a chance." Diane coughed and tossed her lit cigarette at Jane's shoe. "Pardon me, but I've got to thank the preacher before he takes off."

So much for forgiveness. Jane used her shoe to grind the cigarette so far into the grass the tobacco and filter nearly disintegrated. "He's not a preacher."

Diane scowled and took off toward him, trying not to sink her heels into the grass. Jane couldn't help but wonder what kind of thanks Diane had in mind.

A car blazed down the cemetery drive and came to a shuddering stop. Jane raised a hand to shield her eyes from the sun. She watched a woman in a white pharmacy smock pull her hair out of a bun held together with a ballpoint pen and let it drift onto her shoulders.

Georgia Lee.

Their first date had been at the old drive-in on Midland. When rain started during intermission, Jane had scooped up Georgia Lee despite her protestations and carried her back from the snack bar so her white flats and yellow dress wouldn't get muddy. In the car, Georgia Lee pulled at the front of her dress, embarrassed by what might be revealed. Restraint kept Jane from placing her lips on the drops that fell off Georgia Lee's wet ponytail and onto the skin of her long neck.

As Georgia Lee made her way to the funeral tent, Jane noticed a few wrinkles around her eyes and lips. Lipstick instead of lip gloss. No longer slim, but strong. Giant sunglasses, presumably a disguise, her purse clutched tightly along her shoulder. She need not have worried. All but the cemetery crew had faded away from the grave.

Jane had seen photos of her throughout the years thanks to her internet searches. But to see her in the flesh? Surreal. Like looking at someone you knew but only online. Or like a character who stepped out of a movie or TV show.

Jane could ignore her. She could hide behind a column as she'd done after the fight with the Ingrams. But a twitchy feeling overtook all others. Something like excitement, something like fear—what had drawn Jane to Georgia Lee in the first place. Fear and curiosity. Danger. No one would've believed it by looking at Georgia Lee, but Jane had known as soon as she first saw Georgia Lee that she was crossing a line she couldn't uncross, and she knew it now.

See Jane run. Run, Jane. Run.

Jane stepped toward her. "Hey, Georgia Lee."

Ten

GEORGIA LEE

The way the woman said Georgia Lee's name was like hearing a familiar song, one from youthful days that pulled her right back into a day or a dream. Recognition washed over her.

Jane. My God. What is she doing at the funeral?

Jane stood a few steps away and then eased closer. Smiled after a spell, while Georgia Lee tried to recover from the shock of seeing Jane right there in front of her. Georgia Lee approached her for a hug like she'd always done, like no time had passed at all, but stopped herself.

"I didn't recognize you." Georgia Lee lifted a hand to her hair, absentmindedly making note of the missing ponytail Jane used to wear because she couldn't be bothered with things like hair products or mirrors. Even with what appeared to be a bloody nose and a roll in the dirt.

"It's good to see you," Jane said after a too-long pause. The ends of her words were clipped, gone were those valleys of southern speech. She proceeded to take in Georgia Lee. Georgia Lee could only imagine what she must be thinking. Her outfit: an embarrassment. Her makeup: too subtle. Her shoes: might as well be a mall walker. At least her hair looked halfway to fine. She crossed her arms and positioned one leg in front of the other, heel raised slightly, in an effort to make her legs appear longer and thinner, as magazines suggested.

The only sentence her brain offered was "How long are you in town?"

Jane's eyebrows lifted in surprise. "Uh. I don't know. Until they ship me to McPherson, I guess."

"Oh. Oh, I'm . . . yes, of course." Prison.

"Jesus fucking Christ," Jane muttered. Georgia Lee tensed beside her. "Sorry."

Georgia Lee glanced in the direction of Jane's gaze. Diane steadied herself against a man and wobbled her way toward his car in her heels. Georgia Lee clutched her purse and tried to stem the rage once more. Five thousand dollars tucked inside. Five thousand dollars for Diane's silence. It'd taken hours of pacing and psyching up for Georgia Lee to walk into the bank and request it. Anonymous donation, Georgia Lee had said when the bank teller asked. Then she plastered on the most authentic smile she could muster.

"You know him?" Jane's focus remained on Diane and Gerry. Georgia Lee hadn't forgotten how quickly those twin pangs of Diane's neglect and rejection could darken Jane's mood.

"Gerry Hardgrove. Works at the dam. He found Warren." She didn't mention that she'd seen them together at the liquor store.

"Awkward," Jane said, so softly she might as well have been talking to herself.

"Are they dating?" Georgia Lee asked.

Jane shrugged. "Never seen him before today." Finally, she faced Georgia Lee. "What are you doing here?"

Georgia Lee hadn't prepared for the question. "I thought I might see you here."

"Well," Jane said. "Here I am."

Georgia Lee paused. Longer than she realized, apparently.

"Okay then," Jane said and looked around. "I need to find a ride home."

"Sorry. I don't know where my head's at." Georgia Lee tried to laugh off her awkwardness. "I can give you a ride."

Georgia Lee reached out to touch Jane's arm, a friendly gesture. But something woke within her. A tiny glimmer. A vestigial bit of ancestral code, unlocked. A pebble, really. But big enough to upset her balance, to render logic and reasoning out of her control. Something her teacher had mentioned in middle school when he separated the boys from the girls and a film clicked on, talking about babies and hormones and how their bodies might start feeling, looking different soon. That teacher didn't talk about what Georgia Lee had felt when she talked to Jane for the first time. When she saw her now.

Eleven

JANE

As soon as Georgia Lee's fingertips hit Jane's skin, it was like mainlining lost memories.

"What the fuck?"

Georgia Lee and Angie and Jason had begun to talk at once, launching words at Jane. She couldn't focus. Her brain bounced all sorts of things off her skull. Random words that didn't fit into any logical sequence. She was scared. Scattered.

Water rushed through the dam in the distance. Tree limbs reached out toward them like hands, snatching at their hair with the uptick in wind from the impending storm. Angie and Jane had left the house for twenty minutes to talk. Another dumb fight about Georgia Lee that ended with another earnest promise to spend more time together before they walked back to the trailer and noticed the door wide open, shit knocked to the floor, and neither Georgia Lee nor Jason anywhere to be found.

And now Warren was at their feet. Blood clotting the dirt beneath his head.

"What the fuck?" Jane asked again. The only words she could think to say.

Words spilled out of Georgia Lee's mouth, frantic. Something about Warren coming home, them having words, Georgia Lee running out of the house, Warren's hand around the arm that Georgia Lee rubbed, the same way Jane had sometimes caught herself rubbing her neck from where he'd grabbed her.

"What did he do?"

"I'm fine. He didn't hit me. Jason . . ." Georgia Lee stopped. Her face went ashen.

"What about Jason?" Jane turned to him. Blood covered his hands.

He held out his hands as if he was worried she might rush him. "I didn't mean to."

"What the fuck!" Jane's voice reverberated through the woods and across the water.

Angie clasped a hand to Jane's mouth. "Keep your voice down." Panic edged her words.

Jane should've kept her mouth shut. But she had to say things, do things. Antagonize Warren beyond the point where it was okay or safe. Finally, Angie removed her hand.

They stood and stared at Warren's body as if an answer would come to them.

"What are we supposed to do?" Jason asked. He could barely stand still. He twitched head to toe, like something had gotten inside his skin.

"We?" Angie asked. Even in the shadows, Jane noted the flush on her skin. "No. No, no, no."

"Angie, please." Jane gripped her hand. "You can't leave."

Angie shook her head, not looking up from the sight of Warren on the ground. "I can't have anything to do with this."

"You can't unsee a dead body," Georgia Lee said. She stood rigid, hands at her sides, slightly shaking as if from a chill. The perfect picture of a horror-movie heroine with her makeup askew, hair in her face, and blood on her shirt and hands.

Angie didn't have a retort for Georgia Lee, maybe for the first time ever.

While they stood and stared at Warren's body, Jane banged her head against every option but kept landing on the only one that made any sense. The only option that would keep the cops from taking Jason in.

"Grab his arms," Jane said.

"What? No." Angie leaned in to whisper to Jane, casting a glance at Jason first. "Don't you think we should call the police?"

"No," Georgia Lee said. She slowly turned to Jason, who was staring at her. He faced Angie and Jane.

"No," he said. "We can't call them." *What the fuck,* Jane kept repeating in her head.

"But it was self-defense," Angie said, her words rushed. "Right?"

Jason stared at Warren's body some more and then at Angie. "They won't help us," he said to Angie. "You know that."

He was right. How many times had they shown up at the trailer park claiming someone had done something? How many times had Angie's uncles and brothers and father been stopped and questioned when doing something as simple as walking down the road? How many times had they laughed with Warren after a neighbor had called them because it sounded like someone had put their fist through a wall—which he had—and then just walked away like nothing had ever happened?

"He's right," Georgia Lee said. "They won't believe us."

"Us?" Angie asked. Her voice hitched into disbelief. "Please. You'll be fine."

"You're both right," Jane said. Then she looked at Georgia Lee. "They'll burn us alive."

No matter that Georgia Lee was from Maud Proper and they weren't. They'd all get caught up in this one.

"Grab his arms or leave." Jane couldn't look at Angie. She didn't want to see her face, her pain, her disappointment.

After a while, Angie said, "There's the boat." The abandoned flat-bottom boat. Teens from the trailer park partied in it, sometimes took it out at night and drunk dared each other with how close they could get to the dam before getting caught—by the lock and dam engineers or the currents that could suck you under the lock and crush you.

Everyone in Maud had heard stories about the missing men in the river. How they wandered into the water, presumably drunk. Or jumped off the bridge right into the lock—probably drunk, maybe just lost. Sometimes, their bodies would be found floating downriver. Most times, nothing resurfaced.

Everyone also knew that Warren was a drinker. Everyone would believe he fell in, became one of the lost men. No one would know any different. Angie and Jane and Jason had watched the rescues from the river. The boats that dragged the bottom. The ones they did find were considered drownings. Accidental. Even with an autopsy. Any head trauma a matter of how hard they had hit the concrete walls of the lock.

Georgia Lee held Warren's arms aloft, waiting for Jane and Angie to lift his legs. It would've looked comical if not for the streaks of blood and dirt and the sheer determination on her face. When Jason moved toward the body, Jane intervened.

"No. Go home," she said.

"But I—"

"After you clean up here. As much as you can. Get rid of everything. What's left on the ground." Blood, so much blood. How would he get rid of it? Where would he put it? "And then get home." She paused. "Where's Diane?"

He shook his head. "I don't know."

"Make sure the house looks normal. She'll freak otherwise, especially if Warren's not there."

"What if she asks—"

"You'll think of something," she interrupted. "You're smart. She'll listen to you."

His eyes pleaded and pooled with imminent tears, his fingers danced with nervous energy, fear, something else.

"It's okay," she said. "I'll take care of it. I promise."

"Okay," he finally said and stepped back so they could lift Warren's body. But before he could get far, she called after him. "Wait."

They all faced one another, fear clouding their faces.

"When the body's found, you can't say anything," Jane said. "Not a word. The cops will ask us when we last saw him." She turned to Jason. He no longer looked scared but like he wanted to say something. "We tell them we saw him tonight. That he was drunk. That he was yelling—"

"What about us?" Angie asked.

"You and I went out for a walk. It's not a lie."

"And her?" Angie pointed at Georgia Lee, a look of irritation below the fear. "What if someone saw her at the house? The hoarder?"

"I'll tell them I ran after Warren and Georgia Lee and found Georgia Lee alone," Jason said. "She hid from him. He didn't find her. I did."

Jason and Georgia Lee shared a look whose meaning Jane couldn't decipher.

"It's true," Georgia Lee said. "Jason did find me."

Angie blew air out her nose and crossed her arms. "But then what? What do they say when the cops ask if they saw Warren out here?"

"We lie," Jason said. He'd calmed. His body no longer shook.

"We lie," Jane repeated. "We don't know what happened to him. When we last saw him, he was drunk. That's all we have to say. Don't offer any more information unless they ask. Don't say anything more." She looked each of them in the eye. "We don't know what happened to him after that."

Finally, Jason broke from the group and headed toward the dark area of ground where the grass had been pushed down and soaked with Warren's blood. The three girls positioned themselves around Warren's body.

None of them spoke as they labored under Warren's weight and inched away from Jason and where he'd begun to kick the wet dirt toward the nearby riverbank. Georgia Lee pushed forward from behind Jane and Angie, nearly tripping them in the process. Jane refused to turn toward Angie, though she could see her looking her way and could feel the heat of her blame.

Jane's arms burned, and she almost dropped Warren at least five times. They walked a ways and came to a stop.

Jane ran into the bushes to confirm the boat was there and then motioned for them to join her. Once more, their arms burned as they hefted the boat toward the water. The lights from the lock and dam wouldn't be an issue tonight. Not with the storm. They wouldn't be noticed at all. That's what Angie had said and Georgia Lee confirmed and Jane convinced herself was true.

"We're gonna have to lift him again," Jane said.

Georgia Lee and Angie nodded. After Jane quietly counted to three, they heaved and almost managed to get Warren's body into the boat, but Georgia Lee's arms gave out. His body thudded to the ground. Angie cursed under her breath. Georgia Lee started crying. Jane wanted to hug her, comfort her, apologize. But if she paused, she'd lose her nerve.

"It's okay. Pick up his arms," Jane said.

Georgia Lee wiped her eyes and nose on her sleeve, and they all tried again. This time, they succeeded.

Angie studied the boat and Warren in it. It rocked side to side in the shallow water, the metal scraping lightly against the rocks. When Jane lightly touched her arm, she jumped.

"I should help Jason," Angie said.

"Okay." Jane couldn't force her to stay.

"Thank you," Jane said, which felt like the worst kind of thanks she could possibly give. She didn't know how things had gotten so out of hand. They'd only gone for a quick walk to talk. They'd come back, and everything had changed. "Do you think we'll be okay?" Jane asked, even though she couldn't remember a time when she'd ever believed things in her life would be okay.

"We'll never be okay," Angie said, making her way into the woods.

When Angie was out of sight, Jane tried to return her focus to what lay ahead. She wanted to cry, be consoled. To be in bed, asleep. She wanted to wake up to normalcy.

"Get in the front," she told Georgia Lee. "I'll push you away from shore and then hop in the back."

A question lodged in her throat, wanting to come out but lacking the nerve. Wanting to ask if this could be fixed. If there weren't some other way. Now that the moment had arrived, Jane wondered if this was the line. If they'd end this now, call the cops, or keep going. Before Jane knew what was happening, the boat floated away, out of reach.

"Wait!" Panic surged. Currents swirled below the surface, winds churned above.

Georgia Lee's arms expertly worked the paddle, left to right, as she steered the boat away from Jane. Jane rushed into the river, up to her chest, chopped her arms through the water.

"No!" she gasped. "Stop!"

Georgia Lee and the boat grew smaller until finally they disappeared into the distance and darkness.

Clouds covered the moon, providing a dark canvas on which Jane could cast her thoughts. After Georgia Lee had taken off, Jane had hurried to brush the ground where they'd walked with a stick to try to cover their footprints. No need now. The rain had begun. Light at first, and then steady. Now she had nothing to do but wait.

Everything had happened so fast. The fear. The fight. The solution.

A wave of gratitude and guilt and horror flooded her. How could she look at Georgia Lee and Angie again without that swell of guilt that felt like it would crush her? What kind of girls would help you out of a situation, even if it meant doing something against the law, against God?

Wasn't it? Against God? But these girls had saved her and Jason. They'd done more than anything God or Jesus had ever done for them.

There was no turning back. God willing, Georgia Lee would come back.

After what felt like hours, Georgia Lee finally stepped out of the dark edges of the woods toward Jane. Her drenched clothing hung on her body. Her hair clung to her skin. Her whole body trembled, wrecked and weakened. She wouldn't let Jane touch her, comfort her. Neither of them said a thing. They took a well-used trail through the woods and toward the road and the trailer park without speaking. Their river-soaked sneakers squeaked even more in the mud.

The party a few trailers down that had been in full swing and at full volume earlier that evening despite the impending storm had wound down. The only chatter came from the rain hitting the metal siding. The sky hadn't yet revealed whether it'd unleash its full wrath.

The trailer was dark. No sign of Jason or Angie or Diane. Georgia Lee stopped at her car. Warren's car was parked off to the side. That's what had set this off, Jane realized. Georgia Lee had parked in his spot.

Georgia Lee opened her car door and settled into the driver's seat. Rain ran in rivulets down their faces. Georgia Lee looked at her with an expression she couldn't decipher. Not anger, something else.

Like she'd done in the boat, she drifted off without a word. The crackle of stones under the tires and the soft hum of the motor faded.

All that was left to do was wait for someone to find the body. Or, if they got lucky, wait until everyone forgot about Warren and turned their attention to the next man who went missing.

Twelve

GEORGIA LEE

Georgia Lee remembered the precise day and time her high school—and subsequently, college—swim career had come to an end. She hadn't been able to eat all day. Her stomach tumbled and threatened. Sweat ran down her back and stomach, wet her suit before she even entered the pool. This water, calm. The room lit with fluorescents. Filled with people. Not her alone, debating when to bail out of a boat, how close equaled too close to the dam. If her body could fight the current and return to the riverbank. If her muscles would falter due to fears she couldn't tamp down no matter how well she had mastered her breathing. If she'd get sucked through the lock along with Warren and tumble out the other side, alive, or get caught and drown. None of her teammates noticed how she stood near the edge of the pool, breath shallow, panicked at the lack of air. She became so unnerved she rushed back to the locker room. Her mother found her after the announcer had called Georgia Lee's name three times and the gun had gone off without her. She lay down in the back seat on the way home. Her mother reached behind her at the stoplights to pet her and tell her there would be more swim meets. There wouldn't be. In the weeks after, instead of Georgia

Lee returning to the water, her mother returned the new swim cap and suit she'd bought her for that year's competitions.

For years, Georgia Lee had given excuses about not going in the swimming pool or a lake despite her swim career, preferring to sun on a towel instead. She'd let her mind tuck the reasoning away alongside the night that Warren bled into the earth.

It'd been a little over a week since she'd learned of Warren's remains. Now she stood inside a pizza parlor next to Jane, an uncaged suggestion that had escaped her mouth before she'd had a chance to stop it. She told herself she needed to learn more about why Jane was in town and what would happen next. But an old haunt of days past also tugged at her, a fear of watching Jane walk away, not knowing what might happen while they were apart, if Jane would be there the next day, or gone or in prison. She wanted to put everything on pause. Take a break. Go somewhere alone where they could talk, where she could stare at her face and hear her voice and see how much had changed, how much hadn't. But then she'd realized her mistake. They weren't like everyone else. They couldn't go just anywhere. And not within Maud. She should've given Jane a ride home and left it at that.

How could she sit with her and act like old friends, knowing that Jane was about to suffer the consequences for someone else's crime?

But Jane had agreed. As soon as they left Maud city limits, Jane asked if Georgia Lee meant to kidnap her or if she was embarrassed to be seen with her. Georgia Lee had pressed play on Beyoncé, thinking that would make an impression on Jane, how hip and with it Georgia Lee still was—or at least work as a lubricant to conversation, maybe trick Jane into singing along as she'd done in the past—but Jane only stared out the window, aggrieved at the passing scenery, or at something else.

Pizza in Fort Smith would be fine, she tried to convince herself. Safe for an evening out. Anyone from Maud Bottoms would go to Maud Proper for a change of scenery. Anyone from Maud Proper would go to Fayetteville. No one would go to Fort Smith. Georgia Lee only went occasionally for a conference. They were almost thirty miles from Maud. No one knew her here. That was a city, not a town. Dinner with a friend was normal behavior, she told herself. Nothing suspicious. She breathed in. Dough baking in the oven. The sizzle of just-baked pepperoni and sausage. The fizz of carbonated soda in the mouth. Better than a spa. Food had always been their comfort. Just what she—they—needed.

Jane hesitated after they entered the building. "Did you bring me to Jesus Pizza?"

Georgia Lee followed Jane's gaze across the vast building that had once been an equipment warehouse and then a nightclub before giving itself over to pizza, to where large letters on the wall read: *For God so loved the world that he gave his one and only Son, that whoever believes in him shall not perish but have eternal life.* Georgia Lee hadn't really noticed before. Bible verses were a bit of a thing in Arkansas. On walls. In yards. On shirts.

Maybe they could abort the plan for pizza. It'd been a long, hot day. Jane couldn't have been comfortable in all black at the cemetery. Not to mention the dirt and her nose. She considered canceling right there on the spot. Maybe claim a sudden stomach bug. But then what? Georgia Lee had nowhere to go but home, where Rusty had probably bought another item they could barely afford in his attempt to trick himself and everyone else that they had as much wealth as appearances would have people believe, that their faith and marriage were stronger than they were. Tim and Tate had probably left their laundry and empty soda glasses outside their rooms again like she was hotel staff. All those irritations, and she'd still have those nerves knocking on her insides.

She nudged Jane forward. "It's really good pizza."

Jane looked around. "Does it come with a side of homophobia?"

"No one will bother you." She exuded enough confidence to convince herself it was true.

"Until I go to the bathroom," Jane muttered. Georgia Lee plastered a smile on her face and walked up to the girl waiting at the register, who gave Jane a once-over.

Really, if Jane didn't want to be confused for a man, then why dress like one and get her hair cut like one? That made no kind of sense to Georgia Lee. Still, if she was being honest, when she'd noticed this person in the cemetery staring at her, she'd thought it was a man and even gotten a little thrill when the alleged man looked at her with what she'd perceived as interest. Back in school, Georgia Lee would sometimes wonder what it'd be like if Jane were a boy, or if Georgia Lee were. And if they could have real pictures displayed for the world to see, like others did. Hugs, kisses, hands placed on knees, arms around waists. Pictures people didn't consider against God, or porn, just because they saw two girls. Georgia Lee wondered what it'd feel like to be voted Most Romantic, like Christlyn and Jake. She wondered what it'd be like to see themselves in the yearbook, holding hands, standing in the way normal couples do.

"Pizza's on me," Georgia Lee said and handed Jane a cup and tray. Jane begrudgingly took them.

Georgia Lee navigated them through a nest of metal tables topped with glass containers of shake cheese and hot pepper flakes until she found one near the back, away from the few people scattered among them. The whole walk, she agonized about Jane comparing and contrasting what Georgia Lee's butt looked like then versus now. What she wouldn't give for those compression tights. Eyes shifted in their direction. She searched every face for a match to her memory.

"Crowded for a Monday night." She didn't know what she had been thinking, bringing Jane here. Even outside Maud. What a fool. Once again, Georgia Lee had gotten it into her head that she was right. Once again, she was wrong. She was getting real tired of being wrong. But they were here now. No point in beating herself up over it. She busied herself with her napkin and silverware, explaining how the servers would bring all varieties of pizza right to their table, including dessert pizza like chocolate chip and Bavarian cream, because she didn't know how to even begin. What conversation could they have that did not lead to the very thing they needed—but she truly did not want—to discuss?

"Where are you staying?" Georgia Lee asked after she'd run out of things to say about pizza. She wanted to look at Jane, really look at her, take her in. But she didn't want to stare. She let her eyes bounce from one table to another and then back to her silverware. She recognized no one, thankfully.

"With Diane."

"Really? I'm surprised."

"Me too. There was a misunderstanding." Jane took a sip from her cup. She declined to say more or use a straw. Georgia Lee couldn't very well use one, the latest harbinger of Earth's destruction, if Jane didn't. Ice cubes clinked against her teeth, and soda spilled along the edges of her mouth. Annoying.

Jane studied her. A little smile appeared. Was she making fun of her? Georgia Lee had to look away.

"What?"

"Nothing," Jane said, tilting her head to the side. "Been a while, is all."

What was that supposed to mean? "Where have you been hiding all these years?" It'd come out wrong. Like Georgia Lee had been waiting on her to finally make an appearance. Like Jane were a fugitive from the law. She had meant to ask a pedestrian question.

"Boston," Jane said.

"Boston!" Too emphatic. Nerves. "Fancy." She picked at a seam on her shirt and let her eyes wander toward Jane's hands. No ring.

No wife. No girlfriend? She had to focus.

Georgia Lee was a married woman. A happily married woman. Mostly. Sometimes.

Jane shrugged. "Not really. It's mainly full of people fleeing the sources of their insanity."

"I imagine so," Georgia Lee said, trying to sound politely interested. "How'd you end up there?"

Jane considered and then lifted her eyebrows, shrugged. "Bus rides. Free rides. Girlfriends got jobs. Girlfriends broke up with me. Just kept going till I hit the coast, I guess."

Georgia Lee stalled on conversation topics after that. Jane did not exhibit the same curiosity about Georgia Lee's life, which disappointed her. She should've gone somewhere that served liquor. A drink would've done them both good. She could've gotten away with it, friend from out of town and all. People did that. Drank after funerals.

"Where's Jason these days?" Georgia Lee asked. As sorry and low as her spirits had dropped, she hoped Jane would say he was gone. Gone gone. Then this whole mess could be swept away with a quick phone call to John.

"Up in Maud Proper somewhere."

All that hope, though fruitless, dissolved. "I'm surprised I haven't seen him."

"Even if you had, you probably wouldn't know it. You know how guys are. They barely look the same as they did in high school. Besides, he changed his last name. He goes by Jason Tran now." Bitterness edged her words, a surprise given how overprotective and adoring Jane had been of him. Georgia Lee had sometimes teased Jane when she fussed over Jason. Called her Momma Jane. The boy couldn't leave the house without Jane worrying after him, asking if he had his key and where he'd be, what he was going to eat. "He's an MMA fighter. Apparently."

Georgia Lee couldn't place the name, but she knew all about MMA thanks to the boys. That was the one thing they could talk about endlessly at the dinner table. That and football. "I thought he didn't know his father?"

Jane waved a hand to dismiss the topic. She paused and leaned forward. "We should probably talk about that other thing."

Georgia Lee straightened a bit in her seat to look around and waved a server over to distract from the topic Jane did want to discuss. Something trickled into Georgia Lee's thoughts, something she couldn't put her finger on. She brushed it aside. "Usually they come right over."

Jane downed her drink and did that not-smiling-but-smiling thing. "What? Can't talk murder on an empty stomach?"

Georgia Lee whipped her attention around them to see if anyone had heard. The people who'd ogled them when they walked in had returned their attention to their pizza or to reruns of NASCAR races that played from the projector TV over the stage.

"Could you please not use that word?" Georgia Lee had murder in mind with Jane's attitude. Georgia Lee lacked her ability to find humor, even dark, in the situation. "You seem awful jovial for someone headed to prison."

"I'll cry if you prefer that. But seeing as this might be my last meal, I should probably try to enjoy it."

"So it's happening then? No updates to the story? No altered confession?"

"Nope," Jane said. "I confessed. And now there's a body. The one ingredient that was missing. It's only a matter of time."

"I'm sure this will all blow over," she whispered, swallowing down her guilt. "There's nothing to be worried about."

"It's not going to blow over," Jane said. "Just promise me you won't give a different story than the one we agreed to when it's confirmed that you were my girlfriend."

Was that a threat? Why else would she mention it? What did she know? Was Jane Lovelace? "No one is—"

About five servers with five different types of pizzas came round to ask if they'd like a slice of this or that. Georgia Lee's appetite had steadily declined the longer they sat there, but she grabbed slices of ham and pineapple and pepperoni and taco and Buffalo chicken. They'd already paid, after all. And she needed to get food in her mouth. Shove it full. Figure out what to say. Remember how to talk when everything inside her screamed that something was wrong. Something was very wrong. But she didn't have the words to say what.

"Aren't you Georgia Lee Lane?" a cute white gal with a button nose asked. My God, how'd she recognize her here? She prayed she wouldn't recognize Jane as well. She was young. Probably hadn't even been born yet when Jane had left.

Georgia Lee threw on a smile despite her desire to lie. "I sure am."

"I thought so. I seen your face on posters all over town."

"Oh, do you live in Maud Bottoms?"

"Yeah. I can't find any work there."

Nonsense! There were plenty of jobs if you knew how to look.

"That's me!" Georgia Lee said to avoid further complaints about the lack of employment opportunities in Maud. Jane watched, amused. The way Jane didn't drop her gaze made Georgia Lee uncomfortable. Her undivided attention was a lot more enchanting as a teenager. "I sure hope you'll consider honoring me with your vote on November 5."

"Oh," the girl said. "I don't even know if I'm registered." Jane chuckled and yanked a handful of napkins out of the receptacle.

"You be sure to find out. Every vote counts, you know."

"If you say so," the girl said in that sarcastic teenage way that got under Georgia Lee's skin. She had this conversation about once a day. People like this girl sat on their couches and complained about life, but when it came to actually doing something about it, they couldn't be bothered to show up for five minutes to cast a vote. That's all it took. *Five minutes!*

"Every vote counts, honey. And don't you forget it." She dug around in her purse for a flyer and a customized campaign pen and gave them to the girl. "November 5. Don't forget."

"Remember, remember, the fifth of November," Jane sang as she examined her pizza.

The girl looked at Jane quizzically, along with Georgia Lee. "Hey, you're Lezzie Borden, aren't you?" Her face lit up. Georgia Lee's stomach plunged. "Can I get a selfie?" She had her phone out and the picture snapped before Jane had a chance to consent. Right after she got her shot, her fingers danced across the face of her phone on her way back to the kitchen. She left an empty pizza pan and Georgia Lee's flyer on the table. Didn't even bother to carry it to the kitchen and throw it in the trash in private. She kept the pen, though. Heathen.

"If you had kept your mouth shut, she wouldn't have even noticed you!"

"You're the one who decided it'd be a good idea to go out in public together."

Georgia Lee decided not to respond and rage ate her pizza, barely bothering with taste. Tear, chew, swallow. The sooner the pizza disappeared, the sooner she could drop Jane at Diane's house and then go sit alone in an empty parking lot somewhere to scream. Jane was right, though. It had been stupid to go out in public. What was the matter with her? Why did *she* feel guilty and strange? It wasn't her fault Jane had confessed. No one had forced her. She'd made those decisions for herself—for all of them, after harassing them about not saying a word!

From her peripheral vision, she noticed Jane examining the flyer.

"What?" Georgia Lee demanded. Good thing that girl had taken the pen. She had a mind to stab Jane with it. Inspection complete, Jane dabbed a slice of pepperoni pizza with her wad of napkins. As if that made any kind of difference. Orange blots blemished the paper. So much for saving the world by avoiding straws. Typical. "I know that look. You're judging me."

"I'm just looking at your flyer." Jane took a bite and made a face. She doused the pizza in red pepper flakes and salt. Not to her exacting standards, apparently. "I'm a graphic designer. Was."

"That's nice. You were always doodling." Georgia Lee bit into her pizza, grease and all.

Jane had spent hours, days sketching pictures of fields full of flowers with mountains in the background, dogs sleeping on rag rugs in the sun, blackberry bushes, and honeysuckle vines—all for Georgia Lee, who plastered them across her bedroom walls. She had planned to take the small honeysuckle drawing to a tattoo artist once she turned eighteen, place it low on her stomach for only Jane to see. After Jane had left town, she had ripped the drawings off her wall and thrown them in the trash.

Once again, silence. This time, Georgia Lee welcomed it. She brushed the hair out of her face and smiled at the server who offered her another slice of pizza.

When she left their table, Jane finally spoke. "Do you remember what you promised?"

The pizza went down hard and rough. Georgia Lee worried for a moment that she might need the Heimlich. Thankfully, it passed. She downed her drink. "I remember."

Easy enough: Jane did it.

Alone.

End of story.

If that's what Jane wanted, that's what she'd get.

Seemingly pleased, Jane continued eating and glancing around them. "Why'd you go into politics?"

Georgia Lee considered the question. Instead of offering a stump speech out of habit, and as Jane no doubt expected, she said, "I didn't like driving through Maud feeling like I had to lock my doors. And it was an eyesore. It's as simple as that." The words weren't entirely true, but they weren't entirely false. There was a meanness in her that came out when she felt judged. She forced another bite down her throat.

"At least you're honest. I guess." Jane pushed back from the table, one lone pizza crust on her plate. Her demeanor transitioned from not-so-playful banter to melancholy. As long as Jane poked at Georgia Lee, things could be resolved, controlled. When despondency descended, she acted rashly. Georgia Lee never allowed herself to despair. Jane's lack of fight angered her, even as Georgia Lee harbored an odd, selfish glimmer of hope for herself. And all so no one would associate Georgia Lee with Jane. What a terrible thing to think.

An itch worked its way up her throat. Georgia Lee coughed and sipped her drink. Smiled at no one in case they watched. "You shouldn't go to jail. Warren was a horrible person." The first night that Georgia Lee had met Warren, he had barged through the door and declared it steak night. Jane looked confused at the mention of steak, but Jason got excited. He loved steak in all its forms: plain, on rice, in a stew, in a flour tortilla, on a salad. But come dinnertime, the only steak was the one on Warren's plate—though he'd fed Diane bites off his fork while smiling at Jane, Jason, and Georgia Lee and their pitiful plates of box mac and cheese with a side of canned corn. Georgia Lee had taken them to the Dairy Queen for dessert. "The world is a better place without him in it."

"Wow." Jane gaped. "Didn't expect that of you."

"And I didn't expect you to confess. But you did. And here we are." Words she'd longed to say. Been afraid to say, without even realizing it. And now they were out. "This is Maud," Georgia Lee said. "Their attention to detail is not great, their motivation less so. They wouldn't have done anything." Georgia Lee shoved another piece of pizza toward her mouth and chewed with vigor. Jane had brought this on herself. And now she'd have to pay the price. *So be it,* she told herself, even as her guilt for feeling off the hook flamed. "You ruined your life for nothing."

"My life was already bad."

Georgia Lee was in the process of swallowing another bite. Jane's words made her food scrape all the way down to her belly.

"I didn't plan to confess," Jane said. "It just happened."

All that guilt mixed with her bitterness. "You were supposed to keep your mouth shut. That's what you told all of us to do."

"I know." Jane stared at her pizza crust. "I panicked."

"Why? What happened that forced you to do the very thing you begged us not to do?"

"Jason got scared." Jason. Always Jason. What about Georgia Lee? She'd been hurt that night too. "They came to the house. The cops," Jane said. "They kept asking us all these questions. Diane was hovering, getting agitated. Jason started to say something." Jane looked off into the distance, as if recalling the details after a long time without thinking of them. "I stopped him by saying something first." She picked at her abandoned pizza crust. Jane had always called them her "bones" and joked that she used them to keep track of how many pieces she'd already had to prevent herself from getting sick. "I just didn't want Jason to go to jail. Shit was bad enough. I didn't want him to go through more than he already had."

"So that's that? You're just going to go to prison?"

Jane shrugged. "I thought so, but I guess they have other plans." She shoved her plate away from her. "I wish they'd get on with it."

Georgia Lee ate the remainder of her pizza in silence. Everything felt unfinished. Was she supposed to say bye and then wait to see if Jane would actually be arrested, or were they looking for more evidence, more suspects? They had Jane's confession, the body. There was no need to wait on an arrest—unless there was something else the police had learned. Something that would point away from Jane and toward someone else.

Georgia Lee hated to wait. She liked action and to-do lists, but in this situation waiting was all she'd been doing. Doing more meant placing a target on her own back. Maybe if she asked John and Benjamin the question head-on, they'd never suspect she knew the things they wanted to know.

"I'll try to get more information from my contacts at the police station. See what's going on and why they're waiting. I can't guarantee anything. But I'll try."

Jane wadded her napkin into a tight ball, not looking up at Georgia Lee. "You don't have to do that."

"I want to." She had to. All this waiting around had her on edge.

"You know a Detective Hampton?" Jane asked. Georgia Lee nodded. "Best thing you could do is try to convince him I did it alone. He seems to think that's not the case."

"It's not," Georgia Lee said.

Jane leaned back in her chair and gave a little laugh while stretching. "I've been alone with this for twenty-five years. I might as well have done it on my own."

◆　◆　◆

As soon as Georgia Lee veered the car into the trailer park's one-way road, recollections of that long-ago night swarmed into her mind like inanimate objects in cartoons come to life after years of disuse and dust. She tried to ignore the jarring images and focus on the present. That wasn't great to look at either. Maud Bottoms Estates held on to decay like a badge of honor. Tree branches hung over the road, creating a tunnel to block the sky. Every time she'd come here to visit Jane, she had worried a tornado would drop down and carry them off in its funnel, never to be seen again. But wintercreeper and honeysuckle tentacled the vinyl siding and slats of wooden porches, ensuring the mobile homes' permanence until the vines pulled it all back to nature.

"Is Angie still around?" Jane asked when they passed her old trailer.

"I have no idea," Georgia Lee said. "We didn't speak after that night." Angie would rather be waterboarded than affiliated with Georgia Lee. Their worlds had collided, with Jane at the center, and neither had been keen on giving up the time they spent with her. Georgia Lee wished she'd been nicer. But she'd been so wrapped up in Jane and afraid for anyone from Maud Proper to find out.

"Do you think she'll stay quiet?" Another loose thread, along with Jason.

Jane spoke without hesitation. "Of course." Georgia Lee had been jealous of their friendship. Their secrets. Their utter trust in one another.

"You should find her. Just to be sure. If she deviates from the story, we all go down."

Jane nodded at the words she'd told them years ago parroted back to her. Their pact broken a week later by Jane.

Without anything else to offer and with nothing more from Jane, Georgia Lee continued on the road that circled the trailer park until it curved and she came to the place that had brought her equal amounts of joy and heartache. She hesitated and let the engine idle in the empty parking spot in front of Diane's trailer. The last time she'd stepped inside the trailer, the local reporters had moved on to the next story because Warren had not turned up and Jane had left town after the police let her go for lack of evidence.

Georgia Lee's parents had barely unlocked her door before she headed to Jane's house. At that point, the media had stopped swirling. Trailer park neighbors had stopped contacting the local news with "inside scoops" and visions of becoming minor celebrities within their social circles. Everyone had stopped coming by with sympathy cards or casseroles. Everyone finally accepted the rumor that maybe Warren had actually run off because, remarkably, there was no blood, no evidence of a crime. At least that's what she gleaned from a drunken Diane after she answered the door. Jason slumped on the couch, watching TV. With her entrance, he sat up straight, eyed her in a way she couldn't decipher.

Georgia Lee pushed past Diane and her objections, opened Jane and Jason's shared bedroom door. If someone hadn't spent a lot of time memorizing everything about Jane and the world she built around her, the little trinkets and notes and drawings, then they wouldn't have realized anything had changed. An uncanny feeling slunk under her skin, like the earth slipped half an inch off its axis.

When she turned, Jason stood behind her. Diane listened from down the hall with a peculiar look on her face.

"She's gone," Jason said. "She's not coming back."

Georgia Lee didn't cry. She didn't fall apart at the sight of a mostly empty closet and photos of them shoved into the edges of the dresser mirror, friends having fun at the mall. Or any of the innocuous items Georgia Lee had left on Jane's side of the room as reminders, to let her know not to forget Georgia Lee in the hours they were apart: a pair of cheap red sunglasses; a bottle of glitter nail polish; the overnight skate ticket, where when everyone was sleeping, Jane had propped Georgia Lee against an arcade game and kissed her hard. And those socks with black and brown cats that crawled up the yellow fabric. Jane didn't even like cats. She thought they were annoying and loud. But she had worn those socks. The faces of those cats looked up at Georgia Lee from the drawer, along with everything else Jane didn't prize. But the other photo booth pictures. The ones they were nervous about people seeing. They were gone.

That means something, right? Georgia Lee had thought it meant something.

But maybe that was what happened when you fell in love. You forgot that people might not feel the things you thought they should.

Georgia Lee had left the trailer that day and never gone back. She'd never seen Jason again either, not even at school. It was as if they had both vanished. As if the previous months hadn't happened at all. A beautiful dream and terrible nightmare.

Jane fiddled with the car's door handle, running her hand over it but stopping short of pulling. Maybe she didn't know how to say goodbye either. More likely, she didn't want to go inside.

"Maybe we could have a proper dinner sometime," Georgia Lee said. "Really catch up."

Jane dramatically rolled her head to the side and faced her. "Pretty sure that was our last opportunity for a proper dinner. Everything's gonna get turned upside down soon." She let out a long, quiet sigh. "Thanks for the ride." She cracked the door open, and the smell of the nearby river, the dirt and trees along its banks, greeted them.

"Wait," Georgia Lee said. Words brimmed on her tongue but refused to surface.

Now. The word startled her. Locked in her bedroom with "mono," Georgia Lee had considered that maybe God had put Warren in her way to take Jane out of her life. But Georgia Lee couldn't figure why God would let someone like Warren run around the way he did, hurting Jane and Jason, hurting Diane—even though Diane seemed to dish it out as much as she took it.

What did it mean that Warren had returned, as had Jane? What plan could God possibly have for her now?

A head rush, like when she came up too quickly after a handstand in the water, knocked her equilibrium. Faces. Flashes of that night, but not in order. Memories that didn't feel accurate. But memories that didn't feel wrong. She felt all kinds of strange in her body and uncertain in her mind.

"If they arrest you—"

"I don't think it's *if* but *when*," Jane interrupted.

"If." There could be another way. There could be a gift from the universe, some beautiful legal loophole, some fantastic technicality that would keep Jane out of prison. If it existed, Georgia Lee would find it.

"If what?" Jane asked. "If they arrest me? What were you going to say?"

She paused, swallowed down saliva, tried to work up the courage to say the words. "Could I come see you?" Georgia Lee could practically feel the heat from hell work its way up her toes and through her body.

"Oh." Jane stared out the window. "I don't think so," she said. "I don't think that'd be a good idea."

Time collapsed between them, and Georgia Lee was transported to the girl she'd been their last night together. Sad. And sorry. Willing to do anything to stop the world from rushing on without the two of them facing it together. Though Jane looked so far from the girl Georgia Lee had known, there were traces of her in that face. A face she'd spent hours looking at, dreaming of, touching, kissing. A surge of want came over Georgia Lee. Loss. There was so much about this new Jane that Georgia Lee wanted to know, and she despised Warren all over again. Imagine what their lives might have been like if Warren had slipped in and out of the house without caring about what anyone said or did. What might've happened with her and Jane?

Jane placed a foot on the ground. "Thank you for dinner. It was good to see you again," she said before shutting the car door.

Biting down on her emotions, Georgia Lee offered her goodbye and waited for Jane to go inside. Once assured of her absence, she conducted a round of deep meditative breaths to clear her thoughts and steady her after an emotionally assaultive afternoon. Despite her growing uneasiness about where Benjamin's focus might be headed, it couldn't push beyond the other thoughts at the head of the line.

She hopped on to Instagram for a quick check, found the photo that had been taken at the pizza place (annoyance thick on Jane's face next to the overly enthusiastic server's), and scanned the caption and tags: #LezzieBorden #OMGyall #TrueCrimeCelebrity #TrueCrimeJunkie #MaudMurderMystery #ColdCase #Obsessed #OnlyInArkansas

Comments flooded the photo, littered with knife and black heart and skull emojis. Several women wrote *HOT*, followed by fire emojis, desires for conjugal visits, and promises to fight for Jane's release. And #illbeyourbonnie.

Bonnie and Clyde. Those old rumors of an accomplice still swirled, no matter how many times Jane insisted she'd acted alone.

No mention of Georgia Lee.

She paused to collect herself, consider what she was about to do. Erase herself from Jane's past life. Hush money. Her nerves prickled.

She'd find a way to help Jane. Some other way. It wouldn't help Jane to be outed as her accomplice.

For now, she had to get the money to Diane. She couldn't hand it over at Cloverleaf Liquors. Not with all the store cameras. And she didn't have Diane's number. After a moment of panic, she settled on hiding the envelope of cash under a broken pot near the trailer hitch and leaving a note on Diane's car at the liquor store. Despite her better instincts and the fear of theft, she handled the problem and hoped for the best.

Finally, she navigated the car toward home. She didn't get far before a flood of emotions overwhelmed her. She pulled the car as far into the ditch as possible without getting stuck, put it in park, switched on the hazards, placed her head on the steering wheel, and let all her tears come. She wept until her head ached and the fine membranes in her eyelids swelled and her lips and limbs felt bloated to unnatural proportions.

When she was a teenager, crying had been her reaction to pain, shock, happiness, anger, frustration, and other feelings she couldn't name and that could not be controlled. She hated crying. Her mother had always told her crying was a good thing, though, like a flood that could erase all the bad. She knew her mother alluded to Noah, and that made Georgia Lee even angrier. The madder she got, the more she cried and the more her mother thought she was being helpful.

She wiped her eyes and blew her nose with a used tissue she found in her purse. She half expected to see blue lights flash from behind. When she clicked on the engine, the AC blasted her face, and a voice in a commercial on the radio screamed. She slammed the buttons on the dashboard and finally found the one that stopped the noise. Eventually, she calmed. Maybe the crying had dehydrated her. Maybe talking about the thing she'd not been able to talk about in years finally released built-up stress and tension. Perhaps that was all she needed to get through this, a good cleansing cry. She checked her mascara in the rearview mirror and tested her ability to smile as if nothing were the matter, as if everything were fine, as if her heart didn't race at the turn her day had taken.

Jane Mooney.

She held two fingers to her neck, closed her eyes, and waited for her pulse to normalize.

Instead, her heartbeat spiked as a memory clawed to the forefront of her mind.

Thirteen

GEORGIA LEE

Georgia Lee heard Warren before she saw him. The yelling. The footsteps up the stairs.

"Whose car is that?" Warren yelled again. Georgia Lee had gone to the bathroom and watched from the hallway, afraid to step out of the shadow. She hated to be in the same room with Warren.

Jason sat straighter on the couch and turned down the volume on the TV. He'd told Georgia Lee that Warren had once threatened to take an axe to it when he came home and saw they were watching music videos that Angie had taped for Jane. God forbid they have a measure of fun in their lives.

They'd been having a good conversation. Talking about sports. She'd been trying to convince Jason to join the swim team. Get out of the house. For hating it so much, he never seemed to leave, like there was some force field that kept him trapped there. He'd said he wasn't interested in wearing "tiny shorts."

Jason pinned his gaze on Warren, startled like prey in those animal shows they sometimes watched.

"It's my car," Georgia Lee said and walked into the room. Her heart thumped. She looked to the door, hopeful that Jane and Angie would return from wherever they'd gone to fight today.

Warren turned his attention to her. His mouth had a slick, bloody look about it. What looked like vomit trailed down his chin and the front of his shirt. And his eyes didn't seem to focus too good. He gripped his head and winced.

"Where's Mom?" Jason asked quietly.

Warren swung his attention to Jason. ". . . you say to me?"

"Mom," Jason repeated. The word thrummed with anxiety.

Warren rubbed his head, as if just noting her absence. "Your mom's at the bar. Where I left that crazy bitch after she hit me with a goddamn beer bottle."

Georgia Lee's keys were on the kitchen table. She'd have to move closer to him to grab them. Too close for her comfort, but what other choice did she have?

"Where you going?" Warren asked.

"To get my keys. To move my car."

"You better get your fucking keys." Warren gripped the doorknob as if to prevent himself from falling or doing something stupid. But that's all he ever did or said: something stupid. "Why the hell are you in my spot?"

"Jane said you'd be gone all night. Sorry." She bolstered herself for the walk to the kitchen table.

"I don't give a rat's ass if I'm here or not. Don't park in my god-damned spot." He rubbed his head again. "You fucking women. Think you can just walk all over me. You, Jane, Diane." At the mention of her name, he sneered. "Fucking cunt."

Though Georgia Lee went to church and didn't cuss herself—nor did her parents—the word did not shock her. She'd heard plenty of "good" boys and men unleash their otherwise chaste tongues over the smallest perceived slight. She couldn't help but roll her eyes. He scared her sometimes, but she wouldn't let anyone talk down to her just because she was a teenager and a girl.

"Calm down," she muttered. "I won't park in your spot again."

"What'd you say to me?" The words came out slurred.

She edged closer to the table, heart pounding, and grabbed her keys. "I said I'll move my car."

He slung an arm across the width of the door, still keeping one hand on the knob, effectively blocking her from leaving. The buttons on his short-sleeve shirt hung open almost to his stomach, and she could see his chest bones jutting out like weapons he could wield against her. His eyes seemed to misalign in their sockets, like a cartoon character's. He squeezed them shut for a moment before shaking his head like a cat with an ear itch.

He stood there and gripped the door handle, so drunk, she imagined, that he'd fallen asleep standing up.

"I can't move my car if you're blocking the door," she said.

Finally, his eyes flickered with renewed consciousness. He didn't budge, didn't smile, didn't stare at her the way lots of men did, with their eyes like tongues, ready to strip her of dignity top to bottom. She didn't know why, but this felt worse. She could walk away from whistles and low grunts and shit-eating grins from boys and men who knew better. But there was something worse in Warren's eyes, something that didn't want to consume her as much as destroy her. A man who would threaten a woman over something as simple as a parking spot was a man she didn't want trouble with. Jane had told her that if he ever said anything to her or tried to pick a fight, she should walk away.

That's how Georgia Lee was raised. That's not how Georgia Lee ever behaved.

He dropped the arm that held the doorframe and leaned against the door, not far enough that she wouldn't come unbearably close to him in the process of her exit, so close she could smell his body odor mingling with the scent of cigarettes, the sourness on his breath and vomit on his shirt, the sweat from his skin. She should've paid attention to her fear. Getting scared might have gotten her out of a whole heap of trouble. But seeing him there in the doorway, taunting her, trying to make her feel small, didn't make her scared anymore. It made her mad.

"I need you to move," she said.

"Just let her go," Jason said quietly behind her.

"Go on, then." He spit out the door onto the porch floor, swaying a bit in the process. "Ain't nothing stopping you."

She tried not to harbor hate in her heart, but every bit of hate she'd ever held about anyone roared through her bloodstream. She bolted for the door. He blocked her with his arm, strong despite his appearance. She slammed into him, caught off balance.

"Sorry." He smirked. "I thought you was planning to stand there some more."

This time, she shoved his arm away and ducked underneath, pushing him into the door.

He laughed, like she was just a toy to him.

A fire grew within her until she couldn't bear to hold it inside any longer. "You're no better than what gets put out on the curb on trash day. You're nothing but trash. Through and through. And a coward. That's the only reason you beat on women and kids." Behind her, she heard Jason gasp or move. She couldn't be sure. Her heartbeat pounded in her ears.

Warren clutched her arm, squeezed it so tight it burned.

"Well, ain't you a snotty little bitch?"

She spit in his face.

Stunned, he released his grip and swiped at his head. His shock flared to rage, and he raised his hand as if to slap her.

Before he could, she took off running down the porch steps, past the cars, across the road, and into the woods near the river, swatting at branches as she raced past them, instinct kicking in and telling her to run like the devil was after her because that's what his footsteps sounded like as they crashed behind her. She ran as fast as she could, and then she was on the ground, twisted and tangled in his limbs. They thrashed together. Twigs and pebbles ground into her bare skin. Dirt gathered in her hair, but she wouldn't stop. She would keep fighting, and she would keep kicking until he was off her and in the dirt instead. But her strength was no match to his. He straddled her.

"You been talking to Diane? Been taking lessons?"

She kept fighting, tried to scratch and claw. Warm liquid hit her face and found its way into her mouth. She gagged and spit to the side.

"How you like that, huh? Y'all think you can just hit me and spit at me and get away with it? Like I'll just take it?" He laughed and winced, even though she hadn't done anything but try to squirm out of his grip. "You got a death wish if you think you can fuck with me, bitch."

Her elbows jabbed the earth as she tried to buck him off even as her energy waned. His bony knees pinned her shoulders to the ground. She rocked her head side to side, but he caught her and shoved his fingers into her mouth. His dirty nails screeched across her teeth and scraped her gums. She tasted blood and fought to clench, bite down, but he managed to pry and keep her mouth open. He gathered his phlegm with a great hocking sound. His face hovered over her, lips puckered for another round, this time straight into her mouth.

As he opened his mouth and his tongue pushed through, Jason's voice came through the din. She yanked her head to the side. Warm spit coated her neck and slid down her skin to wet her shirt.

She clawed at the space where Warren's body had held her down, looking for purchase. But he wasn't there. She scrambled to her knees and struggled to see in the dark. Grit irritated her eyes, her mouth. The pounding in her ears and rush of water in the nearby dam muted all other noise. She searched the ground for a weapon, anything to fill her hand, but found nothing.

She clambered to her feet on unsteady legs. No one there but her. Confused, she pulled at her clothing, confirmed the smears of dirt, blood. She ran a hand along her neck, felt the wetness on the top of her shirt, in her hair. She spun in a circle.

Where was Warren?

Someone, something, moved behind her, and she turned to meet it, heart racing, hand in the air, ready to strike.

"No!" Jason screamed and clutched her arm before she could send it down on his head.

She'd been alone. She could've sworn it.

Jason looked older. Stronger. Calmer. Slowly, she dropped her arm. Behind him, Warren's lifeless body seeped blood onto the ground. Air caught in her throat. Her arm ached. Something slipped out of her hand and hit her foot.

A blood-covered rock settled against her once-white shoes.

Jason bent over and picked up the rock, examined it, analyzed its heft. Blood transferred from the rock to his hand. There was so much blood.

She blinked and blinked. Slowly. Each time hoping that what she saw on the ground—who she saw on the ground—wasn't real. Finally, she found her voice. "Is he . . . did I . . . ?"

Before he had a chance to answer, Jane and Angie came running through the trees and stopped abruptly once they saw who was on the ground. But Georgia Lee didn't need Jason to say anything. The look on his face and the way that Warren's blood seeped and his body stilled were all the confirmation she needed to know that she had done a very, very bad thing.

Fourteen

GEORGIA LEE

The lights burned bright in the living room despite the hour. Rusty reclined in his easy chair, playing some game he'd gotten addicted to on his phone. The boys craned their heads toward the TV screen, controllers in hand, hats backward, shouting obscenities at each other and the virtual players on the screen. All distracted and disinterested even as Georgia Lee entered the room, hours later than normal. The pharmacy long since closed.

She had to be alone, to think. She couldn't think. Images of that night spun in her head. She examined her hands, expecting to find Warren's blood.

My God. What kind of monster was she?

A tiny gasp from her mouth surprised her. They drew their heads toward her.

Tim and Tate searched Rusty's face for a sign of what they should do or say. He didn't offer a word. They sat in confusion when she didn't respond, as if she lived to guide and serve and provide words for them. And she did. She had. She'd spent so much time ensuring they were comfortable and fed and clothed. And here they were now, her three men. All taller than her. Stronger, if physicality were the judge. More than capable. She couldn't remember the last time they'd done something for her. Not one of them had texted to see why she was late, to ensure she hadn't been hurt or harmed or died in a car wreck. Usually, they all spoke at once. Three mouths morphing into one giant want she didn't have the energy or inclination to fill anymore.

Not one of them asked if she was okay.

She gripped her purse strap, readjusted it on her shoulder, commanded her voice to sound normal. No cracking. No crying. Upstairs. She had to get upstairs. Now.

"I'm not feeling well. I'll sleep in the guest room tonight." She paused, remembering those long weeks locked in her bedroom as a teen after Jane had confessed. "Probably a few days." She rushed into the kitchen, scrambled through the cabinets, grabbed the thing she was looking for, and shoved it into her purse. Back in the living room, they continued to wait. Silent, at last, when she least desired it. "Please keep it down. I have a terrible headache and don't wish to be disturbed."

Upstairs, she gathered some clothing from her and Rusty's bedroom, walked along the hallway to the guest bedroom, and locked the door behind her. She ran the water as hot as it would go in the guest bath.

She sank into the water, head and all, and let her skin cook. She'd thought about drowning often in the months after she'd bailed out of the boat with Warren in it and given it one last push toward the dam.

She had meant to bail earlier but got scared. She didn't want to go through with it. She'd gone in the boat alone, without Jane, because she didn't want her to have to fix one more problem. The problem Georgia Lee had created because she couldn't keep her mouth shut, her temper in check. She stared at the dam as it inched closer.

From the bow of the boat, where Warren's body rested, she thought she saw him move.

Terror shot through her, and she lunged over the side without taking a full breath. She fought against the current with every kick and stroke. Her arms started to give out, the current began to take her under. She held her breath until she couldn't anymore. This was it. The cold water would rush into her lungs. She'd be gone.

But somehow she found herself on shore. How, she couldn't say. The same way she couldn't recall how there had come to be a rock in her hand and then at her feet, next to blood on her shoes. Warren dead. Because of her. Even though he was terrible and had tried to hurt her, her spirit was crushed with the idea that in the span of five, ten minutes, she'd caused a heart that had been beating—even one as dark as his—to stop.

And so she'd told herself to stop. Stop thinking of the water. The rock and the blood. Because what use was it to consider something that she'd survived, something that was accepted as fact? Warren had disappeared. Jane had left town. No one had come to ask any more questions. End of story.

She'd stopped thinking. Stopped remembering. Stopped everything.

You shall not murder. Exodus 20:13. The easiest commandment to obey!

She gasped out of the bathwater, wiped her eyes, and blew her nose into a stream of toilet paper, which stuck to her wet hands. She grabbed the hand towel and screamed into it.

After a while, she bit down on the cork in the wine bottle she'd brought up with her, loosened it with her teeth, and spit it out. It landed in the bathwater and bobbed up and down, floating among the bits of soggy toilet paper she'd rinsed off her hands.

If only the recent flood hadn't drowned the town—or hadn't insisted on being so historic. The worst in recent memory. She might have gone the rest of her life without having to answer any questions. Without knowing or facing what she'd done. She gulped straight from the wine bottle, both hands clutching the glass, and almost threw it across the room to shatter against the wall.

She'd agonized over so many things over so many years. Little mortifying things in the moment that meant nothing in the grand scope of life. Undercooking the turkey and overcooking the sides the first and only time she hosted Rusty's parents for Thanksgiving. Clogging the toilet at Christlyn's house and lying that it was like that already. Going all morning one day in fifth grade with her dress pulled up into her tights. But murdering another human being and letting her girlfriend take the blame? Apparently, that was back burner material. For years, she'd simply forgotten. Until Warren's body rose from its watery grave.

She wished her memory could be wiped again. Or that she could be like a cold, heartless TV vixen and not care. She wished Jane were dead. Then she could blame everything on her and not be crushed by the agonizing weight and guilt of what her mind had decided not to remember. If only she could wish that into existence. Maybe that was how she had forgotten everything. Maybe she could wish for all that knowledge and history to leave her brain and it would.

In bed, the covers pulled up to her chin, she closed her eyes and wished for the world to go back to what it had been like before the flood. Before Warren's and Jane's returns.

Before she remembered that she was a killer.

Fifteen

JANE

A chain-link fence surrounded Family Fun's miniature golf course. Jane had once asked why Angie's parents hadn't renamed the arcade *Pham*ly Fun when they took over ownership. Angie had given her a look that told her to not ask stupid questions.

Located on the other side of the trailer park, the arcade and miniature golf had been an oasis to Maud Bottoms youth, especially after their mall had flooded beyond repair. Family Fun, with its sun-faded zoo animals that lined the course and its fake waterfall, sat at the entrance of Levi Perry Park, *park* being a generous term. It didn't even have a playground. Just flat patches of severely mowed grass, hardly any trees, and only three picnic benches. But they did have a statue for the park's dead Confederate namesake. For their after-school and weekend shifts, Jane and Angie took a shortcut over Indian Mound, where kids played hide-and-seek and pretended ghosts were after them, and then trudged through the vast, barren acres of the park to get to work. At first, Jason would hang out in the arcade during their shift. Angie let him play free games and gave him free drinks. But then he stopped for some reason. Jane didn't fight him on it or ask him why. He'd become good at making himself scarce. And he was getting older. Maybe he'd made friends of his own. She was glad to have some alone time, which was in short supply given that they shared a room.

These days, the mound was protected by a barbed-wire fence due to conservation efforts and given the more appropriate name Caddo Mound. Without the shortcut, it took thirty minutes longer for Jane to arrive by foot from Diane's trailer.

Inside Family Fun, the frenetic dings and robotic voices of arcade games clashed with the classic rock that blasted through the overhead speakers. Donkey Kong, Ms. PAC-MAN, Space Invaders—the same old games she'd fixed when kids came crying to her about eaten tokens. The carpet had been replaced. Used to be light red. Now it was straight up dark red to hide the stains. And a new addition had been placed smack in the middle of the room: a bar. The girl behind the counter barely looked old enough to serve alcohol.

"Can I help you?" she asked with a look that said she'd rather do anything but.

"Yeah. I'm looking for Angie Pham. Is she still around?"

Without losing a beat, the girl turned away and yelled, "Mom!"

Jane hadn't expected a fruitful visit, not this easily or quickly. Not after searching for Angie online and finding nothing. Within minutes of entering Family Fun, Angie—allegedly—stood in front of her. The girl at the counter had called her Mom. But she looked nothing like Angie. Weird. But then no one recognized Jane either.

"Hey, how are you?" She couldn't think of anything else to say.

"I'm fine," the woman said, confused. "Who are you?"

"Jane." She paused. "Angie?"

"No. I'm Kim." The woman said it with a tight smile, clearly bothered by the interruption. Jane could tell where the girl inherited her disposition. "Angie's my sister. We look nothing alike."

"Oh Jesus. Sorry. I just assumed when she called you Mom that you were . . ." No point in continuing her embarrassment or apologies. The girl who had called out for her mom snickered and walked off with a dishrag and an empty glass.

Jane and Angie used to watch Kim pull on black-and-pink striped tights, adjust her neon accessories from Claire's, and yank her bangs sky high to set them with a full can's worth of aerosol hairspray after her shift in preparation for a night out in Maud Proper with her friends. The mall, movies, cruising, the works. Kim's life was a Saturday night special at the drive-in to them. To Jane, she'd also been the desirable older woman, though she was only three years older.

"It's Jane. I used to work here. I was friends with Angie."

"Oh, right. Sorry. All her friends look the same." Kim smiled curtly, but Jane could tell she had no idea who she was and only smiled to extract the thing Jane wanted so she could go back to what she'd been doing. She tried not to be disappointed that Kim didn't remember her even though she and Angie had been nearly inseparable before Georgia Lee came along.

"Is she around?"

"No. But she usually drops by after her spin class."

Angie had hated PE, absolutely abhorred it. They'd both gotten changed in the showers to avoid undressing in public—especially after they got shipped to Maud Proper their senior year and were surrounded by all those awful mean girls.

"Do you happen to know when that might be?"

Kim laughed in an exasperated way that sank Jane's self-esteem. "I don't keep up with her schedule." She smiled again. "I'm sorry. I'm really busy right now. You're welcome to buy a drink and wait." *Buy a drink.*

Jane bought a cheap beer and a pretzel with cheese and navigated outside to a bench in the cordoned-off miniature golf area. A kid screamed about another kid cheating while she contemplated her conversations with Jason and then Georgia Lee and whether Benjamin was planning to arrest her anytime soon. Seemed to her he'd want to get it over with sooner rather than later, but that might just be the influence of crime shows.

She didn't know what evidence they had, if suspicion and a confession and a dead body were enough, though it seemed like enough. Could they tell that a man had been murdered on the riverbank instead of getting busted up going through a dam? Could they still find fingerprints after all these years? Could they convince a jury without a reasonable doubt that they had been a bunch of scared, dumbass kids who overreacted and didn't want to get caught?

She ripped off a curve of her pretzel. In happier days, she'd held out the other half to Angie. They'd dip their pretzel pieces into the melted cheese, hold them aloft, and tap them to toast. She wished Angie sat next to her now. She could use a friend.

But she'd lost that after what happened. Angie avoided her in the hallways at school. She didn't answer the door. She wouldn't come to the phone. When Jane stood in front of her, trying to force her to talk, she stared past her as if Jane were a ghost. Angie already hated Georgia Lee, and then Georgia Lee had kicked the hornet's nest.

The warm dough and cheese melted onto Jane's tongue, and the pretzel salt cracked between her teeth. Now, despite all that had gone wrong in the last few days, she found herself fully in Maud's embrace, remembering good times that had come before the bad. The long walks with Angie to work. Long rides on the school bus. Saturday nights watching horror movies. Flipping through records at the mall.

She mopped the sides of the paper cheese container with her finger. Wallowing in the past felt productive in a therapeutic way. She ordered a second pretzel and proceeded to sweat through her shirt and wait.

The money thing. A hard habit to break, especially when it came to food. Of all the upper-middle-class luxuries a life with her last ex had brought, the guilt-free acquisition of good and plentiful food was the thing she missed most. Now that she couldn't afford such frivolities, she couldn't stop herself from eating. Things were bad enough and likely to get worse. Might as well enjoy herself now. She stopped short of wondering whether food in prison would be better or worse than the food in juvie.

Three hot hours and a dead phone later, Jane gathered her trash and returned to the air-conditioned and clang-filled arcade. Her flesh prickled at the change in temperature. After a quick trip to the restroom, she exited to find a woman whose identity she could guarantee. The snickering young server greeted her with more warmth than she had the handful of other midafternoon customers around the bar. The server nodded in Jane's direction. Angie still wore the silver hoop earrings that nearly brushed her shoulders. The blue chunk of side bang that had covered her inch-thick black eyeliner was gone. This older version wore jeans and a black T-shirt.

Angie's smile morphed into a frown.

During Jane's walk and while sitting on the bench, she had recited various versions of what she would say and contemplated what token she might offer to ease the telling. The week she had waited for the coroner to release the remains, she'd fought boredom and taken the bus to the mall in Maud Proper where she and Angie had spent their days off. She'd wandered the corridors and seen the Fudge Factory. She'd carried the white paper sack with her to Family Fun that day. As if week-old fudge, melted from her walk and looking like dog shit, could smooth the way for a discussion about a dead body.

She took a deep breath and waved.

Angie approached her, planted a smile on her face. "You shouldn't be here." Her whisper came out like a knife.

"I know, but—"

"What if someone recognizes you?" Angie asked through gritted teeth. All the more ominous when she smiled. "They might think I'm your gal pal, or whatever."

"I'll tell them you didn't have anything to do with it." Angie had suggested the abandoned boat instead of just tossing his body in the bushes. They could've never come up with that without her. But Jane suspected Angie would not take the recollection as a compliment.

Angie seemed to weigh a decision. Jane worried she might bolt. Instead, she directed Jane to follow her outside to the miniature golf area Jane had just departed. The humidity hit harder after the reprieve. They sat on the bench next to the pale brick wall, facing the course. The artificial turf and splashes from the fake waterfall made everything look and feel slightly less oppressive in the blinding sun. The trash can positioned next to the door wafted its odors to her nose, a mix of caramel and rot. Sweat dripped down Jane's back once again as she waited for Angie to speak.

Finally, she did. "Why'd you come here? Did you assume I'd take over the arcade for my parents? That I wouldn't do more with my life? No offense to my sister. She only took it on so my parents wouldn't be upset. As soon as they die, we plan to sell it."

"If you wanted to hide from me, maybe don't show up at the family business."

Angie half snarled and faced the course, as if she couldn't be bothered with full-on rage. "Shouldn't you be in jail?"

"Yes." Jane shrugged when Angie wrinkled her brow. "I brought you these . . . this." She held out the white paper bag full of melted fudge. The bottom looked greasy and brown. What could she do? She'd already offered them.

Angie glanced inside the bag and looked away. "I can't eat that anymore. It'll make me fat." She pulled her shirt back and forth a few times to cool off. "I'm not getting involved. You can't bribe me with sugar."

It worked for others. "I certainly hope not. I was just trying to be nice."

"Why are you here? What exactly do you want?"

Silence. But that sounded like a mafia thing to say. "I don't want anything. I wanted to let you know that nothing's changed. I told the police I was the only one involved. I just want to make sure you won't say anything if anyone asks."

"Why would I say anything? You think I'm Lovelace?"

"Who?"

"You know, the 'little bird.'" She used air quotes. "The person who's yapping to those boneheads at Let's Talk About Maud." Angie's words came through pursed lips, tone low and angry even though the course was empty. "It's not me. I told them that too."

"You talked to the police?"

"Yeah, they're talking to everyone who knew you." She said it like it was no big deal, like Jane shouldn't be surprised. She shouldn't be. Of course they'd talk to people. "I know how to keep my mouth shut. I've done it all these years. Unlike you."

As soon as Jane had confessed, she'd known she wouldn't be able to look them in the eye knowing that she'd done the exact thing she'd told them not to do. "Okay, I'm just checking."

"You don't need to check on me. Why would I talk? I have kids. A husband. A good life."

Jane bristled at the insinuation that unlike Angie she had no life to lose, even though she didn't. But if she did, it was her own fault if she lost it. "I do too."

Angie smirked. "You have a husband?"

Out of habit, Jane popped her on the thigh. Angie responded by smacking her in return. Hers always stung more. She didn't hold back like Jane did. Both tried and failed to contain their smiles.

"Asshole," Jane said.

Angie let a smile slip but then shook her head. "They're just rehashing old rumors."

"Well, they're not wrong."

"Even so. Who's to say it's not Jason doing the talking? Or Georgia Lee? You're the one who should've kept her mouth shut." Angie leaned back against the building and stretched. "And your legs."

"Jesus, Ang."

"Look, I told you Georgia Lee was no good. You can't trust her. How many times did I tell you that?"

"Yeah, but why?"

"Because she's a white girl from Maud Proper. What more do you need? They're monsters. They used to terrorize me in gym class. Don't you remember?"

"Dodgeball?" Georgia Lee wasn't in their gym class. She was always on some special sports team that kept her away from the plebes who had to do step aerobics and dodgeball.

"Among other demeaning activities, yes."

"I thought we got hit on purpose to get it over with."

"No, dummy," Angie said. "I mean, maybe you did. But I certainly didn't. They grabbed those tiny rubber balls and whacked me on purpose."

"Shit. I'm sorry. I didn't know. Why didn't you tell me?"

"Because I thought you knew. I thought you were being supportive," she laughed. "At any rate, beyond that, you can't trust her. She's a politician."

If there was one thing Maud could rally around, regardless of which part of the city one occupied, it was the universal hatred of anyone in an elected position. They'd even booed the high school class president for suggesting a blood drive. Probably because the Maud Proper kids did Molly; Maud Bottoms, weed. One could lead to grounding; one could lead to lockup.

"I think it's more like an honorary position," Jane said. "It's not like she's dealing with real problems."

"Well, she's friends with cops"—she pointed at Jane—"another reason not to trust her. They always endorse her. But not this year."

"What's that have to do with anything?"

"If they're not willing to support her this year, that means they might have something on her."

"Like what?"

"Oh, I don't know. Accessory to murder?"

Jane didn't think Georgia Lee would talk. Well, she might. But so would Angie if things escalated.

"What makes you think she wouldn't turn on all of us?" Angie asked. "Sell out your brother? We don't even know what happened. Not really. Only Georgia Lee and Jason do. For all we know, she could've dealt the final blow and tricked your brother into saying he did it."

"What?" Jason had been quieter than most, but he wasn't some dumb kid who could be swayed. "That's ridiculous . . . we know what happened. You're being paranoid."

"Am I?" Angie tipped her head, flashing back to all the times she had been right about something Jane had insisted was not true or could not happen, not even in a million years. Like every horror movie they'd ever rented from Maud-ern Movies and More. Angie predicted the plot of *When a Stranger Calls* after the first ten minutes. She knew the old woman in lot 14 had probably died inside because the feral cats had stopped coming around. "Have you been to see her? Are you sleeping with her?"

Jane paused, tripping on the idea of what Angie suggested.

Angie grumbled. "We're all going to jail."

"Nobody's going to jail. Nobody but me," Jane said. "And I haven't slept with her. She's married."

"Like that matters," Angie said.

"She wouldn't."

"Sell out your brother? Or sleep with you?" A smile lit Angie's face. It didn't last long. "You don't know her anymore. You can't predict what she'll do. And I predict she'll turn on us in a heartbeat. Her name is already out there and attached to yours, thanks to Let's Talk About Maud. It's only a matter of time before she tells all in exchange for a deal. Probably also get a book deal in the process."

"I don't think she would." The look on Angie's face told Jane everything she needed to know about how she felt about that. "In the unlikely event you're right—worst-case scenario, it's three against one. We'll say she's lying. That I'm the only one to blame. Again. Shouldn't be that hard this time. There's a body."

Neither talked for a while. The sun hit its peak and slowly began to cast shade from the building, offering some respite. Across the way, the fake mountain with the waterfall gurgled, the only sound other than a few passing cars from the nearby highway and the dings from video games inside. The life-size giraffe stood in a shallow pool of water, staring at Maud Proper in the distance. Even the animals wanted out.

Back then, Jane wouldn't have believed that she and Angie wouldn't be friends forever, still complaining about work, still rolling their eyes at teenage boys who thought they were the first ones to come up with the brilliant idea of taking a picture of themselves fake humping the faded gorilla statue on the course, still talking every day.

"Believe what you want, I guess," Angie said. "It's our word against Georgia Lee's. Maud Proper against Maud Bottoms. You know who will win."

"Sounds like something we watched in the '80s." Jane hummed the *Rocky* theme.

Angie laughed. "I never liked those movies."

"You still watched them."

"Only because I felt sorry for you." Warren had refused to pay for cable. Angie breathed in deeply. "Look. Georgia Lee may live in the Bottoms now, but she's not from here. She only wins her election every year because no one runs against her. Once the foreclosures started, the developers swooped in. Her husband helped all his friends and their friends buy their McMansions. The ones who could stomach it. But they're closer to Maud Proper, so . . ." She scowled. "People up there may not like her or vote for her, but they'll believe her over any of us. Like sticks with like. And Jason and I—even though I have nothing to do with it and won't be involved—don't look like you or Georgia Lee. You do the math."

That was why Jane had confessed that day. She had seen the way they looked at Jason, the way they focused all their questions on him. Nonwhite teenage male. Murderer. Obviously.

"None of this would be happening if you hadn't turned yourself in." Angie looked at Jane in that precise Angie Pham way. "But you just had to save the golden boy."

"Why d'you call him that?"

"What? Golden boy?" She laughed. "You know why. Like, how many times would you let him get away with murder?"

Jane scrunched her nose and mouth in complaint. "I never let him—"

"Please. You saw him swipe that pocketknife and M&M'S from the gas station. And then he turned around and went back after that to use the restroom and stole that camo hat! Kid had some nerve. I'll give him that."

"When?"

"When? When was he not stealing shit right out from under your nose? And anytime I mentioned it, you said, *No. No. He must've used the money I gave him for lunch to buy those things. He would never.* Heh. You're such a sucker. He was always pulling one over on you." Urged on by memory, she continued, "Remember when Warren had his back to him, and Jason spit in his drink? Like, really spit."

"I don't remember any of that." Jane felt like Angie was recalling a friendship with someone else.

"Are you kidding me? We laughed for days." Angie smirked. "You gotta get your head checked. But then, you've always had a selective memory when it came to him."

Maybe Jane had been too protective of Jason. She'd acted out of love. That's what older siblings were supposed to do. All the boys did for their younger brothers. Why couldn't she? She glanced at the crumpled, not-quite-white-anymore bag of conciliatory fudge. How could she not remember any of this?

The heat suddenly felt more unbearable in the shade. Jane pushed away from the bench and stood.

"Where are you going?" Angie asked.

"Nowhere." She had wanted to run away. Get some cool air. Think on what Angie had said about Jason a bit more. "Why are you trying to shame me for protecting Jason? You would do the same for your little brothers and sisters."

"Um, no. If they commit a murder, they're on their own. I'm not going to get rid of the body or hide the evidence or confess that I did it. One hundred percent no."

"Then why'd you do it for me?" Jane asked.

"I didn't do it for you. I was stupid and confused and scared of getting caught with a dead body. Like, how do you even explain that to a cop? As a teenager?" She shook her head. "The whole thing was stupid. So stupid. I should go to the cops now. Spare us the pain of waiting."

"So go." Jane swiped the fudge off the bench and threw it into the trash.

Angie rolled her eyes. "Sit down. You're making a scene."

Jane swung her hands out at the empty course. "There's no one here!"

Angie reached out to pet Jane's arm, like she would a petulant child. To be fair, she felt like one. The heat made her cranky, along with trying to get arrested alone, which really shouldn't be that hard. But Maud had a way of making everything more stupid and complicated than it needed to be.

"Sit down," Angie said. "Please."

Jane plopped onto the bench. "By the way, I didn't hide evidence. That was your job." Which she and Jason had done stunningly well. The cops hadn't found shit.

Angie stopped talking when a customer appeared behind the chain-link fence on his way to his car. When he left the parking lot, she continued, calm as could be, as if there'd been no interruption. "I didn't hide any evidence."

"Um, yeah, you did," Jane said. "That's the whole reason why you left and didn't get in the boat."

"Um, no, I didn't. It was already done by the time I got there."

No way Jason had cleaned it all up. Even with the storm. There would've been something left behind. Some little bit of shirt or blood or skin. Recognition or something like it crossed Angie's face. She focused on the waterfall and bit down on her bottom lip.

"What are you not saying?" Jane asked.

Angie shook her head. "Nothing. It was a long time ago."

"Not so long ago and nothing for you to bring it up and then pretend it doesn't matter. Spill it."

Angie scrunched her nose and then blew a long stream of air out of it. "If I tell you, you have to promise not to say anything."

"Jesus, that sounds ominous." When Angie paused, Jane spoke. "I promise. What is it?"

"I saw your mom there," she said after a while. "She was helping Jason."

"What do you mean, helping?" That didn't make sense. If Diane had helped Jason clean up, did that mean she knew that Jason had killed Warren, not Jane? She'd never have lifted a finger for Jane. "Are you sure?"

"I'm sure," Angie said. "I'm sorry. I should've told you. But like everything else that night, it got messed up. And I got scared."

"What was she doing?"

Angie looked off into the distance as if to remember. "She had a shovel. She was shoveling the ground." She mimicked the action with her hands. "Or more like scraping off the top layer of blood."

"To do what?"

Angie shook her head. "I don't know. Maybe toss it in the water? Get rid of it."

"Did you talk to her?"

"I had to. She saw me."

"What'd she say?"

Angie paused again. "Said if I told anyone I saw her, even you, that she'd make sure I paid." She shook her head and stared at the ground. "I believed her. She scared me. Stupid."

"It's not stupid. We were kids. She was the adult."

If only Jane could go back and fix things. A time machine to help her reset everything. She would've graduated soon enough. She could've taken Jason with her. Her money from Family Fun wasn't much, but she would've figured it out.

She could never fix the knowledge that Diane had made a choice about which of her children to save. Diane knew Jane was innocent. She *wanted* to sacrifice her. Her own daughter. She had screamed for them to kill Jane as they led her away in handcuffs. To erase the child who had ruined Diane's life. Jane felt sick.

All that humidity coalesced with the rising heat under Jane's skin. Her tongue got heavy. The smell of the trash can beside her made her sit up straight, an attempt to keep the vomit at bay.

"You got pictures of your kids?" Jane asked, changing the subject before she spiraled.

Angie relaxed for the first time since she'd sat down. Still, she sneered jokingly and then pulled out her phone to swipe through her photos. She held the phone out to Jane.

Three kids, all under ten, Jane guessed. Cheesing on the couch in their pajamas with a giant bowl of popcorn. "Cute."

"Thanks."

"You in Maud Proper?"

"No. I only come here to check on things. We moved outside of town. Better jobs."

"So I've heard. And your husband?"

Angie swiped, held out the phone to reveal a photo of her in a bikini and a white guy in psychedelic board shorts on a pontoon boat in the middle of a lake. Aviators on both. Her torso twisted slightly, leg posed. Her hand on his trim waist, his arm around hers. Friends in the background midlaugh. Beer koozies in hand. Sunshine glittering off the water in the background. The American dream. "Handsome."

Angie smiled. "I know." She tucked her phone away in her purse. "I should go." She stood and headed to the door.

Jane stayed put on the bench. She needed a moment alone.

"It was good seeing you," Angie said.

Jane nodded and locked down any desire to ask Angie for more. She'd already done so much. "It was good to see you too." Before she forgot, she added, "And thanks for giving Jason my shifts after I left."

"Well, someone had to scrub the toilets, and it wasn't going to be me." She laughed and grabbed the door handle. But then the smile faded and she paused. "I'll stay quiet as long as I can, but there's only so much I can control. If things get intense, I need to protect myself. And my family. I'm sorry. I really am."

Jane nodded, waved her hand as if it were totally understandable. Because she'd been in Angie's shoes. When things got intense, she'd protected herself and her brother.

But why had Diane done the same?

Sixteen

GEORGIA LEE

Georgia Lee should've canceled the barbecue. She hadn't felt right for a week. Not since she'd seen Jane. Since the memory. She'd called in sick at work. She still slept in the guest room. How could she sit with a bunch of cops, knowing that she had killed the man whose death they were investigating?

Georgia Lee glanced out the kitchen window at Rusty and the other guys in the backyard while she washed dishes. Trading "war" stories. Big talk about so-and-so getting in their face and how they got right back. Cheap jokes about shooting guns being better than sex even though the boys were right there. Laughing along like they were grown men. And Rusty let them. If they'd had daughters instead of sons, Rusty would probably have them in chastity belts. Pose with them in uncomfortably similar-to-wedding photographs after they made virginity pledges.

Not five minutes after the guys from the station walked in the door, Rusty had pulled out his new toys. The manufacturer name followed by his pet name for each gun: The Terminator, Rambo, John McClane, and Sweetie (named for her, he'd said that morning with a genuine smile). As if that were any kind of gift. As if their recent conversation had never happened. The cookout had been intended for the station only, but Rusty had invited several of his about-town buddies. Probably for the best—that way it didn't look like Georgia Lee was trying to buy their support or endorsement, even though that's exactly what she was doing. Only a handful of the station had made it. All but Benjamin silver haired and wary of unfamiliar or heavy spices. Spouses and girlfriends welcome, but none of them had shown—a relief. Most of them were at least twenty years older than her and about as fun as watching someone crochet a single-color blanket. That's probably what they were doing right now while she entertained their should've-retired-by-now husbands.

What did any of them know about murder? Mayhem? They patrolled the streets of Maud, where the only excitement came courtesy of the occasional burglary or drunk and disorderly. They had no idea what it was like to get their hands dirty. To do something hard. Something that could come back to hurt them. They had no idea what women like her could do. What women like her had done. What women like her would do to keep men like them from learning what she knew.

She ripped open a bag of tortilla chips, poured them into a bowl, and noticed a text that had popped onto her phone screen. Susannah.

Where have you been?

I've been calling you.

Rusty said you're sick?

Why aren't you answering my texts?

It's been over a week.

Another text. Christlyn this time.

Do you have mono again?

Georgia Lee swiped her phone off the counter, fully intending to lash out. Ask Christlyn, a.k.a. Lovelace, how long she'd been spreading rumors about Georgia Lee anonymously to Let's Talk About Maud and if she'd sold her out to Benjamin for money or for free.

Instead, she tossed the phone back onto the counter, opened a fresh bottle of wine for herself, and threw the bottle opener back into the drawer. She tried to slam it shut for effect but couldn't because Rusty had insisted on quiet cabinets that "whispered" when they closed.

She scooped an avocado out of its shell and plopped it into a bowl. She couldn't stop thinking about Jane, searching for her online, even though there was never anything new. Her eyes stung, and tears wept down her cheeks. From the onion, nothing more. Her father's voice rang in her ears, loud and clear: *Georgia Lee. There's no need to cry about it.* He was long gone now, felled by his own fool refusal to quit smoking cigarettes.

"I'm not crying!" she had screamed back at him and pointed at the onions her mom had cut for supper.

Georgia Lee had been home and bored and irritated about it. Jane had not called her as much in the days after Warren's "disappearance." It didn't help to ask why. Some things weren't allowed in Jane's world: speaking to anyone about what they did when they were alone, asking anyone else for help, and asking Jane if she was okay, which Georgia Lee did one day after that night despite knowing better. A brief and heated exchange in the school hallway followed. Amid the angry postfight haze, she heard the whispers of classmates after Jane passed them. Words her dad had said before he'd told her to stop crying. He said them about Jane, but he also meant them about her.

"Georgia Lee, I'm not going to tell you again. You are not to see that girl, or any other girl, again. That's final." He also whispered the words, as if Georgia Lee's mom might slip back into the kitchen after her pee break and die of shock.

They'd been so careful.

"I'm not like that! We're just friends!" Desperation and shame crawled from her belly and clawed at her throat.

"Even so. I don't want her in this house. And I don't think it's a good idea that you hang around her at school." He rubbed his eyes, exasperated. "Please don't mention this to your mother. I don't have the energy for that conversation."

As soon as her dad left the room, Georgia Lee swiped an arm across the counter and watched the onions fall to the floor. It felt good to do something. What she really wanted was something to throw or smash. Eventually, she retrieved all the onions and placed them back on the cutting board before her mother returned from the bathroom.

Her mother didn't die of shock, even after Jane was arrested and she learned what Georgia Lee's dad had correctly assumed about her and Jane. She had gone full Mother Superior, but without the temper. Locking Georgia Lee in her room and lying to everyone that it was mono was done out of "love" and "protection," she'd cried (and cried). Alas, she'd died a few years after Georgia Lee's dad from a heart attack she'd complained was heartburn.

Georgia Lee couldn't stop the panic that rose and settled in her chest, hovering near her throat, coating her thoughts and coming words with the desire to make things right after doing so much wrong. That's what she'd always been told. In church, in school, at home. Be a good Christian. Do the right thing. And she had done the right thing, hadn't she? She'd protected herself. But then her memory came loose, and she wasn't sure what to believe.

"Bathroom?" Georgia Lee startled at the interruption. One of Rusty's buddies. Bart? Barry? Something like that. "Upstairs. Rusty still hasn't fixed the one down here."

She needed a task to refocus her. A to-do list.

1. Find out what John and Benjamin know.
2. Keep them from learning what you know.
3. Stay away from Jane.

Simple.

On the way outside, she banged her foot on the patio door to get Rusty's attention. He couldn't hear her over the sound of his own voice. Benjamin noticed and ran over to open the door for her.

"Thank you, Detective. You're too kind."

She placed the chips and guacamole on the table and settled into a chair next to Benjamin when he sat down. He'd been hired after the lieutenant retired. Not without a fight. Others on the council had balked at hiring a replacement. They claimed money as the cause; Georgia Lee suspected it was race. Though Maud was rich in youth and diversity compared to most towns in Arkansas due to its proximity to Fort Chaffee, the council and police force were not. But Benjamin had been the best applicant, what with his actual on-the-job experience. She could not have accepted the other options, most of whom were related to council members or other cops and had no experience beyond fast-food and under-the-table construction jobs. She encouraged the other council members to change their minds and gave them an ultimatum: Benjamin or they'd lose their hiring opportunity. A majority vote was required. Georgia Lee had hoped John and the others would remember the favor come election time. She'd seen no evidence they had.

"How are things going for you, Benjamin?"

Georgia Lee nodded as he recounted the past few months living in Maud. House hunting, gym going, paperwork. Boring story, but he was handsome. Single. The sleeves of his plain black T-shirt fit nicely around his biceps. Made the listening a bit more bearable. She wondered if she knew anyone he might grow fond of. Maybe a girl from church?

John joined them. He'd already enjoyed several of the burgers and snickerdoodles she offered him. Everyone had taken bets as to when the next heart attack would occur. Georgia Lee's mother had died of hers relatively young despite all that focus on diet and exercise, yet here he sat, indulging and ignoring his health. Perhaps today would be his lucky third. After all, he had gone behind her back to befriend Bollinger. She still couldn't believe John had told him about the discovery of Warren's body before her.

"French onion dip?" She offered the prepackaged, do-nothing dip to him instead of the homemade guacamole. "How's the heart?"

John laughed, mentioned the food plan Pat had him on. Pat wanted him to retire, spend more time at home. If only Pat knew what it was like to have her husband home all day. A week into retirement, she would probably change her mind. But perhaps Pat enjoyed his company.

Across the yard, Rusty had his hands out, talking animatedly about something. The other men laughed, and his face brightened in response. She couldn't help but smile. She'd been too hard on him. Perhaps it was hormones after all. The change? So early? She would try to be nicer.

She returned her attention to John. "And the case of our washed-up man?" Despite her need for action, she'd been loath to ask for fear they'd suspect she knew something only a guilty party would know. But the news of Warren's bones and the growing rumors of a new twist to the crime in Let's Talk About Maud had electrified the town and kept the story alive, which she didn't appreciate one bit. "Any news?"

"Now, Georgia Lee," John said. "You know I can't comment on an ongoing investigation—"

Investigation. So it was active. "And I can't comment on your funding for next year. Should you ask. Again."

"Fair enough." John crunched a potato chip loaded with dip.

Georgia Lee leaned back in her chair. Somehow she had known, deep down, this day would come, even when she didn't remember that she had played the lead role in Warren's death. The shock of it coming to fruition still unsettled her.

"Why on earth is this an open case?" she asked. "You've got the confession; you've got the body. Surely you've got enough to convict." The words came out of her mouth so easily it made her stomach turn. But she couldn't let him believe she cared for any specific reason.

"There's always more to the story than what gets released," Benjamin said.

"Oh, please don't tell me you've been suckered by those idiots at Let's Talk About Maud too?" she asked. John chuckled; Benjamin did not. "Here's what I think," she said. She'd thought a lot about this moment since she'd gone to pizza with Jane, lying in bed all day thinking about her soul and her busted brain and her future. She had come prepared. "I think what Jane Mooney said is true." She punctuated her sentences with a pointed finger. "I believe she hit that man over the head like she said and she truly believed she had killed him, but what really happened is that he got knocked out due to drinking more than anything and then stumbled into the river and drowned." Benjamin didn't disguise his skepticism. "Wouldn't be the first time." She turned to John. "How many bodies have they found up and down the county in this decade alone?"

"I'm sorry, what?" Benjamin asked. Now he looked alive. Nice little spark in his eyes.

"The river takes a lot of our men," she said. "The currents are swift, and the men a little too certain of their skill. That or they fall down drunk, like Warren."

"All men?"

"Hashtag all men. As far as I know."

Benjamin shook his head at her joke. "How many men?"

"A normal amount," John added. "Don't get too excited."

Benjamin considered the comment with what Georgia Lee recognized as pure astonishment. "And what do you consider norm—"

"She's exaggerating." John gave her a look.

"I'm not! There have been several accidents near the lock and dam. Look it up."

"Nobody from around here," John explained, as if that made it okay. "Just folks upriver. Out-of-towners."

"Not true," she said. "Warren lived in Maud. And there was that one guy—"

Benjamin retrieved his phone to swipe and type.

"It's nothing to get worked up about. Georgia Lee's just yanking your chain." John leaned in and shook his head at Georgia Lee like he would a rotten but playful puppy. He hated when she brought up anything that alluded to the job responsibilities he and the station preferred to shirk, like investigation or interrogation—not that there was much to do, mind you. About the only thing they were willing to do without complaint was collect overtime for off-duty detail assignments. She'd never seen a lazier bunch. They reminded her of the guys who had come over for her dad's poker nights. All bluster and no bite. At least their inaction allowed Maud to keep the crime stats down. And, fingers crossed, away from her involvement in a murder.

Benjamin, though, exhibited a different work ethic from his peers. Competition had always been her strength and weakness. And now she'd have to walk it back to ensure Benjamin didn't get too excitable about potential additional crimes.

"Regardless," she said. "Everyone's talking about this like it's some big mystery and conspiracy, especially Let's Talk About Maud," she said. "I've no doubt the final conclusion will be that he simply suffered a tragic yet preventable accident by getting drunk and running his mouth." Not untrue.

Benjamin narrowed his eyes at her. "Weren't you friends with Jane Mooney?"

The chip Georgia Lee had grabbed nearly shook out of her hands. She quickly popped it into her mouth, wiped her salty fingers on a napkin, and shoved her hands between her crossed legs in case they decided to shake and give her away any more than her mouth already had.

"That's not news." She crunched as she talked, held a hand to her mouth. "Let's Talk About Maud already mentioned it. There was only one functional high school back then," she said. "It's not hard to know someone."

"I heard you spent some time at her house, over at that trailer park."

Who had told him? Christlyn? Susannah? Perhaps Jane had turned on her after all. Or Jason? Angie? Perhaps they'd all cut a deal to protect themselves.

"Everyone went to the trailer park. That's where they held all the parties." She grabbed her wineglass. Something to hold, to do, while her mind spun. Examined it like it was a misplaced narcotic someone had left lying around. "But yes. We were friendly for a time." No point in hiding the fact, especially after she'd been to the funeral and the pizza parlor. "As class president, I made it my job to be kind to new kids. I felt sorry for her and her brother. There were rumors of trouble at home. Neglect. Serious neglect," she added. "Then she got arrested, and that's the last I saw of her." She tried to keep her voice even, her tone mildly disinterested. But she got shaky, and her throat constricted in that prevomit way. "Even Let's Talk About Maud doesn't believe I could be the gal pal." No fun, they'd said. The straightest person ever, Christlyn had said. She wanted to smash the glass into tiny pieces and scatter them inside Benjamin's shoes.

Benjamin held up his hands, all smiles. "I'm only doing my job, trying to figure out who might've known something and who might've been around the family at that time."

"Now, Georgia Lee," John said. "Don't give Benjamin here too hard a time."

"A hard time? I'm simply answering his questions." They were so sensitive. She swept the air with a hand. "Oh, have another beer and loosen up. The both of you."

"Shit, you think I don't want to?" John said. Benjamin returned his attention to his phone. "People got it in their heads that something criminal happened, and they're demanding answers. We never fielded as many calls and messages in all my time in Maud. I blame all them damn shows and them radio things, what do you call them?"

"Podcasts?" Georgia Lee offered. She'd never listened to one herself. Who had time? Christlyn and Susannah, probably.

"Yeah, them podcasts. They got people thinking everything's a crime."

Georgia Lee watched Benjamin scroll away. "Better to blame Let's Talk About Maud."

"Hell, I blame them all," John said. "Unfortunately, I can't ignore people when it comes to my job."

"Can't you, though?" Georgia Lee asked. John laughed along with her.

Benjamin tucked his phone into his back pocket. "Call me old fashioned, but I'd say it's important to follow up on what appears to be a more complicated picture of what actually happened to Warren Ingram and also to a rash of men who've died over the years with no explanation," he said, not a trace of humor in his tone. "Set the town at ease."

"You confirm the exact number?" She gestured toward his pocket. Thrown off guard, he paused. "The drownings."

"A few missing and presumed dead. But that was earlier, late '80s and early '90s," he said. "After that, most were found along the shore, drowned. Several. A lot. I mean, we're talking decades of data, so . . ."

"There you go," she said and snapped her fingers. "Drowned and found, not murdered. End of story."

"Well, not so much an end for the families of the men who are still missing."

"End of story for Warren, I mean. As for the others, you're presuming they were murdered. Where are you from?"

He looked surprised by the question. "Outside Atlanta."

She nodded. "Went that way once. Nice people. Good food." She brushed away the freshly mowed grass that had drifted onto her pants. "Anyway, Maud loves to talk about the missing men. They want to be like Texarkana. Have their own Moonlight Murders. Or a ghost, like the Gurdon Light. That's a thing, you know. In Arkansas. We like our stories. You'll learn. But everybody born here knows that, excepting Texarkana, the rest of it is all just a bunch of tall tales. Those men that haven't turned up probably drowned too. Probably got carried off down to the Mississippi. Good luck finding them." Before he could interrupt, she said, "But by all means, knock yourself out. Open up every cold case you can find." She'd not even considered how useful that would be. If she could get him focused on something more interesting, he might let this case lie. "As for more recent events, is there any reason to even suspect there's more to learn? You have the confession." She aimed for the role of City Councilor Setting the New Guy Straight as opposed to Guilty Party Seeking Insight.

Benjamin enacted his best Hollywood police stance for her: leaning in, eyes direct, elbows on knees. He looked at her with an intensity that made her mouth go dry. "Is there a specific reason you're interested in this case?"

Georgia Lee retracted. She'd shown her hand. Asked too much. "Do I need to have a lawyer present? Is this an interrogation?" Both John and Benjamin examined her like she was serious. "My God, look at you two. I'm only kidding." She laughed to disguise the way her chest seemed to rise and fall as she neared hyperventilation. She glanced across the yard at Rusty to calm herself. The gun show continued. This time, the cops showed Rusty and his buddies their guns. She wished she had the luxury of relaxation. "I'm heartened to know I can count on you to take this seriously and that our taxpayer dollars won't go to waste," she said, trying to change the subject away from her. "Maybe Maud can get worked up about something besides me."

John chuckled. "You never cease to amuse me, Georgia Lee."

"At any rate, I don't plan on stopping until I figure out what happened," Benjamin said.

"Well, all right." He was about as exhausting as Bollinger, but better looking. "Just make sure you stay within budget, honey."

John laughed and slugged Benjamin on the arm. "Like the lady said. Loosen up, Benny boy."

Benjamin tightened his posture. He didn't appear to be the type of individual for whom loose was a personality trait or *boy* was a joke, yet he focused his attention on her instead of John. "I imagine you're interested because of the election."

He wanted to get ahead. Make an impression. Nothing more than that. No need to worry. At least she hoped. "It's certainly not ideal to have a murder investigation during an election year. People make strange associations. But as long as it's taken care of in a timely fashion, neither you nor I will suffer too much. And I'd be lying if I said I wouldn't mind the distraction."

They took too long to respond, and they certainly didn't laugh.

"Of course I'm thinking about the election," she said. "I'd be a fool not to. Bollinger is already using this nonsense to his advantage, claiming that I'm somehow responsible for something that happened over two decades ago." She sipped her wine as if untroubled.

John reached for another beer from the ice chest near where he sat. "Ah, I wouldn't worry about it ruining your election. Folks round here are always mad about something. But they always do right."

"Do they?" Georgia Lee asked. She hoped her nerves didn't reveal her irritation but rather sounded like an insecurity. But there was that look on Benjamin's face. "What is it?"

Benjamin raised his eyebrows. "Maybe people just want a change."

The signatures on his job offer and lease were barely dry. Hardly enough time to have an opinion on the state of their city or its citizens. Georgia Lee couldn't wait for his shine to wear off. And to think she'd gone to bat for him. "Meaning, a change from me?" She looked to both of them for confirmation.

John squirmed in his seat. She was glad to see it. But Benjamin might as well have scanned her and decided she was someone who required extra screening.

"Change is an illusion," she said. "And messy. It doesn't happen without hard work. Money can't buy everything, despite what Bollinger would have everyone believe."

"Yeah," John said, "but maybe it can buy some influence. Sure would help to recoup what we lost with that factory. And our budget's been the same for years."

The nerve of John to bring up K-Parts. "Why would you need a budget increase? Maud is one of the safest cities in the state."

"What about all those missing men?" Benjamin asked.

"I mean violent crimes. We've had none of those." Except Warren, but that'd been justified, she assured herself. And long ago. It didn't count. It was practically a public service. Jane had mentioned how she suspected Warren of killing their pet parakeets. She'd probably taken out a serial killer. "There's been no indication those are even crimes, as you just confirmed." She fanned herself with a napkin and expelled all the worry she tried to disguise as exasperation. "I know you and Bollinger are golf buddies. But we all have to think about what's right for the city—"

"Come on now, Georgia Lee," John interrupted her. She hated to be interrupted. "Let's not ruin the day with politics."

Why on earth did he think she had invited him and the station over for a barbecue? Because she enjoyed their company? Because she had nothing better to do?

She took a long sip of her wine. She'd not planned to have this conversation. That was the worst thing about politics: keeping everything she wanted to say inside. Like telling John he'd been invited to her house precisely for politics. That he kept his job despite his obvious deficiencies because of politics. That Benjamin had been hired thanks to her politicking. Neither of them would be sitting in her backyard drinking beer and eating too much food were it not for politics. To them, politics only happened during election years. Change, not hard work over time but a businessman who only saw numbers—not realizing that to him, they were both expendable. She couldn't say any of those things. Instead, she asked the one thing she could.

"Do you plan to endorse Bollinger?"

The top half of John's body seemed to sink into the bottom half of him.

"You *do*." She let the words drip out of her mouth, full of accusation. She'd seen Bollinger the night before, and he'd been slaphappy when he walked into the store. Georgia Lee's poll numbers hadn't been great. Bollinger had taken a slight lead, but she still presumed she had a shot as the incumbent because no one would vote. They hardly ever did. In a city of over thirty thousand people, they usually got a 1 percent turnout. She was banking on that and had told him so. He'd told her turnout would be bigger this year. Now she'd confirmed why.

For years, she'd had John's back. More than that, they'd been friends. When she brought him treats, it had not been because she wanted something but because she genuinely enjoyed his company, their shared jokes, their laughter. All gone now. And for what pleasure or access or power, she couldn't fathom. He already had a pension, plenty of time off, season tickets for the Razorbacks, a new band saw. He definitely didn't need more money for the department. They were already overstaffed as far as she was concerned. The only reason she could land on that would explain why he'd endorsed Bollinger over her was that they could share the same locker room. Because how could he possibly pick a woman over another man?

She raised her glass. "To politics. Ruining parties since time immemorial."

They raised their glasses and laughed quietly, not knowing what else to do. At least their discomfort could bring her joy.

"Will you gentlemen excuse me? Time to refresh the party dip." She bit down on her anger, but her words tinkled out like a song.

"Actually, I should get going." Benjamin followed her into the kitchen. She grumbled and let the screen door he'd opened for her earlier accidentally close on him now.

Inside, she set the dip bowl on the kitchen island. Before she had a chance to turn to the refrigerator, he placed his hand on the island. He leaned in closer, didn't blink.

"I know you know Jane," he said. "And I'm going to find out what you're hiding."

As he made his way to the front door, dark scenarios consumed her. John and Benjamin would arrest Jane. Jason would swoop in and save Jane. Tell them that Georgia Lee was the one responsible for Warren's death. They'd lead her away in handcuffs, and she'd rot in jail for life. She would lose everything. She'd already lost her mind by forgetting that she'd bludgeoned a man to death. She'd been "washed in the blood of Jesus" and promptly gotten on with her life. Even if Jesus had forgiven her sin, how could she forgive herself? Especially with Jane's imminent arrest.

Each minute that passed, the weight of what she'd allowed Jane to believe in the moment and then forgotten suffocated her a little more.

Seventeen

JANE

Jane turned the information Angie had told her over in her mind. Kim kept coming outside to check the trash (read: Jane). She sat outside by the mini golf course until the outdoor lights kicked on, waiting for a reply from Jason she knew wouldn't come. Finally, out of rage and spite, she fired off one last text:

> HELLO again. SO GOOD to see you at the funeral . . . Before I forget. That was SO NICE of Diane to help you clean up! ;) But ALSO, what the fuck?!?!?

If Angie learned of her broken promise, she'd find some extravagant way to apologize that didn't involve week-old fudge.

The long walk back to the trailer from Family Fun did nothing for Jane's sobriety or mood. A truck Jane didn't recognize sat alongside Diane's car in the driveway. No reason for her to recognize it, though. She didn't know anything about her mom. Not then, not now. But she recognized the anxiety that bubbled up. An unknown vehicle meant an unknown man. No telling if he was the good kind or the bad kind. Sometimes, they hid their bad behind something good, not showing their true selves until later. She had always hoped the missing-finger man would come back, but no luck. Probably too normal to stick around long. Any man with any kind of sense would only need one solid hour with Diane to know that he should pack up and get out while he could.

Her nerves lit up when she touched the door handle. Every time, she expected the door to be locked. Wouldn't be the first time Diane changed it without telling anyone.

The handle twisted easily. She walked into a cover of "I Heard It through the Grapevine" and a cloud of smoke. Diane and the guy she'd gone home from the funeral with glanced at her from the spot in the living room where they danced—or whatever you'd call what they were doing, kind of dancing, kind of just holding each other up so they wouldn't fall. *Oh God,* she thought in horror, *are they fucking?*

As soon as a glassy-eyed Diane recognized Jane, her lips drooped into disappointment. She laid her head back onto the guy's chest. "It's just Jane," she slurred. "Back to fuck up something else."

If Jane had been holding a glass, she would have crushed it in her hands and scraped the shattered pieces down Diane's cheeks.

Gerry had a bit more decorum and lucidness to him. He nudged Diane away. She frowned and slipped her fingers through his belt loops. He tucked his button-down into his jeans, checked his zipper, and ran a hand across his hair.

"How do you do?" He smiled and held out a hand. "I'm Gerry. With a *G.* Work down at the dam."

"Jane. With a *J.*" She looked at his hand and lifted hers in greeting instead. "Murdered my stepdad."

He slowly removed his hand and placed it in his pocket. "I should probably be going."

"No," Diane whined. "Don't you let her scare you away. You said you was gonna take me out tonight." She tugged his belt loops again. "Take me out."

Jane cringed at the way Diane draped herself onto him, drunk and horny. But Gerry gently moved her away.

He adjusted his glasses so they weren't so low on his nose. He wasn't bad looking. Seemed to be nice. What the hell was he doing with Diane? Especially if what Georgia Lee said was true.

"Heard you found the body." Jane was intent on making Diane suffer. "That true?"

Diane loosened her grip on Gerry, launched daggers at Jane with her eyes, and wandered to her pack of cigarettes.

"I know how this may look," he said.

Jane raised her eyebrows. "No worse than my mom letting me stay with her after I confessed to killing her husband."

He wasn't sure what to say. He looked back and forth between her and Diane.

Jane walked to the cupboard where Diane kept her liquor and drank from the first bottle she could find. The liquid slipped and leaked down her chin. She wiped it with the neck of her shirt.

"Y'all headed to Crawdaddies?" she asked. The booze hit her hard, especially after day drinking and then sweating and then getting riled up during her long walk from Family Fun. "I always wondered what it was like, seeing as it's basically my mom's second home." Primary, more like it.

"You never been?" Gerry asked, trying to redirect the conversation away from the fact that he was dating the widow of the dead man he'd pulled from the river.

"Nope," she said.

"Ah, I bet you'd like it. Real nice bunch. Why don't you join us?"

Diane looked like she could put a knife through his throat.

"Well shit, Gerry. That's about the best idea I heard all day. I'd love to." Jane let her voice get high, so high it screeched. "Might be my last chance for a hurrah before they ship me to the big house." The room felt hot, her teeth throbbed. "That is if you don't mind, *Mom*." She emphasized the word, drawing it out nice, long, and sharp.

Diane glared at her, so quick that by the time Gerry looked to her for the A-OK, she'd already clutched her head, her cigarette so close to her scalp Jane prayed she'd catch fire and burn the whole place down.

"I got a headache," Diane said to Gerry. "Some other time."

Berated, Gerry backtracked. "Oh, I was . . . we could just—"

"Not tonight." Diane headed toward the hallway and her bedroom at the end. Before she disappeared behind the wall, she gave a stone-cold look to Jane.

Jane turned to Gerry. "Welp. Guess it's just the two of us. You driving?"

The inside of Crawdaddies looked like everything and nothing. For years, while Jane and Jason did homework, watched TV, and then slept (or tried to) in this home or that, Diane had made her home within these ripped-posters-of-random-people-Jane-had-never-even-heard-of walls. Lights flickered randomly. In the corner of the room, a group of middle-age men flipped their hair like girls did in the '80s to refeather it and then tuned their instruments. If any of her former coworkers in Boston had seen this, they would have called it authentic as fuck. Authentic meaning sticky, smelly, and full of patrons who looked as pickled as the eggs in the jar that a woman on a barstool dipped her bare hand into for at least a minute before finding the perfect specimen to pop into her mouth whole.

Vomit spiked Jane's throat. A hand touched her arm. She jumped. Gerry's eyes grew big, concerned.

"Sorry," she said. "You got any Rolaids? TUMS?"

"Uh," he patted his pockets. "I'm sure someone will have some. There's a table over there. Why don't you go sit, and I'll see what I can scrounge."

He pointed. Smiled. What was he doing with Diane? Had to be a serial killer. No other explanation.

He bought the first round, and they talked that special nontalk that all bar patrons knew and engaged in: *Oh, I love this song. How's your beer? Good, how's yours? Good. The burgers are good. The fries are good. Buffalo wings are better across town. Check out ole fancy pants over there cutting a rug.* Occasionally, Gerry would brighten and wave at someone familiar to him. He introduced her to a few folks on their way to or from the restroom. Never her tabloid nickname, always "This is my friend Jane."

That made her cry. The alcohol didn't help. Or the knowledge that Diane had learned what Jason had done and instead of being proud of Jane for protecting Jason, she'd pretended not to know. She'd called her names, screamed, told her she was going to rot in hell. Damn near pushed her toward the electric chair. Would probably ask for a front-row seat if she got the chance.

Why? That's what she didn't get. Even if Diane did hate her, did she hate her enough to want her to die?

At the sight of her tears, Gerry sucked in some air, patted her hand, pushed a fresh drink toward her, and asked if she wanted to talk about it. That only made her cry harder.

"Why are you being so nice?" She yelled the words through her tears. Everyone was drunk. The band was loud. And at least three other women were crying at their tables. The bar felt like a protective womb. No wonder Diane spent so much time here. "Are you gonna murder me, Gerry with a G?"

Gerry sat back, aghast, and then sort of laughed. "What?"

"Why are you with Diane?" Cry. "She's a horrible person. A worse mother. She hates me. Wants me to die." She choked back her drink and licked the insides to get the last drop. "You seem like a nice person."

Cry. "I just don't understand, Gerry. I really don't." Cry. "Could you please explain it to me in terms I can understand?"

Even with the shitty lighting, she could see him redden. Laughter replaced her tears. The room shifted colors, volume.

"Oh, bless your heart." She laughed, wiped her eyes, scooted her chair next to him, and slung an arm around him. "As good as the sex might be with Diane, it's not worth it. Trust me. There are women out there who are just as good. I would know. I've been with a lot of women." So many women. Anytime they wanted more, she said good-bye. How could she say yes to a future knowing that hers might be cut short by a conviction?

"Goodness," he said and checked his watch.

"All I'm saying is . . ." She couldn't complete her thought because she started to cry again. She couldn't control it. "My mom doesn't love me. And you seem nice. So how can you love someone like that?"

"Love?" Now his face was downright flaming. "Did she mention?" He stopped himself. Gathered his composure. Refocused on Jane, which pleased her. "That can't be true," Gerry said in the comforting old man voice she'd longed to hear so many times in moments of pure misery. Maybe her dad had been a nice guy. Tough, but tender. Ironic. She'd never know, though. Maybe she could get one of those DNA tests after all.

"I'm sure your mother loves you very much," he said.

"Are you fucking kidding me? Trust me. You don't know how she is. And then my brother? I mean, fuck that guy. All I've ever done is love him and protect him." She poked Gerry to ensure he was listening. "I mean, really protect him. Like, above and beyond. And he just shits on me. Just like Diane. Like mother, like son. I fucking kid you not. What's that saying about the apple and the tree?" Her thoughts fuzzed. "Whatever. The real takeaway here, Gerry with a G, is that I love them." Her nose clogged, her eyes streamed. "And they don't love me back. They really, really don't."

He petted her hand again. "I'm sure it's not as bad as all that." His tone was kind, but his gaze wandered to the exit. Jane clapped her hand on his back to keep his attention on her. How needy. How drunk. How Diane.

"It is bad, Gerry. It's real bad." He offered her a napkin that smelled like sopped-up beer. "She loves my brother more than me. Even though I'm her firstborn." On and on she went. Detailing her woe. Drinking all the while from the pitchers that kept arriving. Who had bought them? Gerry? She didn't know. She didn't care. She drank what was offered.

He folded his hands on the table and paused until she stopped whining. "Is that why you killed Warren? Were you upset about your mother?"

Laughter pealed out of her mouth. The room got spinny. Her eyelids heavy. The sticky table invited her head and she accepted.

"I didn't kill him," she said.

Eighteen

Georgia Lee

Every morning since Georgia Lee had left the trailer park and remembered what she'd done, she'd gasped awake and flung the weighted blanket that had piled against her throat off her body. Today was no different. She sat upright and tried to flush a nightmare of drowning from her mind.

Two questions continued to haunt her: What did Jason remember? And why hadn't he said anything?

Surely he remembered what had happened? Perhaps he'd blocked out the night as well? It had been traumatic, after all. Why hadn't he said something by now? Would he let Jane go to prison? Would she?

Have nothing to do with a false charge and do not put an innocent or honest person to death, for I will not acquit the guilty. Exodus 23:7.

If only she could get that verse out of her mind.

The little bit of hope she marshaled every morning dwindled with each new post on Let's Talk About Maud that drummed up Lezzie Borden fever. Finally, they'd united around something. People had nothing better to do than speculate on the means, the motive, and the opportunity of the murder of a dreadful man—even though Jane had already confessed! Everyone thought there was more to the story.

Everyone thought they knew the truth. If they'd met Warren—which most had not—they would've seen that his fate was more than fitting and they'd not waste time on "justice" or whatever it was they were doing. Playing puzzles. That was all.

Even Diane had asked people to move on and do something more productive with their lives than harass her at home and work. Apparently, KMSM had taken to staking out her house for interviews. She'd even pleaded with the cops to come and arrest Jane. She told them Jane was sitting right there on the couch. The more everyone continued to insist there was more to the story, the closer they were to finding Georgia Lee.

She needed to get her plan together. To figure out what on earth she could do to stop the train coming in her direction. But she'd been too panicked to think.

It didn't help her mood that her poll numbers had declined even more since the last attack ad from Bollinger. In this one he yelled, "Georgia Lee Lane's Greatest Hits!" and placed bull's-eye targets on each supposed service or good business deal she'd killed. He even included a photo of the one pothole that had gotten missed in the annual street repair. One pothole! Often, on the drive to or from work or while conducting mindless inventory or washing vegetables, she'd fantasized about murdering Bollinger. She'd already committed the Big Sin, why not add one more? Truly, the election might be the thing that sent her to jail if Warren's death didn't. If prison was in her future anyway, then why not take a rock to Bollinger's head as well?

She was kidding, of course. Even so, during her nightly prayers, she asked for forgiveness.

Her move to the guest room had made her bold in thought. Even hopeful for the future. Maybe the cops would close the case for lack of evidence. If they had any, they'd have arrested Jane by now. Teenage confessions were so unreliable. Everyone knew that. Maybe they'd all finally be free. Maybe at the end of election day, Georgia Lee would fold her pharmacy smock and place it on the desk along with her store keys. She would pray it all into existence.

She made a mental note to review online job postings to prepare her body and mind for the experience of leaving a place she'd stayed too long. She had enough in savings to get by for a short while. Her experience in store management and on the city council would matter to someone. Maybe not to employers in Maud Bottoms, but certainly someone in Maud Proper had a spot on their staff for a woman of her aptitude. Or Fayetteville. Maybe over in Fort Smith. Little Rock? Too far? Maybe for the old Georgia Lee. The new one . . .

Two weeks left. Two more weeks until she was free from the election and expectations and putting on a happy face for the world. She was done with all that. Done with Maud Bottoms. Every day, she imagined what other, non-Rusty-related changes she would make once released from the confines of her life in public service and with Warren's case finally behind them. It'd been foolish of her to try to improve Maud Bottoms. They hated the housing developments. They accused her of gentrification. They laughed at her. Maybe they were right. Maybe all she'd done was try to reclaim her spot on the top of the social ladder, but in Maud Bottoms this time. Perhaps that had been unfair of her to attempt to change Maud Bottoms instead of herself. She would consider it.

She dressed as usual, ate her cereal at the kitchen table, and drank her coffee. The boys had left early that morning for a game in a neighboring town, leaving the house blessedly quiet, with the exception of Rusty as he walked back and forth in their bedroom upstairs.

She braced herself when his footsteps sounded down the stairs and toward the kitchen.

"Good morning," he said, cheerful, though forced. She echoed his words back to him and tried to appear her usual self. He wore his around-the-house pants, a ball cap, and a T-shirt with holes and a hint of body odor.

He poured a cup of coffee and sipped it at the kitchen sink. Birdsong drifted inside from the open window. Annoyingly chipper, like him. "Lovely day outside."

She mumbled agreement. Before long, he placed his cup on the counter and his hands on either side of the sink.

"Are you going to tell me what's going on with you?"

Cruel to ask for elaboration on his meaning, but she did. Crueler still to watch him agonize over what he'd done wrong when the fault belonged to her.

She coughed. "I still feel terrible," she said. It was true. Her soul felt absolutely terrible. On the verge of complete collapse. "I think I'll be staying in the guest bedroom awhile longer. I don't want to infect you or the boys, and I don't want to wake you up coughing. Or tossing and turning. I know you have work to do." The hurt in his eyes at her jab showed. She didn't just feel terrible. She was terrible.

"You ain't gonna infect—"

"I'm the one who works in a pharmacy."

He sat down at the table, steepled his hands. She steeled herself.

"You haven't been to church in a while," he said.

"I'm busy."

"I know. I know," he said. "But maybe—"

"Please don't tell me that going to church will solve all our problems." They'd been short with each other for a while. They barely spoke about anything but the weather.

He flinched at her use of *our*. "It could help."

When he reached for her hand, she lifted it to her mouth and coughed.

Some other thought percolated, and she braced herself. It was painful to watch him and be in his presence with the memory of what she'd done fresh in her heart.

"Is it true what they said?"

"Who?"

"Let's Talk About Maud." He sheepishly glanced at her. "About knowing that girl, Jane Mooney."

This again. "Yes, I knew her."

"Is that all?"

She became impatient. "Is that all what?"

"Is that all it is, knowing her?" When she glared and didn't respond, he added, "Everyone's talking how . . ." He struggled to say the words. "How maybe." He cleared his throat. "Were you more than friends?"

Prior to her recent revelation, Georgia Lee might have kept her mouth shut. Now, defensiveness overcame her. "What if we were?"

His mouth opened wide in surprise. He yanked his cap off his head and ran his hands through his hair. "So it's true."

She couldn't, wouldn't deny it. "What does it matter?"

"It matters 'cause you never told me."

She cracked her neck and fought the indignation that grew within her. "What reason would I have to tell you about other relationships? Have you told me about all the girls you dated in high school? I recall you bragging with your buddies about being quite the ladies' man back then."

"This is different."

She examined her nails. About on par with how she felt. Wretched. "How is this different?"

"You know how, Georgia Lee!"

"You're making that abundantly clear."

He threw his cap behind her. She flinched. "Have you seen her recently?"

"Yes."

"Oh my God." He pushed away from the table and gripped the kitchen counter, away from her. "Did anyone see you?"

"Probably." No need to lie. "We went for pizza."

"For pizza?" He practically screamed the words at her. "You went for pizza with a murderer?"

"Are you worried that I went to pizza with a murderer or a lesbian?"

He thrust his hands every which way, like he was trying to find the words. "Both!"

She rolled her eyes. "You're so old fashioned."

"Well forgive me if I don't want my friends seeing my wife out with that woman."

"Your wife? I have a name. And let me remind you that none of this has anything to do with you or your friends."

He slammed the table with a hand. She jumped in response. "It has everything to do with me and the kids."

"You said friends, not kids." Maybe everything coming out was good. Maybe it was just the thing she needed. Maybe a change would come over her. Like when she was younger. Right before she met Jane. Maybe she couldn't wish the past away. But maybe she could alter what happened next. "This is why we have a problem, Rusty. *This* is why I need space."

"I'm sorry." He sat down at the table and tried to clasp her hand, but she crossed her arms. "You know I would never hurt you. But I shouldn't have raised my voice. And I shouldn't have hit the table."

"You don't get to dictate my life."

"I know. You're right."

"I think I need a break. From us."

That rendered him into a puddle. She'd mentioned it in the past. She'd mentioned it more in recent years. She'd felt bad about it, looking for good reasons for feeling the way she did. But all she came up with was *Because I'm bored. I'm tired. I need something different.* At last year's holiday gift swap at work, someone had given her a copy of *Tiny Beautiful Things*, a book of advice on love and life. Probably one of the girls. Probably meant it as a lark. A big joke on Georgia Lee, ha ha, Miss Cheesy Advice Book Target Audience. But she'd read it. And it wasn't cheesy. It was beautiful and funny and it'd almost made her cry. She'd learned that wanting to leave is enough. That's all that was required to separate, to divorce, to leave.

She solidified herself against her desire to comfort him. Comfort would not be useful. She grew impatient and coughed. He pulled himself together.

"We can fix this," he said, pointing back and forth between them.

"Can we?" There were all the things he didn't know. All the things she barely knew herself. Confusing thoughts in her mind about that night and what she'd done. She wasn't sure she wanted to tackle them with him. She doubted he would understand. His life was simple. Hers only looked it. It hadn't been simple since she walked out the school doors and spoke with Jane Mooney for the first time.

"What are you saying?" he asked.

"I don't know if I want to fix it." Her hands and voice shook as the words she'd been wanting to say wrestled their way onto her tongue. "I just want to be alone."

"You've had nothing but time alone this past—"

"No," she said and reached for his hand.

"You're just reacting. With everything going on—"

"No." She gripped his hand.

He slumped into his chair. "Is this about Jane? Did you—"

"Did I what?"

"My God, Georgia Lee. Don't make me beg you to tell me if you and her . . ."

She gathered more air into her lungs. "There's no one else," Georgia Lee said. "There's only me."

"Then why would you . . ." He let the question trail off. But she knew what he was thinking: *Why would you leave this if not for someone else?*

If there was no one else, they would have no one to blame but themselves.

She had loved Rusty. She had not settled for him after Jane. There had been other boyfriends, even other girls in college. He was not bad. He was not "Not Jane." She hadn't put Jane on a pedestal after she'd left. She hadn't compared every lover to her. She and Rusty had simply grown apart. That was the hardest part.

When anyone she'd known had mentioned they were getting a divorce, she'd immediately wondered who had cheated on whom and what nefarious activities might have led to their demise. Now she knew that in most cases there was nothing as sinister as that. They were simply people, flawed but still loved and loving.

"I guess I can't be surprised," he said and wiped his eyes and nose with his sleeve. "I know you haven't been happy." You. She bit down on a response. Many of her friends had not questioned their own happiness even as they outlined all the ways in which they hated everything about their lives. She didn't want to be that woman for whom her husband was the butt of jokes, the target for her disdain while out drinking with friends. There was more. She wanted more. For her, and for him. He deserved more, even as she broke his heart.

"I'm sorry," she said. Things were better this way, she told herself. He deserved someone who loved him all the way through. Someone who would not be disappointed when he came into the room because he'd invaded her quiet. Someone who didn't become enraged at the smallest things. Someone who wouldn't murder another human being.

She'd been unfair and unkind to him. That was no way to live—half-loved, half-resented.

He sniffled and rubbed her wedding ring as if it were magic and could fix them.

Tears, those enemies, charged again, as if they were an army inside her, unleashed and finally breaking the seawall Georgia Lee had built to try to keep emotions from overtaking her. She would face whatever happened next with Warren's case. She'd protect Rusty and the boys by removing herself. It was for the best.

"I don't care about the other girl. Girls," he corrected. "I just want you to be happy."

Georgia Lee wondered what information had come out of the woodwork since Let's Talk About Maud had insinuated an association with Jane. She couldn't imagine any of the girls from college coming forward and admitting to a relationship. Those girls had been like Georgia Lee. They'd only been having fun. They'd all meant to eventually settle down and get married to a man. That'd seemed the only option. One that Georgia Lee had taken to readily. She recalled a verse from 1 Corinthians 7, one she'd read in their early days, one that felt prescient, if she'd only paid attention: *It is better to marry than to burn with passion.*

Times had changed, though. If she were that same girl now, she'd think on her options a bit more. Not that she'd eschew Rusty for a woman, necessarily. She had loved him. But after almost two decades of an ember, she might choose instead to burn.

"We can still make this work, Georgia Lee." He reached out to hold her hand again. His voice faltered, but he restrained any tears. "I'll change. I'll do whatever it takes to keep you happy."

Part of her was with him, part of her wanted out. It was a confusing place to be. She wanted to rush into his embrace, the security of him. But she imagined herself driving up to their house once again and feeling her heart sink. Her life, she hated to admit, would feel over, especially after coming this far, speaking what was in her heart. But here was Rusty, so tried and true. Anything else, uncertain, risky. She teetered on the possibilities. Perhaps a different woman would've swallowed her pride and her desires and would have leaped at the chance to be held once again in those strong arms.

"Will you just think about it? Stay in the guest room awhile. And then we'll see how things are going. After the election."

He was right. She couldn't do anything before then. Too messy. She had enough on her plate. She nodded. She'd deal with this another time. First, she had to deal with what to do now that she remembered what she'd done.

◆ ◆ ◆

At work, she went about her morning duties, ensuring Billie and Cassidy had their register drawers and all the aisles were cleaned, the shelves straightened.

Everything was going to be fine. No, everything was going to be *great*.

As the afternoon ticked down, the store remained quiet as always. Nothing but the adult alternative station and the incessant chatter from Billie and Cassidy.

Even when the pharmacy wasn't busy, there were things to do, clean, take care of. The illusion of work even when work proved hard to find.

She walked to the front and caught them looking at their phones, whispering. As soon as they saw her, they got this look, the kind she and Christlyn and Susannah wore when they were caught talking about the very person who had walked up to them unawares.

"What's so interesting?" she asked.

"Um. Nothing." Billie slipped her phone into the back pocket of her jeans. Cassidy trained her eyes on the doors. She recognized those looks. She had perfected them back in high school.

"Let me see." Georgia Lee held out her hand. She had no authority—it was probably illegal to even ask—but she was an authority figure to them, and they tended to do what she asked out of fear.

Billie slid the phone toward Georgia Lee, who couldn't help but roll her eyes at the drama. She pulled her reading glasses from the pocket of her smock and picked up the phone as if it were the greatest inconvenience of her life. By the time Georgia Lee had it in hand, the phone screen had gone black.

"It's locked."

Billie unlocked the phone and handed it over again.

Even without her glasses, she'd recognize that photo booth strip anywhere.

The photos on Let's Talk About Maud's page looked mild compared to what Billie and Cassidy and her own teenagers were exposed to—and no doubt participated in—on the various screens to which they were addicted. Nothing but heavy petting and kissing. Messing around in a semipublic space for the fun, the danger of it. Their hands tangled around each other's bodies. Jane's face clear. Georgia Lee's head almost entirely cut off in all the shots due to the angle of their awkward groping and a case of the giggles that had erupted when the camera clicked four times. The last photo was quite fetching, she had to admit. Like a movie poster of two lovers meeting again after years apart. She couldn't remember the movie name, but she could see the poster clear as day. But two girls making out, no mistaking that. Panic spread across her body like a hot flash. Who had found this? Where had they found it? There was only one answer.

She calmly removed her glasses and returned the phone to Billie. "At least give a woman some warning before you expose her to alternative lifestyles." The girls didn't say anything and tried not to look at the phone again. She stiffened her posture. "Is that all?"

Billie sucked in a breath. "Let's Talk About Maud said that's you in them photos."

A frenzy of lies and excuses clamored for release.

"My sister's gay," Cassidy offered. Billie smacked her arm.

How could she lie? Again? Without another word, she walked to the back office, grabbed her purse, and headed to her car as quickly as she could without breaking into a full run.

As soon as she exited the pharmacy, reporters shoved near her and lights flashed in her face. There weren't many. But three of them seemed like a lot, even if one only used the flash on her iPhone.

A reporter she didn't recognize shoved a mic in her face. "Is it true?" Her nerves crackled. She'd expected something bad, but not this.

"Is it true you're the companion of Jane Mooney?" They couldn't prove the girl in the photo was her.

"Are you in contact with her?"

As much as she wanted to run to her car and fly out of the parking lot, muscle memory—her old friend—kicked in. She'd handled outrage before.

She paused, told her body to stop shaking like a fool, faced the reporters, and put on her best smile. "My goodness. Give a girl some room to breathe." She smoothed her smock and cursed that she'd forgotten to remove it. Maybe it'd give her that folksy look people sometimes liked in politicians. She was working class, like them. Not that she cared anymore.

They waited, mics held out, the lot of them vibrating with the frenetic energy that only small-town scandal could create. That special sauce of insularity that allowed people to say they knew so-and-so and they were this-close to the facts and the details. The glow of something bigger than them finally shining a light into their sad little lives. Whoever got up on a pedestal was sure to be knocked down. Only a matter of time, and here she was, up to bat.

"What's this about?" She couldn't lie. But she couldn't admit to being the other girl from the photos either.

"Can you identify this woman?" James from KMSM—one of those men who called his wife *Mother* and didn't seem to believe in birth control, not even the rhythm method—held a printout. Georgia Lee had never liked him. All he focused on was gossip, nothing of substance. Feeding the Let's Talk About Maud cretins. He squirmed and tried not to look too close at what he shoved in her direction. She would never understand how someone in his profession could consume photos of crime scenes or show up at the house of someone who had died and decomposed on the toilet or from an overdose and be fine but become squeamish at a couple of girls kissing. The world made no sense some-times. Defiance—something she'd not expected to feel—built in her. He'd probably never experienced in his whole life what Georgia Lee had experienced in one minute with Jane. Probably groused about two girls like the ones he saw in the photos with his buddies or his work colleagues but did deplorable things while staring at the pictures when alone. By God, if he'd come all this way to accuse her of something, then he darn well better accuse her of something specific.

She took the printout. "Which underage girl are you inquiring about?" At the phrase, James blanched. Good. For that's what they had been.

His finger hovered in the white photo border, presumably trying to find a spot that didn't alarm him now that she'd reminded him the girls had been minors.

He settled on the top of the first image, right outside the border, above Georgia Lee's head. "Her."

Georgia Lee tilted her head to the side. "The headless girl?"

He took great pains to keep his focus on Georgia Lee's face, not her breasts or the swell of breast in the photo near Jane's mouth and whether or not the two clothed breasts were a positive match.

"We know the identity of the other one," he said.

"And who would that be?" If he wanted to draw this out, then she was going to make him squirm.

The unidentified reporter, a young woman Georgia Lee didn't know, thrust the mic toward her. Maybe the high school? The U of A? Perhaps journalism wasn't dead yet. "Were you friends with Jane Mooney, the dead man's daughter?"

"Stepdaughter. I'd expect you to get your facts correct. According to everything that's been published thus far, she was not his daughter." The student journalist rolled her eyes. She told them she knew Jane from high school, as did the other students when Jane was thrust into the spotlight. Nothing but the truth.

Katrina from the *Maud Register* raised her pen. "You didn't answer the question. Is that you?"

"Let me see," she said and pulled on her reading glasses to examine the pictures once more.

Georgia Lee might as well have been the Headless Girl, some sideshow attraction for the citizens of Maud to laugh at and marvel at how she'd lost her head after an accident and had been kept alive, but not by science. By her own ingenuity and grit. That was what.

"I suppose it could be if you looked hard enough and wanted it to be me so you could get your story."

The flashes nearly blinded her. She lifted a hand to block them. My God. She didn't know which admission might be worse: being in the photos with Jane or being an accomplice to murder.

"Are you a lesbian?" James shoved forward. Rude. And hateful the way he said it. Like it was a dirty word, something someone should be ashamed of. Maybe if people like James didn't say it that way, people wouldn't be so afraid all the time.

"Of course not." Not a lie. She wasn't a lesbian, technically speaking.

"That's what Let's Talk About Maud is reporting this morning," the student reporter said.

"Yes, I've seen. Along with the absurd and unfounded speculation of some vast and detailed crime when the perpetrator has clearly confessed," Georgia Lee said. "I support the police in their pursuit of justice and will do everything in my power to assist them should they find additional evidence in relation to the existing crime, which I don't believe they have." *Dear Lord, let there be no evidence.*

James wouldn't let up. "What does your husband have to say about this?"

Katrina had lost interest and wandered away to check her phone. That's when Georgia Lee noticed Bollinger standing next to his car, arms crossed, a pleased look on his face. He wiggled his fingers to wave. Of course. He'd set this all up, no doubt. But how'd he get the photos?

Or did he simply know about their impending release? Either way, she would not let him get one over on her. She returned her attention to James.

"This unsubstantiated claim by a couple of mechanics in a garage?" she asked. "You care more about that than the fact that a murderer is walking our streets and the police have done nothing to arrest her?" A low blow. The quip immediately festered in her stomach, but she was an animal, backed into a corner. She promised to retract it later.

Who cared about crime when you had two women doing something people thought they ought not do? Perhaps she should feel shame, like people were wont to do when they were confronted with the indiscretions of the past. But she didn't feel shame. She had been young, and she had been in love. She had been happy, and it showed. She'd been aglow with something rare. What everyone wanted but few found, the absence of which made people bitter or complacent or maybe both. She'd had it, and then it had slipped away. But this—this was a reminder of what she'd once felt, who she'd been, who she might be again. The thought alternately thrilled and terrified her.

She put on a big smile and ignored further questions as she made her way toward her car. Before she shut the door and all of them behind her, she yelled out, "Don't forget to vote!"

Nineteen

GEORGIA LEE

Georgia Lee drummed her fingers on the steering wheel. She couldn't go home. She couldn't face Rusty. The boys. The video of her in the pharmacy parking lot with a salacious headline running over and over as the sole enticement to watch the five o'clock news.

Those waves of thrill and terror, calm and chaos from earlier in the day continued. She sat in the parking lot of the Walmart for a while before sitting in the parking lot of the Taco Bell awhile longer after going through the drive-through. She downed the emergency bottle of wine she kept in the trunk. No point in worrying about anyone seeing now. The election, all but lost.

Involved in a murder? She might have a chance. Making out with another woman? Not in Maud.

She'd been too frazzled by the photo to read the full details from Let's Talk About Maud. She pulled up the post to assess the damage.

SECRET LOVERS. YEAH, THAT'S WHAT THEY ARE!
Is that Holier Than Thou City Council Member Georgia
Lee Liar
getting down with a girl? But not just any girl.

That's the infamous Lezzie Borden, aka
Jane Mooney, stepdaughter of Warren Ingram,
the man who went missing 25 years ago and turned up
all dancing skeletons
down at the Lock and Dam a month ago.
Like y'all needed the reminder. Lol.

We'd of never thunk it.
But our secret source Lovelace claims it's the God Honest truth.
(Georgia Lee would probably sue us if we agreed.)
Lovelace wouldn't say where or how he or she (gotdam
y'all,
we're gonna have to use THEY) came upon these photos, but THEY sure as shit are
convinced the Headless Girl in them there pics is our
very own
Georgia Lee Lesbian.

SAY WUT?!?
We didn't believe it at first, but
with that gal back in town, eating pizza with a certain
city councilor we know,
we gotta accept the facts where they lead.
(That tip came free of charge from the great gals down
at Tommy's Pizza!)
Could Georgia Lee be a person of interest, NAY an AC-
COMPLICE, in a . . .
(insert an image of a lady in a floofy gown gasping
right here, folks)
MURDER?!
We ain't saying she is. But we ain't saying she ain't.

Georgia Lee Lane, you got some 'splaining to do!
#OhShitYall #MaudMurderMystery #LesbiansLesbians-
Lesbians #SinnerSinnerChickenDinner

She scrolled through the comments even though she knew better. They contained a mix of shock and vicious glee and out-of-context Bible verses condemning her alleged sin.

After sitting there awhile to let the food settle and to make the inside of the car stop spinning from all the wine, she wound up at Jane's door, lips still buzzing from her overindulgence. She knew better than to drive toward that doomed part of town in her intoxicated state. She knew she shouldn't be standing in front of the door of the woman whose hands had been all over her in those photos. How compromised she would look. How they'd laugh. Anyone—John, Benjamin, KMSM, Katrina, even the college reporter—could show up at any time.

"Well hello to you too," Jane said after Georgia Lee knocked and then pushed through, shutting the door tight behind her.

Before knocking, Georgia Lee had rushed to the trailer hitch and overturned the flowerpot. The envelope of cash, gone.

Jane looked annoyingly good in her sweats and braless T-shirt even though she also looked hungover. She hated how Jane's breasts hadn't drooped with age or childbirth. More than that, Georgia Lee hated how her own body responded to Jane's. She squelched her traitorous biology and let anger take its rightful place. But the room began to spin.

"Diane!" Georgia Lee screamed.

Jane gripped her head. "Jesus. Why are you yelling?"

"Diane. Your mother. Where is she?"

Before Jane could answer, Diane wandered in from the hallway, her whole demeanor a far cry from when Georgia Lee had last seen her. She sauntered into the kitchen in a black, sleeveless sequined top, tight jeans, and sky-high heels, a trail of perfume following her. Probably still had the tags on everything she wore. Probably bought it with the money Georgia Lee had given her. Probably would return it all after she'd sweat in it at the bar and after it'd been crumpled on some man's floor all night.

"Should've known you'd show up eventually," Diane said.

"I paid you." The room darkened like she was looking through a pinhole camera as Georgia Lee's anger narrowed on Diane and her betrayal. "I did what you asked, so why are there reporters hanging outside my workplace?"

Jane watched them, suspicious. Georgia Lee couldn't worry about her right now.

Diane paused as if to think. "I'd remember if you'd paid me."

"I left the note on your car." She gestured toward the front of the trailer. "I left the money outside. I hid it under a flowerpot." Five thousand dollars. Cash. Taken from her personal savings account. One she'd hidden from Rusty. Her voice edged higher. "I left a note on your car!"

Diane contemplated, shrugged, and then stared into a cabinet. "Maybe it blew off."

"I taped it on the underside of your door handle so it wouldn't blow off and so no one else would see it." She wasn't stupid. She wouldn't have left the note on the windshield for all to see.

Jane looked back and forth between Diane and Georgia Lee. "What are you talking about? What note? What money?"

"For the funeral. Your . . ." Georgia Lee's throat tightened as her pulse quickened. "She blackmailed me."

Jane's mouth fell open, and she looked to Diane. "I paid for—"

"Blackmail?" Diane slammed the cabinet and launched herself at Georgia Lee, which made her jump back, startled. "I kept my word to your parents, didn't I? For over twenty years. Yet you come into my house, accusing me of blackmail? If it weren't for me, you'd've been locked up just like her."

Jane scrunched her face in confusion. "What the fuck is going on?"

Georgia Lee grumbled and scrambled through the depths of her purse for her phone. An onslaught of text and phone notifications had popped up since she last looked. She'd have to deal with all that later. She showed her phone to Jane while glaring at Diane, daring her to move closer. She refrained from showing Jane the post from Let's Talk About Maud that mentioned Georgia Lee as Jane's accomplice. She'd learn soon enough. For now, Georgia Lee wanted to know what had happened to her money. Savings that had taken her years to collect. She had no plan for it. But she needed it. She needed to know it was there if she needed to . . .

Run.

She needed the money. Her money.

Jane rubbed her eyes. "Why are these photos online?"

"That's what I'd like to know." Georgia Lee directed the question to Diane.

As if a switch had been flicked, Diane had gone from rage to calm. She tossed an arm across her chest. A cigarette dangled from her free hand. "Let me see."

"You've already seen it! You gave it to them." Georgia Lee shoved her phone into her purse. Despite her trepidation at angering Diane again, she added, "You lied. And you stole my money. And I want it back."

"I didn't get your note. And I didn't give no photo to no one."

"Then how'd they end up online?" Diane smoked; Jane blinked. Georgia Lee didn't know what to believe. Maybe Diane was right. Maybe someone had taken the note. Maybe it had somehow blown off. This was worse than telling Let's Talk About Maud. This was showing them. How had the photo even stuck around this long? Did Jane know what had really happened? Had Jason confessed to her? Were they plotting with Benjamin to get Georgia Lee to confess to the crime?

Before she could stop herself, she punched Jane's arm, but it did little to assuage Georgia Lee's desire to afflict pain on her. Her arms were all muscle. Infuriating. Georgia Lee hadn't meant to do it. But Diane's lies lit her like a match.

"Why are you hitting me?" Jane rubbed the spot.

"You told me no one would ever see those photos." Georgia Lee's voice cracked an octave higher as she tried to wrestle her emotions. When she noticed how closely Diane listened and how a slight smile had crept up, she whispered to Jane, "You said they'd be our secret. You promised. Did you give the photos to them?" The words came out too whiny, girlish. She wished she could take them back.

"They arrested me," Jane said by way of explanation. "I didn't really have an opportunity to grab personal items."

"They wouldn't have arrested you if you hadn't confessed," Georgia Lee said. Bitterness lined every word.

Diane took a drag off her cigarette and propped a hand on her hip. "But she did, didn't she?"

Georgia Lee glared at her and then returned her attention to Jane. "But you got out. You came back, right?" Jane nodded, thinking. "Did you see the photos? Were they still here?"

Jane held her gaze. "I don't know. I don't remember."

"You don't remember?" As Georgia Lee's voice slid up the scale of hysteria, Diane looked on calmly. Of course she hadn't taken them. As soon as they'd released her, she'd left town. Without notice. Without so much as a goodbye. "How could you forget? How could you not take them with you? Or destroy them?"

Jane was sober and awake now. "So sorry I didn't grab a bunch of photos. I was trying to get out of town before the cops changed their mind or my mom tried to kill me."

Georgia Lee looked to Diane. She shrugged as if to confirm.

Diane sauntered closer, blew smoke toward Georgia Lee, and slung her purse strap on her shoulder. "Looks like someone's chickens finally come home to roost." She nearly spit out the words. They trailed behind her as she slunk toward the front door and slammed it on her way out, causing Georgia Lee to jump.

She swirled in the memories of the last night she'd spent within these walls. The room began to spin again. She closed her eyes and reached out her hand until it found a kitchen chair. She sat down and waited for the spins to pass before she opened her eyes.

The scratched table she sat at looked the same as it had the night she'd fought with Warren. "Do you have something to drink?"

Jane rifled through the cabinet they used to raid. Diane never seemed to notice her missing wares. After filling two glasses from a cheap bottle of whiskey, Jane slid one toward her.

Georgia Lee downed it, grimaced, stood. She paced in front of the couch. The walls and carpet were darker than she remembered. The space more cramped. Her hands shook. She shoved them in the pockets of her smock, whose removal kept slipping her memory.

She grabbed the whiskey bottle, poured herself another drink, downed it, and grimaced once more. If only she'd parked somewhere else. Warren would've complained at her presence like always but would not have chased her down. Her life would be so different. She and Jane would probably have broken up over some petty thing, their lives no worse for wear. Georgia Lee sulked into the kitchen chair she'd recently vacated.

"I didn't give them the photos," Jane said. "I swear."

"Because you forgot about them."

Jane stared at her without blinking. "I just got out of jail."

"Juvie," Georgia Lee corrected.

"What do you think juvie is? Summer camp? It's jail for teenagers. Same fucking thing."

"If not you and not Diane, then it had to be Angie." Suddenly, it became clear to Georgia Lee, the one other person who knew something and had a motive. Little bird. "She's the only one who has a reason to point the finger at us. Maybe it's a plea deal."

Jane closed her eyes and tilted her head backward in exasperation. "She's not up to something. She hasn't said anything."

"How would you know? Did you find her? Do you believe her?" One look at Jane's face said it all. "Of course you do."

Georgia Lee walked to the couch and plopped onto it, purse still hanging from the crook of her arm. She dropped her head between her knees and began her breathing exercises even though taco- and alcohol-spiked bile burned on its way up her throat. She wanted to cry again.

No, she wouldn't cry anymore. Crying only ruined her makeup.

The cushions depressed when Jane sat down next to her. She waited for a hand at her back, rubbing out the pain, but it didn't come.

"Why is everyone talking about this?" Jane asked.

"Why do you think?" Maud's only claim to fame. Georgia Lee lifted her head and smoothed the jeans that didn't need smoothing, but it seemed like the thing to do.

"Shit." Now Jane was the one with her head propped in her hands. She focused forward, lost in thought. "What's the latest?"

"They got everyone thinking Warren had some problem with you and your lover." She hated the word. "And that meant we murdered him so we could run away together and live happily ever after."

Jane inhaled and exhaled into her fist. "If only he'd had a problem with us instead of everything else." A motive that people could understand. If only things had been that easy.

"Why did you give her money?" Jane asked.

Georgia Lee stared at the carpet. Stupid, stupid woman. She never should've believed Diane or left the money there. Now it was gone. "She promised me she'd keep my name out of the papers if I paid for the funeral."

Jane groaned.

"What?"

"I paid for the funeral."

"Looks like we're both suckers."

"Looks like."

Jane's thigh was warm against Georgia Lee's. She wanted to move away, she should move away. She was compromised. By the photos. By alcohol, emotions, holding everything so tight within her. Any minute she'd burst like a tomato shot through with a gun like in those slow-motion videos.

"Have they talked to Jason?" Georgia Lee asked.

"Yeah, but he won't say anything." Some other thought bubbled underneath Jane's assurance.

Would Jason stay quiet as they led his sister away in handcuffs for a murder she hadn't committed? Would Jane? They all had much more to lose as adults than they ever had as teens.

"They haven't confirmed it's me in the photos. They don't have any additional evidence. Or any, for that matter," Georgia Lee said. "At least none that I know of. Just your confession."

That stupid, stupid confession.

Jane faced her, exasperated, tired, ready to give up. She might as well have written *I surrender!* on her face. "It's not like I wanted to. I made a mistake. There's nothing I can do about it now."

Here Jane was, willing to take the fall for something she didn't do, again. *Praise Jesus* came to mind before Georgia Lee had time to admonish her wicked subconscious self. Jason had never told Jane anything else about their fight with Warren. That could change, and quick.

"Don't turn yourself in again before they even show up to your door. That's insane."

Jane glared at her. "I didn't say I would."

"Well, good. You need to see what evidence they have before throwing in the towel. Even with your confession, it's possible they won't be able to convict you. You don't have to admit to anything until you find out what they even know. It's all speculation. It could fizzle out any minute." Though she spoke the words to Jane, they were more for herself as the certainty of Benjamin's tenacity, the weight of everything, and what her brain told her had happened pressed on her conscience. How could she come clean now? After saying all that? Jane would never forgive her.

"I'm sorry I didn't get rid of the picture," Jane said. "I didn't know it'd come back to haunt us." Jane leaned closer to Georgia Lee to whisper, to comfort. It tore at Georgia Lee's soul. "And I'm sorry your husband and kids have to go through all this. To see that photo. That can't be easy. Not in Maud."

Georgia Lee's wedding ring glinted up at her, still there even though she wasn't sure she wanted it or what it represented anymore. That morning, she'd slipped it halfway off but then stopped. Not until after the investigation concluded, with or without that photo. Depending on how Rusty responded to this latest reveal from Let's Talk About Maud, she might not have a choice.

"I'm not ashamed." In that moment, unbridled from alcohol and despair, Georgia Lee could say those words. But they weren't altogether true. She'd heard nothing but how wrong girls like them were. But a small part of her, the one that had opened herself up to Jane back then, fought to get out, to be heard, to be seen again. "What I hate is that other people think I should be ashamed. I'd like to at least have the option to choose what I share and have the opportunity to explain it rather than respond to it."

"How do you want me to explain us when the cops show up asking questions and pull out those photos? You want me to lie?"

"I don't know." She hadn't outright denied it in front of the reporters. "I'll say it was a fling. Long before anything to do with Warren. So you can keep your story intact."

Jane offered a withering look. "Thanks. I'm sure your husband would be delighted to hear that."

Georgia Lee wrestled herself out of the busted sofa cushions she'd sunk into amid Jane's apologies and entreaties to stay. Once she extricated herself from the couch, she slung her purse onto her shoulder. She'd never been one for soap opera theatrics, but the wine and the whiskey and the circumstances had put her in a mood for just that. At the door, she held on to the handle. For drama and also to assist in her efforts to not fall down. But it only reminded her of Warren. She snatched her hand away as if the handle were hot liquid.

"One day, you're going to regret that you responded with sarcasm instead of kindness." She lifted her chin, defiant. Let Jane know what someone else leaving was like for a change.

Twenty

Georgia Lee

The tap at Georgia Lee's window about scared her to death. Only one exterior light lit the laundromat parking lot that sat at the entrance to Maud Bottoms Estates; the interior loomed in darkness. Georgia Lee had parked off to the side and in the shadows. Appropriately, near the dumpster. She'd been in no condition to drive and decided to wait awhile to sober up. She'd fallen asleep and dreamed of tumbling under the lock, over and over, her breath held, her lungs screaming.

Jane stood at her car door, sweat glistening on her forehead from the stuffy night air.

After pulling herself together from the fright, Georgia Lee checked the time—a little after ten o'clock—and rolled down the window. "What are you doing out here? How did you find me?"

Jane paused and then laughed. "You didn't even leave the trailer park. I went for a walk and saw your car," she said. "You shouldn't leave the car running."

"It's the outdoors, not a garage. I'm not trying to kill myself."

Jane smirked. "I meant that someone might see you. And it's bad for the environment."

Georgia Lee smirked right back. "Get in the car," she said. "It's hotter than Hades out there."

Once settled in the passenger seat, Jane positioned the air vents toward her face. Thunder rumbled in the distance. They sat awhile without talking. Eventually, Jane froze herself with the AC, closed the vent in front of her, and hugged herself for warmth.

Georgia Lee turned down the air and tossed a Maud City Council fleece jacket from the back seat at her.

Jane wrestled her arms into the sleeves and propped her head on the window. Finally, Georgia Lee could look at her without accidentally drawing her eyes downward.

"I hate sitting here," Jane said. "Waiting, when I know any minute they could show up and escort me to my new lodgings." As soon as Georgia Lee opened her mouth to protest, Jane interrupted her. "I'm not going to turn myself in before they come and get me."

"You promise?"

She waited awhile before speaking. "I promise." It was the first time since they'd reconnected that Jane looked at her without a hint of disdain or disappointment or dread.

Jane narrowed her eyes. "What was all that about Diane and your parents?"

Georgia Lee sighed. "As soon as they learned about your arrest and the rumors of an accomplice, they locked me in my room."

"Really?" Jane asked. Georgia Lee nodded. "How long?"

"A month? They let me out after they let you go and you'd already left town."

"Jesus. That's like something out of the '50s or '60s." Jane considered. "And Diane got them to pay her for her silence?" After Georgia Lee nodded again, Jane laughed and shook her head. "God. What an asshole."

Georgia Lee didn't have the heart to laugh. Not with the memory of being locked in her room for a month and the sting of losing $5,000 still fresh in her mind. Diane had played her.

They sat in silence again before Georgia Lee had to break it or she'd go mad. "I'm sorry about rushing out of the house. It's . . ." *I'm guilty.* "I'm thinking of leaving him."

If Jane felt any kind of way, she didn't reveal it on her face. "After the election?"

Georgia Lee looked away. She didn't want to see if Jane was teasing her. "Of course. I'm no fool."

She rummaged around the back seat and took a swig of what was left of her wine, then held the bottle out to Jane. Georgia Lee hated to drink alone, something she'd been doing for a while now, trying hard to be the good woman she was supposed to be. The upstanding citizen and public servant. It got to be real tiring.

"He's a good man," Georgia Lee offered, even though Jane had not asked. "But it's been a long time coming."

For a moment Georgia Lee panicked that she'd made the wrong choice by telling Jane about something as intimate as her homelife. She felt wretched for even letting the words slip out. Like it was a betrayal of Rusty. Thinking it was one thing, saying it out loud another. But then she contemplated what it'd be like to pull up in the driveway and face the house again. Those feelings that something was missing. A life with a hole in it was no life at all.

As the silence gathered between them, bits of hail began to ping the windshield. When they were younger, they'd said the silly things young people in love said. Like *I love you.* Like *forever.* Georgia Lee had once believed in such a thing as forever. Forever was a concept for the young. Still, even with those words, Georgia Lee had not quite captured, not spoken, what Jane had truly meant to her. She doubted she would have been able to find the right words back then. And perhaps the words, this feeling, could not have come if Jane had not left. Even if she had been able to stay in Maud with all that notoriety, maybe she and Jane would have also drifted into that shallow bit of love she and Rusty now found themselves in. Her aching for something more after settling in for so long.

It did no use to wonder.

Georgia Lee never would've been able to be seen with Jane. Rumors would've felled Georgia Lee. She'd not had the fortitude to withstand scrutiny back then. She wasn't sure she had it now.

But Jane had mattered. That was what Georgia Lee had longed to share when she drove her home after pizza.

"I don't know what'll happen," Georgia Lee said.

"I'm going to jail." Jane offered a sad smile before turning toward the window. "I didn't mean what I said the other night, after the funeral. If you wanted to write or visit, that'd be fine."

Georgia Lee choked down the urge to come clean. What good would it do now? But she ignored another part of her, one that said to hush and behave and let things go, that not everything needed to be said. Not every truth had to be voiced. At least not all at once.

"You didn't just mean something to me." Georgia Lee could barely contain the emotion in her voice. She focused on her lap instead of Jane so as not to lose courage. "You were everything to me. And then you left. Without a word."

Georgia Lee had a bad habit of blurting out the truth when the truth rattled so strong inside her it felt it might crush her bones. She shut down the oncoming tears. She succeeded, but it made her nose run. She grabbed a tissue from her purse and wiped it.

"You were my first love," she said. "You only get one of those. I'm glad it was you. Thank you."

A laugh escaped Jane's mouth.

"That's . . ." Georgia Lee crossed her arms. "I was being sincere."

Jane reached out and took Georgia Lee's hand. "I know. I'm sorry."

Embarrassed, Georgia Lee shoved the tear- and snot-covered tissue into the side pocket of the door. "You never take me seriously."

Georgia Lee's words hung in the air, drowned by the summer downpour the skies finally unleashed. But then Jane put a hand to Georgia Lee's cheek. It was cold from where she'd previously held it up to the vent. A smile lingered. Georgia Lee's body tingled; her mind raced with warnings. She should turn away from that hand, from Jane. She should tell her she had to get home.

It was dark. It was late. Reporters had been hanging around Diane's trailer. The last thing Georgia Lee needed was another photo to upend her. Everything she'd worked for could disappear. Her life. Her home. Her family. She should go home, beg Rusty for forgiveness, ask to be welcomed back into the comfort of their home, their routine, everything she knew and understood. Everything that didn't challenge her. She should let Jane move forward, do what she'd always planned to do. And then forget her. Georgia Lee had done it before; she could forget again.

Instead, she welcomed Jane's mouth when it was offered, without pause or shame. She let Jane pull her onto her lap and undo her jeans, recline the seat, and position her hips. While the residents of Maud Bottoms Estates settled into their bedtime routines or late-night shows or last drinks, their representative, Georgia Lee Lane, the one who fought for them even though they were unaware and mostly unimpressed, unzipped the fleece jacket Jane wore, lifted the T-shirt, and once more cooled her tongue against the skin that had teased her all night and long ago.

Twenty-One

JANE

Jane definitely should not have had sex with Georgia Lee in the front passenger seat of a car like a teenager in an '80s flick. Things were messy enough without adding extra helpings of emotion on top. However. Considering Jane's potential imminent arrest for the murder of her stepfather—again—who could blame her?

Outside, the brief thunderstorm had dissipated. They untangled their half-naked bodies and groaned in response to their backs and necks having been forced into uncomfortable positions their joints and muscles no longer tolerated. Georgia Lee settled into the driver's seat and smoothed her hair. She rubbed away the steam on the windows and peered outside. They avoided eye contact, but not in any way that made Jane's stomach plunge. It was almost charming, Georgia Lee's shyness and hesitation and paranoia.

Jane had had plenty of lovers. Enough to know a good one from a bad one. The last ex had been the former until they'd both become the latter out of boredom and disinterest. It got to the point where she would have rather been forced to watch a *Bachelorette* marathon all day than have a five-minute quickie with her ex. She could barely muster the energy for a romantic comedy and assumed she'd reached *that age.*

But one glance from an emotionally compromised Georgia Lee in the seat next to her and Jane fell under the spell. Her hair and skin smelled like what Jane imagined sunshine would. There were soft curves in the places where her ex housed muscle. Roughness instead of smoothness, though no less exciting to Jane's palm.

Georgia Lee sat quietly with her eyes closed, dozing off, after they'd exhausted each other in familiar ways Jane had never thought possible when she first started thinking about other girls with both alarm and excitement. After their first night together, so long ago now, Jane distinctly remembered thinking, *If this is what it's like to be in love, to be happy, then I never want to leave Maud.*

Jane. Plain Jane. Nothing but a nobody since the day she was born. No one, in all the lunchrooms where she had eaten at the end of a long table way at the back, all the playgrounds where she'd found a spot against a wall, all the classrooms where she'd kept her head low. Elementary school, middle school, high school. Jane had let herself feel invisible. But then she'd met Angie, the closest she'd ever come to a best friend. And then along came Georgia Lee, the closest she'd ever come to love.

She'd been seen. She'd been liked and loved. In Maud. And then she'd lost both. She'd lose them again soon.

Past tense, present. It all collided. Emotions raced across Georgia Lee's face, and Jane's heart hammered.

"Let's leave Maud." A foolish notion, but she'd done a foolish thing. "Let's run."

Twenty-Two

GEORGIA LEE

Nothing had ever felt so good to Georgia Lee as those moments of climax, when every nerve ignited. In the moments before and after, her guilt and shame swelled. Didn't matter the gender of her lover. A needling voice rushed at her. Two opposing devils, one on each shoulder, not even an angel to balance her out. They whispered all the thoughts and deeds Georgia Lee embarked on, not willing to stop, not willing to say no to the moment, that big burst, the one minute of her day when the devils dispersed and there was nothing but that blinding, beautiful sensation.

She breathed in that heady remembrance of yesterdays, tried to keep herself from tripping into the present, where nothing waited for her but hurt. The air thick with their scent, reminding her of how primal they were. Another animal on the food chain. At the top, with no predators, so they'd created them out of each other to compensate. Her body, her mind, her desire a weapon to be used against her.

God hadn't made weapons; man had. But he'd made rocks. And she'd wielded one.

The lie had become the truth. And now she barely remembered the details herself. Wasn't that something? How quickly and efficiently the mind manipulated trauma. But here those devils sat once again. Threatening. One telling her to take Jane up on the offer of retreat. Run. Even if it meant leaving her husband, her children. The other telling her to let Jane go. Let her do what she had always wanted.

If only she knew what Jason had planned.

She twitched.

"Are you okay?" Jane asked.

Georgia Lee opened her eyes. Concern colored Jane's face.

Now or never, she'd thought back then. Tell her the truth. But now had become never the minute Georgia Lee saw Warren on the ground and the look on Jason's face. Like he'd been bested, like she'd stolen something from him. Jane had seen it too. She'd made an assumption. An incorrect one. Georgia Lee had wanted to speak, tell her the truth, but she couldn't. Things happened so fast. They made a plan, executed it, and then made a pact. Days passed, and Warren's body didn't show. Georgia Lee thought everything would be fine. The truth unnecessary. She didn't feel compelled to scan the riverbank or worry that Warren would return like some horror movie villain. He was gone. Never to bother them again. She knew that. Deep in her body.

There'd been no need to tell Jane. But then Jane had confessed, and never had become forever. The truth, lost. Until now.

"I'm sorry," Jane said, interrupting Georgia Lee's thoughts. "I shouldn't have mentioned it." She rubbed at her eyes and then shook her head. "It's stupid."

Now. Those devils sat on her shoulders.

My sins, O God, are not hidden from you; you know how foolish I have been.

Georgia Lee's throat itched. She wormed a hand around the floorboard and found the wine bottle, which had rolled into the back seat during their activities in the front. She popped the cork and tipped the bottle into her mouth, but nothing dropped onto her tongue. She tossed it behind her and chanced a look at Jane. Her hand gripped the door, but she didn't move. Only her bottom lip, like she too wanted to speak but couldn't find the words or the courage.

Jane, sweet Jane. The next time she saw her might be behind bars.

Before Georgia Lee could stop herself, she blurted out, "I killed Warren."

Twenty-Three

JANE

Jane had to have misheard. "Wait. What?"

Georgia Lee took a long breath. "I killed Warren. Not Jason."

"No," she said, not understanding the words. She'd been there. She'd seen her brother. She knew him, better than anyone. His eyes had told her all she needed to know. "That's not what happened."

"In the moment. Right after it happened. You thought Jason did it." Georgia Lee clutched her chest as if horrified by her own admission. "Neither of us actually said he did it, of course. That's just what you believed."

"What I believed?" Jane repeated the words slowly. Like she had believed Angie had helped Jason. Like she had believed Diane had no idea what had happened.

Georgia Lee nodded. "Correct."

Jane repositioned herself to face Georgia Lee. She had to see her mouth say the words because what Jane's ears heard made no sense. "And what I believed, according to you, is that Jason murdered Warren."

Georgia Lee nodded again. "That was my understanding of events."

"Was?" Jane asked.

"Correct. Well, is. I suppose."

"I see." Had Jane hit her head? Had she been blackout drunk that night? Every new revelation made her believe either was possible. She'd come across Jason and Georgia Lee in the woods. She'd seen Warren on the ground. She'd seen blood on both of them. She'd seen the rock in Jason's hand, the anger in his eyes before he noticed Jane, before alarm spread across his face. She'd told him not to worry. That he must've done what was necessary. That she would take care of him. She would protect him.

Neither Jason nor Georgia Lee had said anything. They had just stared at her while she stared at the bloody rock.

Georgia Lee scanned the stations on the radio, which had been playing low the whole time they'd been in the car. She blinked. A lot. Turned up the volume and then adjusted it lower.

Jane smacked the power knob. Georgia Lee startled. Stilled. "You let me believe that Jason killed him instead of you. Is that also your understanding of events?"

"I didn't mean to mislead you." Georgia Lee stared at her hands, which were sweetly clasped in her lap as if she were sitting in church, as if they hadn't been all over and inside Jane moments before. "I believe I was in shock."

The events of that night unraveled on repeat in Jane's mind. There was no new information. No new images or insights by replaying it. Her pulse quickened. "Let me get this straight. Just to be sure. You were so shocked by committing murder yourself that you let me believe my brother did it instead, not you. And you let me confess to a murder I didn't commit and one that Jason didn't commit, and you never said a word until now."

Georgia Lee clenched her hands in her lap. Her lips pursed. "I know, it sounds terrible."

Jane gaped at her. "Because it is. It's terrible. Really shitty, in fact. I confessed to save Jason. I went to jail for him. I'm about to go to prison for him. And you're telling me he didn't even do it?" Jason had never said a thing. Why would *he* lie? Why would he let Jane go to jail—twice—if he knew what Georgia Lee had done? "Are you fucking with me? Is this some kind of joke?"

Georgia Lee breathed deeply and pushed back against her seat. Little pops rang out from her spine. "It wasn't intentional. Everything happened so fast. With Warren. With you assuming Jason did it . . ." She rubbed her face. "I reacted. Poorly. Certainly."

Georgia Lee's tone was earnest, but her words made no sense. "Sounds like your intention was to let someone else take the fall, then and now. Even if you were in shock back then, you still said nothing after I confessed—"

"I couldn't!" Georgia Lee looked pained. "I told you my parents locked me in my room and wouldn't let me out! Your mom blackmailed them into not mentioning my name."

"You never said a thing when we talked about it when we went for pizza after the funeral. You asked me if you could fucking *visit* me. In prison. For a crime you committed." Jane yanked her arms out of the fleece jacket and threw it on the floor. The air in the car had become hot, suffocating. She glared at Georgia Lee. "Forgive me, but I find that more than a little psycho."

"Don't say that." Georgia Lee gripped her head, fingers pulling at the roots of her hair, which reminded Jane of an ex's grandmother, who'd had a stroke and got frustrated when no one understood what she was trying to say. "I didn't know."

"Didn't know what?"

Georgia Lee seemed to struggle with the answer. "That I murdered him."

The proper response would be anger, but Jane was too baffled by what Georgia Lee had said. She could only stare, wide eyed and open mouthed. "You forgot that you murdered him?"

"Yes," Georgia Lee said, as if relieved to finally be understood. She placed a hand on Jane's thigh. "I'm so sorry."

"You forgot? You just tore me a new asshole for leaving behind a photo of us after being arrested for a crime you committed." Jane lifted Georgia Lee's hand off her thigh and shoved it away from her. This was not how things were supposed to go. They were supposed to have a reprieve. At least for ten goddamn minutes before the world came crashing down again. "How the fuck could you forget that you murdered someone?"

"I don't know!" Georgia Lee took a moment to collect herself. "I'm sure there's some literature out there to explain—"

"Literature?" Jane repeated, stunned at what she heard.

Flustered, Georgia Lee yanked her hair behind her ears. "You know. About trauma. The things it can do to the mind."

"Did your parents also send you to a therapist? Ask them to implant some memories of Jason killing Warren instead of you?"

"No! I swear."

"How would you know? You can't remember shit."

Georgia Lee's eyes began to swell with tears.

Jane pressed her hands in front of her, trying to organize everything into logic. "You're telling me now. That means you recently remembered."

Georgia Lee paused, too long. "Yes?" she said, but as if it were a question.

"When?"

Another pause. "That night I dropped you off. After the funeral and pizza."

"And you had, what, a flashback?"

Recognition lit her face. "Yes. I suppose you could call it that."

Jane counted the number of days it'd been since the funeral. A week, maybe more? Time got harder to track the longer she spent in Maud. A week. At least a week, Georgia Lee had known. And she'd said nothing. Without those photos coming to light, would she have admitted it at all? Would she have let Jane believe the lie indefinitely?

Would she have let her go to prison? Anger rippled under the surface of her calm.

"So did you think that fucking me was going to keep me quiet? Or that it would somehow persuade me to go to prison for you because, shit, if I would do it for Jason, I'd do it for you? Was that your big plan?"

Georgia Lee flinched and sat up straight. Her fingers wove in and out, as if trying to put the pieces together. The omissions. The lies, old and new. "I never lied."

"Not telling the truth is the same as telling a lie."

"A lie would have been me telling you, in these words: 'Jason killed Warren.' I never said that."

As the confusion cleared and fury rose, Jane gripped the door handle. "Use whatever wording you'd like. The fact remains: You kept this from me. You only told me when your ass is on the line with those photos, fresh off of fucking me."

"I'm sorry. I don't know how many times I can say I'm sorry, but I will." Georgia Lee placed a hand to her head. Her brow crinkled. "I don't know what happened. I don't . . . I don't know how to explain this to you. I don't understand any of this." She collapsed her head onto the steering wheel to cry.

Jane waited for her to pull herself together. "What does Jason have to say about this? Did he forget too?"

"I don't know." Georgia Lee rubbed at her eyes. "We never talked about it. But something happened. He looked at me—"

"Who?"

"Jason. It's like he didn't want me to say anything."

"When?"

"That night!"

"Why?" Jane tried to trap her irritation given the tears that continued to streak Georgia Lee's face. She failed. "You're not making any sense."

"Neither are you," Georgia Lee said. "You confessed to something you didn't do. You were supposed to keep your mouth shut, but you didn't!"

How many times had Jane beat herself up over that same thing? An impulse decision in the moment that would follow her forever. "Because he's my brother. Because I didn't want him to spend his life in prison for something I caused. Because I love him."

"And I love you!" The words seemed to shock Georgia Lee more than her murder confession. Her face went pale.

"Please." Jane cracked the door but didn't step outside. She wanted out, but more than that, she wanted to inflict pain. "You only ever loved yourself."

"I loved you enough to risk everything. I thought you deserved a better life. One without Warren. I protected Jason that night, same as you. I didn't say anything because I didn't know what to say. I was scared about what I'd done and what would happen. And then you confessed but were released and left town. And then something happened, and I forgot. But I've never loved anyone like I loved you. I would do anything for you. Then. And now."

"So you're going to turn yourself in?" The color drained from Georgia Lee's face. "Yeah, that's what I thought." She'd fallen for it. She'd let Georgia Lee slip under her skin like an infection. "Would you have let them arrest me again, after what happened tonight?" When Georgia Lee didn't respond, Jane's anger grew. "If you killed Warren, then you should've come clean back then. But you didn't, and you have no excuse for that. None." She slapped the back of one hand against the palm of the other, accentuating every point. "Even if your parents did lock you up as you say, you had plenty of time after I was released. You could've admitted it, and the cops would've believed you. They would've gone easy on you. You're a girl from Maud Proper. *You* could've gotten off."

"That's not fair. I can't help where I'm from." Georgia Lee gasped and cried. "And you don't know that. You don't know what they would've done. It would've been anyone's fault but Warren's. You know that better than anyone else. I only meant to hurt him, to stop him from hurting Jason. And me! He hurt me too! Did you forget about that! I didn't know what he would do. He could've killed me!" Georgia Lee's voice cracked. She paused, tried to catch her breath and calm her pulse. "I didn't mean to kill him. And I didn't mean to lie. I'm so sorry, Jane." She gasped out the words. "I'm so sorry."

"You never answered me." Jane pushed the door all the way open, and heat and humidity filled the car. The rain had stopped.

"About what?" Georgia Lee searched her face.

"Did you think fucking me would help you somehow? That if Jason ended up telling them the truth about what you did, I might be more forgiving and go to prison for you?"

"My God, Jane, no. No, of course not. I don't regret it—" Before the words could leave Jane's mouth, Georgia Lee stopped her. "Of course I regret not telling you the truth! But not tonight. Not us. This. Warren hurt you. I told you because I know what I did was wrong. And I will never forgive myself for that. And I don't expect you to either."

"Trust me. I won't," Jane said. "Forgive or go to prison. Not for you."

Twenty-Four

GEORGIA LEE

Everyone said the third time was the charm, but even Georgia Lee had doubts when it came to her salvation. God might forgive her, but what of the rest? Rusty? The boys? Not to mention the one whom she'd harmed the most. She left the laundromat parking lot with every intention of going home and waiting for her fate, delivered either by Jane or Jason. But waiting had done no good thus far. Every time a new Let's Talk About Maud emerged with some new rumor, she felt as though a fist had ripped through her diaphragm. She truly believed she could be suffering a heart attack like her mother. Earlier that week, she'd mentioned it to Dr. Irwin (minus the root cause, of course), and he'd calmly told her it was probably heartburn. After her initial rage at his dismissal, she'd come around to the idea he could be right. But that's what her mother had thought. Then she couldn't help but think perhaps the Lord was trying to tell her something. Or trying to get her to tell something. To use a particular word: guilty.

Even saying the word made Georgia Lee swallow down hard. Despite Jane's admonishment to the contrary, things hadn't been easy for Georgia Lee. Nothing catastrophic, of course. Nothing like what she imagined Jane had gone through, thinking that Jason had been guilty the whole time, being locked up, even if it was juvie. Georgia Lee had been locked up as well! But she often considered her memories of that year as though someone had put stones in her shoes. Reminders of her bad behavior. She'd ignored it for so long she'd told herself discomfort was the price of being a person in the world trying to do good, not willing to believe it was because she'd not taken care of the bad she'd done in the first place.

She'd put them all in an impossible position, begging them not to go to the police. That had been her idea, one that gained traction after Jane wrongly assumed that Jason had killed Warren. Georgia Lee had broken her mind to avoid facing what she'd done. No amount of church or public service could help, and she'd tried. She'd tried to reconcile with Jane, even though it was wrong. She'd squeezed her hand and kissed her and shared something once more in the car, but she knew every time Jane looked at her now, thought of her, Georgia Lee's lie would sit between them. Though Jane would never hear it, Georgia Lee hadn't planned what had happened in the car. But what Georgia Lee had done to Warren was an act of love too. What Georgia Lee had done was for Jane, who so loved her brother that she took the blame for him. But it'd sapped every last bit of love between them. There was no going back. There was no going forward. Not together.

Where had things gone wrong? She considered as she took the ramp onto the highway instead of the road toward home. Had she overhelped? She had. She had overhelped. She had overhelped when her help wasn't wanted. Even though it had seemed like life or death to Georgia Lee. It had. Warren had come at her. He had raised his hand to her, and then Jason had yelled at him to stop. But he hadn't stopped, so Georgia Lee had stopped him. Hadn't she? Her memory clashed with all the lies. When his body didn't show up, they should've gone to the police right then. Georgia Lee should have told the truth. But how were they to know that then? They were young and scared and so had covered their sin. That was their mistake. But Jane had made the mistake to confess. That was all on her.

She pulled into the police station, locked her door and any emotion that might betray her, headed inside, and asked for John. While she waited for him to finish his "business in the back," she chatted with some of the guys about the election. The chat anchored her in the moment, kept her from running out the door, which she considered with every lull in conversation. She crossed her arms to still her shaking body.

They also had lots to say about the news coverage of the photos that were, allegedly, as far as they knew, her. Lots of jokes about them suspecting her of murderous intention all along and how they couldn't wait to see what other juicy details Lovelace would reveal to Let's Talk About Maud next. She fake laughed along with them, except Benjamin. Not the laughing sort, she supposed. Maybe he knew exactly why she was there. Maybe he knew everything.

Just as her resolve had begun to crumble and doubt crept in and led her feet to creep toward the exit, John wandered in from the back room. He gave her a smile.

"What brings you in this late?"

Georgia Lee cast her gaze toward Benjamin. A wave of fear and finality rushed through her. There was no now or never. There was only now or soon, when she was least prepared.

Georgia Lee placed her purse on the counter and took a deep breath. "I'm here to turn myself in for the murder of Warren Ingram."

Twenty-Five

JANE

The trailer was empty, Diane nowhere to be found. Probably out with Gerry, that traitor. Jane had spilled her guts, and he'd gone back to Diane anyway.

She paced the floor, trying to think of what to do with the information Georgia Lee had told her. She texted Jason.

911!

Emergency!

What the fuck?!?

He hadn't responded to the drunken and incendiary text she'd sent from Family Fun, so she doubted her latest round would produce results.

She loosened her shirt, which bunched at the waist. She pulled the fabric to her nose. She could still smell Georgia Lee all over her.

She ripped off her shirt and pants and underwear and threw them on the floor. In the shower, she scrubbed until Georgia Lee was off her skin. Afterward, she returned to the couch, grabbed her laptop, and clicked on the TV. She flipped through the channels in between texting Jason and googling local news. Nothing but reality shows and old episodes of *Law & Order*. She left it on the latter with the volume low enough that it didn't agitate her—and high enough that she didn't feel all alone. She was hardly that. Next door, she could hear a couple talking loudly. Someone somewhere nearby listened to Spanish versions of American pop songs. In the distance, a subwoofer signaled the start of a party. Above it all, she swore she could hear the steady roar of water in the dam.

She turned up the volume on the TV, but it only heightened the questions in her head. How could Georgia Lee have forgotten what happened? Why had Jason let her think he had killed Warren? Did Diane know she hadn't killed Warren?

A tornado of questions with no answers intensified in her head.

She wondered what Georgia Lee was doing at that moment. What she might be thinking, doing. Probably plotting against her. Had she done that already, gotten Jason to go against her, as Angie had suggested?

How the hell was she supposed to convince the cops that Georgia Lee had done it, not her or Jason, after Jane had already confessed?

She needed to calm all the nervous energy that vibrated through her. She needed a distraction, but the only thing that calmed her was going all in on the thing she most wanted to avoid but could not.

She typed *Lezzie Borden* and hit "Search."

For hours, she pored over whatever details she could find about her original confession, about her prospects now. She didn't know what she was looking for, so she wandered down a long and winding trail that led her to web sleuths, people who helped solve mysteries and cold cases from the comfort of their homes. Why the fuck didn't she have web sleuths?

That goddamn confession.

She drank shitty coffee and read through forums and discussion groups. Learned the types of things web sleuths wanted to know when trying to figure out who really killed so-and-so and whether the alleged murder weapon was really the murder weapon.

At 5:00 a.m., blurry eyed and at a dead end, she grabbed a generic-brand yogurt from the fridge and returned to the couch. It'd been hours. No texts from Jason.

Tired but wide awake, she engaged in another futile social media check to see if anyone knew something about her case that she didn't know, which would be a lot considering she didn't know shit. Georgia Lee's last Facebook post was an election flyer. Visually assaultive and predictable. Red, white, and blue all over in mismatched fonts and sizes. About as compelling as a bowl of unseasoned, unbuttered quick grits.

Jason Tran's last Facebook post was the announcement of a fight in Hot Springs at the end of the month. And, as she'd suspected, photos of rock-hard abs and adoring fans.

She yawned and stared at the TV awhile. Finally, she navigated to the Facebook group with which she'd become deeply familiar since landing in Maud, scanned the most recent post, sat straight up, and dropped her yogurt, which splattered strawberry splotches all over the carpet.

"Shit. Shit. Shit."

HOT OFF THE PRESS:
LEZZIE BORDEN'S ACCOMPLICES (!!) CONFESS!

Twenty-Six

GEORGIA LEE

It took Georgia Lee a long time to remember a worse morning than waking up in jail, but she did: the year after she and Rusty had gotten married. The boys had just been born. They wouldn't latch and cried without pause. Her boobs hurt. Her feet were swollen. Her butt was big. She'd not had a good night's sleep in so long she'd forgotten what it felt like. All she wanted was to head down to the Waffle House alone, order a cup of coffee, and eat some bacon and eggs in peace.

She'd let herself shift to darkness. It'd come on swiftly with the boys. Wanting to be the best mother and seeing that perhaps she was not. Wanting them to love her in ways they didn't. Becoming angry with them for not appreciating her the way she wanted.

She stared at the concrete walls, which had been painted white and stayed white. She imagined it'd been some time since the Maud Police Department had locked up anyone longer than the usual overnight stay. Possibly the last person who'd stayed longer than one night was Jane. They had no procedure for what to do with an extended-stay guest such as Georgia Lee. They let her use the real toilet in the hallway instead of the not-at-all private one in her cell. Her privilege afforded her such gifts. She vowed to ensure future residents would also be handled with such courtesy should she be allowed the opportunity. The cot was perfectly fine. She'd always preferred a firm mattress to Rusty's insistence on one that sank "as if on a cloud." Tom even delivered her a bacon-and-egg sandwich on an english muffin, which was as close to that Waffle House dream as she'd come in as long as she could remember.

Tom was older than the rest of the squad. You'd never know it from his soft voice and agreeable personality, but he was a sworn believer in vigilante justice. Charles Bronson was his favorite actor, after all—a random fact Georgia Lee had gleaned from years of dropping by for chats. He'd been kind enough to tell her that if his daughter or granddaughters had gone through the same situation as she claimed she had, he would've encouraged them to act in the same way.

Though no one would believe her if she were to confess it, she felt light. Lighter than she had in some time, what with the weight of what she'd done and how she'd lied to Jane off her shoulders, out of her mind, and into the public realm. She was ready to face her judgment from her family, her friends, her town. Jane, the person she'd hurt the most. That was all that mattered. The only bruise to the day came when Tom escorted her to the interview room, where John and Benjamin waited. How she hated to see Benjamin in the room. How he'd pursued the case when there were plenty of drowned and dead bodies to prove that none were special. No one but Diane missed Warren. She supposed she could give him credit, though. He'd been a good, competent hire. No one would give her credit. Of that she could be sure.

"Handcuffs?" John asked. "Really, Tom?"

Tom opened the cuffs. "She asked for them."

Georgia Lee rubbed her wrists, though it'd been no trouble at all. A quick walk down the hall. It seemed the right thing to do.

John shook his head and told her to sit down, which she did. On second thought, the cot could use a bit more cushion. Her back was in a way.

"You know you're free to go," Benjamin said.

She folded her hands on the table. "I did the crime; I should do the time."

"What kind of sense is this?" John held his hands out on the table, flustered. "What on earth has gotten into you?"

Tom returned to the room and gingerly placed a plastic bottle of water on the table for her. He'd been good to her, bringing her the fresh bottles from the fridge instead of tap.

"You're wasting city resources," Benjamin said.

She uncapped the bottle and drank it all in one fell swoop to spite him. "I'm wasting resources? You're wasting resources! And my time. I told you what I did. I told you how. I told you everything. And I'm not leaving here until you charge me with murder."

"We've already got our murderer," Benjamin said.

He looked at her in the same manner she'd sometimes looked at certain constituents who had no end of complaints about the plans for a new green space and public park as a waste of city resources. The plans had been put permanently on hold; the complaints continued.

"Well, Jane's lying. I did it. Alone. Not her."

Benjamin shifted in his chair, propped his elbows on the table, and rested his chin in his hands. "Funny how you all come in here claiming to have acted alone."

His use of *you all* was peculiar. She refused to respond.

"It seems to me like everyone's lying. And I think I know why." Everyone? What did he know? He opened a folder on the table, found what he was looking for, and pushed the photo of Jane and Georgia Lee from the picture booth toward her.

"We fooled around in a photo booth. So what?" She shrugged and frantically searched for an excuse while trying to act cool-girl calm. "I told her what happened because I knew I couldn't tell any of my friends in Maud Proper. I only knew him through her. She felt bad for me and sorry that he attacked me. She didn't want me to get in trouble for what happened to him because I had protected myself. Honestly, I think she was jealous that I got to him first, which was why she confessed. She was obsessed with me. Said she'd die for me. I didn't tell her to confess. She did that on her own. To impress me." Only a little of what she said was a lie.

"And you were good with that?" Benjamin asked. "Just let that shit ride for twenty-five years without saying a word?"

She could've spit she was so mad. She aimed to make amends and come to justice whether they liked it or not. "I got sick and didn't even know what was going on! Check my school records," she said. "Once I found out, I wouldn't have let her die in prison. I'm telling you the truth. If you recall in your notes—" Here she stabbed the table with a finger and recounted what she'd confessed the night before. She'd left out all the parts that included anyone helping her. It was the least she could do for involving Jane, Jason, and Angie in the first place—even though Jane had already confessed, and it had been Angie's idea to put the body in the boat and send it toward the dam. She'd give her credit for that, but never out loud and never to her face.

Benjamin smiled at her. "As Jane is also aware, based on our conversations, we don't believe either one of you could've taken him down and then hauled his body out to the boat all by yourself without dragging it and leaving a trail behind for someone to find," Benjamin said. "And they did look." Beside him, John nodded like a fool. Instead of investigating Warren's death, Benjamin should investigate how John and his fellow officers had missed all that blood years ago. They'd done nothing but conduct a few halfhearted interviews before Jane got spooked and confessed.

And of course Georgia Lee hadn't done it alone. But she could have. It riled her that they didn't believe she—or Jane!—had the strength. She'd concede the beating she'd given Warren may have been less enthusiastic in reality than her telling, though.

"Never mind swimming against the current near the dam," Benjamin added. "From the notes, it looks like there was a storm brewing that night."

"I was a competitive swimmer in high school. Look it up."

"You didn't weigh but a fraction of what Warren did," John said. "I gotta be honest with you, Georgia Lee. I don't see how you or Jane would've been able to pull off none of it—"

"Unless . . . ," Benjamin interrupted. "You had help. Jane, for instance. Someone else?"

Panic spiked. They weren't supposed to believe anyone but Georgia Lee had committed the crime. They were supposed to end their suspicions. She was supposed to clear Jane's name, keep Jason and Angie out of the spotlight. Take the blame. For all of it. They may have helped her dispose of the body, but she had killed Warren. No one else. Maybe she'd been too weak then to face it. Maybe that was why her brain broke. But she could, would, be strong now. She would face the consequences.

She crossed her arms and focused on a spot on the wall behind them. "Sexism is alive and well in Maud." She was certain they rolled their eyes. It only made her more resolute. "Warren was nothing special. Tall. It was all me. I had no help. Not even from Jane."

"Bigger than you, and all dead weight?" John shook his head. "Why are you telling these lies, Georgia Lee? Is this some sort of stunt?"

Georgia Lee clamped down on a reply, removed her hands from the table, and folded them into her lap. She burrowed her nails into her palm at the implication she could be so stupid as to admit to a crime to win an election. Or lose, to save face, if that's what he was getting at.

"Am I still free to go?" she asked.

"If you want. We've got no use for you until you tell the truth, which is that either you and Jane killed Warren, or you and someone else killed Warren. Or . . ." Benjamin smiled again. "You're covering for two other people." He narrowed his eyes. "Not quite sure why you'd do that, though." He glanced at the photo of Georgia Lee and Jane in front of her. "But I'm sure you have your reasons."

She huffed and tried to further bury her fingernails into her skin to keep them away from his eyes.

John grumbled and walked to the door while Georgia Lee and Benjamin continued their stare down. Finally, Benjamin left the room, too, and didn't return. Rude, especially after she'd consumed all that water. But she did hear him yell at Tom to come and get her—or get rid of her. Either way. The nerve of that man.

She aimed to stay bolted to her spot, facing forward, but her bladder had other plans. After a quick bathroom break, she sneaked back along the hallway and to the interrogation room to begin a sit-in. But the room was no longer empty.

"What are you doing here?" she asked in shock.

Jason startled at the sudden noise and then groaned. "You have got to be kidding me."

He rolled up his sleeves to bare tattooed arms and cut muscles underneath his business casual. He reminded her of the type of guys sororities hired for "sex parties" in college: way too hot to be pizza delivery. After their faux deliveries, they ripped their faux pants off and thrust their groins in screaming women's faces before those same women disappeared into another room to buy sex toys and giggle when they returned with their glittery, content-concealed bags. Despite their mismatched fathers, he and Jane looked an awful lot alike. He smelled like cake icing. And sex. Her knees stung in heady remembrance of youthful nights, but she shut it down before her mind wandered too far. He slung a hand across the back of the chair next to him and watched her.

When their impasse became too much, she spoke. "I confessed."

"To?"

"Murder."

"Jesus Christ." He dropped his head back and let his chin face the ceiling. "It wasn't murder. It was self-defense."

"Same thing."

"It's not," he said and righted himself.

"It's not what?"

"It's not the same," he said, rubbing his face. "Murder is an act of intention."

"I intended Warren to be dead after he attacked me." Now that she could say the words out loud, she couldn't help herself from saying them repeatedly. Emphatically. Lean in, as the business lady said.

"What we committed was noncriminal homicide," he said and tapped his index finger on the table with each word. "As such, I believe a jury of our peers will let us off on the basis of self-defense."

"Who do you think you are? Coming in here defining murder for me like I'm some bumpkin Bottom Feeder and telling me about what *we* committed and what *our* peers will do?"

Finally, he returned his gaze to her and let out a quick laugh that let her know they were so, so screwed.

"Because we all confessed to the same crime."

Twenty-Seven

JANE

Chuck practically trembled.

"Do you need help with that?" Jane asked. Clouds crossed the sky, a holdover from the previous night's rain and hailstorm. All along her frantic run from the trailer to the funeral home, she'd thought, *Maybe I'm wrong. Maybe my brain is playing tricks on me.*

Too late to go back now.

"I shouldn't be doing this." He fumbled with his keys. "You should probably wait around back." He looked around the empty lot. The grass was dew topped. The predawn streets quiet. Not even the birds bothered to sing. "What if someone sees us?"

Her urgency and irritation grew. "They'll think you're my lover and you helped me kill Warren and you can tell them you didn't and you'll be all the rage for a while and then you'll just go back to being plain old Chuck, the funeral home guy. No one will remember it in a month."

He paused his door-opening attempt and stared at her. "Do you want my help or not?"

She snatched the keys from him and opened the door. "Do you want your testimonial?"

He grumbled and rushed inside after her, securely locking the door behind him.

"Follow me." Chuck brushed past her as if they were about to journey through a vast and cavernous crypt full of secrets and booby traps.

"You could have emailed it," she said.

"And leave a paper trail for the police? I don't think so. And if you—"

"I told you. I won't."

"Surely your attorney could provide you with—"

"I don't have an attorney. And I don't have time."

His chest rose and fell in jagged spurts. He analyzed her face, maybe to gauge whether or not she was lying.

"You should get an attorney." Perhaps he'd seen the latest Let's Talk About Maud too. The one that had prompted her to call Chuck.

HOT OFF THE PRESS:
LEZZIE BORDEN'S ACCOMPLICES (!!) CONFESS!

As they say at the start of southern fairy tales,
Y'ALL AIN'T GONNA BELIEVE THIS SHIT!
In a turn of events none of us here at the LTAM saw
coming,
rumors are flying that Jane Mooney's teenage lover,
our very own
Georgia Lee Felony done turned herself in!
For the murder of Warren Ingram!
But WAIT! THAT'S NOT ALL . . .

First. A Programming Note:
According to one of our loyal followers, the proper
term for Georgia Lee's shenanigans is
BISEXUAL.

(Look it up! We did! HOT!)
End Programming Note.

Not only that! Jane's very own brother, local MMA
superstar,
JASON MOTHERFUCKING TRAN
also turned himself in!
(HOLY SHIT! WUT EVEN, Y'ALL?)
On the same night!
[slams fist on microphone]
CAN WE GET A WUUUUUUUUUT?!?

We didn't even know Jason Tran was related
to Jane Mooney. What other secrets are they hiding in
their closets?

Now, we ain't so good at math, but we do know how
to count
to three. That's THREE people who have now confessed
to murdering that man.
Dang. Looks like everybody had it out for that dude.
Must've been a
real sonofabitch. But like we said, murder is murder.

We can't wait to hear what Jane's IRON MAIDEN,
aka Georgia Lee, has to say for herself
(Whatchall think o' that nickname? Throw up some
horns, fellow bangers!)
... and what REALLY went down that night
other than Lezzie Borden and "Bonnie" Lee Lane!
(Another option. Hit us up in the comments with yer
fave!)

[rubs hands together]
IT'S GETTING GOOD, Y'ALL!

#MaudMurderMystery   #BisexualsBisexualsBisexuals
#AndJasonTran #ConfessionSessions

Jason had likely confessed because of the text Jane had sent him about knowing Diane had helped him. There was no other reason she could find. And then there was Georgia Lee's confession in the car. At least she'd come clean before they arrested Jane first. But now she had no idea what they would say about that night and if they'd implicate Jane and Angie as well.

Somehow, everything had spiraled, and someone had gotten the information out to Let's Talk About Maud, and now she was standing in a funeral home with Chuck after going down an internet rabbit hole trying to learn more, anything, something that might help them. Otherwise, they were all looking at murder one. And the crowd was rooting for death.

"What are you waiting for?" Jane asked when she regrouped and got her bearings.

Chuck began to protest but must've thought better of it. He rushed down the hallway past open doorways for rooms meant for mourning and stopped at the end in front of a door located next to a built-in shelf for displays. A gigantic vase of orchids was lit like a painting in a museum. The smell overpowered her. She sneezed. A headache was sure to follow.

Once again, he fumbled with the keys.

She reached for them, but he held them away from her.

"Don't rush me."

She smirked and leaned against the wall to wait for him to figure out how to unlock his own door. She yawned loud and big and swiped at her leaking eyes. The manic energy that had kept her up all night had begun to fade. Across from her, inside one of the dimly lit rooms, a coffin perched on its bier. What Jane could see of the body inside looked like a mannequin. Plastic features with a manufactured tan.

Death penalty.

Somehow it hadn't felt real before. Before seeing it online and from other people. Even though they were comments. Even though everyone knew not to read or believe those or let them get in their heads. But they had.

She wouldn't die for Georgia Lee. Or Jason. Not now.

"Are you coming?" Chuck sneered.

"Sorry. I fell asleep waiting on you." She pushed past him into his office and held a hand to her eyes when he flicked on the lights.

"What are you looking for in this anyway?"

She didn't know. But she did. It was something the web sleuths wanted when they were investigating crimes.

"Don't ask questions," she said.

Chuck grimaced and sat down at his desk. He found the file quicker than he'd been able to unlock the doors. Must've had it resting right on top in case Hollywood came calling. She bet he stared out the window during his lunch break and fantasized about his giant head on a screen, his name and title below, Helvetica Neue, flush left: Chuck Yancey, Funeral Home Director, Maud, Arkansas.

He held the folder to his chest. She rolled her eyes, yanked a piece of paper and a pen off his desk, and scratched out the first thing that came to her head: *Looking for someone to bury the asshole you hated and then murdered? Well, look no further than Yancey Funeral Home! Chuck will get you all settled—and with a smile! —Jane Mooney, aka Lezzie Borden, Maud's famed murderer.*

She thrust the paper at him. "There. Now hand over the file."

He continued to hold the folder to his chest with one hand and inspected her testimonial with the other.

"I can't use this!" He handed it back to her. "This isn't appropriate!"

"Edit it however you want."

"I . . ." He huffed. "You said you'd write a testimonial. This is a joke."

"I don't have time for revisions, Chuck. Write whatever the fuck you want. I don't care about the content. I'm probably going to die anyway."

He thought about it for a bit and then handed her the folder. "Fine. But this is not to leave this room. Not me meeting you here. And not me showing you this file." She grabbed an edge of the folder and tugged, but he held on. "If you try to run away with it, I will have no choice but to tackle you. I played defense in high school."

"Just give me the damn folder." Finally, he let go.

She sat in the same chair she'd sat in to negotiate Warren's funeral service. Chuck wandered to the window and peeked out the shades.

Before she even had a chance to flip the cover, he said, "Don't take too long. I need to get home before Annie wakes."

She ignored him and opened the folder.

The coroner's report. Web sleuths treated it like a holy grail. The dead talking to the living, telling all their secrets. What secrets would Warren's body reveal?

She squinted to try to decipher the coroner's handwriting. Her eyes seemed to jump around the page. She swiped at them and held the paper behind her, toward Chuck. "What's this say?"

He stepped away from the window. The shades hushed closed behind him.

"Let me see."

While he examined the report, she yawned again and stretched her neck, pausing to stare at the ceiling. She opened her eyes wide to try to get them to function properly, but it didn't help.

She blinked rapidly several times before casting her gaze back on the folder in her lap. Behind a cover page, the corner of a photo peeked out.

"Blunt force trauma," Chuck said behind her.

She lifted the cover page slowly, afraid of what she might see in the photo after the gradual reveal of the tile floor in the room where Chuck prepared bodies for burial.

"Murder weapon inconclusive. Officially. Meaning they can't tell from the remains."

There on the metal table, bones. Not like in the shows or classrooms. Not crisp white. But brown. A little busted. A little sad.

"What'd you say you used?"

"I don't remember," she said.

An odd sound escaped his throat. She turned to him.

"How do you not remember how you killed a man?" he asked, incredulous.

She stared at him awhile and then returned to the photos. Something about them. Maybe she was overtired after being overstimulated, but she felt almost sorry. Emotional in a way she couldn't pin down.

She shuffled through the handful of photos taken from different angles and distances. Chuck stood quietly behind her, probably judging. But he probably had never felt fear when walking through the door of his home.

"Are you done?" he asked.

"Yeah." She sniffled and chewed a nail. She didn't know what she had thought she'd find. Evidence. Maybe she was looking for absolution. Or courage. "I just wanted to see."

"Well, you have. And there's nothing there. Nothing to know or tell anyone should they ask . . ."

While he reminded her of her promise not to tell anyone that he'd shown her the report and photos, she put the photos back in what seemed like their original order, but she couldn't be sure. And it didn't matter. She was wasting time, hesitant for reasons only her body, not her brain, had access to.

"I should really get back home," he said.

Something about the bones.

"My wife is going to kill me if I'm not there when she wakes up for coffee."

Something about the arm wasn't right. The hand.

"It's our little tradition. Coffee and buttered toast and . . ."

The missing finger.

Twenty-Eight

Georgia Lee

"Are you awake?"

Tom had installed a sheet between Georgia Lee's and Jason's cells for privacy. He'd also moved their beds to the opposite sides of their cells like they were young, unmarried lovers who couldn't be trusted to sleep in the same bed or room. The lights were out, and the sun had yet to rise after a long, anxiety-filled night. A long night where Jason refused to talk to her. There was nothing to do but contemplate her situation.

Nothing from the other side of the sheet. Not even a bit of snoring for pretend. Georgia Lee eyed her hands. There should be cuffs around her wrists.

She wished she had a drink.

She wrapped the thin blanket around her, padded across the cold floor, pinched a bit of the rough sheet, and rubbed the fabric between her fingers.

"Are you awake?" she asked again. Earlier, before they had a chance to discuss the particulars of their individual confessions further, Benjamin had rushed into the room and separated them. They'd kept Jason in the interrogation room for hours. When he returned, he wouldn't talk to her.

Probably because she'd thwarted his plan to be the hero—which he clearly thought he'd be—and now he applied the silent treatment. He'd mapped out his defense and everything. She wondered if he had a whole wall at home full of note cards and string tying together the plot and outcome and a wall dedicated to his story of revenge and redemption.

She couldn't figure why he'd want to take credit for killing a guy—even to protect Jane—unless he was deeply disturbed about everything that had happened. That being the case, he should go to therapy, not confess to her crime.

She'd spent all that time fretting about the truth coming out and then fretting some more, and here came Jason, stealing her thunder by telling John and Benjamin that *he* had hit Warren on the head, not her. Men were always taking credit for her actions in business, in politics, and now even when it came to her crime. If Jason wanted to take credit so bad, then why did he wait until after she'd gone and done the thing? He'd had years to confess! She'd not let that stand. She'd not let Jason or anyone else take credit for what she'd done. She'd fought a predator. She'd rowed the body in a boat toward the dam. She'd bailed out at the last minute and kicked her legs and cut her arms against the current, terrified that it'd take her under with Warren. Her legs, her arms, her lungs screaming for air. She'd shivered on the riverbank. Grateful to be alive. Terrified of what would come. Her, alone.

With Jason in the picture, no one would believe her. She was simply the body person. Not the hero who had killed her attacker. An accessory, like a purse. Georgia Lee got so wound up she could barely stand still. Her jaw ached from clenching down on the patriarchal oppression under which she suffered. She wished Jane was in the cell next to her instead of Jason so they could commiserate. Maybe they could have gone to McPherson together. Been lovers like in the TV shows. Though she knew that was fiction.

Jason could play the part, but he was no killer. His pants were slim and pegged at his bare ankles. He wore shoes without socks.

"You don't even look like a murderer." Her whisper hit the sheet and puffed it away from her before it stilled.

"Jesus Christ." The sheet puffed back and startled her. How long had he been standing there, so close? "I'm not trying to take credit for it. I'm trying to get us out of this without life in prison. My story makes the most sense," he said. "Or at least it did, until you showed up."

"I showed up first," she said.

"It's not a competition."

"Tell that to the mirror."

He sighed again. "I was there. I saw what happened. Jane and Angie didn't. And we're here now. We have no choice but to figure out how to make this work with the both of us." He paused. "There's a simple solution."

"Oh, I can't wait to hear all your smart ideas and solutions."

He blew out a long stream of air. "I've already told them that Jane lied to protect me, which is the truth. And that I killed Warren and dumped the body."

"That's a lie."

"You're lying by saying you did it all. What's the difference? Besides, I can probably gain the support of the public better than you. You're not exactly a fan favorite."

"Oh, and you are? You think your adoring fans can save you?" After Tom had escorted Jason to his adjoining cell and locked the door, he had asked Jason to autograph something for his grandsons. Quick as a finger snap, Jason sat straighter, smiled wider. The full charm effect. No wonder they didn't believe her.

"I'm not trying to grandstand," Jason said. "And I can't go home. They believe my confession, whether you like it or not."

"But why? Why confess now? Or at all?"

"Why did you?"

She paused. "Because I don't want Jane to go to prison for something she didn't do."

"Well, neither do I."

"But what about me? Were you going to tell them I was involved before I walked into that room? Did I ruin your big plans?"

"No. I wasn't going to say anything about you."

"Well, you should have. You should have told the truth. You and Jane. What's with your need to take credit for something you didn't do? Never in my life have I met two people more invested in being . . ." She searched for the right word. "Martyrs? Heroes?"

Now he was the one to pause. "You weren't the only one who lied to Jane."

"Why did you?"

"Same as you," he said and paused. "Anyway, it doesn't matter. We're both here. We both confessed. Self-defense isn't the issue. What happened to the body is. And I have the background to convince people this is something I would and could do because I fight for a living. People will understand." He laughed cynically. "Some will probably even love it. The point is, I can get off the easiest of all of us. They've made it clear they don't believe you could've done this alone—"

"They said that? They told you all about me?" She'd known nothing of Jason's confession, yet they'd talked all about hers. Laughing. She was a joke to them. "Why would they believe you over me?" she asked, even though she knew the answer.

"I don't know, Georgia Lee. But they don't believe you, okay? Can we agree on that? We're at a standstill. We have to do this together. It started with us, and it needs to end with us."

Us. We. He kept using those words.

Everything had gone exactly the worst way possible. All she had wanted was to lift this burden off her soul. Come clean. Now everything was a mess. She cursed the day she'd broken down and cried again after holding off the tears. Now she hovered on the brink of losing it every minute of the day, no matter what the emotion. She wasn't afraid, though. She was angry that Jason had decided to do the very thing she had done. And on the very day! Worst luck ever.

She didn't know what weighed on his conscience, but she doubted it weighed as heavy as hers.

She managed to stop the threat of tears, but her voice still cracked. "You shouldn't be here. It's not right. I've already messed up once, and I don't want to mess up again. I don't want them coming after anyone else. You've all been through enough, especially Jane. It has to stop. You have to go out there and tell them you had nothing to do with this. That you were being nice. And so was Jane. That's all you're doing, being nice to me. I did this. I shouldn't have antagonized Warren. Jane had warned me. We all knew—"

"Fuck warnings and what we knew. You were just a kid. We all were. He was the adult." Something broke in Jason's voice. He sounded distant, like he was talking to himself, not her. "You didn't do anything wrong. You're not to blame for what anyone did to you. You had to protect yourself."

Tears, dreadful tears. For her, for him. "I'm sorry, Jason. I'm truly, truly sorry."

The sounds of her trying and failing to trap her emotions filled the space. After she succeeded and silence settled, he said, "I'm sorry they didn't believe you."

Tears hovered, but she choked them back. "Thank you. I am strong enough to have carried it out alone, you know."

A pause. She stared at the white sheet and waited.

"You're a woman. We all know how emotional you can be." The sheet fluttered with their sudden bits of laughter. Welcome after all that silence. "But not so emotional you could murder a guy."

"Of course not," she said. "Murder is for men, acting on their desires to protect their property, which happens to still include women. You're the man of the family. You must protect us all." Laughter felt good. Calming. Leveling. She let it course through her until she had no more laughter to give. "I did it. I bludgeoned him to death. Not you. I'm not backing down on that. That's what my attorney will say and what your attorney needs to say despite the Maud Police Department's sexist views on a woman's physical ability to kill a man."

Jason chuckled, his surrender a surprise given his ongoing adamance. "You've always gotten your way."

"I try," she said. "I was mad, you know. When I saw you in that room earlier, after you'd confessed. I'm sorry for what I said when I was angry. I promise I won't tell anyone that I saved you and that you were wearing footie pajamas that night even though you were fourteen, or what have you." She had gotten a bit carried away in her anger. "I'll tell them you tried to stop me, but I was out of control. Blame my hormones if you must."

"That's not necessary."

"It is." She put her lips to the sheet to get as close as possible. "It is necessary. I'm sorry you got pulled into this. I never wanted that to happen. I want to apologize to you, Jason." She straightened her posture and took a deep breath. "I apologize."

Jason paused long enough to worry Georgia Lee, but then he laughed. "You're really very weird sometimes."

Georgia Lee would never understand Jason or Jane, or anyone really, how they found the things she did and said so funny but not in a normal funny way. It hurt sometimes, to be that misunderstood. To be laughed at when all she wanted was to say sorry. To be good. To be kind.

"I'm asking you to forgive me. You don't have to. I know that. But I have to ask."

"Isn't that an AA thing? Asking for forgiveness? Making amends?"

"It's a Christian thing. Perhaps they stole it."

"Are you decent?" he asked, which startled her.

She had certainly tried to be, to varying results. "What do you mean?"

"Do you have clothes on?"

Puzzled, she looked down until she caught his meaning. She'd not changed out of her clothing but had slipped off her bra. She pulled the blanket tightly around her shoulders. "Yes."

He pulled the sheet aside and stood before her. "I, Jason Tran, forgive you, Georgia Lee Lane, for involving me in a murder."

She gripped the blanket tighter. "You're making fun of me."

"Yes. I am. It's the least you can allow me."

"That's fair." She couldn't shake how similar he looked and acted to Jane despite having a different father. Diane's genes were as heavy handed as her. There was the dry humor and sarcasm. The way they could make fun of her but she could still laugh and like them afterward. The way they looked at Georgia Lee. Not unlike a zoo exhibit, but still.

As if reading her thoughts, Jason asked, "Does Jane know you're here?"

"No. You?"

"No."

"Well," she said. "That'll be a fun conversation."

Not that Jane would speak to her about it. Georgia Lee would need to hear the particulars from Jason, including, most likely, Jane's suspicion that Georgia Lee had tried to trick her with sex. But what Georgia Lee had felt in the car was real. She'd thought it'd been real to Jane as well. But to Jane it was only sex, brought on by fear and an uncertain future. She had to remind herself of that. They might have worked in the past, but they would not work in the future. It helped to tell herself this. It soothed the ache.

"Can I tell you something?" he asked.

The request surprised her. "I suppose."

"I actually thought I murdered him that night."

"With the rock?"

He shook his head no. "I put roach killer in his food for weeks. Even his Bud Light."

"You did?" She remembered the time he had spit in Warren's drink behind his back. Seemed he was doing more than that.

He laughed. "Yeah. Fucking hated that guy."

"Did he not know?"

He shrugged. "He and Mom were always so wasted. I could've put a gun in his mouth with his own hand and pulled the trigger, and he wouldn't have noticed." He paused. "I should've done that instead."

She'd never heard him talk this way. But then, she barely knew him now, as an adult.

"And you thought that's why he died?"

"Of course. I was young and stupid. I didn't think it would do anything that bad. I just wanted to make him sick. But then he died, and I thought for sure they were gonna arrest me and blame me."

"Does Jane know? Is that why she confessed?"

"Of course not. I'd never tell her. Besides, she'd never believe it."

Georgia Lee could hardly believe it. The sweet, quietly funny kid who sat next to her on the couch and shared popcorn? Impossible.

"Warren did look a little rough that night. Perhaps it did affect him." She recalled the vomit on Warren's shirt. A vague recollection of him saying that Diane had hit him over the head with a beer bottle. The confused looks. It hadn't affected his ability to hunt her in the woods. Some things were innate, she guessed. "No wonder you feel so responsible for my crime."

"Well, you could say I loosened the lid for you."

"Loosened the lid?" She didn't catch his meaning. And then she did. "How dare you!"

Before she could object further, the lights burst on in their cells.

She and Jason held their hands over their eyes and squinted. Tom walked to Georgia Lee's cell and unlocked it. Then he unlocked Jason's. Neither one of them was offered handcuffs.

"You two," Benjamin said, as if they had cellmates and might be confused as to whom he was speaking. "Let's go."

"What time is it?" she asked Tom.

He checked his watch. "'Bout seven a.m. or so, ma'am."

Too early for anything but bad news. My God. McPherson. They were sending her to McPherson, Jason to wherever they sent the men. She had expected this, but not so soon. She'd just confessed. She held both hands to her diaphragm and tried to slow her breathing.

"Where are we going?" she asked Benjamin. "What's happening?"

He held the door open with one hand, the other held a manila folder. No answer.

Tears dropped onto her shirt. "Where are we going?" she asked again, the panic creeping higher in her voice.

"It's gonna be okay," Jason told her.

How could he say that? What did he know?

For the first time, his smile didn't seem forced. So calm. Not a shadow of doom on his face, like he knew something she didn't. Like everything would actually be okay.

For him.

Twenty-Nine

JANE

Jane's knuckles hovered above the door handle. As a kid, she had kept a close eye on the door, waiting for the slightest turn of the knob to reveal a figure who meant her harm. Either a stranger or whichever man walked through the door, trailing after Diane. One time, Jane almost hit Jason with a metal baseball bat when he slipped into their room in the middle of the night after using the bathroom or doing whatever. Maybe reading comics on the couch. The terror she experienced standing at that door now felt no less than when she was a child.

Though it was warm out, her breath fogged the dirty glass. Anxiety and adrenaline and doubt surged through her. Maybe she was wrong. She could be overtired. Tired people did dumb things all the time.

She heard the TV on low, turned the handle, and entered.

Diane sat on the couch. She didn't say hello or offer any other words. The blankets and sheet and pillow Jane used every night were smashed up in one corner of the couch. Diane propped her cigarette on top of her crossed legs. She stared at Jane but didn't make a move.

Jane looked around the room. "What are you doing up this early?"

Diane responded with what amounted to a low snarl. She reminded Jane of chained dogs she, Jason, and Angie had passed on their walks to school. Their chains looked sturdy, but their mouths told Jane they could snap those chains like twigs.

"I went for a walk," Jane offered, even though Diane hadn't asked. "Couldn't sleep." She made a show of yawning and stretching even though she felt wired, as if on uppers. "I'll probably try to get a few hours in, though. In case."

In case they arrested her alongside Jason and Georgia Lee. The whole lot of them now cast in the same crime.

Diane didn't move when Jane grabbed her blanket and headed to the hallway. Her ears buzzed with adrenaline.

"Where are you going?" Diane shouted behind her.

"To my old room."

"Why?"

Jane paused and turned to her. "To sleep."

"I told you there ain't no bed in there."

"I know. But you're in here. And—"

Diane stubbed out her cigarette and stood. "Nobody's stopping you from sleeping in here."

"I thought maybe since you're up you—"

"I've got somewhere to be anyhow." Diane looked around as if searching for the place she had to be.

"I'll just grab my things from the bedroom, and then I'll come back out here."

"What things?"

"My clothing." Jane tried to pull on her usual mask of exasperation and sarcasm, but she couldn't hide what she felt certain was fear coming through her voice. Her tongue practically vibrated with it. "I thought I'd change before taking a nap."

Diane eyed her. "Why do you need to change?"

"I just need some clean clothes." Despite her nerves, Jane rushed through the hallway.

Diane followed closely behind. "What are you doing putting your clothes in there?"

"There was nowhere else to put them," she said. "I didn't want them to be in your way in the living room."

Diane made it to Jane's side faster than Jane would've ever expected. Her eyes had that particular raged look in them she got before a fight. The kind she got before every final blowout with a boyfriend that sent them packing. "You should've asked me before putting your stuff in there. I told you there's no room."

"What does it matter?" Jane grasped the door handle. "It's just a bunch of shit you don't use."

"You don't know that! There's nothing for you in there."

"Yes, there is. My clothes." She had to get in that room. Find that shoebox. That photo of the old boyfriend. The one with the missing finger. The one who had disappeared. But they all had, hadn't they? Every boyfriend. Impossible and outlandish possibilities rang like sirens in her mind. They left. They all left. Sometimes they stayed for months, other times only weeks. But they had one thing in common: there one day, gone the next. Without a word. As if they'd never existed. None of them returned. There was never a moment of kissing and making up.

She'd actually cried when Missing Finger left. She'd liked him. She and Jason had begun to think of him as their dad. They talked about how amazing it would be when they could all live together. They would be a family.

Diane had shrugged when Jane asked where he'd gone and what had happened and said, *Good riddance.*

What had happened?

If she could just see that photo. Confirm which finger. It was madness. Pure madness. She'd been up all night, drinking coffee. Her brain was going haywire. But she had to see. "I'll just be a minute—"

Diane grabbed her by the arm, yanked her off balance. She wedged in front of Jane, blocking the door. "I told you not to put shit in there!"

The cold stare coming from Diane nearly choked Jane's courage. "Okay. Calm down. I'll grab my suitcase and then there won't be anything in there." When Diane didn't move, she grew bold. "Are you gonna let me get my suitcase?"

Rage flared on Diane's face. Before Jane knew what was happening, Diane had opened the door and rampaged through the room, throwing shit every which way until she found Jane's open suitcase and threw that out the door at Jane, hefting it easily despite the size.

Jane held her hands up to block it. "Jesus Christ."

"Here!" Diane threw a shoe, a pair of pants, an empty bottle of lotion that didn't even belong to Jane. "Take your shit and go!"

Jane dodged an unidentified flying object coming her way. "You don't have to be—"

"There! There's your shit!"

An empty tape dispenser hit Jane's face. "Ow!"

Shirts and underwear and socks confettied around Jane. She tried to see inside the room, to locate the box with the photos, but Diane stormed out and slammed the door shut. Hair fell over her sweat-beaded face.

"There. There's all your shit. Now stay out of there." She started down the hallway but then paused. "Why are you even here? You should be in jail. Why don't you take your shit and just go on and get out? I'm sick of looking at you."

Jane's hands shook as she gathered her clothes off the floor. But she could only fight one battle right now, and that was how to get inside that room.

As soon as she closed her suitcase and prepared for a conciliatory speech—something, anything to get in that room—Diane's hands were at her throat.

Thirty

JANE

Startled, Jane scrambled for something to throw, something to defend herself with, but all her hands found was a shoe. She raised it above her head and started hitting behind her.

Diane clenched Jane's neck tighter as she screamed, "All this time you knew Georgia Lee killed him!"

Jane struggled to breathe but finally managed to break free from Diane's grip. She scrambled away from Diane and ended up back in the living room. She rubbed her throat, shocked.

"You knew." She raced toward Jane, finger stabbing the air, shrieking out her words. "And you hid it from me. You didn't say a thing. You lied to me. All these years. You knew all along. You were protecting her."

"I didn't—" Before she could say more, Diane pummeled her with her fists. Though her limbs were twigs, the punches landed in sharp little stabs. Jane batted her away. When that didn't work, she hurried into the kitchen, the table between them. They stood across from each other, both panting like wild animals, daring the other to make a move.

Finally, Jane was able to catch her breath. "I didn't know until last night. Jason didn't even tell me what happened. Georgia Lee did. She never meant for anything bad to happen. Warren attacked her."

"Warren would never touch her! She's a lying bitch!" Spit flew across the table. Diane continued to rail against Georgia Lee. Sometimes coherent, mostly not. How she'd probably come over in a seductive outfit—which would've made Jane laugh if not for the tears and snot rolling down Diane's face and the throbbing pain in Jane's throat—and had come on to Warren and then gotten mad at him for not wanting to fuck her. "He'd never touch her!"

"She defended herself," Jane said. "And Jason."

"Of course she's gonna say that." Diane yanked her purse off the chair and threw it at Jane's head. "I'm going to make sure they fry her ass."

"What about me?" Jane's whole body pulsed, fight or flight. "You were willing to let me fry, too, even though you knew I didn't do it and thought Jason had. You *knew* Jason had done it. You helped him."

She repeated the words until Diane acknowledged them.

"What are you talking about?" Diane gasped for breath.

"I know you helped Jason hide what happened that night."

Briefly, the mask fell, and Jane caught the truth before the lie. "You're lying! You've always lied! You lied all the time because you were jealous of me and my boyfriends. You're a lying liar!"

"Jason knew Georgia Lee killed Warren. He's the one who lied to you about everything. Not me."

"What?" Diane shook her head in confusion.

She still wanted Diane to want her. To feel something, to love her, to hold her, to mother her. If Diane offered it, Jane would take it. She'd forgive her. She'd love her back.

"Jason lied?" Diane crumpled to the carpet in tears.

"Yes, your beloved son. He lied to you." Jane wielded every word like a hammer, wanting to inflict as much pain as possible. "He let me take the blame even though he knew Georgia Lee killed Warren. He protected her." It pained her to say those words out loud. "He lied to me too."

Diane sniffled and wiped her face on the bottom of her shirt. Little ripples of belly flesh hung over her pants. Jane hated to see the scars and ruined skin that childbirth had wrought and that had never left despite her thin frame. Jane and Jason still clung to her, no matter how hard she'd tried to rid herself of them.

"Why would he lie? To me?" The volume and pitch of each word grew as it escaped her mouth.

"You're upset that Jason lied about Georgia Lee but not me?" She tried to tamp down the incoming anger, but it swarmed. "You told me you hoped I'd fry in the electric chair. Even though you knew I didn't do it." Tears poured down her face. "You knew I didn't do it. And you said those things to me."

Diane shook a finger. "All you had to do was behave. But you couldn't do that. You had to egg him on. Make him mad. And then you turned Jason against Warren. Against me."

The words whiplashed Jane. "How could you say that? You watched us cry and worry about every little thing we did. And when Warren hit me, you told me not to tell anyone!"

Diane's face didn't crumple. Instead, she burrowed down into resentment. Her frown lines deepened along her mouth. "He never hit you."

"Now who's lying?" Jane squatted in front of her. She didn't need a barrier now. She wasn't a little kid anymore. "He hit you, and you asked us to lie. He hit me, and you asked us to lie. Then he hit Jason. If you'd seen it, you would have asked him to lie too."

"He never touched Jason." Little bits of spittle hit Jane's lips. She swiped her arm across her mouth.

"He did. But the last time was down by the river. He hit Jason. And Georgia Lee did what you should have done all along but never had the courage to do. You've never been a mother to him, and you certainly haven't been one to me."

The slap came as a shock. Then the next and the next. The flurry of Diane's hands startling and propulsive. Jane finally captured both of Diane's arms and pinned them behind her, not without catching an elbow to the eye and another to the ribs. Diane struggled like a catfish on the line. Jane wrestled her to the carpet, and all the while they simultaneously yelled at each other to stop. A cacophony of wallops and words.

At last, Diane stilled.

Jane let herself believe their struggle had come to its end, but as soon as she loosened her grip, Diane headbutted her. Jane collapsed backward and gripped her forehead. Stars spotted the ceiling. She snaked her way to the couch and slumped against it. Diane strung her limbs haphazardly against a kitchen table chair that had been knocked askew and on its side. Her hair hung in strands across her face. Her cheeks flushed with rage and exertion. Her chest rose and fell in rapid succession. She looked like a trapped animal.

"Warren never hit you. He never hit any of us," Diane said.

There was no fighting her. No winning. No logic or reasoning.

"He wasn't the one who gave you a concussion either." A string of spit fell from Diane's mouth onto her shirt. "That was me."

Jane didn't want to feel anything. She wanted to be dead to this world and this woman. Despite everything in her that shouted to be calm, try to reason with her, Jane's heart pounded with want.

"Mom . . . ," she pleaded. Her throat tightened around the question she'd always wanted and been afraid to ask. "Do you really hate me so much?"

The pause said it all, but Diane lifted her head in defiance. "I don't hate you." Diane's mouth curled into a snarl. "Most days, I don't even think about you."

The love of a mother was something everyone talked about. Like it was a promise. A guarantee. A foregone conclusion. If this were a movie, Jane and Diane would somehow figure out how to resolve their differences. They'd have a difficult but heartwarming reunion. The audience would understand why Jane was mad, but they'd still ask her to forgive Diane so she could be forgiven herself for harboring such ill will toward her mother. After all, Diane had been a battered woman. Sure, she'd done some battering herself. If Jane didn't reconcile, she'd be the bad guy. Not Diane. Because maybe Diane hadn't known any better. Maybe her parents had not loved her enough. Or maybe they had loved her enough, and Diane was simply flawed. Who didn't love a flawed character? Movie Diane, unlike Real Diane, would fall to her knees and cry. She'd proclaim her sorrow and sorries about the things she'd let slide. The things she'd done. She'd been emotionally compromised. And Movie Jane would go to Movie Diane. They'd embrace. They'd cry. They'd forge a new life out of the ashes of the old.

But this was real life.

Jane stood. Diane mirrored her. They faced each other.

"What happened to the guy with the missing finger?" Jane's chest tightened from nerves. "Your old boyfriend. What was his name?"

Panic shadowed Diane's face and then disappeared as quickly as it'd come. "Who?"

"The guy with the missing finger. Remember him? He was a nice guy. But then he disappeared."

"I don't know who you're talking about." Diane swiped the hair out of her face. Her gaze darted around the room. "I don't know what you want. But you—"

"What happened to him? I saw his picture in that box you keep, the one with all the other pictures of all these other men." Her face heated. "I saw his photo. I saw it in the box. What happened to him? What happened to the others?" Madness. Her mind had turned to madness. But she had to know for sure. "What did you do?"

"What did I do?" Diane practically cackled. "I didn't do shit. They're the ones who—"

"The body." She thought she might collapse from lack of air. *Say it,* she told herself. "It's—"

Out of nowhere, Diane brushed the hair out of Jane's eyes, startling her. She held onto Jane's shoulders and looked at her with what Jane could only interpret as pity. Then she grasped the back of Jane's head and pulled her close, so close, her fingers twined so tight the roots of Jane's hair felt liable to give and fall to the floor. Pain pulsed at her scalp.

"Nothing happened to him or them," Diane said, her grip tightening. "And nothing happened to you."

Before she could pause to think about what Diane meant, survival took over. Jane yanked her head away. Searing pain followed from the tuft of her hair left hanging in Diane's grip.

She rushed down the hallway, knocking pictures off the wall as she tried to keep from stumbling. Inside the room, she pushed the clutter out of the way until she found the shoebox. It was still there. She grabbed it, held it in front of her, and raced to the bedroom door.

She ricocheted backward and almost fell but managed to stay upright.

Diane looked as stunned as Jane felt. They both looked down.

A small box cutter was lodged in the cardboard.

"What the fuck?" Jane whispered.

Before Jane could recover, Diane yanked and yanked until she released the box cutter. Then she lunged for Jane.

She cut her finger. Her hand. Her face. Any strip of skin she could find.

Jane wielded the box as a weapon and shoved Diane into the wall repeatedly. Diane screamed and shrieked, but Jane kept shoving her. Again and again. All the while, Diane lashed out with the box cutter, slashing Jane's exposed skin.

Jane held the box away, closed her eyes, and hit and hit and hit, and then the box slipped from all the blood and Jane dropped it. She scrambled to grab all the photos that had spilled out.

She ran out the door.

She ran into the street.

She ran until she almost got run over by a car, whose driver jumped out and screamed.

But Jane kept running. Because she had the box.

She had the box.

Thirty-One

Georgia Lee

"Tell us again." Benjamin glared at her.

"We told you." Georgia Lee gripped her head. "There's nothing else to say."

"What was Jane's involvement?"

"For the last time, she wasn't there," Jason said.

Benjamin's chest rose and fell with irritation. "You've all said a lot of things, none of them consistent, which leads me to believe none of them are true."

"Jane was protecting me," Jason said. "She thought the police were going to lock me away, so she took the blame. That's the truth."

Georgia Lee clasped her hands. "It's true. I swear he's telling the truth."

"None of you have told the truth," Benjamin said. "Why did Jane lie? Why did you both decide to confess last night? What prompted that?"

"Nothing!" The agony of Georgia Lee's conversation with Jane still ached. Now she fully understood why Jane had confessed to the crime years ago. "I told you. Nothing!"

John shifted uncomfortably in his seat. "Let it go, Benjamin. They confessed. It's enough."

But it wasn't enough for Benjamin. He was chasing the truth. A confession was hardly that. It was just words. Words were easy to tear apart, unlike proof. Evidence. And from all Georgia Lee had seen, they had none of that.

"We confessed," Jason said, still calm. He eyed Benjamin almost as if he were staring at someone across the bar, contemplating whether or not to buy them a drink. He glanced at Benjamin's manila folder and lifted an eyebrow. "Unless you have something to share."

They locked eyes. The clock ticked down the seconds of their show-down. John and Georgia Lee watched them, waited. Any second now one of them would explode.

The door flashed open and slammed the wall. Georgia Lee screamed and dropped to the floor, covering her head with her hands. John joined her. From her vantage point, she could see Benjamin and Jason in mir-rored positions, hands clutched to their chests from being startled. Also from her vantage point, she recognized the shoes, the pants of the per-petrator who had crashed into the room and nearly scared them all to death. Georgia Lee raised her head. Eyes level with the table, she witnessed a panting, bloody Jane, a box in front of her.

"It's not him," she said, ragged breath barely getting out the words. "The man you found. It's not Warren."

Thirty-Two

GEORGIA LEE

"Jane," Georgia Lee eased herself off the floor, where she'd collapsed in fright. "What happened to you?"

Her face and arms and clothing were slashed as if she'd run into a field full of barbed wire and just kept going, never stopping, until she reached her destination. A variety of red lines, some light, some deep. Blood had wept in rivulets and dried on her skin. Her hair stuck to her scalp from blood and sweat, as if she'd run the whole way. Her eyes were red, wild.

"It's not Warren. The bones. They're not Warren's." Jane dropped the box on the table. The metal table legs rattled. Their plastic cups of water spilled. "I know whose bones they are, though. And I know who killed him."

Not Warren? "What?" Georgia Lee whispered.

Jason's eyes landed on the box. He rushed to Jane and put a hand on her arm, but she shrugged it off. What did she mean, not Warren?

Laser focused on Benjamin, she kept repeating, "It's not Warren."

Benjamin said nothing. John looked like he had entered a scene he didn't belong in.

"It's not Warren."

"Jane." Jason petted Jane's arm, tried to get her to turn toward him, but she glared at Benjamin. "Maybe you should sit down."

"No. I'm not going to sit down!" Georgia Lee had never heard Jane yell at Jason. Not once. She'd always been comforting, motherly.

"Can we get her some water or something?" Jason's veneer of calm shattered.

The whole room fell silent. They watched Jane. Finally, she unlocked her eyes from Benjamin and noticed Jason as if for the first time since she had rushed into the room, even though she'd just yelled at him. He held her by both arms. A smile full of relief broke on her face, giving her the appearance of some disaster survivor.

"It's not him," she told him, soothingly this time. And then she turned to the others, joyful. The words coming out maniacal.

It's not him!

It's not him!

Not him? How could it be? Georgia Lee dribbled a bit of saliva out her mouth, like a fool. How long had she stood there with her mouth open?

"Then who is it?" Georgia Lee asked quietly.

Jane ignored Georgia Lee, grabbed Jason's hand, and pulled him with her toward Benjamin. That manic smile still plastered on her face. "It's not him!"

"Maybe we should sit down," Jason said. He tried to remove his hand from Jane's, but she held on tight. Georgia Lee didn't understand what was happening. "She's obviously under duress. We should—"

"There." Jane pointed to the box. Between her wide-open eyes and the slashes that covered her, she looked possessed. "In there. There's a photo of a man with a missing finger in there. He's—"

"Let's all just take a beat," Jason said. The vein at his temple looked like it wanted to uncage itself from muscle and skin. Why did he keep interrupting her? What was going on? Georgia Lee felt like she'd been drugged and couldn't keep up with the conversation.

Meanwhile, Benjamin pulled the box toward him. "What's this?"

"You don't know what you're saying," Jason said to Jane, his voice full of urgency and pleading, though it was obvious he was trying and barely managing to stay calm. He rubbed his thumb across Jane's cheek, wiping a swath of blood. "You've clearly been through something. We should get you checked out. Make sure you're okay." He turned to Tom, Benjamin, John. "Could we get some help here? A paramedic? She's lost a lot of blood. She's—"

Georgia Lee found her voice. "Are you okay?" she asked Jane.

"No, I'm not fucking okay." Jane wrenched herself away from Jason and avoided Georgia Lee. She planted herself in front of Benjamin. "Our mother came at me with a box cutter when I tried to get this box out of the house. There's only one reason why." Her eyes blazed. Georgia Lee swapped her attention between the three of them, trying to make out what was happening. Tom stood vigilant as ever, awaiting instructions. John stood in the corner, motionless. "She tried to kill me. Just like—"

"She doesn't know what she's saying." Jason closed his eyes briefly, swallowed as if it took great effort, and then planted that forced smile on his face again. "She's clearly been through something traumatic—"

"You need to go arrest her before she takes off and you can't find her."

"Arrest her for what?" Benjamin asked, the only one in the room who seemed to understand what was happening even as he asked the question. It's almost like he was teasing it out of her. Getting Jane to say words he already knew.

Georgia Lee watched, her head spinning with questions about what Jane held in the box and why she'd run over here. But mostly why Jason wanted Jane to stay quiet.

Jason yelled at them, "Can one of you do something? She's lost a lot of blood."

"What are you waiting for?" Jane screamed. "She lives at number fifty-one Maud Estates, out by the river, in case you're not fucking familiar with where we live. Do you want her phone number too? 'Cause I can give that to you." No one moved. "You have to go get her before she runs away!"

Georgia Lee watched it all in confusion. Her blood beat so fast she thought she might pass out. John and Tom looked about as confused as Georgia Lee felt. Jane was a tornado, Jason the frantic one trying to contain the storm. Benjamin the outside observer, taking it all in, asking the questions. On the edge of something.

"What is this?" Benjamin asked again and removed the lid from the box.

"A box of men." Jane's eyes lit up, as if finally being heard after years of speaking without anyone hearing her. "From our mother's house—"

"A box of men?" Benjamin asked. The question came out tentative. "Like she's collecting them?"

"Photos, all these random men. Other things too. Like, mementos."

"Stop talking." Jason glared at Jane. "Don't talk unless you have a lawyer."

"I don't need a lawyer." Her words were lashes off her tongue. "Diane does."

Jason's chest rose and fell. What was going on?

Benjamin flipped through the photos. "Who am I looking for, Jane?"

She plunged her hands in the box and searched. All the while, Jason held his hands on his head, elbows spread out at the sides like a bird, looking like he wished he could use them to fly away from there.

After a while, Jane found the photo she was looking for. "Him."

"Who is he?" Benjamin asked.

"I don't know his name. But it's him. The guy you found. I don't remember his name." She turned to Jason. "Do you?"

Jason blinked but didn't respond.

"Why do you think it's him?" Benjamin asked.

"The missing finger."

Benjamin stopped looking at the photo of the man and focused on Jane.

"I saw the photos," Jane offered before Benjamin could ask. "From the coroner."

Benjamin kept whatever he was thinking concealed. He grabbed a handful of the other photos from the box. "And these men? Who are they?"

Jason held his hand over his mouth.

"Old boyfriends, or whatever, of Diane's," Jane said. "They came in and out. They never showed up again."

Georgia Lee stepped forward to get a closer look. There were maybe twenty or so in all. Random. Some posed with Diane, others alone. They sat on Diane's couch. At the kitchen table. At a bar with Christmas lights strung haphazardly along the walls. The man in the photo Benjamin held sat by the river, his arm wrapped around Diane. His hand making an okay sign. His ring finger was missing after the knuckle.

Benjamin's eyes met Georgia Lee's, and recognition washed over his face. He tried to telegraph something to her, some shared knowledge, but she couldn't parse his meaning. Her mind went blank. What was he thinking? What did that look mean? Then she remembered the conversation from her backyard: the missing men.

He lifted the box and handed it to Tom. "Take this into evidence. And get these two out of here."

The look Benjamin had given her unmuted Georgia Lee. "What's happening?" She didn't know why, but she started to cry. "I don't understand what's happening."

Georgia Lee, Jane, and Jason surveyed each other in silence for a while, which brought to mind imagery of deer in the woods, caught by hunters, waiting to see what fate would decide. Then Jason's face changed, a look Georgia Lee couldn't decipher.

Finally, Jane spoke. "It's not Warren."

"I know," Benjamin said and looked at John in a way that reminded Georgia Lee of when the boys were young and screamed, *I told you so, I told you so* over and over. Tom gripped the box. John wrenched the hat in his hand.

"What do you mean you know?" Georgia Lee asked.

"She's right," Benjamin said flatly and tapped the manila folder on the table. "We got the DNA results this morning. The remains aren't Warren's."

Georgia Lee stumbled back into a chair and nearly tipped over.

If the bones weren't Warren's, then whose were they? And where was Warren?

Thirty-Three

JANE

Jane didn't want to see a medic, she wanted to see Benjamin arrest Diane. Whatever love she'd wanted from—and wasted on—Diane was gone after what she'd discovered and what Diane had done. She'd tried to stab her. She had really tried to stab her.

She brushed the medic's hands away, but that didn't do much to stop them. The medic had given her something. Maybe a sedative. Jane felt calm, no pain. But desperation clawed under the surface.

"Where's Benjamin?" The medic didn't answer. "Could you find Benjamin?"

"Drink this," the medic said and shoved a bottle of something in her face.

"What is it?" Jane asked.

"Electrolytes. You're dehydrated." They wiped at another slash. Jane jumped at the cold sting of alcohol along one of the hundred little cuts that Diane had inflicted on her body. "And you should be at the hospital."

Jane didn't remember details, just great swaths of action that could be summed up as fighting, running, yelling, sitting, resisting any efforts to remove her from the police station until Jason was released. All the things in between were a little fuzzy, like when Jason and Georgia Lee had left the room. What happened after that was a blank.

"Do I need stitches?"

The medic examined Jane's cuts. "Probably."

"Will I die if I don't get them?"

The medic grimaced. "This should hold you for a while. But you need to go to the hospital when you're done here. You might have other injuries. Understood?"

Jane nodded halfheartedly.

After the medic finished with Jane and packed up their things, Jane sat in the interview room alone for an indeterminate amount of time. She wondered if they had locked the door but didn't have the energy to get up and check. The room was bright as hell from the fluorescents, like a work conference room. Not at all like in the TV shows. All white walls with stains and broken ceiling tiles. No two-way mirror in sight. She glanced at the camera mounted from the ceiling. Still broken. Just like the last time she'd been in this room.

"Fucking Maud," she whispered.

When Benjamin came in some time later, Jane lifted her head off the table. She must've fallen asleep. She felt like a pincushion, head throbbing.

She wiped her eyes and mouth. "Did you arrest Diane?"

"It's in progress," he said.

"For murder?"

"For assault. On you."

She groaned. "It should be murder. When can Jason leave?"

Jane refused to acknowledge Georgia Lee. She wouldn't. Couldn't. One detail she did remember: the look of shock on Georgia Lee's face when Benjamin confirmed what Jane said was true.

Benjamin tilted his head as if not understanding her.

"Are you going to let Jason go now?"

"No."

"Why not?" Maybe her blood sugar was crashing because she got woozy and gripped the table. "You said the DNA doesn't match. And I gave you the photo of the guy whose body Gerry found."

"Just because you say something doesn't make it true. Your confession is plenty evidence of that."

"Well, if the bones don't belong to Warren, then why is Jason still being held?"

He cleared his throat, looked down at the paper, and took a deep breath. "Because he confessed to murdering Warren."

"I know," she said. "He confessed. But to that murder. Not this murder." His irritation at her irritation irritated her. "And—"

"There's no body?" Now he held her in a staring contest. "Is that what you were going to say?"

She stared right back. "Yeah. I was. Because how can there be a crime if there's no body?"

"Because—"

"He confessed. Got it. But technically . . ."

"Technically, you confessed to murder. Then, Georgia Lee confessed to murder. And then, because this is the most ridiculous town I've ever worked in, Jason confessed to murder but then changed his story and said that he didn't commit murder but helped Georgia Lee get rid of the body. And they both said that you had nothing to do with it, despite your confession."

"Well, they're wrong."

He steepled his fingers. "Are they?"

She didn't know what to say to that.

"So you're not going to let Jason go?"

He stared at her.

"Sorry. Just wanted to be clear. I assume this will be a lot like what happened to me. And maybe he'll be out in like, a week, or something." She held up her hands to stop him from interrupting her. "Pending your investigation, of course."

He shook his head and went back to his notes for a while. "Are you sure there's nothing you remember about this guy?" He held up the photo of the missing-finger man, who'd been so kind and fun.

What life might Jane and Jason have had if Diane had been normal and hadn't murdered him? And what about the others? The other men in the photos? Had she assaulted them like she'd assaulted Jane?

"Do you know who this guy really is but are wondering if I know so you can pin this on Jason too?" He wouldn't manipulate her with his polite manners and good looks. "Did you guys even do forensics before you arrested them? Or whatever it's called?"

Benjamin put down his pen and clasped his hands. "I didn't arrest them. They confessed."

Right. The details had begun to get lost among the lies they'd told. What she remembered had been wrong. No. What she had assumed had been wrong. And she still wasn't even sure what was right. Everything was as close to the truth as she knew it, except how she'd sent Jason home with Angie and she'd helped Georgia Lee, not Jason. Had Diane helped Jason? The truth she did know was right there on her tongue. All she had to do was open her mouth and let the words fall out. But she was tired of admitting to things she hadn't done. And things she had.

"I don't remember anything about him except he was nice."

Now he looked like a disappointed dad. After jotting down one more note, he rested his chin on his fist. "Is it true? Did you lie about killing Warren to protect Jason?"

"Yes."

"So you lied? Is that your final statement?"

"Yes."

He wrote it down and then outlined her consequences. False confession, technically, which meant she was looking at three to ten years in prison for perjury, plus a fine, if the court decided to convict an adult of a false confession made as a juvenile—according to Benjamin, who advised her to speak to an attorney. At least it wasn't life. Or death at the hands of the state. Maybe Jason's attorney had a referral discount.

After writing some more, he settled back in his chair. "Are you sure there's nothing else you want to share?"

She didn't know what to do with the question. "Like what?"

He shrugged. Something about him made her trust him. Master manipulation and side effects of sedatives, that's what. But she couldn't help herself. She felt like he wanted not only the truth (which she wouldn't give) but also the why (which she could and had). That something, whatever it was, emboldened her to ask the question that had begun to haunt her.

"Do you think Warren's still alive?"

He offered a little *hmm*. "Do you?"

"I asked you first."

"I'm not at liberty to discuss my thoughts. But I think these two cases are linked. I think that this guy, whoever he is, had something to do with Warren, wherever he is."

She shook her head. "No, this guy was around years before Warren. I was just a kid then. I don't think they knew each other." She recalled the conversation with Angie about Diane helping Jason get rid of Warren's blood and the signs of the struggle with him in the dirt. "Maybe Warren's not the missing piece. Maybe Diane is. Maybe she had something to do with both of them going missing."

"Why do you think that?"

Jason would tell her to stop talking. But he wasn't here. "I don't know. A feeling."

"Did the guy or Diane say anything back then that would make you think that?"

Jane tried to think, but clarity scattered as soon as she almost reached it. "No. Not that I recall. He joked about my mom cutting off his finger."

"Did she?"

"Maybe. He never said, and then he never came back."

"Was he violent with you or Diane? Jason?"

"No," she said. "Never." That she knew for a fact.

He wrote something down. Without looking up at her or stopping his pen, he asked, "You didn't answer your own question. Do you think Warren's alive?"

"I don't know." There was never a reason to think he was until now. "I know Georgia Lee and Jason thought they killed him. Accidentally." She made a point to emphasize that. "And when he didn't show up, we all thought he either washed out to sea or took off. It'd happened so many times before with the other men. For less interesting reasons." Her eyes got heavy. She thought about Georgia Lee. How Georgia Lee had rowed the boat near the dam. How she swam back to shore alone. It played in her head, almost like a dream. "You got a Coke or something? Coffee?"

He nodded, stood, and asked someone, maybe the tall old guard, if he'd bring her something. Task dispatched, he returned to their table. A kinder, gentler, less agitated detective. He even smiled before returning to his notes and scribbling something for a while.

Finally, he set down his pen and looked at her. "I'm sorry that happened to you."

"What?" she asked.

He kind of shrugged as if to say, *Everything.*

"You get used to it." She regretted letting that part slip as soon as she said it. She was usually more careful, but with the way things were going, that old melancholy resurfaced, one that sometimes receded during good days but always waited there in the background, ready to make an appearance. Her voice cracked. "It's not that big of a deal."

"I'd say it's a big deal."

His tone sounded genuine. He was either the most empathetic cop she'd ever met, or he was a really good actor. Probably the latter.

Though she didn't want to and tried not to, Jane found herself wiping at her eyes. No one had been upset by her and Jason's circumstances before. No one else, that is, except Georgia Lee and Angie.

Benjamin returned his focus to his paper and began to make little notes. A kind gesture. At some point, Jane had stopped telling people about her childhood. About Diane. She always ended up comforting the other person instead of being comforted. It was easier to keep quiet; then at least she wouldn't have to watch them cry and carry on about how unfair it was when there was absolutely nothing they could do to help her or change the past.

She grew embarrassed that Benjamin had seen her cry and tried to shake it off. She felt compelled to apologize and excuse her tears as a result of being overtired and frustrated.

"Sorry," she said and blew her nose on the napkin placed underneath the Coke the guard had brought while she was crying.

Benjamin told her not to feel sorry, but she did. She felt sorry for everything that had happened. Sorry for herself, mostly. And angry and hurt. Then she felt embarrassed for apologizing like some dumb girl. People always put the blame on girls, but then they always told girls not to apologize. And then she felt embarrassed for feeling embarrassed. And then she remembered something she should've thought of sooner.

She wiped her eyes and pretended that the past few minutes hadn't happened. "What happens now?"

"We have to ensure Georgia Lee and Jason have nothing to do with the guy we did find. And then we have to do our due diligence with Warren."

She'd heard that term used before. Recently, in fact. Jason. "Could you guys do your due diligence in the correct order this time?"

He lifted his eyebrows but kept his eyes on his paper. Scribbling. Guy loved to write longhand. Her hand hurt watching him. Finally, he stopped.

"Can I speak to Jason?" she asked.

He put down his pen, stood, and walked toward the door. He hesitated before leaving.

"I'd be okay with that," he said. "But he told me he didn't want to see you."

Before she could process what he said or the weight of her emotions in response, a crashing noise came from down the hallway.

Benjamin raced out of the room. Jane followed.

◆ ◆ ◆

Staplers and metal files and trays and everything else Diane could get her hands on crashed to the floor after she launched them at walls and people.

"We buried him!" she screamed. There were new lines on Diane's face, darker circles under her eyes. Fury bubbling under her skin.

The officers looked to Jane as if she could control her. The best thing for the situation? Let her rail. She'd calm eventually. But who could blame her? The body buried under the headstone for Warren Ingram belonged to someone else, a man none of them knew. No one but Diane and Jane and Jason. A man passing through town. A man who had somehow ended up in the dam and gotten dislodged years later. How? No one could confirm that yet. But they knew who he was not, without a doubt, despite Diane's protestations otherwise.

Other officers ran into the room. Soon, the older guard followed. They circled Diane, who grasped a pair of scissors and held them above her head. They all looked to Jane, as if gauging how they might look if they decided to engage her. Intent to harm a police officer—nay, a precinct—with a deadly weapon. That'd get Diane even more quiet time and a reprieve from the liquor store and the long hours of standing she loved to complain about than an assault charge on Jane. Anger puffed and reddened Diane's skin.

"You said it was him. You said it was Warren."

"You should've waited for the results before letting us bury that guy," Jane said to Benjamin above the noise.

Benjamin shook his head, not taking his eyes off Diane. "I tried. Trust me."

One officer, maybe the chief, moved closer to Diane, hands up in surrender. "We didn't have reason to believe it was anyone else. Your daughter told us what she'd done and where she'd done it. Now, let's be calm."

"You be calm!" Diane pointed the scissors away from the officer and then at Jane. Jane flinched. "She confessed. And so did Georgia Lee." She left Jason out of her complaints. Why? After learning that Jason had lied to her? And why would he protect Georgia Lee? Why would he tell Diane he had killed Warren?

The officer moved his hands, palms down as if pressing them to the floor. As if that would calm her. "We don't have any—"

"They confessed!" Her breath came out her nose in gaspy spurts. Her words screeched into the room and bounced off the ceiling. No one moved, but no one seemed all that worried that she'd do something stupid, like stab them. Maybe they *had* dealt with her before. "They should burn. The two of them. Those fucking cunts."

Jane refrained from reaching for Benjamin's hand, an odd impulse. Maybe because that's what she'd done with Jason when Diane railed and got violent, even though she couldn't protect him from all that he had to see and hear from Diane.

She felt Benjamin's hand on her shoulder. A wave of emotion washed over her.

"It's almost over," he said.

She clamped down on her insides screaming at her. Diane didn't look well. Sound well. Her sentences slurred and stuttered beyond comprehension. Jane's heart couldn't help but reach out to her despite her deep urge to hate her, her desire to see her arrested. Biology, she supposed. Everyone talked about the bond of a mother's love. But that wasn't true. It was harder the other way around. Harder to separate and let go of the first person who knew her; the first to hurt her. She knew now that Jason could handle it far more than she could. He'd learned how to separate his feelings into something he could manage. He'd learned how to separate Good Mom from Bad Mom.

Finally, Diane threw the scissors onto the floor—and very nearly stabbed her foot in the process.

Officers rushed toward her, almost in a tackle formation. Smart. Diane didn't struggle.

A collective sigh went around the room, and all those tensed shoulders fell.

"Fuck you," Diane said to the room, head raised high. Four guards held her and walked her toward the back of the station.

As she passed Benjamin and Jane, she spit at her. "Fuck you too."

Jane wiped the spit from her face.

"Are you okay?" Benjamin asked.

She nodded. He said something about needing to do something or go somewhere and asked her not to leave, but she had to leave. She had to get out of there. Away from Diane. And Jason. She looked around her, not sure what to do or where to go when she heard the officers laughing.

They'd talk and laugh about this for days. Years. The feral woman who came at an officer with a pair of scissors. Jane hated that. Maybe she hated herself more for still thinking such a thing, especially after Diane had tried to stab her and if what Jane accused Diane of turned out to be true. In the comedown of her sedatives, she wasn't even sure. It all sounded ludicrous now.

Maybe one day she'd be okay with the idea that her shit with Diane was complicated, as the kids said.

The officer who'd been on the other side of Diane's scissors looked familiar. Too familiar. Clarity washed over her. He'd come out to the house the night Warren—or Diane, as it turned out—had hit her after someone had called the cops about a domestic disturbance. Now she could see: he'd made chief.

He caught her eye, asked if there was something he could help her with, which was funny because she'd asked him for help many times.

"You came to our house," she said. "Back when we were kids."

"Well, that's not surprising, considering." He gestured toward the hallway they'd led Diane down and laughed again, as if not able to shake the earlier fit. The other officers quieted and adjusted their postures.

"You think it's funny?" she asked. "Did you think it was funny then? When Jason and I had no say in the matter? No power to do a thing about it?"

The chief tucked his hands into his belt. "Now, listen here. I don't know what you're getting at or the particulars of your situation, but—"

"You got called out to the house all the time, and you didn't do a thing." She glared at him. "I remember you smirking at Warren. Joking about women, how they're sensitive, how sometimes things get out of hand. But it was no big deal, right? These things work their way out on their own. In the home."

"I don't know what you're talking about—"

"After you left, Diane hit me. Gave me a concussion. I didn't go to school for a week." Her whole body shook at the release of the truth after telling a lie for so long. "If you'd done your job, Georgia Lee and my brother wouldn't be back there in cells. Maybe that guy you found would still be alive. Hell, maybe even Warren. You're as responsible for this as anyone."

She looked around at all those men. "All of you. Every time you do nothing. You're all responsible."

Thirty-Four

GEORGIA LEE

Georgia Lee didn't know what to expect once she relinquished the cuffs and her time was her own again. According to Tom, she and Jason had been the talk of the town, followed by Diane's arrest and then Georgia Lee's subsequent election loss, but the town would move on to other news as quickly as they did everything else. A formerly disgraced, now free political figure only held so much allure, even one with crimes as serious as hers had been.

"You're done here," Benjamin had said an hour prior. "Done done. Unless you'd like to admit to another crime we can't verify. Perhaps one that involves a grassy knoll." The last part he said with a teasing smile, not dissimilar to the ones Jane and Jason had always given her.

"Really?" Georgia Lee asked.

Benjamin leaned against the wall. He appeared to enjoy her confusion.

"But I confessed."

"No body. No evidence. No crime. Yet." He pointed at her. "I've got my eye on you, though." Before she could argue further, he'd given her a final incomprehensible look and walked away.

Free to go. She could go. Anywhere.

All the cops had to go on was what Jason and Georgia Lee and Jane had told them and what they all agreed to accept as truth: Georgia Lee had gotten into a fight with Warren over his parking space (stupid, but true); she'd run across the street to the river (also true); when Jason had seen Warren attack Georgia Lee (with violent intent, Georgia Lee had insisted), he'd jumped in to help (perhaps true); and after, Jason had helped Georgia Lee carry Warren's body to the boat and shoved it in the direction of his assumed death (super not true, but she had agreed not to argue the point).

She would trade a criminal defense attorney for a divorce attorney. She would find a new job. A new place to live. Things she'd thought about while there was nothing else to think about or do in the quiet hours since Jane had charged into the interview room with her box. She couldn't say how long ago it had been. A week? Now that it was here, the future loomed like a blank slate. She took a deep breath. She'd figure it out. She always found a way.

They had processed Jason first. She hadn't even gotten the chance to say goodbye. No doubt their paths would converge again. All it would take was another historic flood.

"Climate change, you fucker," she muttered to herself and laughed. She hoped Bollinger enjoyed his new responsibilities as city councilor, all the new complaints. Perhaps he'd love it.

Once Tom gave the all clear, she gathered her things and said her goodbyes to everyone at the station. They'd been good to her, which she had not expected, not with being held in connection to a murder. She told them she'd be by soon with cupcakes, to which they all laughed. Except Benjamin. Probably because Georgia Lee had thwarted his plan to arrest his top suspect. The brother and ex-girlfriend of the top suspect weren't quite what he'd had in mind. You'd think he'd be pleased to have caught his criminals. Though *caught* was generous, as they'd both confessed. He wouldn't be long for Maud now that the notoriety had died down. Someone somewhere would snatch him up. He'd chase the next thrill in the next town now that he'd gotten a taste of it. "You're welcome," she whispered.

"You head on home," John said and nudged his head toward the door. "I bet Rusty's ready to pop some champagne."

Georgia Lee glared at him. "I pop my own champagne bottles."

"Same old Georgia Lee," he said as he leaned against the counter. He smiled warmly at her, as if they were friends again. His betrayal stuck at the forefront of her mind.

He was right, though. She was the same; their perception of her had changed. She didn't mind, for once. In fact, she found it quite meaningful they could all now see exactly who she was. There was nothing to hide, though she'd never had to really hide until the past few months. But now they better understood her. Even if it no longer mattered in the public realm, it mattered to her personally.

She was a woman who had faced down a monster. Even with her future as uncertain as Jane's had been when she'd been released years ago, not a bad way to walk out the doors. She pulled her sunglasses out of her purse and slipped them on. Her car was waiting for her in the same spot she'd left it when she'd confessed.

Outside, she greeted Rusty with a small smile. The last time they'd spoken, she'd said she wanted alone time. Funny.

"Thank you for bringing my things."

He handed over a small suitcase she'd asked him to fill with clothing and a few personal effects. They'd both agreed it would be best if she found another place to stay. He'd been hurt when she declined his visits, if not his phone calls. She'd answered his questions as best she could:

Yes, it was true.

No, she had not meant to kill a man. (If he was indeed dead.)

Yes, she was genuinely sorry. (She was sorry she had hurt Jane.)

No, she had not planned it.

No, she was not coming home soon.

Which is why she had encouraged him to date, what with their recent talk of divorce and her expectation of being locked up until she died. He had agreed it might be best. For closure. Christlyn and Susannah, whom she had allowed to visit, had relayed that he'd wasted no time jumping on dating apps as soon as she'd confessed, according to their sources, whom Georgia Lee suspected were their husbands. That stung a bit. He could've at least waited until she'd known for sure she wouldn't die in a state women's prison. But she had not communicated that, so she would not blame him.

"You sure you don't want to come home? The guest room's all made up."

"I'm sure," she said. He looked relieved. "How are the boys?"

He shrugged and looked at his watch. She couldn't tell if he was still hurt, didn't want to be associated with such a wicked woman as her, or was late for a date.

"Oh, you know," he said.

She didn't. Perhaps they were upset, or embarrassed. Probably embarrassed. Mothers were embarrassing enough to teenage boys without adding a murder charge on top. But maybe they were like Tom and Susannah. Maybe she could be a hero to them at last. "Are they terribly disappointed in me?"

Rusty scratched at his chin. "They were excited that you know Jason Tran."

She gritted her teeth. They probably bragged about it at school. Not her role, of course. She regretted believing for one second that they'd care.

"Do let them know I'm thinking of them. And that I'll call them soon. When things have settled." A rush of motherly feeling came up. She wanted them there, and she didn't want them there. She wanted them to care. "Tell them I love them."

She hoped they would forgive her for what she had done once they realized what she had done was wrong and not equal to what they watched on Friday night wrestling—and nothing to either cheer or high-five, which they'd apparently done during a KMSM interview, to her horror. And for not being there through critical moments of their senior year, their childhood. For not being the mother she should have been to them. But there would be time, years, to untangle that mess.

For now, she released Rusty from his chore and let the sun and wind grace her face for what felt like the first time in years.

She stood there for as long as she wanted, not caring what anyone in the station or anyone outside would think. A small, habitual part of her had hoped a news crew awaited her release, but she stood in the parking lot alone. Birdsong flew along the breeze like the birds were saying welcome home.

Home. She didn't know where that was anymore. It wasn't the house she'd driven to for years.

Maybe she'd leave Maud. Her dreams felt big, yet small. The more she had sat in her cell, her release almost assured and imminent, the more she pondered that dream of hers, the one with a small house, alone. And the more she wanted it. In quiet moments, she tingled in anticipation of what that place might be. Who she might meet there. Who she might be. The real her. The one who didn't worry about what other people thought. Whether or not she was too old for the kind of happiness she'd dreamed of in youth. But she was willing to see. Even if it was only a dream, never to become tangible or true.

Underneath all that, Diane's threatening whispers from that one night they held her for assault on Jane. Jason caught between their two cells, unable to stop Diane's chants.

Georgia Lee, Georgia Lee, nothing but misery.
Especially when I get done with you.
Don't fall asleep.
I'll slit your throat.
I'll shit inside your body.
I'll feed it to your boys.

She shuddered at the recollection.

From the corner of her eye, she caught movement. And then the person Georgia Lee had once pledged forever and ever to stepped away from the station wall, where she'd been waiting.

Thoughts of Jane had not subsided. Rather, they settled over Georgia Lee like a warm summer day. A remembrance of a good place she could return to in the dark days that she had assumed awaited her.

Georgia Lee could tell it was hard for Jane to be near her. It was hard for Georgia Lee as well, and unsettling to know she had the capacity to do such a thing. Murder and lie.

"Can we talk?" Jane asked.

Georgia Lee breathed in deeply to prepare herself for the next bad thing.

Thirty-Five

JANE

The motel hadn't changed much since Jane's first sojourn years ago. A brief stint of courage in her youth, before she'd ever met Georgia Lee or even Angie. For a week now, she had pinched pennies and hand-washed the two brand-new outfits she'd bought at the Walmart—Benjamin had requested her tattered, bloody clothes as evidence—because she'd been too anxious to walk back to Diane's trailer and grab her clothes or laptop or anything else. All she had was what she'd had on her the night of their fight.

Jane picked at something on the faded bedspread and then looked over at Georgia Lee, who sat at a small table in front of the window, glancing at the carpet, the bedspread, the bedsheets. Probably not the place she'd envisioned stepping into first upon learning of her release. Cigarette smoke emanated from the fabric. The room was dark. The walls were water—and who knows what else—stained. Impenetrable dirt lodged in corners. The bathroom sink smelled of rust. Even after Jane had scrubbed everything and aired out the room.

Jane had a great ability to pretend everything was clean and nothing could hurt her.

"You said you wanted to talk," Georgia Lee said. She looked tired, resigned. Ready to sign over her life for a little sleep.

"Jason won't talk to me."

Georgia Lee sighed heavily. "He stopped speaking to me the moment you burst in the station claiming the bones weren't Warren's."

Never in a million years would Jane have believed they weren't. And never in a million years would she have believed someone if they'd told her that an officer in the Maud Police Department would've had the sophistication and foresight to confirm not only the identity of the bones they'd found but also the time frame of when he'd gone missing and the time frame of his death, both of which ruled out Jason's and Georgia Lee's involvement in one Keith Lindsay's death.

Keith Lindsay. After a news blast of the photo, a family from Missouri had claimed him. He'd worked construction in both states. Went missing back in '89. His DNA matched theirs.

Keith Lindsay. Jane had turned the name over in her mind so many times in the past week, trying to remember more. She wanted to tell the family more, but she didn't remember anything other than that summer day at the creek, his warm smile, his teasing and joking about his missing finger. Turned out he'd lost it as a child in a lawn mower accident.

As for Warren? Maybe he was dead. Maybe he was alive.

It'd all been a matter of three young, dumb teenagers, one alcoholic asshole, and self-defense.

Perhaps, Benjamin had said. Jane's accusations about Diane had worked their way into his brain.

"Is that all?" Georgia Lee asked.

"No. It's not. I don't know why he lied about it," Jane said. "Do you know why he lied to me?"

Georgia Lee wiped her eyes. "I don't know."

"And I still don't know the truth."

"I told you the truth."

"Yeah, you told me you did it. But not why you both lied to me and let me go to juvie and then probably prison. Not to mention spending the bulk of my adult life in fear and anxiety and unable to have meaningful relationships or stabil—"

"I know. I'm sorry. I . . ." Georgia Lee scratched her head before folding her hands together. "It all happened so fast, with Warren. And then you took over, and everything snowballed."

"What's that supposed to mean?"

Georgia Lee sat there calmly, but a hint of anger flashed on her face. "It means: the 'tough' butch who thinks she has to save everyone even though they don't ask for it confessed even though she told everyone else to keep quiet and then felt tortured and resentful about it afterward."

She might as well have slapped Jane. She felt sure Georgia Lee had referenced Tough, Jane's father's nickname, on purpose. "That's mean."

"And you're being nice?"

Her pulse quickened at what she'd brought out in Georgia Lee. So calm, but her words were knives. "Why did Jason lie to me?"

"Probably because you assumed he did it. Maybe it made him mad." She began to speak but then stopped.

"Why did you confess to the cops?"

"I didn't want you, or Angie, or Jason to go down for something you didn't do." Georgia Lee leaned forward, arms resting on the table.

Jane tried to sort her words into logic but failed. "Did you and Jason plan this?"

She grimaced. "Definitely not."

"But why would he confess?" Jane rushed through her memories, tried to pinpoint moments that would bring the night into focus. "I already told them I did it." Jane searched Georgia Lee's face and waited for clarification. "Did you ask for something in exchange for his confession?"

"No. I didn't even want him there. I had the same problem you did. No one believed me. I wanted to take the full blame. But then Jason showed up."

Jane considered everything she'd said. "You must've said something to convince him to go along with you, even if you didn't mean to. To make him feel guilty." To make him believe he'd killed Warren. Maybe he'd lost his grip on reality. Maybe he'd always believed he'd done it. Maybe that was why he started boxing, or whatever it was he did.

"Give him—and me—a little credit, okay? I didn't persuade him or force him or manipulate him. We're both capable of making our own decisions."

"You're both idiots for confessing. We don't even know if they would've come for me." The same thing they'd said to her. Jane's head pounded, and her whole body urged her to expel a scream. Georgia Lee sat patiently, waiting for her to finish talking. "Why would you throw away your life if I already confessed? You have so much to live for—"

"And you don't?" Georgia Lee breathed out heavily, as if her burdens had been released and were actually physical things that had weighted her down. "I'm sorry I didn't speak up sooner. I have no excuse. I was a stupid, stupid girl. I wanted this off my conscience. I was responsible. That's why I confessed. That's the only reason."

Jane stared at the cracked paint on the wall and tried to catch her breath. She was too angry with them both and worried all that anger would trip off her tongue and end in regret.

"Okay," Jane finally said. "I just thought maybe you could shed some light on why, is all." She looked to the floor. "You were with them both. Before they released Diane."

On bail. Someone had posted fucking bail. For the aggrieved widow and mother. Lots of people had mentioned that they would have done more than slash Jane. They said she got off lucky. She hadn't left her motel room except to meet Georgia Lee for her release. Benjamin wasn't all bad. He did keep her updated on that at least.

But she felt unmoored not knowing where Jason was or what he was thinking. She wanted the opportunity to bang on his chest and ask *What the fuck?!* in elevated tones. Jane wandered to the window to stare at something that didn't make her feel complicated feelings.

"Why haven't they arrested Diane for Keith's murder yet?" she asked. Benjamin hadn't been forthcoming on that. "I gave them the photo. I was right about that."

"But there's no evidence she did anything," Georgia Lee said behind her. "He could've disappeared without her help."

Jane turned to Georgia Lee. "Is that what Benjamin said?"

"John. The police chief."

Jane returned to staring out the window. "I've never met a police department less interested in solving crimes." She'd left the station with hope. But nothing had happened since.

"Maybe John's right. Maybe it's all a coincidence and there's nothing more to it."

Jane couldn't concede that. Diane knew something. And Jason too. The thought ate at her. Every waking minute, she burrowed into what she remembered, what she thought she remembered, what may have happened, and what Jason knew.

"I just thought . . . I just wish I knew why Jason never told me she helped him clean up. If maybe she threatened him too." Georgia Lee didn't express confusion at what Jane said or ask for details. Maybe she knew. Maybe Jason had told her. Jane swiped at her eyes even though no tears fell. She felt shriveled from releasing them throughout the week, the comedown of what had happened, how Diane had attacked her, Jason's continued silence. "Everything's fucked up."

"I'm sorry," Georgia Lee said. Anguish broke through her facade. "That's my fault."

Jane choked up at the sight of Georgia Lee's pain. She'd been so angry at her. "No, it was fucked up long before you ever arrived."

"I'm sorry I can't help you. I really am. And I'm sorry I lied."

"It's okay," Jane said. She couldn't stay mad forever. Georgia Lee had done a stupid thing in youth. All of them had.

Jane scrubbed her palms along her face and then dug around in a bag and pulled out a bottle of red wine. She sat at the table and held the bottle out to Georgia Lee as a question. Georgia Lee hesitated but then nodded.

Georgia Lee took a long swallow and gagged. "That's terrible."

"I know. I stole it from the front office," Jane said.

Georgia Lee smiled at the recollection. After another stint in the principal's office for fighting with another girl, Jane had emerged with a bottle of whiskey she'd stolen from his drawer when he wasn't looking. The only other person wandering the school hallway was Georgia Lee.

"Wanna go for a joyride?" Jane had held up the bottle and given it a little shake. They'd only spoken in the parking lot a week before. But Jane had watched her from the back row of fifth period, and in the hallways. There was something about Georgia Lee.

To Jane's surprise, Georgia Lee said yes. They found a spot out near the lock and dam to sip and talk. After, back at Jane's trailer, the night closing in, they sat awkwardly in the car with the windows down. Spring had blossomed hot after a long bout of cold, biting rain. The fresh air felt good on Jane's skin because she burned with what she guessed was desire. But that seemed like such an adult thing to think.

Jane got that feeling where she wasn't sure if she was supposed to lean in and make a move.

"We should do this again," Georgia Lee had said, all polite and professional but with a slight shake in her voice. Jane had smiled, thinking, *What a surprise*. Her senior year wouldn't be so bad after all.

They'd been so innocent then. So young. And new. Here they were once again.

Georgia Lee stared absently at her wine. She'd barely touched it. "Are you okay?" Jane asked.

Georgia Lee raised her eyes to the ceiling and crossed her hands on the table. "I lost my election. I no longer have a job. At least not that I'm aware of. Bollinger has never been great at communication." The words rolled off Georgia Lee's tongue so easily, so casually. Shock, maybe. Resignation. "I have two teenage sons who hate me. That was before all this, mind you. A husband whose heart I absolutely broke. So no, not really okay. But I will be." She continued, "Let's see. What else? I'm a murderer. Maybe?"

Jane shrugged. "Let's go with yes."

As quick as a thunderstorm, emotions roiled across Georgia Lee's face. "I'll be okay." The words seemed like a mantra more than anything. Soon, Georgia Lee covered her face with her hands and began to sob.

Jane scooted her chair over. Georgia Lee collapsed into her lap. Slowly, Jane reached out and let her hand rest on Georgia Lee's head. She ran her hand in slow circles along her hair until the room grew dark and Georgia Lee's breathing regulated. They stayed like that for a while longer until finally Georgia Lee lifted her head, her face inches from Jane's. Jane rested her hands along Georgia Lee's cheeks.

"Georgia Lee. Georgia Lee." Jane sighed. "What are we gonna do with this mess we've made?"

The catch in her own voice startled her, so she looked away. She might lose her nerve to ask and receive comfort from the one person who could understand her better than anyone. Georgia Lee might see doubt in Jane's face. After all these years, she didn't want her to see that. Even if she felt that. But those were ancient emotions. Fears she no longer had to carry. They didn't need them anymore. They didn't need to put their fists up to the world.

Georgia Lee gripped Jane's hands with hers, leaned into Jane's palm and kissed it. An accident, perhaps.

"We could run away," Georgia Lee said, her mouth inches from Jane's. "If your offer stands."

Thirty-Six

GEORGIA LEE

Georgia Lee stepped out of the bathroom after her shower, fully spent and intending to collapse into the bedsheets she'd just untangled herself from and get some sleep. Jane sat at the table in a T-shirt and boxer briefs, checking her phone. An innocuous activity, but one that stirred Georgia Lee in its normalcy. No matter that Jane had already exhausted her body in ways she hadn't felt in years. She wanted more of her. She'd always wanted more. Now that they were older, it was a different kind of want. Deeper than what they'd had before. They had new secrets to keep.

Jane must've sensed Georgia Lee staring at her because she looked up and smiled.

Georgia Lee unwrapped her wet towel and flung it onto the carpet. She straddled Jane and slung her arms around her neck. Jane ran her palms along her back and kissed her ear. Then she went back to her phone.

Georgia Lee tugged at Jane's briefs. "Why'd you even put these back on?"

Jane laughed, distracted, and swatted at Georgia Lee's hands.

"I need to go get my things," Jane said.

"What things?" Georgia Lee positioned herself along Jane's thigh and then slid her hand inside Jane's briefs.

"The things at Diane's."

"That's insane." She nuzzled in the crack of Jane's neck, held the back of her head close with her free hand, the other working on Jane.

"I have no clothes. I need my laptop," Jane said, her inhales and exhales intensifying before she gently pulled Georgia Lee's hand away.

"Don't go," Georgia Lee whined. She didn't want to leave this cocoon. The dream world of only them. Her husband. Her kids. The untangling of all that. Another day. "Your mommy's mean."

Jane laughed and leaned back in her chair. "I have to."

"Is this about Jason? Do you think he's there? Do you think that she'll give you some insight into why the brother you love so much and protected doesn't want to speak to you?"

Jane ran her finger down Georgia Lee's bare shoulder and twisted her hair between her fingers.

"She can't give you anything but pain," Georgia Lee said.

"I know."

"Fine." Georgia Lee extricated herself from Jane's lap and bent over to unlock her stiff hip joints. "We'll go together."

"You don't have to punish yourself anymore."

"You need a ride."

"That's not necessary. I can get a cab."

"You can't get a cab in Maud. Don't be silly. That would take hours. And she tried to stab you. I'm coming with you in case she tries again."

Jane considered the offer. "Okay. But only if you stay in the car."

"We'll see." Georgia Lee grabbed her dirty clothes off the floor. She also needed to make a trip home at some point. Rusty hadn't packed her anything but socks and underwear. Maybe she could borrow some clothing from Susannah and Christlyn. Susannah would take clothing from the house for her if necessary.

Jane leaned over to reach for her hand. "You really don't have to do this."

"I've already helped you get rid of a body."

Jane laughed and smacked her on the butt. "Get dressed so we can get this over with and come back here and lay around in this filthy room some more."

When Georgia Lee returned from brushing her teeth, Jane still sat at the table. She stared at her phone, not blinking or scrolling, as if in shock.

"What is it?" Georgia Lee asked. Jane didn't respond until she asked a second time.

She held out the phone. "Fucking Gerry."

It took Georgia Lee a minute to remember the name and why it sounded familiar. Stress. Trauma. Short-term memory loss. She'd not been wrong about all that.

Georgia Lee took the phone from Jane.

LOVELACE—UNMASKED AND READY TO REVEAL ALL!

Welp, folks. We did NOT see this one coming!
As you all know, we've been able to bring you the latest news in town
thanks to loyal followers like you. But ain't no one in town more loyal
than Lovelace, who's been at the forefront of hot goss in Maud's greatest,
most epic story of all time: LEZZIE BORDEN AND HER IRON MAIDEN.

. . .

Y'all ain't gonna believe this shit.

. . .

Lovelace, our best and most famous source is . . .

GERRY HARDGROVE.

!!!

GERRY FUCKING HARDGROVE, LADIES AND GENTS!

!!!

Let's give a round of gotdam applause for the man's
service.

Not only did he keep us a-BREAST of the details, he
tipped

us off to her gal pal, our very own GEORGIA LEE
VIGILANTE.

How exactly did Gerry know all this you might ask?

Aside from finding and pulling up the remains, good
ole Gerry

found it within himself to do the Lord's Work and slid-
ing right

into the grieving widow's DMs.

(Gerry said he didn't mean for anything to happen and
just wanted

to send his condolences.)

LOL, GERRY. LOL.

So why come forward as Lovelace now?

That's exactly what we wanted to know!

Hoooooooboy. Sit down for this one.

After Diane Ingram's arrest for assaulting the daughter

who confessed (falsely, apparently)

to killing Warren (and who could blame her?),

Gerry bailed Diane out and ushered her home.

But that's where, he says, things got weird.

Diane Ingram started going through the house and
tossing shit.
WHY? GERRY ASKED.
But Diane wouldn't give an answer. She just kept mut-
tering about
MURDERING HER OWN DAUGHTER.

Freaked out, Gerry got the hell outta there and since
learned from his
own secret sources that Jane Mooney, Diane's own
daughter,
ACCUSED DIANE OF MURDERING KEITH LINDSAY, THE
MAN WHO
IS NOT WARREN!!!!

Can y'all keep up? Cause we're having a hard time.

Gerry went on to say, generally speaking, we ain't so
good at the details or
stenography round here:

"I have turned over what I know to the po-lice,
and I reckon they're drawing up a warrant as we speak.
Y'all know I don't like to speak ill of people, and it's not
my place to
cast someone as evil, but I do believe that woman has
a
darkness in her heart. And I do believe,
she has lost everything.
AND NOW SHE'S LOST ME."

Oh, Gerry! You heartbreaking sonofagun.

My man, you are lucky you made it out of there alive!

The Chief already pulled his usual bull crap when we
asked,
saying how this is another tragic and unexplained
drowning that
he ain't gonna do shit about. Well, we call bull on that!
Put Detective Benjamin Hampton on the case!
He seems to be the only one who cares about the *Missing Men of Maud!*

As for the fate of the man who started this all?
Did former city councilor Georgia Lee Lane and Jason
Tran END that motherfucker, along with Jane Mooney?
Is he hanging out on the bottom of the Arkansas River
somewhere?
Or did he get up and scootch on outta here as some
suggest?
We can guess. But we may never know.

But, hey Maud, we'll keep digging until we do!
In the meantime, if you want to Lace us with some
Love, don't be shy.
Give us a little ring-a-ling.
#MaudIsMurderCity   #LovelaceRevealed   #KillOr-
BeKilled #FuckinGerryAmirite?

"We have to get over there." Jane hopped out of her chair and
grabbed her wallet, her phone, her motel key. "Now."

Georgia Lee checked the post date. It'd just gone live. "That place
is about to be swarmed with people."

"Which is why we need to go now."

"That's exactly why we shouldn't go."

Jane threw Georgia Lee's purse toward her. Georgia Lee barely caught it. "One. My shit's there, and I don't want it to be taken into evidence. Or two, have her take it and hock my shit on her way out of town," she said. "I'm not letting her leave Maud. She'll have to kill me first."

"Based on what I've seen, she might."

Jane ignored her and opened the door. "Let's go."

Thirty-Seven

Jane

"Maybe Diane drunk herself into a stupor and you'll be in and out like that with your things and we can just wait in the car to ensure she doesn't leave," Georgia Lee said. "Like a stakeout. Until the cops show up."

Jane tried to smile. She grasped Georgia Lee's hand. "Don't leave."

"I won't." Georgia Lee squeezed in return. "Not ever. Just promise me you'll be careful. You don't know what you're walking into."

Jane's stomach sank at the thought. It was one thing for Georgia Lee to have killed Warren, a knowable rage and response. But for Jason to have also confessed after lying to Diane for so long—a whole other level of unknown.

Jane took a deep breath and expelled it through her nose. She eased the car door shut and inched her way toward the trailer. Despite Georgia Lee's predictions, no one surrounded the trailer. Not the neighbors, not the cops. Everything was eerily quiet. She blamed it on the time of morning or the day, even though she didn't really know what day it was. Maybe everyone was off to work, not paying attention to social media. And the trailer park didn't get going till about noon.

Walking up the stairs, she glanced at the trailer next door. Yellowed scraps from the *Maud Register* still covered the windows. Somehow, she'd stepped in and out of Diane's trailer for weeks and hadn't noticed until now. Part of her felt relieved to know that whoever lived there might call for help if they heard something today like Jane suspected they'd done all those years ago. But those calls never did anything but create more trouble.

Unlike the last time she'd opened the door, she didn't hesitate. She rushed right in. Only after did she realize she should've brought some sort of weapon.

"Jesus fucking Christ," Jason gasped, looking like he could jump out of his skin.

After collecting herself from her own shock, Jane said, "Of course you're here. Mommy's little boy." Golden Boy, Angie had called him, and she was right. So right. And Jane was part of the problem.

He held a bottle of whiskey, which was odd. According to Diane, he never came over. Now, after confessing to killing her husband, they'd become drinking buddies?

As if coming out of a waking dream, he reanimated. Smiled that speaking-to-a-difficult-client smile. "I didn't expect to see you." And then, oddly, "You shouldn't be here."

"Yeah? Well, neither should you. But here we are." All the worry and anger and confusion at his silence stewed inside her, tunneling her vision onto her target. "What the fuck, Jason?"

"Calm down." He held out his hands in surrender. "I can imagine what this must feel like for you."

"I fucking doubt it. I've been texting you for days. Don't you get a phone call or something in jail? Why didn't you call me?"

"I called my lawyer." Fine. Appropriate. The right thing to do. But Jesus, she was pretty sure he got more than one phone call.

"Did it ever occur to you that I might be curious as to what you had planned? How it might affect me personally? That I might be, I don't know, interested in the idea of not going to prison?" They had a brief eye-contact standoff. "Why didn't you tell me that Diane helped you that night?"

He didn't have an answer for that, just a hangdog offering on his face.

"What I don't know is why you've been avoiding me. The only reason I can come up with is you feel bad about letting me take the blame. And I don't get why you thought it necessary to confess when Georgia Lee was guilty. Unless you couldn't bear the thought of letting Georgia Lee tell everyone what really happened that night because it'd make you look weak, which doesn't exactly square with the image you've crafted for yourself."

He gave her an Angie Pham special: that look of utter exasperation at her dramatics. "Fuck you."

"Fuck you more for lying to me. And to Diane. And for having her help you clean up the mess. And for letting her treat me like shit. And you, for treating me like shit too." Her eyes grew glossy despite her desire to stay calm. "I just wanted to protect you, and that's what I get in return."

"I didn't need your protection."

"You sure? You seemed pretty in need of saving that night."

After a moment, he adjusted his shirt. "Just because I didn't react the way you did doesn't mean I didn't know how to take care of myself. You don't always have to push or shout. Jesus." He looked away, maybe to calm himself. "You've got some fucked-up version of the past. Like I was always in the corner in the fetal position and you had to come to my rescue. I never needed you to protect me. I protected myself."

They stared at each other for a moment before both dropped their eyes.

"Why are you even here?" The tone, his face—both dripped with condescension. As if she were the one who needed help.

He'd never tell her the truth. She looked around the room. "I need to grab my shit."

"I can get that for you," Jason said and bounded after her. Just like Diane had.

"I can get it my goddamn self."

Jane found her laptop on the end table where she'd left it. Miracle it hadn't been thrown at the wall. Bigger miracle would be if it still worked. She pulled the power cord and her phone cord and assorted other cords into a plastic bag she'd found in a cabinet. Jason stayed close behind her.

"Why are you following me like you're with the DEA?"

She shoved past him. Only then did she notice Diane sleeping on the couch, turned away from the TV and toward the back of the couch. The blankets and pillows Jane had used covering her and under her head.

"Oh my God. Are you kidding me?" She gaped at Jason and pointed at the couch. "She's been here this whole time? Fucking blackout drunk? And you're what?" She examined him. The whiskey still in hand. "Bringing her booze, like a good fucking boy?"

"Keep your voice down," Jason said, his voice all quiet and weird. "You'll wake her."

"I don't give a fuck if I do!" She shoved him. It felt good. Like something she'd wanted to do for a long time. He dropped the whiskey. Dark spots from the spill covered his shirt and the carpet. "Fuck her! She's the worst, and so are you." She glared at him. "They're coming for her. It's only a matter of time. Let's Talk About Maud said they have a warrant. They're coming."

"Jane, please. Just leave."

"Why?"

A mix of anguish and panic played on his face. "Be quiet."

"Why?"

She rushed to where Diane lay on the couch, fully intending to pull the covers off and start whaling on her, but Jason stood in her way.

"Stop it," he said.

She pushed him again, but he barely moved. He tried to capture her arms.

"Why should I leave? Why should I be quiet?" Her screams echoed in her ears. She burst around him and launched at Diane.

"Don't touch her!"

Jane slammed into Diane, lost her balance, and rolled onto the floor. She scrambled to her feet, ready to fight.

Diane didn't move.

"Fucking USELESS." She screamed the words right in Diane's ear. Nothing.

"Why isn't she moving?" Jane asked, her voice still high and ragged.

"Jane." Jason's voice registered. Calm. Declarative. He put his hands on her shoulders in a comforting gesture. "You should leave. I'll take care of it."

Take care of it? Take care of what? He wanted to distract her. He wanted to make peace. Make the bad things go away.

"Wait. What?" The room began to spin.

"Mom," he said. "I'll take care of it."

She thought she might collapse from lack of air.

"What do you mean you'll take care of it?" Her eyes wandered the room, as if the answer to her question could be located somewhere within those walls. A bottle of pills sat on the kitchen table.

She raced toward it. But Jason grabbed the bottle before she had a chance to examine the label. The patient name.

"I found her like this." Small, almost imperceptible veins along his temple jumped.

Jane shook her head. "She doesn't take pills. She drinks." She thought back to the medicine cabinet. There had been nothing she could OD on. Nothing she could even use to escape.

He seemed surprised, caught off guard. "I didn't think so either. But I came in, and I found her." He searched for words. "I'm so sorry. I'm sorry for everything. I didn't know. I didn't mean to . . ." Sadness shadowed his face, but he locked it down. "You have to go. You didn't see anything."

"What?"

"I'm sorry I didn't do more, okay? Or speak up. You're right. I'm a fucking coward. Now go. Before they get here."

"Who?"

"The police, Jane. The fucking police."

"I don't . . ."

The pills, the booze, the body. Her mom's body.

Oh my God.

Without warning, he pulled her into him. He held her so tight she could barely breathe.

She scrambled to release herself from the cage of his embrace. Her lungs closed in. Air felt difficult. Wooziness unsteadied her. She didn't know what was happening. Right when she felt certain her body would hit the floor, Jason let go.

She bent over and gasped for air, hands clutched on knees. She squeezed her eyes shut and then opened them, as if that might make a difference, might encourage air into her lungs.

When she lifted her head, he held her gaze. "Go," he said. "Leave Maud. Don't come back."

"No." It was too final. "I don't want to leave you here." Who was she if not Jason's big sister, protector?

"You have to. We can't both be here when they find her."

When they find her? The way he said it scared her.

Something within him seemed to break. He released great gasping cries in between suffocating squeezes of remorseful sorries. The fury and then the anguish had been assuaged, replaced by defeat.

"You know, you always used to tell me we weren't like other kids," he finally said. "That we had to grow up too soon. You were right. You just didn't know how right. How different I was from them, and even you."

"What do you mean?" She began to cry too. "How were you different? What are you talking about?"

He grabbed her face. "Everything's going to be okay."

Georgia Lee's favorite line. She never believed it. Not when Georgia Lee said it. And not now, when the words came from Jason. None of this was okay.

"I never asked you for anything, but I'm asking you to promise me," he said, still gripping her face. "I'm asking you to leave."

"But what about her?" Panic crept into her voice. "What about Warren?"

"They're not going to know anything other than what you see. An overdose. On the eve of her arrest." He stared at Diane's lifeless form on the couch and then looked at Jane. "And they're not going to find Warren."

How could he know that?

"Jason?" His name came out as a question. "What did you do?"

He started to laugh, and then it turned into a cry and his face looked more peaceful than she'd ever seen it.

"I saved myself," he said.

She shook her head. "I don't understand."

"It's better this way."

"No . . ." She shrugged out of his grip. "I'm not leaving." He swallowed and sighed and did all those things he and Angie did when they were exasperated with her and couldn't get their way. "What did you do?"

He grabbed her arm and tried to push her toward the door, but she dropped her body weight and hit the floor.

"Jesus," he said. "Get up!"

"No! Tell me why. What do you know? What did you do?"

Now the room seemed to pulse with their tension. Her head pounded, and she felt like she might vomit. But she refused to move, even as he tried to pick her up and bring her to her feet. She squirmed away.

"Goddammit, Jane! Why do you always have to be this way?"

"Because you always have to be this way! Shutting me out. Not telling me things. Things like what you did. Why you know that Warren won't be found."

"Because we took care of him!" he screamed, but then stood still as if he'd startled himself. "He's gone. He's not coming back."

She shook her head in confusion. "Who took care of him?"

He lifted his head to listen. "You need to go."

She didn't move.

"They're coming."

"Who? Tell me!"

He ran his hands through his hair. "They'll be here any minute."

"I'm not going anywhere."

He stared at her, blinked. Everything in her ached. But mostly not knowing, confusion at the smallest things. She'd endured a lifetime of that. No more.

Finally, he crouched down to her level. Fear and anger flicked across his face. His breathing was ragged. Sirens called out in the distance.

"I stopped him." Jason looked at her, but it was like he was watching a movie in his mind, recalling events.

"Who?"

"I heard them."

"Who?" she cried. "Who did you hear?" But he was lost in the memory.

"I thought he was hurting her. He always hurt her. She had a black eye. That night. I grabbed your bat."

"What night? What—"

"He wasn't . . ." He laughed and gasped at the same time. He shook his head. "They were having sex." He stared into the distance. "I hit him. A lot."

She grabbed his hands, absorbed the information as quickly as she could. But she still had no idea what he was talking about. "I don't understand."

"Rick." She almost asked who when it came to her. The one who had told them he hated kids the first day he met them. "I was only seven," Jason explained, still lost in thought. "I didn't mean to—"

"It was an accident, then?" She squeezed his hand. "An accident."

"That time." Then he looked at her. This time, really looked at her. "It wasn't an accident the other times."

"What?" she whispered.

"I'm sorry. I didn't want to." His eyes shifted to the couch. "She made me."

"Made you do what?" And then a spark of a memory. The image of him in the police station when she'd run into the room, alarm in his eyes, trying to get her to stay quiet. "Is this about the box of photos?" She couldn't be sure, but she thought his pupils pulsated. "Did she . . ." The words stuck on her tongue. "What did you help her do?"

"Warren." He looked at the dirty carpet, not at her. "She knew what I did. She helped me that night . . . she made me. So many times. So many men. It . . . so I made her help me." He cleared his throat, but it came out dry and painful sounding. "He was the last. I didn't have anything to do with the others. Until . . ." He looked over at Diane and choked back a sob. "I had to. I had to do it."

"The others?" She sobbed. "What others?" She looked behind her at Diane, dead, and faced him. She thought about the twenty-three men in the shoebox. She thought about the Missing Men of Maud. About the whispers. The rumors. "You did this? Why did you . . . what did she make you do?"

Tears stretched along the contours of his face, so much older now. But still there, in his eyes, the boy he'd been then. "Real bad things."

Everything in her collapsed. "Jason, no." She muttered no repeatedly under her breath, tears mixing with the words to create the most mournful sound she'd ever made. He managed to get her to her feet. She could barely see from the tension in her head, the tears.

No. No. No.

Sirens drew closer. "I'll call you. I'll find you. When everything is settled."

"No!" Familiar lies she'd heard before and knew not to believe. "No, I'm not leaving! I don't believe you."

He gripped her face again. "Listen to me."

"No!"

He gripped harder until she stopped. "Listen to me. You're going to leave. You're going to get into Georgia Lee's car, and you're going to leave Maud. You're not going to come back. Not ever. You and Georgia Lee. You're going to find a new town. You're going to start all over. You're going to grow old together. You're going to have a beautiful life. Promise me."

She squeezed her eyes shut, wanting to end this nightmare. "No."

"Jane," he whispered.

Finally, she opened her eyes. "I promise."

His eyes watered, and he smiled. "I love you, 'kay?"

The words she'd longed to hear, had never heard from him because that's not what brothers and sisters did unless it was too late and there might not be another chance.

As he whisked her away, toward the door, she shoved her fists to her eyes like a child and began to sob.

Before she could pause to think or feel, he rushed her out the door, and then she stumbled down the porch. At the car, she threw her suitcase and the plastic bag of electronics into the back seat and then herself into the front seat. Stunned, she stared ahead of her at the trailer.

"What happened?" Panic surged in Georgia Lee's voice. "What did she say to—"

Georgia Lee's terror shook Jane out of her current state. She blinked back the tears. Wiped her face. Turned to Georgia Lee. Cleared her throat and said as calmly as she could, "Start the car. Now. Get us the hell out of this godforsaken town."

Georgia Lee put the car in reverse and looked behind her to see more clearly. When Jane looked up, she saw Jason there on the porch.

He waved, like they were happy relatives parting ways after a long-overdue but bittersweet reunion.

Later, tucked safely away from Maud in the security of another town, in Georgia Lee's arms, Jane would begin to tell her what she'd seen. What Jason had done. But then she would reconsider and decide that belonged to her alone. Not even Georgia Lee. She didn't want to watch her face, see or hear the confusion when Jane relayed the last words Jason would ever speak to her.

How Jason had told her, as calm as he'd ever been, "Run, Jane."

Then he had gripped Jane's shoulders and cut his fingernails into her skin before whispering, "Run."

ACKNOWLEDGMENTS

Thank you to the readers. I owe so much to you.

I'm so grateful to the folks at Thomas & Mercer for their passion and thoughtfulness, including Grace Doyle for the enthusiasm, Nicole Burns-Ascue for the deadlines and structure, Sarah Shaw for author-handling me, Brittany Russell for publicity, Rex Bonomelli for the amazing cover, Dave Andrews for audiobook expertise, Andie Davidson for enduring my commas, Susan Stokes's eagle eye, and all the folks I haven't met who are working hard behind the scenes to make this book the best it can be. But mostly, a gigantic thank-you and one thousand praise hands emoji to Jessica Tribble Wells for her shared creative vision and unfailing support for this book.

Many thanks to my agent, Chris Bucci, who took a chance on a story I thought would have to be shelved, brainstormed edits with me, and never doubted its ability to reach readers. Thanks as well to Allison Warren and Shenel Ekici-Moling at Aevitas.

Thanks to Katrina Escudero at Sugar23 for saying the nicest things and telling me to dream big.

Thank you to everyone at my day job, especially Adam Fisk, Aaron Stallings, Max Furst, and our fearless leader, Mike Oh. You've made it possible for me to avoid being a starving artist, create space for my writing, and are also just very nice people, for which I'm endlessly grateful.

Thank you to the Encyclopedia of Arkansas, an invaluable resource for all my stories.

The highest of fives to the Novel Incubator community, led by Michelle Hoover. To current students and alum who make me feel like a rock star: my fragile ego thanks you and blesses you with good book fortune. Special shout-outs to the following folks who have improved my writing and extended kindnesses over the years: Susan Bernhard, Marc Foster, Stephanie Gayle, Carol Gray, Kelly Robertson, Emily Ross, R. J. Taylor, and Milo Todd.

A big toast to my Shay's Pub Thursday-afternoon "writing" club: Rachel Barenbaum, E. B. Bartels, Michele Ferrari, and Elizabeth Chiles Shelburne, my longtime critique partner and southern sister.

Thank you to the crime fiction (and adjacent) community, who welcomed this genre-confused author into their ranks at various festivals, conferences, and events. I'm ever grateful for the introductions and invitations they extended that helped me in big and small ways: E. A. Aymar, Daniel "Cuz" Ford, James D. F. Hannah, Gabino Iglesias, Eryk Pruitt, Alex Segura, Shawn Reilly Simmons, and Kristopher Zgorski.

My Bouchercon "Branson" buddies who provide the best of text: Amina Akhtar, Matt Coleman, S. A. Cosby, Penni Jones, and John Vercher. And of course, my fellow "Bad Gay" P. J. Vernon. To say that this book would not be what it is without you is an understatement. My friendship with you is one of the best things to come out of launching my debut.

I'm hashtag blessed for friends old and new who make this weird-ass timeline more tolerable: Greg Adams, Natalie Baumgardner, Henry Burden, Janet Reindl Edgar, Maria Ferlick, Walter Gadecki, Pearly Leung, Jenna McAuley, Brian Olson, Gina Sartori, Christel Shea, Amelia Thomlison, Tim Wisniewski, Jennie Wood, and Alice Wu. With special thanks to Cindy Nguyen, who endured me when I asked her to read a draft and enumerate all the ways I could fail. *Nobody beats your meat!*

Thanks to the Pruski Clan for welcoming me into the family and making me feel like a proper redneck Pole. *Na zdrowie!*

Love to all my Ford boys, but especially Jesse, my first friend. Thanks for taking care of me. And Anita for texts, fingerless gloves, and assurances that I didn't fuck it up.

Thanks to Linda for providing shelter, security, and stability to us Wild Dog Fords all those years ago.

My love of stories (especially the weird ones) came from my dad, Glen Ford. Thanks for answering every single text I send about various ways to die and get dismembered in Arkansas.

And Sarah for #allthethings. Thank you for agreeing to join Poor Dead Bob, Simon, and me for this game of Life. We spun the wheel and picked the right pegs. None of this means anything without you. #LLL.

ABOUT THE AUTHOR

Photo © 2021 Sarah Pruski

Kelly J. Ford is the author of the award-winning *Cottonmouths*, a novel of "impressive depths of character and setting" according to the *Los Angeles Review*, which named it one of their Best Books of 2017.

An Arkansas native, Kelly writes about the power and pitfalls of friendship, the danger of long-held secrets, and the transcendent grittiness of the Ozarks and their surrounds.

She lives in Vermont with her wife and cat.